the GOOD THIEF

ALSO BY LEO FUREY

The Long Run

LEO FUREY

the GOOD THIEF

~A NOVEL

FLANKER PRESS LIMITED
ST. JOHN'S

Library and Archives Canada Cataloguing in Publication

Title: The good thief : a novel / Leo Furey.
Names: Furey, Leo, author.
Identifiers: Canadiana (print) 20220181284 | Canadiana (ebook) 20220181292 | ISBN 9781774570364 (softcover) | ISBN 9781774570371 (EPUB) | ISBN 9781774570395 (PDF)
Classification: LCC PS8611.U73 G66 2022 | DDC C813/.6—dc23

PRINTED IN CANADA

This paper has been certified to meet the environmental and social standards of the Forest Stewardship Council® (FSC®) and comes from responsibly managed forests, and verified recycled sources.

Cover Design by Graham Blair

FLANKER PRESS LTD.
1243 KENMOUNT ROAD, UNIT 1
PARADISE, NL
CANADA

TELEPHONE: (709) 739-4477 FAX: (709) 739-4420 TOLL-FREE: 1-866-739-4420
WWW.FLANKERPRESS.COM

9 8 7 6 5 4 3 2 1

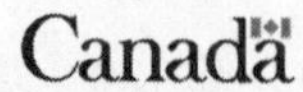

Canada Council for the Arts Conseil des Arts du Canada

Newfoundland Labrador

We acknowledge the [financial] support of the Government of Canada. *Nous reconnaissons l'appui [financier] du gouvernement du Canada.* We acknowledge the support of the Canada Council for the Arts, which last year invested $153 million to bring the arts to Canadians throughout the country. *Nous remercions le Conseil des arts du Canada de son soutien. L'an dernier, le Conseil a investi 153 millions de dollars pour mettre de l'art dans la vie des Canadiennes et des Canadiens de tout le pays.* We acknowledge the financial support of the Government of Newfoundland and Labrador, Department of Tourism, Culture and Recreation for our publishing activities.

To the memory of George Sanderson
March 21, 1935 – November 4, 2005

AUGUST 1967

I

I was a son to my father . . .
And he taught me and said to me,
"Let your heart hold fast my words . . ."

— Proverbs

1

MY FATHER HAS DECIDED TO KILL HIMSELF. And he wants me to put him in the ground. No funeral home, no undertaker, no clergy. "Only you, me, and Mother Earth, Sonny. Nobody else." And he has his reasons, one of which is to protect me.

He doesn't really believe taking his life is suicide. But I do. I mean, what else do you call taking a pill that'll prevent you from ever waking up again? He's determined to cross the river, as he calls it, because his number's up.

"We all gotta go sometime," he says. "I'm one of the lucky ones." He lights a smoke, squints at the flame. He chain-smokes unfiltered Camel cigarettes. "I know my time's come. And it's your time to help out."

We've been arguing about this for months now. He says he needs help to *do the deed*. I don't want any part of it, but whenever we're working in the garage, he brings it up. We live in Portugal Cove, or "the Cove," as everyone calls it, about eight miles from St. John's. He runs a small garage called Charlie's Auto. He loves the name, insists I always call him Charlie, never Dad—even when I was a child, in private and in public. Everyone calls him Charlie. Charlie the mechanic can put an arse in a cat.

He swipes at a trail of cigarette smoke, points the torque wrench at me, then at the yellowing photograph of my mother, one arm around me, the other snugging a napkin up to my chin as I blow out the candles on my fifth birthday. In the photo it's hard to tell where my mother's long pale hair ends and mine begins.

A wheezy chuckle and Charlie lifts his greasy baseball cap, looks away. "Your mother was alive she'd want you to call her Lucy." He rarely talks about my mother. I guess he has his reasons. Charlie always has his reasons. Never mentions how she died. Too difficult to talk about, so I let it rest. But whenever her name comes up, I ask about her. His answer is always the same: Lucy was like God—slow to anger, rich in kindness.

My father glances at the photograph. "Were she alive, Lucy'd agree with what I'm doin'. 'Why leave it to an undertaker?' she'd say. 'Someone you don't know.' Hell, she'd be there with the shovel." He rants about the terrible falling-out he had with Lucy's priest, Father McCarthy, who refused to put his name on the burial plot in Mount Carmel Cemetery. "Powers and principalities!" He's angry enough to spit in his soup. "We'll see who gets buried where, Father Almighty McCarthy! Crooked as sin, he is. The stupidity of it! We'll see who gets buried where."

"Charlie, you can't do this. It's too risky." I say my piece and wait. Nothing. "It's a public graveyard, for God's sake."

A derisive snort, then a long silence, different than usual, testing. He bemoans yet again Father McCarthy's refusal to let a Protestant be buried in a Catholic cemetery. "Not like there isn't precedent." He hesitates, glances around: tools, brake and bumper parts of a Chevy truck litter the floor. He snatches a heater gasket from the workbench. "Eighteen-hundreds, the poor Catholics used to sneak into the Anglican cemetery downtown and bury their dead. All that space outside the Anglican church? Dead Catholics!" The corners of his mouth turn down. "If the micks can do it . . ."

"Charlie, you can't do this. You—"

"Oh, I'm gonna do it!" His voice quavers. "Gonna be with my Lucy, and that's that." He turns away, says she wanted them to be together. He's grown frailer lately, thinner, his brows forever wincing in pain. "Need your help, son. Not asking you to shoot me, like some old horse with a broken leg. Just supervise the thing, that's all."

I hate being talked at but can't bear the thought of him gone.

"Be my acolyte. Just—" He coughs, spits. "Every wash, you lose a sock."

He's all head about it, I'm all heart. Sometimes we go days without a word to each other. Furtive glances exchanged, polite grunts in the shop. His way of sticking to his guns. For a religious man it's amazing he doesn't see it for what it is. Respecting his belief isn't easy.

He leans forward, his head over his hands—palm to palm—as if in prayer. "Moses wandering in the desert said to God, 'Kill me now, please, it'll be a kindness.' And Jesus knew why and where He'd die, knew it all. Knew where they'd come for Him—the day, the hour. Even knew how it was gonna happen. Public execution! Capital punishment! Could've chosen to stop it. He didn't."

"Charlie, you know I don't agree with some of your religious notions—"

"I'm in the same boat. Hallelujah! I know how and why and where. Simple matter of when—and the clock's tickin'. I'm no fool, son. I know what spitting up blood all the time means. Don't need a doc to tell me what's coming."

He sighs, looks out the window at Johnny Fabrella mowing the lawn, red hair blowing in the wind. There's a light in his face every time he sees Johnny. "Vietnam will be the death of him. Useless war!"

"He doesn't have to go," I say. "It's his choice."

He gives me an angry shrug.

"Johnny's not earning his pay. He's never in the garage, and when he does come, he quits early. He's a quitter, a school dropout."

"So am I." Another dismissive shrug, a wince of disgust. "Make sure he never finds out about the print shop—Rosie." He gets up, waves to Johnny to stop mowing and come inside. Garage door's always locked, so Johnny knocks. Charlie lets him in, throws out his arms, and hugs him. "My handsome Johnny! And why not? Your mother was beautiful." He opens his wallet. "Here's a sawbuck. Need any more?"

"P-plenty, Charlie, th-thanks." Johnny stutters when he's nervous.

Charlie smiles. "More where that came from."

Johnny reaches in his pocket, hands him back five. "Plenty, Charlie."

Charlie laughs, says keep it.

Johnny lived in New York till he was ten. His parents died and he returned to the Cove to live with his deadbeat uncle. Charlie took him under his wing, treated him like a son. Johnny practically lived at our house. We were raised like brothers. Arlene thinks we even look alike, which is funny because Johnny's the spit of Arlene; they're cousins, after all.

When he was little, Johnny swallowed antifreeze. He thought it was syrup, almost died. Charlie was by his hospital bed all night. He still feels guilty about leaving the antifreeze around and favours Johnny as a result.

"Gotta run, band practice," Johnny says. He'd rather be off playing the guitars Charlie buys him. He avoids the garage, doesn't like grease and dirt, *real* work. When he does the odd job, he gives the money to hippies who always flop at his place. He's too kind.

"Before you go, Johnny, let's go over the most important things about car maintenance."

Good luck, I want to say. He's been teaching him that for years.

"Change the oil regularly. What else?"

"Check the battery," Johnny says.

"Good! Good! Come here, did I show you how to recognize worn-out brake pads?"

"Yes."

"Can you replace this spark plug?"

"Think so. I'll try."

"Just don't put it up your ass."

We laugh.

That's what I'll miss most about him—his humour. And his patience. Just having him around the shop, his being here. He taught me to look at a problem and not be in a hurry. "When your mother and I picked tobacco, she'd always say, 'More hurry, less speed.'"

It gives me a special confidence when I ask him why something isn't working, something as simple as why a rusty bolt won't loosen up after a heavy pounding. He's so easygoing. He stares at the problem, muses for a while, gets his toolbox and a can of lubricant or something.

And I'll miss waiting till he sticks his head out from under a car hood or slides out on his creeper and asks, "What's up?"

"Replace them every 70,000 miles," he tells Johnny and reminds him how to recognize a burnt-out plug. Johnny smiles, nods, but he won't remember anything. His mind's on one thing, guitars.

Charlie finishes up, and Johnny says he's gotta run.

"Stay for supper," Charlie says. "We'll cook our famous lasagna." They're both wonderful cooks, and we have some great meals together.

"Gotta run, Charlie, band practice. Let's cook up a storm Friday night."

That means Johnny will make a special dessert. I wave goodbye, remind him of the oil changes he forgot to do.

"Sheez! Sorry, little brother." He always calls me little brother, the brother he never had. "I'll come back later. Promise."

"Never mind, Johnny, I'll do it." I know he won't be back.

"'Little brother,'" he says. "This is a holy moment." One of Charlie's expressions.

When he's gone, Charlie says I shouldn't badger him about garage work. "He's a musician, has the divine impulse, let him do it on his own time."

"He's never here, Charlie, I do all his work." I think of my great-grandfather, David McCluskey, who started Charlie's Auto. What would he say about a slacker working in the garage? "There are deadlines, Charlie. People expect their cars back on time."

Another shrug. "When I'm gone, give him full-time work, but don't badger him. You know anyone as thoughtful as that young man? He practically runs a soup kitchen at his place."

"You mean flophouse."

"And he's a sensitive soul, gets anxious, depressed sometimes—"

"I'll give him a paycheque, but I won't expect much. He's not a mechanic, Charlie. He hates grease, for God's sake."

"He'll be fine over time. You shouldn't be jealous. You're my real son."

"I'm not jealous."

"Yeah, you are." He grits his teeth in that stubborn way he has.

I'm really pissed off with him, so I let it go. I hate arguing about Johnny, who, as I say, couldn't care less about fixing cars. He thinks a car is a tin can with wheels and a motor. I'm never happier than when I'm in the garage, rolling up my sleeves, and getting down and dirty with an engine. I'm going to be the best mechanic in town. Why not? I've had a great teacher.

"Johnny's come a long way. He's a talented musician and very modest. I'm proud of him. You should be too . . ."

He's talking at me again. It's unnerving. He'll go on and on, and I'm frustrated to no end, so I mention an important date with a girl in my class, gotta go.

"Is it that Arlene gal? From the Trades School?"

"Yeah, she's in my mechanics class."

"You know her father's driving me crazy trying to amalgamate the two garages. Not gonna happen, but he won't give up. Old White would use his own mother if he could. Wouldn't put anything past him. Watch your bobber, son. Don't let her do Old Man White's bidding."

"I'd never let anything happen to Charlie's Auto. I'd never—"

"I like that gal. A bright spark. Not afraid to get her hands dirty or speak her mind. Reminds me of her Aunt Laura, who was one tough *muchacha*. Laura!" he exclaims, his voice high, amused. "Those eyes!"

We argue again about the burial. "What if I get caught? It's Mount Carmel Cemetery, for God's sake, it's on a hill."

"Get caught?" A triumphant cackle. "Nobody hangs around graveyards late at night. We'll do it after midnight. We'll go over there tomorrow and case the joint, see where to park and all. Don't worry, we'll rehearse."

"And what about when you're gone? The death certificate. What am I gonna say happened to you? There's a million details. There's the—"

"All in good time. I've figured everything out. You'll be eighteen end of the month, almost a man." He pauses and looks at me kindly. "A real man. And sometimes a man's gotta do what a man's gotta do."

That crack in his voice again, can't bear to listen; it breaks my heart. And I've already made up my mind—I'm not burying my father, no matter what kind of cockeyed logic he uses. I'm not taking that on, man or boy.

I remove my coveralls and head back to the house to clean up before meeting Arlene at Thelma's Diner. I don't want her to know about this madness. It's our first official date, and I need to pull myself together.

"Don't forget, you promised to drive me to the hospital later."

"I'll be back, Charlie. I never forget a promise."

2

THELMA'S IS NOISY, PACKED WITH STUDENTS—Van Morrison's "Brown Eyed Girl" blaring from the jukebox. Through a smog of blue smoke, I spot Randy Quinn's unmistakable mop-top in a booth by a tall picture window, see his fingers tapping the table. He's the drummer for Johnny Fabrella and the Acid Test. I wave. He's next to his girlfriend, Esther-Marie. She sings background with Arlene, who plays keyboard. Esther-Marie's short hair looks wet, as if she's just come from the swimming pool. She's on the local swim team—his third girlfriend this month. Quinn melts at the sight of a pretty face.

Arlene's next to her cousin Johnny, whose facial features are soft, like Arlene's. With his shoulder-length, fiery red hair, they could pass for sisters. Like me, Johnny has a dimple on his chin, wide lips. He looks uptight, Vietnam's on his mind. He's an American citizen and could hear from Uncle Sam any day.

Everyone wants a music career. Esther-Marie wants to study music at McGill. Arlene's performing on the CBC's Young Talent and wants to cut a record.

Johnny's got the best shot at making it. He's the lead singer, bops around the stage like Mick Jagger, plays a mean guitar. Everyone loves Johnny Fabrella and the Acid Test. They sell out every concert.

Through the smoky din, loud knocking, ringing bells from the pinball machines, I grab a chair, sit at the booth. Quinn flashes a peace sign beneath his rabbity grin. "You're late, McCluskey. Fighting with your ol' man again?"

"Workin' at the garage, had to shower. Better late than ugly."

The girls laugh. Esther-Marie has stained teeth.

"Hi, Sonny!" A slight caving in my stomach as Arlene pushes back her hair. She's wearing a faded Beatles T-shirt, loose and comfortable, her café racer leather jacket. She adores her racer bike, beautifully finished in metallic magenta with black accents, white pinstripes on the fuel tank.

"Ha!" Quinn says, stroking his wispy goatee. "Up all night thinkin' of that one, McCluskey?" His green irises are weepy-looking. I swear to God, if his ears were floppy, he'd be a dead ringer for a rabbit.

Behind the cash register, a yellowed cut-out of Thelma in her diner-girl uniform: Best Home Cookin' in Newfoundland.

"You missed hoops this morning," Quinn says. "Too tired for basketball?"

From the rowdy haze, a nasal drone takes our orders: Cokes, hamburgers, fish and chips.

Johnny asks if I've checked out the stage for our next gig, the Pot Park Concert.

"Not yet, the weekend."

Arlene says, "I'll take you for a spin on my new racer." Our eye contact is electric, her eyes like my mother's, caramel brown.

I manage the band, booking venues, transporting equipment, that sort of thing. Johnny negotiates contracts, resolves conflicts. He's really in charge.

Quinn goes through the concert set list, suggests they make some songs unique. Johnny says he's writing new lyrics, recommends variations of songs, the tempo, chord variations. "Writing a protest song, Johnny g-got his g-gun." He stretches far back in his chair, hands behind his head. He's an imposing figure, over six feet, prominent Adam's apple and that long red hair, bright blue eyes. He wears a rawhide jacket, headband, jeans except when he's playing a gig. He has flamboyant outfits for performing. Everyone calls him Handsome Johnny, and all the girls in the Cove are crazy about him. *Oooo! Johnny Fabrella—Lady Killah. Oooo! Fu Manchella, pretty cool fella . . . Oooo! Oooo! Hollywood Handsome Johnny. Oooo! The Acid Test's playing at Butter Pot Park . . . Oooo! Johnny Fabrella's an American. Oooo! From New York. Oooo! Oooo! Might get drafted . . . A-Ahhh!*

"Can we try some songs in a different key?" Esther-Marie asks. "Do something original to get into the melodies? Buffalo Springfield—"

"G-great idea," Johnny says, "next practice. A knotty guitar riff between the lyrics. Flex our musical muscles."

"And we could do the Joni Mitchell song differently," Arlene says, "experiment with the rhythm, maybe, change the tempo."

"Make it a soul anthem," Johnny says.

Quinn says, "So it sounds like anyone but Joni Mitchell."

Everyone wants fame except me. I just want my own garage, the simple life. Unlike Quinn, who says if he doesn't make it as a drummer, he'll be a cop, just like his old man. His father's a detective, and Quinn fancies himself one. He's always reporting something or other to the school principal. He's famous at school for ratting on people. But I don't razz him. It takes all kinds.

"If we had brass," Esther-Marie says, "we could slip in a little Satchmo. Too bad Sonny doesn't play—"

"I do."

"What?"

"The radio."

"Ha, ha," Esther-Marie says. "I saw a great movie last night."

"Why's it take so long for a flick to come here?" Quinn says. "It's 1967. Spaghetti western in town was made years ago."

Esther-Marie says she loved *Who's Afraid of Virginia Woolf?*

Arlene says they'll never make a better movie than *A Man for All Seasons*.

"*Bo-ring*!" Esther-Marie says.

"No, really, it's a great flick," Arlene says.

The waitress, not much older than I am, arrives with an armload of plates: Quinn grabs a hamburger, chomps. "That movie's crap," he says, a dab of ketchup on his chin. "*In Cold Blood*, now there's a great flick. My father and I saw it last week."

I catch Arlene's eyes for a fraction of a second. "I'd like to see that movie you mentioned."

"I plan on going again." She winks, pulse beating in her neck as she stares at Quinn.

"Serves them right! That's what they get for electing Johnson." Mr. Crenshaw's voice booms as he and his wife enter the diner, a harsh British accent that you usually hear before seeing him. He teaches mechanics at the Trades School. His nickname is Comrade Crenshaw—his first name was James, but he changed it years ago to Vladimir when he became a Marxist. He likes his friends to call him Vlad and insists Charlie always call him that. Eccentric? Yes. And so is his wife.

Mr. Crenshaw nods toward the cash register. "Take our orders, please, darling. The usual, extra rashers, leaner the better. But you know me, darling, I never complain."

His wife calls out their order as they move toward our table. Quinn cringes. He hates Crenshaw. And Crenshaw hates him and his father. Detective Quinn once interrogated Crenshaw about using drugs. Quinn's the only student Crenshaw ever failed.

Crenshaw's a big, middle-aged man in his fifties, a bit stoop-shouldered, with a massive, shoulder-length mane of hair, shovel-shaped beard. Broad, defiant face, large nose that looks like it was broken at one time. His bushy eyebrows hover above alert, close-set eyes and thick, black-rimmed glasses. He dresses formally, always the same, double-breasted suit or sports coat.

He flashes a peace sign, grins, and I glimpse broken teeth. "You all know my wife, Flo."

"Which one got the A plus?" She glances at Johnny with her ferrety, black eyes—framed by a sexy pageboy haircut—then probes my face, her lively eyes challenging mine.

"That'd be me," I say, my face getting hot.

She tilts her head to the side, narrows her eyes. "Your father's a saint, Sonny."

"Mother Teresa of the Cove," Johnny says. He gives a peace sign.

Crenshaw snickers. When I was little, I'd hear him arguing with my father in the garage—first I heard the word communism. Crenshaw claims he went to Oxford, always signs his name with Ph.D., but Billy Ferguson, the director of admissions's son, says that's BS, that he attended Oxford but was expelled for drug dealing. "But his wife has a Ph.D. in physical education," Ferguson says, "from the States."

"Tea, Vladdy?" his wife asks. The tendons in her slender neck look strained. She's dark-skinned, looks Spanish.

"Of course, darling," he says, slicking his hair back with his hand. Mrs. Crenshaw teaches physical education at the university. She's a bodybuilder, coaches the men's wrestling team at school. She dresses simply, always in black, always wears a worn, full fur rabbit hat that her husband bought on a trip to Russia, her Moscow, she calls it. Often, she can be seen twisting it in her large, rough hands. Originally from New York, there's a rumour she killed her first husband during a wrestling match. With those hands you can see how.

"Sonny, there was a little problem with your last mechanics test." His tone is nasty. "Come to my office Friday." A cynical twist of his mouth.

There's nothing wrong with my test. He's peeved with me for challenging him in class. He doesn't like it when a student disagrees with him. Crenshaw turns to the others. "Today's test question, comrades: What precisely is the establishment? Answer, comrades: Powerful politicians who make laws, the media who control the airwaves, financiers who run the economy, and, of course, their puppets, the police, who enforce the rigged laws in favour of the rich. All in the same big happy bed. One rule for the poor, one for the rich, hmm. A poor bloke steals a candy bar, it's jail time. A rich man filches millions, what happens? Nada, comrades. Not a thing. The rich get richer, comrades. Men of England, wherefore plough / For the Lords who lay ye low? The clothes you weave another wears . . ."

Around the time of confederation with Canada, Crenshaw began teaching at the College of Trades and Technology, or, as everyone calls it, the Trades School. He teaches auto mechanics and the only academic elective available, history. When he was hired, instructors were poorly paid and hard to find. Mr. Crenshaw insisted his contract contain a clause stating that he'd teach world history each year. It's really a course in communism. All Crenshaw ever talks about in class is the Russian revolution, Marx's classless society, and the haves and have-nots. He always has full enrolment. Everyone takes it because he hasn't failed anyone except Quinn in over twenty years. You just memorize a few paragraphs from *Das Kapital*, write them on the final exam, and you'll pass.

His wife arrives with their takeout, looks at Johnny. "You've got a great voice," she says. "I used to sing."

Johnny nods, smiles.

"In a choir back in the States."

Crenshaw says, "I see Charlie is socking it to them again." I think he's referring to my father until he says, "Viet Cong have killed over 11,000 soldiers so far."

Johnny bites his lip.

"Fifty soldiers a year killed by snakebite," Mrs. Crenshaw interjects. "*Pfft*! Rather take a bullet to the brain." She jerks her shoulders as if itchy.

Crenshaw turns his hand into a finger gun, aims at Johnny. "Draft board come calling yet, comrade?"

"No," Johnny says.

"Nasty little war. I'd stay put in the New Found Land if I were you, hmm. Most soldiers are working-class lads fighting an undeclared war by a president they can't vote for." He smirks. "And Johnson ran as the peace candidate. God bless America! G'day, comrades." Then he adds as an afterthought, "Oh, Johnny, the Doctor Club meets today. Jean-Luc and Manfred have been asking for you." He's referring to a group he founded to discuss political and philosophical issues. They meet at Eden Farm, a hippie commune on the Bauline Line, a few miles out of town. Johnny dropped out of school to do music full-time. He's the only musician in the Doctor Club. Charlie's a member too. There's a rumour that the Doctor Club is a front for drug dealing—Charlie says that's idle gossip, pay it no mind, Johnny smokes pot but he'd never traffic in drugs.

"Meeting's at Eden Farm, four sharp. Today's topic: proof that Jesus was not a historical person. G'day, comrades." He turns to his wife, flourishing his hand. "After you, darling."

As they leave, Quinn shakes his head. "Ryan says the Crenshaws take mescaline. They're weirdos. And there's a rumour he's cruel to her, always makes her wear black. He's straight out of *Dr. Jekyll and Mr. Hyde*. Split personality. Heartless prick! He's one thing in public, but alone you see another side. Comrade Two-Face. Johnny knows, don'tcha?" Johnny lowers his head. "And his eyes are too close together. Looks like a sadist to me. Kinda guy would swing a cat by the tail."

As Quinn and Esther-Marie leave, Quinn says something about Mrs. Crenshaw wanting to sing with the band, but he's drowned out by the roar of the milkshake machine.

"She wants to join the band?" I ask Johnny.

"No. She wants to sing background at the Pot Park Concert. I said yes."

"She can sing?"

"No. Leastways, not as well as she wrestles." He smirks. "Told her to lip-synch. It's a favour for old Crenshaw." He pauses. "Say, was she serious about fifty soldiers killed by snakebite?"

"It's the Vietnam jungle," Arlene says. "Vietnam'll be the end of the band."

"What my father would've wanted," he stutters.

"It's your choice, Johnny," I say. "My father—"

"Saw Charlie the other day. He looked tired. I drove him to Canadian Tire and took him to lunch."

"You're always taking him to lunch."

"Says he's going to Toronto. To see a specialist. I'm worried about him. He's more of a father to me than Uncle Harry, wherever he is."

"He'll show up," I say. "He always does."

He says he'll get the bill. I wave him off. "You always pay, Johnny, my treat this time."

"See you at practice. Don't forget to measure the stage at Butter Pot."

"Lotsa time," Arlene says.

"Hope it doesn't snow," Johnny says.

"First weekend in October. It won't snow."

"It's Newfoundland," I say, "could snow any time after September."

Johnny winks. "You'll have to share a sleeping bag," he says and throws a buck on the table. "For gas."

"No wonder you never have any money," Arlene says. "Go! Go on."

He flashes a peace sign and leaves.

"Give you his last dime, that one," Arlene says.

3

I HAVE A SPLITTING HEADACHE BUT ASK TO WALK ARLENE HOME. We've been friends since high school, but lately we've been flirting, testing the waters. She lives by their service station, White's Esso, the only other garage in the Cove. White's sells gas mostly but does some repairs. Arlene knows a lot about mechanics, wants to set up a small engine repair shop.

When she stands up, she's tall, thin-limbed, big brown eyes, a freshness about her. Her smile has a slight sideways tilt to it. We walk, talk, and I'm taken by her sideways smile. Everyone in the Cove calls her Ar except me. I call her every letter in the alphabet except R. I say how's it goin' B or C, L or Y. She always gets a big kick out of How-D! And every now and then I growl Arrr, Arrr, which cracks her up.

As we walk, she asks if Quinn is right about Crenshaw being so heartless. "Seems nice enough to me."

"Oh, he can be pretty nasty, can turn on you."

"But Jekyll and Hyde? C'mon!"

I remember what Charlie said about him. "He's two-faced. I've heard rumours. You don't wanna cross him."

"I don't pay attention to rumours. I like facts."

"Well, here's a fact: Quinn's father told Crenshaw he shouldn't be teaching at the Trades School. Quinn failed his course. Only one he ever failed."

"That's awful," she says.

"Watch your bobber with old Crenshaw."

"We'll take my racer this weekend to check out the stage at Butter Pot, okay?"

"Sure."

"Ever been on a racer before?"

"No."

"You're in for a ride." She shoots me a wrenched smile. "Racer's made for speed."

"Fill your boots." But I'm nervous as hell, and she can tell.

"Don't worry, you're in good hands."

Motorcycle riding's not my idea of fun, but now's not the time to chicken out.

"Just wrap your arms around me and hold on tight."

"How tight?"

"Don't touch my boobs, that's all." Mischief in her eyes.

I almost gasp.

"You're blushing, McCluskey."

She likes to laugh. I'd had a crush on her for over a year before asking her out, melted at the sight of her. She picks my brain about mechanics, and I pick hers about books. And she's playful, witty, loves tongue twisters. Lying in bed, I often hold her picture in my mind at night for the longest time before falling asleep, remembering something she'd teased me about or a joke she'd cracked.

It's a hot afternoon, cloudless sky, blue to the horizon as we walk. She takes the shortcut to her place, a path through the woods. We stroll aimlessly, listening to the wind in the trees lining the marshy path. It's special, intimate, and I want to take her hand but don't dare.

After a while we chat about the band breaking up if Johnny goes to Vietnam.

"Why's he so hell-bent on joining that stupid Yankee war!"

"His father. Captain Fabrella—"

"He should marry that girl he's crazy about. What's her name? Celine. He should settle down in Montreal with her. Talk to him, Sonny, he's like a brother to you. Thank God Charlie took him under his wing. His uncle's a flake, always AWOL."

Arlene's heart breaks for her cousin. Her mother and Johnny's mother, Laura, are sisters . . . *were* sisters. Mrs. Fabrella is dead. She moved to the States before Johnny was born, one of the 40,000 Newfoundland women who fell for US servicemen during the Second World War. Johnny's mother was smitten by Giovanni Battista Fabrella, Captain, US Army Air Corps, who was stationed at Fort Pepperrell in St. John's. Johnny has a framed photograph of Captain Fabrella boarding a train. He's in his military uniform, tall, debonair, pencil moustache. Mrs. Fabrella was married when they fell in love, so they met secretly. After the war, they eloped to New York, where Captain Fabrella died. A weak heart, Johnny said. And Charlie said Johnny's mom died of a broken heart. Johnny was twelve when he came back to Newfoundland, but he's still an American citizen.

Arlene once told me that her Aunt Laura was a free spirit. "She had that fiery red hair as a baby."

Her family visited New York when Johnny was born. "He was a very quiet baby. Mother told Daddy that Laura thought he'd never speak." She laughs. "Now he gets paid for screaming."

"Charlie admires Johnny's singing. He calls music a tool of sanctification. Who said that life without music would be a mistake?"

The wind shifts, looks like rain. "Anyway, he and Celine plan to tie the knot. They met in New York, where she was visiting. Love at first sight, he said, couldn't believe his luck. He caught the bus back to Montreal with her. They spent the summer together."

"Johnny says Montreal's a gas, he could live up there."

Out of the blue she points to the scar on the bridge of my nose. "Little early for Halloween."

"Skated into a flying puck the other day. Dumb, huh?"

"It bother you?"

"Hurt like hell at first. I get a lot of migraines—"

"No. I mean the scar. It's for life, right?"

"Never think about it. Don't look in the mirror."

She smiles, a hint of red in her cheeks. "I couldn't live without a mirror." She laughs. "It's all I'd need on a desert island."

I quote my father: "Thank God mirrors only show us our looks." Her mouth hiking up one side knocks me for a loop.

We leave the woods, hurry along crunching gravel, and I think of Charlie's illness, his crazy request to help him cross the river. It tears me to pieces, but maybe it's not so crazy. He'll be reunited with his Lucy, my Lucy too, strictly speaking. It makes perfect sense in a way, to be with the one you love after you die, or, as Charlie says, *especially* when you die. A sadness comes over me, the dread of being without him. Arlene says, "A penny for your thoughts."

I turn to her brown eyes, her skewed mouth. "My dad pisses me off sometimes. He has some crazy notions."

"Join the club. Wanna talk?"

"Another time." I pick up the pace, afraid she'll see my watery eyes.

At White's Esso, I remind her I'll come by tomorrow at one. She and Johnny already agreed to help deliver groceries to poor families out the Brook way.

"Should I bring anything?"

"Just your beautiful self."

"My goodness, aren't you the charmer." She spins, marches off, then quickly turns back. "See you tomorrow."

4

WHILE CHARLIE'S IN THE BATHROOM, THE YOUNG DOCTOR, HAIR PULLED back in a ponytail, drops a clipboard on Charlie's bed.

"Your mother with you?"

"Mother's dead."

"Sorry to hear. Sending him home tomorrow. To get his affairs in order."

My heart pounds, though I knew it was coming.

"Your father have any family members? A sibling?"

"My Aunt Vivian's closest to him, she lives in Stephenville. His cousin Art lives up the shore." I don't mention that Charlie's weirdness has alienated everyone in the family except his brother, my Uncle Ches, who lives in Ontario.

The doctor jots down his phone number. "Tell someone to call me. He shouldn't be left alone. Blood pressure's way up."

"So's mine."

The doctor smiles weakly. "None of this is easy."

"No."

"He's had several seizures, significant damage to the neurological system. Has all the symptoms of lead poisoning: fatigue, anemia, paranoia. What's he do for a living?"

"Auto mechanic."

"His brain's damaged. Exhaust fumes are extremely toxic." He nods toward the bathroom. "I don't give him much time. No cure for reversing the effects of lead poisoning. I'm sorry." He takes the clipboard, writes something, and asks if I'm looking after myself, eating properly, sleeping okay.

"Yeah, my Aunt Vivian's visiting, to keep an eye on me."

"Good. Glad to hear that."

As he's leaving, I say, "How much?"

He turns and looks at me quizzically.

"How much time?"

The doctor shrugs. "A week. Two, maybe."

I think of lead coursing through Charlie's body, his deranged brain, and I choke up. Last week he went missing. I found him wandering around town looking for a street I didn't recognize the name of. Turns out it's a street in one of Louis L'Amour's novels. He's in and out these days. Losing his noodle, he calls it.

Stooped, Charlie comes from the bathroom, stares at the clipboard, and grunts. The hair on the back of his head sticks up. This past year he's aged, shrunk. He's only fifty-eight, but he looks ninety. He pushes the intravenous pole ahead, chattering about no smoking in his room, his voice high and hoarse, but now it's sometimes as high as a choirboy's. I can't remember when his voice wasn't hoarse. We trudge along the hallway, take the elevator to the main entrance.

He nods sharply. "Lord, teach me Thy statutes." He stops, out of breath, flicks a thumb over his shoulder. "Back of the building, so's I can smoke."

A stethoscope dangles from his neck. I ask about it.

He wheezes in his rasping voice, "Resident left it." He winks broadly, says we're gonna need it, he'll explain later. His shoulders jerk, rattling laughter louder than usual. He's a prankster and a pack rat. Even a bit of kleptomania. He built a shed behind the garage to store the things he collects, anything that isn't bolted down. And I love him for it.

Dark circles under his eyes today. Like all the McCluskeys, my father is tall and skinny. He has a swollen nose, small nests of purple veins spreading on each cheekbone. Whiskey maps, he calls them. His chin's always a mess of grey stubble. I've been hounding him for ages to grow a full beard or shave that prickly fuzz. Really, he takes better care of his car.

"They're lettin' me out tomorrow." He tugs his hospital gown, runs a hand through a full head of silver hair. "*Release*, they calls it." Sometimes he slurs his words. He hums, then sings, "Please release me, let me go." He gurgles, stops suddenly, spits. "Release! You'd think the place was a prison. Unhooking this contraption tomorrow, I can leave at noon. Noon!" He spits again, clears his throat. "You know what? Bring the getaway car. Be down soon's I get my pants on."

I ask if he's sure, we can wait till morning.

"Sure I'm sure," he spits out in his rough voice. "Doc says I have a week, two weeks, maybe." He pauses, screws up his face. "To get my affairs in order!

Doctors! They think they decide when you die. God tells us when the time's up. There's but one God who's Lord over all the earth, and His name's not Doctor Almighty Ponytail." He gurgles, laughs. "Affairs in order! What a joke! Would make sense if I was seeing a few women."

I burst out laughing. "The doctor means well, Charlie."

"Doctors! Humph. Good mechanics, bad mechanics." He waves a hand, shuts his eyes, his way of saying forget it. He seems to gurgle again, but I recognize the word *gawgew*, a favourite of his that he uses when he's drinking. He's a great lover of words and, as he often reminds me, whiskey.

5

WE PUSH THROUGH THE HEAVY ER DOOR AND HEAD OUTSIDE. He launches into his rant about how most people wouldn't agree with what we're doing, they'd say it's a sin. "Growing up, John Dillinger was my hero. A real Robin Hood. Like him, the McCluskeys are outlaws." He smirks. "There's no law between the heart and God. When Dillinger died, people begged for a lock of his hair. Had to keep replacing his tombstone because people chipped away at it for relics. Today people worship the Rockefellers and the Rothschilds, the real thieves." He stops, spits, asks if I think that people today know what sin is.

"No."

"They think greed is good, anything that feels good is good." He lifts his head, squints, as if remembering something. Then, with urgency in his voice, he reminds me that my great-great-grandfather, John-Dan McCluskey, was a preacher and a great champion of the poor.

"Most people don't know which end is up, they believe in ghosts but not the Holy Ghost, the spirit of truth. The average Joe leads a life that's nothing but a beeline to the grave, making a lot of little circles and squares to keep his mind off that beeline." People are so confused, he says, they think the rich and powerful are saints. *Woe to you rich, you've had your consolation.* "It's an upside-down world."

"Some rich people are kind."

"Some. Not many! Ha, ha! Never was a millionaire put his head through the eye of a needle. Foul is fair in this world where the poor always get screwed."

I think of Crenshaw, who often comes to the garage to have a swally of whiskey and rap. "Crenshaw's a big fan of Fidel Castro."

"I'm a big fan of Jesus. The McCluskeys have always been on the side of the downtrodden. We've been politicians, union leaders, clerics, and outlaws;

we've never worked for the rich. Never! It's the McCluskey way. Throughout my illness, the Lord's reminded me to love the poor. He's always in charge. Don't ever forget that." He gurgles, spits again, and I turn aside at the sight of blood. "You'll be tempted too. The devil's greatest trick—convincing you he doesn't exist."

We move slowly around the outside of the building as I open a pack of Camel cigarettes, light two, give him one. I only smoke with him or when I'm uptight. He takes a long drag, turns his head away, says, "You thought about it? I need an acolyte. We'll go late at night, nobody around." Another drag. "Ah," he says, "the pause that refreshes." He steadies the intravenous pole, snaps his fingers, orange with nicotine, motions for the pack. Then he hikes up his gown, takes a leak against the building. "Second thought, *that's* the pause that refreshes." He puffs his cigarette, complains his mouth is dry as chips, asks if I've brought the juice, meaning whiskey.

I point toward the parking lot. "Glove compartment, almost empty. Liquor store wouldn't serve me, asked for ID."

He scowls. "Legs feel like marshmallows." He looks shrivelled, yellow.

He flicks ash from his cigarette, stares at me. "You memorize everything I told you about the plates? Plates can take days." A string bean wearing green scrubs throws a garbage bag into a nearby dumpster. It lands with a thud.

"Yes, Charlie, been over it a thousand times." I'm nervous as all get-out, thinking about his death. Can I go through with this? I take deep breaths, the way he taught me.

"Plate-making's not child's play. It's science. Exact. Burn the plates too long, bills are too dark."

"I know. I know."

"Takes days," he says, smoke drifting above his head.

I remind him I've helped with the printing many times.

"Scrub 'em clean afterwards."

"I will, Charlie."

"And be sure to keep that closet really dark when using the camera."

"For sure, Charlie. I will."

He knows I'm uptight, says, "Well, no need to get your knickers in a knot. You're doing God's work." He grips my shoulder. "You know that, so relax. I wrote it all down for you, in the ledger at the office, with the will. Read it over a few times. You'll need to practise hard before I cross the river." His shoulders hunch. "Still a few things you gotta have down by heart. Did I mention having the plate process down pat?" A dreamy look comes over him. "Sorry, so scatterbrained lately, want everything to go as planned when I'm gone. No screw-ups."

"It will, Charlie, don't worry. There'll be no screw-ups. I know how to make the plates, won't make any mistakes. After the burn I'll scrub 'em spic and span with the chemicals, don't worry." I speak fast. He knows I'm jittery, unable to relax, tells me to breathe deeply, let it out slowly.

"Not the plate-making I'm worried about." A thin trickle of saliva dribbles down his chin. "It's the rest of the rigmarole. Why I wrote down the three-F rule: Forget about tellin' anyone. Forget about tellin' anyone. Forget about tellin' anyone."

"I won't tell anyone, Charlie, I promise."

"And the five-N rule: Never ever tell anyone. Never ever tell anyone—"

"I know. I know."

"Especially a girl. You don't have a chance with a girl. Eve tempted Adam—"

"Charlie, you're beating a dead horse."

He lights a cigarette off the one he's smoking. Haven't seen that before. He's rattled. "You'll want to tell someone. Guaranteed. Hard thing to hold inside. But lemme remind you . . ." He looks around, whispers, "Penalty's jail time. Even for an eighteen-year-old. Federal offence. Maximum twelve years, where you'll be makin' a different kinda plates." Rattling laughter again. "Look, I'm handing you down somethin' been in the family for generations. The family legacy. It's a gift, Sonny. A great gift, prophecy. Don't throw it away. We're like Abraham, son, called into exile, we must look after our brothers and sisters. You understand that, don't you? He's put eternity into man's heart. We all have a choice—time or timelessness. I choose the latter—eternity. There's no time with God. Like the Good Book says, 'A thousand years, a single day: it's all one.' The inner law of freedom shouts *life*. Death can't kill us. We need the eternal, the infinite, to be human. You get that, don't you?"

I nod.

"Eternity isn't endless future. It's endless present. Eternal life doesn't begin after death. And when the choice is between life and death, there's no such thing as sin. Remember, the rich own the earth. We can never be satisfied here. Never."

There's a sudden shortness of breath, then raspy laughter. "You remember the time I had it out with Bert White at his Esso station? I thought poor Bert would pass out, with his asthma, his belching. Kept breathing so hard. Said he'd buy me out. Buy him out, more like it. Bert the jerk! Doesn't know the difference between a lug wrench and a hammer. How do you make a million dollars working for Bert White?" He chuckles. "Start with two million! Guy doesn't know his ass from a toolbox. Always asking to team up. Join forces, he says. We'd make twice the money."

Two men stop nearby to smoke. We wander off. When we're out of earshot, he says, "He means he'd make twice the money, and I'd do all the work. Besides, he's a Catholic."

I don't see what religion has to do with it and ask what difference that makes.

"Big difference," he says. "Big, big difference. They don't believe in reincarnation."

"Neither do Anglicans."

"I do," he says. "And I studied to become a priest." He slaps my shoulder, calls me a son of a monk, and cackles.

When he was young, he did study for the priesthood but left because "They didn't understand that Jesus came to destroy class rule, that He wanted to turn everything upside down. Ergo, I do it my way." He follows his own brand of Christianity—the combo, he calls it—bits from different Christian denominations and a lot from the wise East.

I once accused him of creating a smorgasbord religion. He laughed and said what saves him is his cornerstone, Robin Hood, the stone rejected by the builders. "Most people think Robin Hood's a fairy tale, like 'Snow White' and 'Cinderella.' Charity's the ultimate imitation of Christ. Jesus was the first Robin Hood, the first great antiestablishmentarian. Remember Robin of Locksley."

I recall my first fake dollar bill. I still have it. He pressed it in my hand and said, "God made money—the fresh air too—for his children's use. He never made the difference between rich and poor. Right over might. Listen to your inner voice, your conscience, else this sterile world will kill you."

And it's that very thing, my conscience, which won't let me have anything to do with his crazy death scheme. It's wrong, and I know it.

He believes in a thing called the transmigration of souls, says Jesus believed it too: *Whatsoever a man soweth, that shall he also reap*. It's all karma, he says. What goes around comes around.

"We'll always be together, Sonny. The world has it ass-backwards. Death isn't the end, it's the beginning. Death's just a doorway. I've had a full life. I'm ready to go now." He looks me straight in the eye and grins. "Eternity, son! Here and now! Why Jesus became one of us. We've all got the Christ virus now. Whether we like it or not, we live in the fullness of time. It says in the Good

Book somewhere that the things of time are one with eternity. Can't recall where. Mind's shot. Everything changes, dies, disappears . . . returns." He perks up. "Yes, yes, I remember: To everything there is a season. No tears when I'm gone, and never refer to me in the past tense. We'll always be together, Sonny. No need for tears. No long goodbyes. None of that."

I wipe my eyes again, force a smile. "Okay . . . I'm okay."

He flinches, jerks the IV pole toward the emergency exit, and says, "I'll undo this contraption and be down in a minute. You bring the getaway car."

I head to the parking lot, heave a sigh, addled about burying him, how sick he is, how good he's always been to me. Lots of fathers in the Cove lay on the belt with their kids. Not Charlie. He never gets angry. Oh, he can rant about the rich, the unjust rich, and he can pull some crazy capers, but he never frightens me, never makes me fret or feel bad. Never has. He's like a child in many ways, and I guess the child in him always gets along with his own child.

I pull up front; he appears wearing faded jeans and his favourite jacket, a Harris tweed, riddled with holes from cigarette ashes. I tell him to patch those pockets. He says no, the jacket has character. When he plays darts at the Legion, nobody'll steal it. "Love that jacket, feel like a professor," he says. "Maybe I was in a former life. Or will be in the next. Philosophy, maybe, or music, like Johnny." A shadow crosses his face. "You will look after him, won't you? Promise me."

"I promise."

"My fondest wish, you two working together in the garage." He perks up. "Or maybe I'll be a literature professor." He coughs, laughs. "Either way, Louis L'Amour will be required reading." He reads only westerns except for his favourite book, *Robinson Crusoe*, which he's always reading. "All you need to survive in this world. Crusoe was independent, a free man, one of a kind."

He takes forever to get in the car. I'm jittery, check the rear-view mirror for security. On the drive home, he opens the glove compartment and swigs whiskey. "Never make anything over a twenty, Sonny. Cops are hawks about anything over a twenty."

6

NEXT DAY'S WINDY, A FINE DRIZZLE FALLING. I drive to White's Esso in our butterscotch pickup: rear-wheel drive powered by a straight-six engine, manual transmission. She's old, but she's a beauty. A dozen food hampers are strapped beneath a ratty army tarp in the cargo bed.

With an ear-splitting rumble, Arlene's café racer pulls up beside the old bubblehead gas pump, the kind only found in the country these days. You can hear it a mile away because she's souped up the muffler. It's equipped with black leather saddlebags. Her baby, she calls it; you mess with it at your peril. One day after class she found a guy sitting on it and gave him a piece of her mind. He never sat on it again.

"Poor man's Harley," I say.

She sticks out her tongue. "You look lousy. You feelin' okay? We can do this tomorrow."

"Just a headache. I'm okay."

She's wearing her biker jacket, black leather chaps, hair pulled back in a ponytail. She removes her helmet, undoes her ponytail, shakes out her thick, wavy hair.

"Snazzy jacket," I say. "Hop in."

"Where the food hampers?"

"'Neath the tarp, a dozen stops."

"All out the Brook way?"

"No."

"Johnny can't make it. He's helping one of the hippies find his lost cat."

We drive in silence. She turns on the radio. "Little music? Johnny says you should always have a song in your heart."

Radio static, then she sings along with "Four Strong Winds." *Think I'll go out to Alberta, weather's good there in the fall . . .* "One of these days I might just hop on my bike and head out there. Goodbye, Daddy."

More static. I smack the radio. "Sometimes that works." Not this time.

"Mind if I sing a capella?"

"Fill yer boots."

"Song I did last week at church, my favourite:

Amazing Grace! How sweet the sound,
That saved a wretch like me . . ."

I don't usually like people singing solo, but her voice is beguiling: silky, sad. She finishes. I clap, blow the horn. "That was beautiful, and I don't like church music."

"Music is music." She glances my way with puzzled eyes. "It's all beautiful. You sing?"

"Can't carry a note."

She laughs, says everyone can sing, it's just a matter of confidence. "I'm pretty good, don'tcha think?" She glances slyly, that lopsided smile again.

"Oh, you're more than pretty good—"

"Mmm." She looks out her window, trees blurring in the gentle rain. "I'm singing the responsorial psalm at church this Sunday. First time. You should come."

"Maybe."

"We're all Christians, Sonny. We're all singing from the same hymn book. Come, why don'tcha?"

"Maybe." I don't know what hymn book I'm singing from. When you help your father to kill himself, you don't know what to believe anymore.

She reaches over and pokes me. "I'll make a mick out of you yet, McCluskey."

7

BROOK ROAD IS LINED ON BOTH SIDES WITH RAMSHACKLE HOUSES, SOME abandoned, shuttered with plywood windows and doors, paint peeling off, broken-down porches, sagging roofs. Many chimneys have fallen down. Weeds choke the yards, overgrown grass everywhere. It's a washed-out dirt road, plenty of potholes. I'm sad when I come here but always get a lift too. People are grateful, ask about Charlie, make me promise to say hello.

I point to a For Sale sign on what looks like a one-room school and, nearby, what's left of a few houses, jagged bits of concrete sticking out of the ground.

"My goodness!" Arlene says. "*Les Miserables*."

"The poor we shall always have with us."

"Ridiculous that people should live like this in 1967. Canada's one of the richest countries in the world."

"Crenshaw says we'd be better off in a communist state. Cuba has one of the highest literacy rates in the world, free health care, free—"

"A model country in some ways. But they banned the Beatles." She looks around. "Good Lord! Probably no central heating."

"Or indoor plumbing. Yet some of these people are the happiest I've ever met."

The first driveway is owned by the Ricketts family and their deaf German shepherd, Bruno, who heralds our approach with loud barking. Their small house is odd-looking. A few years ago there was a fire, and an anonymous donor (Charlie) paid for the renovation. Mr. Ricketts insisted on building an extension at the side that's bigger than the house.

Mrs. Ricketts's big moon face, crowned with head scarf and curlers, pops out from behind laundry hanging on the line. She's a plump little woman in her sixties, and you can see her big breasts flopping around under her turtleneck sweater as she walks toward us. She points a pen flashlight at Bruno's teeth and pets him. When he stops barking, she gives him a treat.

I roll down the window and holler, "Hello, missus."

She greets us with a smile that's missing front teeth. "How is ya, Sonny? Some good to see ya. I see youse brung your girlfriend." I introduce Arlene. Mrs. Ricketts says, "My, but you has some lovely eyes. The angels knew what they was doin' when they sent youse into the world."

Arlene laughs, unties the tarp.

Mrs. Ricketts says, "Is ye stayin' for a cuppa?"

I tell her we won't be able to, quite a few stops, weather's miserable.

"Well, if ye can't stay for a cuppa, what about a great big hug?" She throws her arms around me, turns to Arlene. "You too!" she shouts. "Youse not gettin' outta here either without a great big hug." Arlene laughs, hugs her, pets Bruno. Mrs. Ricketts stands back from the truck with her hamper as we leave. "Say hi to Charlie. God bless you!"

I toot the horn, drive off. In the rear-view mirror, a pair of long johns jumps cheerfully on the line.

As we drive, the drizzle turns to mist. We pass a boarded-up post office with graffiti: GROOVY, BONEYARD, FREAK OUT. Next stop, half-mile away, Johnny Fabrella's dilapidated old house. He lives at the end of a barren clay road: houses with flat pitch-gravel roofs, siding made of dull asphalt shingles. The faded exterior of his place has a greenish-grime sheen to it; the lot is separated from the road by a rusty fence.

"No car in the driveway," Arlene says. "Probably not home."

We unload a hamper, head to his house. I knock, open the porch door, which is always unlocked, call out, "Special delivery for Johnny Fabrella!" No answer.

The porch is the colour of butter, smells musty. We wait a bit. Arlene says, "Think he'll go?"

"He's an American citizen, old enough to get his head blown off."

Her sideways smile turns to a sickly grimace. "But he's a Canadian citizen too, has dual citizenship, right?"

"He's an American, Arlene. He'll wind up in Johnson's dirty little war."

"But Johnny's a pacifist—"

"Says he'll peel potatoes, carry a stretcher. I told him he's crazy. I'd dodge the draft if they came looking for me."

"That war's so wrong."

"He's torn, doesn't want to be a coward. His dad fought in World War II and Korea. Charlie says all wars are a racket, a way to make the rich richer. And the public gets fooled every time. The rich just run the flag up the pole to sucker people."

"I'll say a little prayer for him. Maybe he'll marry his girl, settle down in Montreal."

"Doubt it." I call Johnny's name again—no answer—put the box on the porch floor, and leave.

We head up the bumpy road, pass a boarded-up store: CLEM'S GROCERIES. Old tires, rusty cans, bottles are strewn along a shallow bank. As we drive, I ask Arlene what she liked so much about the movie *A Man for All Seasons*.

"The man had a conscience." She leans back. "He died for his principles. Rare birds, that kind."

I want to bring up my father's situation without mentioning him, so I make up a lie about a TV movie. "About an old man diagnosed with terminal cancer. He's between a rock and a hard place. Doctor says he only has a few weeks to live. He's in a lot of pain and asks his wife to help him die—"

"You mean to kill him?"

"Old man says it's not like killing someone, not suicide—"

"It's called mercy killing, but it's still *killing*."

"He says he's gonna die as sure as there's poop in a dead cat, can she help speed things up, help avoid the suffering. His wife refuses, says that'd make her a murderer."

"She's right. It incriminates her as an accessory, she'd go to jail."

"But there's a twist. The old man's religious, says Jesus knew when He was gonna die and could've stopped it, but He didn't. Wasn't that a kind of suicide? he asks his wife. If you're gonna die anyway, one foot in the grave, the other on a banana peel, what's the big deal?"

Arlene's eyes widen, her voice shoots up an octave. "What kinda harebrained logic is that? You're saying it's murder to kill someone but not suicide to kill yourself? That's cuckoo. Thou shalt not kill means yourself *or* anyone else."

"But Jesus was God. He could've saved Himself—"

"Jesus was human like everyone else." She shakes her head. "He behaved like a human being even though He didn't have to, He had a divine nature too."

"But what if the person was really suffering? You wouldn't let a dog suffer. Would you let Bruno suffer if he was really old and sick? Wouldn't you put him out of his misery?"

"You're still talking about mercy killing." She's silent for a bit, then says, "I don't agree with mercy killing. Even if I did, that would be for a doctor, a lawyer, the family, a lot of other people to decide, not me."

"But isn't it a matter of conscience? Isn't it the same as that movie you liked so much?"

"No!" She shrugs, throws up her hands. "It's a million times different, other side of the galaxy. Just because someone *thinks* something's right doesn't make it right. There's a big difference between fact and fiction. If I think it's right to take your truck, that doesn't make it right. It's still theft, and that makes me crazy for thinking it's right to steal it. That's why we have the Church to guide us based on tradition and truth, the commandments."

I don't agree with her, but she sounds pretty upset, so I say she's right and drop it. "It was the late movie, I was tired, might've missed something."

"Facts are facts," she says. "Fiction is fiction."

"But aren't all movies fiction? Wasn't *A Man for All Reasons* fiction?"

"Seasons!" She laughs. "*A Man for All* Seasons. And that movie was based on something that really happened. That's called historical fiction."

"I didn't mean to make this so complicated." I hope she doesn't think I'm stupid.

"It's not complicated. It's quite simple, actually. There's fact and there's fiction. Fiction is usually made up, except when it's based on fact, like *A Man for All Seasons*. Thomas More was a real person. He lived in the sixteenth century and was the Lord Chancellor of England. That's historical fact. *Winnie the Pooh and the Honey Tree* is fiction. *Blow-up* is fiction."

"I get it."

"Do you really?" She leans over, touches my arm. She doesn't think so.

"Yeah, I do." I don't say anything else, just drive on, staring straight ahead at the misty road, wishing I hadn't brought up the topic in the first place, and wondering how in God's name I'm going to convince my crazy father to change his mind.

8

I PRETEND I'M SICK, TAKE TIME OFF SCHOOL FOR CHARLIE'S FINAL QUIZ: making the plates, shooting the negatives, mixing ink, and running the offset press. It's all hidden in Charlie's Auto, a garage about thirty yards from our house, a small brick bungalow with a low sloped roof and dormer windows.

Charlie's motto: *I treat every car like my car.* As I say, the garage is always spic and span, a place for everything and everything in its place. It's about 1,000 square feet and has two bays, one for lube jobs and oil and filter changes, the other for diagnostics, exhaust, brakes, suspension and safeties, with paint jobs thrown in when there's time. It also has a small office with a six-by-four-foot steel safe that weighs about 300 pounds, which Charlie says a megaton bomb wouldn't bust open. And in the back there's a 100-square-foot storage area.

One of the bays has a six-foot pit with steps leading down to a dirt floor and cement walls built with thick wooden pilings and two feet of reinforced concrete. On the far wall there's a padlocked, rusting steel door that leads to a soundproof print shop. This is where Charlie keeps the counterfeit equipment, including Rosie, his homemade, cutting-edge offset press, a compact machine with a spinning plate cylinder that inks an image on a rubber cylinder and then transfers it to paper. He rebuilt the offset printer with parts from second-hand A B Dick presses and the plates from sheets of aluminum; they took forever to make. "Plates have to be perfect," he tells me. "One mistake, you ruin the whole batch and have to start the process all over again."

I recall recently watching him work on the press late one night. "I call her Rosie," he said when he finished, "after your great-great-grandmother, who ran the operation for years when her husband got sick. Provides perfect colour reproductions of crisp, clean bills, no spots or streaks. And she always gets the colours dead-on. We can do a large run, 500 or more." He winks. "For big jobs we get more for our money."

The shop is big enough to move around in. It consists of a darkroom for developing negatives and a plate-making station complete with light table—and Rosie. It's designed to use incrementally until you have a fresh sheet of minted $20 bills ready for the paper cutter. There are storage spots for paper, chemicals, ink. Everything in its place.

Against the far wall in the shadows is an ink-black machine, a heavy cast-iron clunker of a press that Charlie calls the old monster. And from a distance it does look like some strange, prehistoric beast. In its day it produced 250 prints per hour. It's in good working condition, but Charlie never uses it. He's kept it all these years for sentimental reasons. It was given to Charlie's father, Aaron, by his father, David McCluskey, whose family used to print the *St. John's Gazette* in the 1800s. Working in the garage, my father would often groan and say why did we move from ink under our thumbs to grease under our nails?

"If you ever have to vamoose, try to save the old monster," he says. "It's an heirloom and a work of art. Been in the family over a century. You mightn't be able to if you have to skedaddle, but save it if you can." He spits blood.

I hang my head, don't want to look. He points to the machine, puts his hand on my shoulder, and says that the old monster helped quite a few poor people in its time.

I nod. "I'll do everything to save it."

9

HE SEEMS CHIPPER TODAY, ONE OF HIS GOOD DAYS. But lately he seems so weak I wonder if he'll need help to *do the deed*.

"Measurements have to be perfect or the negatives won't come out right," he repeats as we go over everything in the print shop for the umpteenth time. He swigs whiskey he keeps handy and rants about mixing the inks properly. "Getting a colour proof is the hardest part," he rasps. "Plates and ink can get expensive. And the ink must be perfect, Sonny. You can botch a lot of paper if you don't mix the inks right." Then he walks me through the process step by step: 1. Turn on the press. 2. Lift the paper. 3. Place the plates. 4. Start the front run.

"Look for fuzzy areas," he cautions, "especially around the edges. Real bills have precise, even borders."

I ask about the lightweight newsprint we use. "How long will the stock last?"

"Enough for your lifetime," he says. "But if you run out or it spoils or somethin', the three paper mills carry it by the ton. Just don't buy too much the once. Don't wanna raise eyebrows. Next thing you know, the cops are in the driveway. Speaking of cops, watch what you say around your pal Quinn. His father's climbing the Constabulary ladder in St. John's. Nice man, but a cop all the same."

Another swig of whiskey. "When you're droppin' the dough"—his name for getting rid of the counterfeit bills by spending them and getting real change back—"remember only twenties, nothing but twenties. That'll keep you from getting too greedy."

He snatches a crisp sheet of bills from the tray and reminds me that the serial numbers are all the same. "That's why you need to get out of Dodge when you're droppin' the dough. Never drop any in the city. And only one twenty per store or gas station, no more. Take a day off, drive around the Avalon, as far as Clarenville, maybe. There's a list of places, with drop-records, for

Conception Bay. Believe me, you'll have a grand in jig time out CBS way. A grand! That's the limit. Greed's the only thing can ruin a man in this game."

He says to head home when I've dropped the dough, stash the clean money in the print shop, and update the records right away. "Lie low for a few months. Read the papers. Listen to the news. Keep your ear to the ground for any announcements about fake bills being used on the Avalon. Never carry any more than a few bucks in your wallet. No need to show off."

His shaky hand slaps my back. It doesn't have the oomph it used to. He says he's proud of me, I seem to have the whole operation down pat. He reminds me that I'll always need the auto shop. He cautions again against greed, pats my shoulder. "Do this for the poor, level the playing field."

He says he wishes he had an estate to leave me, an inheritance. "The garage is an inheritance of sorts, the family legacy! Pass it on when the time comes."

He screws the top on his whiskey bottle. "Give most of the money to good causes—someone loses his house in a fire, that sort of thing. There's an updated notebook in the print shop. You can add a cause, but don't drop any. Coupla hundred dollars now and then, larger amounts when warranted. Real money, of course—never fake. Give to the churches if you like, but don't give them too much, they'll just buy more gold candlesticks."

He brags that the McCluskeys have always been good thieves, that if you traced them back to Sherwood Forest, you'd find a McCluskey among Robin Hood's Merry Men. "If you donate to a church, just put the money in an anonymous envelope. There's a poor box at the back of most churches. Wear gloves. Don't put anything in the mail. It can be traced. There are a million ways to help, as many to get caught. There's a long list in the notebook. Keep good records. Your mother loved to give to the Sally Ann. Promise me you'll do that too, won't you?"

"I promise."

"And Johnny's mother gave to the Red Cross—"

"I promise."

"Good!" He lights a cigarette, squints at the flame. He lifts his head and with one eye closed looks at the trail of smoke, and I recall the story of Lazarus in agony in the flames of hell. He waves the lit match my way, asks if I've thought any more about the burial. "I want to be with your mother for eternity, body and soul."

There's a small lump in my throat. I swallow hard, say, "I'm not doing it. I've made up my mind, Dad. I can't . . . I won't."

It's the first time in a long while I call him Dad, and I'm surprised he doesn't correct me. I'm so overcome, I tear up and head to the house to start supper. As I close the garage door, his bark is loud as a thunderclap: *Charlie*!

10

VROOM, VROOM-VROOM, VA-VA VAROOM AND WE'RE OFF . . . Arlene's in her own world. She's wearing her leather jacket, black leather chaps.

"On my racer," shouting over her shoulder, "is the only time I'm free, really in the moment."

"The here and now," I shout back. "Eternity!"

"You got it, baby. Power is sent to the rear wheel through chain-driven primary." She swerves recklessly to avoid a paper bag. "Four-speed transmission shifted by foot."

The engine revving reminds me of angry bees. The wind is roaring in my ears, both arms tight around her waist, the seat surprisingly comfortable. First time on a motorcycle and I'm scared.

"Stay tight," she yells, "don't wiggle around, throws me off . . . might throw you off. If you get antsy, bite your lip." She turns her head, laughs. "And don't bang your helmet against me. Hate that." She reminds me to put my feet down firmly whenever we stop and groans that she once broke off her boot heel putting her foot down too quickly. "Wait till we come to a full stop."

She taps my knee, lets me know she's accelerating, meaning she'll hit 100 mph. She's installed passenger foot peg extensions to make it cooler on the feet. "Keep an eye out for wild animals," she shouts over the engine's growl. "At sixty mph we're travelling eighty-eight feet per second. Don't fall asleep."

"Don't worry."

"Doing a hundred now," she calls as we zoom up the twisty highway. The fir trees are blurring by, and I'm hoping my face doesn't get windburn.

"Slow down, you'll save gas."

"It does one twenty-five." She speeds up, brakes hard to avoid a rabbit scurrying across the road.

We're on our way to Butter Pot Park to check out the stage for the concert. Each time she passes a car, I think I'll die, endless dips in the road, potholes everywhere. An eighteen-wheeler roars by, the bike shakes in its wake.

At the park, she takes notes as we measure the stage area. Afterwards, we drive along the rocky path checking out campsites, stopping at one hidden deep in the woods. She takes a small sign marked RESERVED from a saddle-bag and stakes it into the ground. "Most peaceful spot in the park," she says. "Nobody wants to walk this far. Sleep like a baby up here. Ver-ry cool." She winks. "Ver-ry private!"

As we head back, she asks how I liked my first ride.

"Not bad, feel a lot better if you'd stick to the speed limit."

She sticks out her tongue, mounts the bike. "Daddy was drunk again last night. Get on." *Vroom*! Angry bees again. "Sometimes I feel like hopping on this thing and just going."

"Where?"

"Anywhere outta this world. Away from the parents. Wanna come?"

"No."

"We could catch the midnight ferry in Port aux Basques."

"No way."

"C'mon, why not? *Think I'll go out to Alberta—*"

"Got a garage to run."

"Chicken!"

Vroom, and we're off. She's in her own world again. We hit the highway, and in no time she's over the speed limit, me hanging on for dear life.

"Speed limit!" I yell.

Her answer: *Varooooooooooom*!

11

I DIDN'T ASK WHERE HE GOT THE PILLS, FIVE OF THEM: three morphine tablets, two cyanide capsules. My father can get his hands on anything, lickety-split.

"It's a crazy idea, Charlie. A movie, you say?"

"Yeah, a western. Saw it quite a while ago. Ten years, maybe." He was always watching western movies. And he read every Louis L'Amour book he could find. Sometimes he'd read a book two or three times. L'Amour's memoir, *Education of a Wandering Man*, was a favourite. He'd often read aloud from it.

"L'Amour dropped outta school at fifteen," he'd say.

"That's something to be proud of?"

"Gawgew! I'm a school dropout. I always wanted to write a novel like him, one with your mother in the leading role. Mister Louis Dearborn L'Amour has written about fifty novels and a ton of short stories. He's sold over 100 million copies. One hundred million! That's a lot of oil changes. I reckon he'll sell 300 million before he dies. They're all still in print, and most of 'em have been made into movies. Not bad for a high school dropout. There's hope for Johnny."

"What about the movie?"

"It starred Alan Ladd. Was it *Shane*? Maybe it was *Shane*. Mind's shot. Or *The Big Land*, maybe. I dunno. Sorry, son, old noodle's not what it used to be. Anyway, it opens with a posse surrounding a house during a shootout. Inside, a cowboy's digging a hole in the dirt floor. 'They'll torch the house soon,' he says, 'one of us should get out alive.' He tells the younger cowboy, his son, that the hole is a trick he learned from his father. 'You get in the hole, I'll cover you with a wet blanket. Before I fill in the hole, I'll stick a punctured can in the ground so you can breathe. When the place is burnt down, they won't notice you're in the ground. They'll think you escaped. I'll crash through the door with both guns blazin'. They'll shoot me but think you got away out the back.'"

I don't bother mentioning that the young cowboy would die from smoke inhalation. You don't argue with Charlie about westerns.

"When the fire dies down, the posse leader inspects what's left of the house. 'The other one got away.' He curses and kicks the can before they ride off. Then the young cowboy rises from the grave, Lazarus back from the dead. It's the best opening of a movie I've ever seen."

He looks at me like I'm supposed to know what he's thinking. I ask what the movie's got to do with him taking the pills.

"That movie gave me the idea about crossing the river," he says. "You know where your mother's grave is. What's special about it?"

I shrug. "The small Celtic Cross?"

"Your mother's grave is near a private corner in Mount Carmel Cemetery where they buried the nuns way back when. The northwest section. Nobody goes there anymore. We'll do it before your birthday. My days are getting short."

"Charlie, we've had this out. There's no way—"

"I know. I know . . . I made a breathing contraption. It's in the shop. Just in case I don't cross the river." He grins. "Wouldn't wanna be buried alive."

"Charlie, you're crazy. Is this another stunt? You can't do this." I recall his Halloween trick-or-treat stunts. We'd dress up as Robin Hood and Little John and knock on poor people's doors, giving out groceries instead of asking for candy. People in the Cove call him Mother Teresa.

"Why not?"

"It's crazy, that's why."

"Gawgew!" A sly glance. "Only right I be with your mother." He clutches my shoulder. "You think that clown Father McCarthy has a right to dictate where a man and woman, *husband and wife*, can be buried? No way! *Never*! I'll show the high and mighty, the powers that be."

He's spitting sparks now, so I clam up, leave it for another time.

12

ARLENE HASN'T RETURNED MY CALL. Is she playing hard to get? Maybe she's upset I didn't say I'd listen to her sing at church. Or maybe she's busy studying or working at the gas station, or she's with Esther-Marie right now working out their harmonies for the Pot Park Concert. Arlene sings country and western, mostly, which I hate, but her rendition of "I Fall to Pieces" gets to me. And she's really good at deliberately flubbing songs. On stage she puns and adds silly words to make people laugh. She plays the guitar, only knows four chords, C, F, G, and D, but says it's amazing the songs you can play with them.

That night she calls, and we talk for hours on the phone: Johnny and Vietnam—will he go? will he stay?—her parents, school, movies. Thankfully, she avoids the amalgamation question. We tell endless jokes to each other. If there's a long silence, she ends it with a tongue twister: I saw Susie sitting in a shoeshine shop. Where she shines, she sits, and where she sits, she shines. She insists that I try it, and of course I muff it.

Everything is looking up. We like the same things. I love that she's into motorcycles and mechanics. Age nine, she wired an alarm from her front door to her bedroom so she'd know when her parents came home. She took her first motorcycle apart when she was thirteen. We like the same music, sports, pizza, and we both hate raisins. But she's sloppy and I'm neat. The other day at Thelma's she said that women do all the work, who cares if the dishes pile up. I can live with that. And sometimes she teases me about my messy hair and clothes. Hey, I work in a garage. The only serious differences between us are religion and our fathers. She's pretty set in her Catholic ways. But she doesn't like talking about her dad. When you grow up with a father like Charlie, you can get pretty confused about religion. He was right about some things—I like the prayers he taught me, like saying them, especially the Our Father. And I like his notion of eternity. Other things—dharma and karma—I'm not so sure.

The choir leader nods Arlene's way, and she sings: *The Lord is my shepherd, there is nothing I shall want.*

The proud parents, he in his business suit, she in her floral, going-out dress, stand in the front row, hymn books open, singing along in unison. They remind me of so many churchgoers, toeing the line. Robots. I don't believe everything Charlie does, but he's right about needing a quiet place if you want to find God. You can hardly hear yourself think in here, such commotion. At least Charlie taught me to think for myself. I could never toe the Church line like Arlene does. Sometimes she can't make a date because of Church commitments. The other day she couldn't come to the A&W because her family was saying First Friday devotional prayers. I mean, c'mon, get a life.

I'm in the pew behind the Whites, nervous, feeling out of place, someone behind me mumbling the rosary. I think of Arlene saying we're all singing from the same hymn book, pick up a hymnal, fumble, and drop it. The Whites turn, shoot me a dirty look.

I gaze at Arlene, a huge statue of an angel, sword raised, towering beyond her. At the altar, Father McCarthy looks my way and nods. The prodigal returned. I remember Lucy talking to him after church. His face reminds me of a newly hatched bird. Red eyes, like he has a bad cold.

I really don't want to be here, rather be in the garage, where it's calm and I can concentrate, but it's Arlene's first time singing the psalm, and she practically begged me to come. I look around the small church. It's a simple gothic design, two Romanesque windows on either side of the nave. Planked walls look like they're from a ship, plain wooden pillars. No interior decoration except for carvings of the stations of the cross mounted on the inside walls, two statues behind the altar. Near the tabernacle, the blood-red sanctuary lamp flickering away; a powerful smell of candle wax reminds me of my mother. I look at the first station of the cross, the carved image of Jesus standing in his crown of thorns before Pontius Pilate.

Then I look around at the people, all the lonely people. The place is packed. Why are they here? And why does Bert White keep coming? There's no money in it for him. Perhaps he's drumming up business. Or keeping up with the Joneses.

I wonder about it all . . . church, religion, if Arlene and her parents are brainwashed. It's all like some fancy formula for finding God. And I don't buy it. You can only live the way you can. There's no single, sure-footed way. If you want a formula, I guess that's what you do, join a church. I believe in going my own way, which is never set in stone, which comes from putting one foot in front of the other each day. Like Charlie, I cut my own path through the woods, not follow someone else. I could never be like the Whites. Charlie was right about one thing for sure. You gotta figure out this religion stuff for yourself.

After the service, Arlene asks me to join everyone for sandwiches in the basement. I tell her I'd love to, but I can't. "I promised to tow a car out the Brook way, guy went into a ditch." A big fat lie. "You sang beautifully, voice of an angel, Johnny always says."

She smiles. "See you at school tomorrow?"

"See you tomorrow." And I'm out of there, lickety-split.

13

HE MOVES WITH A RIGID, PAINED SLOWNESS, LIGHTS A CIGARETTE, SAYS, "I'll dig the hole. You won't have to. Just wrap me in a blanket and lower me down. Is that so hard?" He cocks his head and winks. "We'll dig late at night."

"Charlie, I'm not doing it. I can't." I turn away, look out the garage window, remembering what Arlene said about mercy killing.

"Well, butter my butt and call me a biscuit! Why the hell not?" He stops, out of breath. "It's your mother's plot, what she would've wanted. She was Catholic, but she didn't agree with her priest telling a Protestant where he could be buried."

"I agree, Charlie, it's all pretty silly."

"Hell, it's our plot. If it wasn't for McCarthy. . . . Imagine! The powers that be telling us where we can be buried. And don't you get the logic? It's perfect. We do this late at night, nobody will know I'm gone. It'll buy you time. You're gonna need it till you turn eighteen. Otherwise, the welfare officer will be snoopin' around."

"Tell me you're not serious, Charlie. Please."

"You can tell everyone I went to Toronto to see a specialist. When the time's right, tell 'em I died. I set everything up with your godfather, Uncle Ches, in Scarborough." He flicks his thumb toward the garage. "After our father died, he wanted to leave all this behind. Ches knows what to do. He'll phone you about when to come up, fly back with the coffin. Just do as he says, and remember, he's a man of few words. Take a little trip. See a hockey game, the Maple Leafs, maybe. Stay with Ches, he'll show you the town. Do some shoppin'. Drop a little dough while you're up there. Ches will arrange for a quick burial at the Anglican Cemetery. The coffin will be weighted and sealed. They wouldn't pry it open with a wrecking bar. All the loose ends will be tidied up.

Ches is very thorough. You won't have anything to worry about. All you'll have to do is cry at my funeral." He laughs. "You will cry, won't you, son?"

I'm silent. He slaps my shoulder, chokes back laughter.

"And I left a letter for your Aunt Vivian. Said the will's in the office. Everything's left to you. Ches will print up an official death certificate. No one will ever check. People are very accepting when it comes to dyin'. Deep down they know it's a privilege, payin' God back for the gift of life."

I shake my head, stare at him.

He puts his arm around my shoulder, cozies up to me the way he does sometimes when he really wants something. "I'd appreciate it if you'd do this for me, Sonny. You'll have to fill in the grave, tidy up after so no one suspects anything. Sweep it all clean, just like you do at the shop."

I choke up again recalling what the ponytail doctor said about lead poisoning and his brain. Under ordinary circumstances I'd do anything he asked, but what makes this so difficult is his state of mind. He's daily losing touch with reality. And yet, what he wants me to do is something he would've asked even if he weren't sick.

"I'd hate to be wasting away in a hospital weeks on end." There's a long, familiar silence and a familiar declaration: "I'd like you to think hard about this matter." Another, longer silence, which means he won't take no for an answer.

He makes me so angry sometimes. "Okay," I say, a pain in the pit of my stomach; he's made up my mind. And I don't want him wandering off like a child, getting lost looking all over town for a street that doesn't exist. And I sure don't want him going off and dying alone. That isn't going to happen to my father. "*Gawgew*!" I say.

Rattling laughter at my use of his word. "Thank you," he whispers.

"But Charlie, if we can find some other way—"

"That's my boy! Knew I could depend on you." His voice is childlike. "You're all I've got, Sonny. I don't want strangers taking care of this." He stops short again, catching his breath. "It's hallowed ground, good enough for a simple man like me." His rattling laughter is louder than ever. "Besides, I'll be with a good woman."

14

ALL WEEK I SECOND-GUESS MYSELF ABOUT THE BURIAL. There are a lot of reasons for giving in to him. His being with my mother for eternity gets to me. But the main reason is my love for him. I change my mind every hour, but I know that his crazy idea is going to happen one way or another, with or without me. He'll ask for help from Johnny. I can't let that happen. Or worse, he could pay Mr. Crenshaw, who's always looking for money. That'd be a disaster. Old Crenshaw couldn't dig his way out of a paper bag. He's always huffing and puffing when he enters the classroom and wheezing and whistling when he talks. Charlie often says he'll drop dead from a heart attack one day.

And there's always the possibility that Charlie might try to do the deed and botch it. There's no way out, I must be part of it.

In exchange for helping him, I insist on a coffin, and we spend the weekend making a plain pine box, complete with cover. Burying him in a blanket just doesn't seem right.

After we finish, he shows off his breathing contraption, a metal snorkel mask with a plastic pipe, a little over four feet long. It looks like something from a horror movie. "Plan B," he says, "just in case."

The day of his death is the hardest of my life. I'm a wreck, can't eat or sleep. I tell him I have a test coming up and stay in my room. In the evening, I fight back tears asking what he'll wear. He says his jacket and dungarees are fine. Besides my mother's funeral, I'd only been to my cousin Wilf's. He was smartly dressed in a suit. I want my father buried in a suit too, so before we head out, I hide his Sunday best in a bag under the seat in the truck.

We load the box on the tow truck late at night. I grab the shovels and the small ladder.

"Nice night for it." He looks at the sky. "Warm, calm." He sighs, and it seems to come from his nose.

He sounds anxious, so I don't say anything, arrange things on the truck.

He carries a duffle bag containing rope for lowering the box, a blanket, kerosene lamp, two candles, a Bible, and the stethoscope he stole from his hospital room.

"The mystical minimum," he says as he pitches the bag on the truck. "I'll talk to you about the funeral rite on the way." He's firm about having a burial ceremony. "I'd have the priest," he says, "but it was that clown wouldn't let me in the cemetery in the first place. So, you're performing the last rites."

We drive a long, winding lane to the far corner of the cemetery and park by a row of trees near the gravesite with the bluish-grey Celtic Cross. Just after eleven, by the light of the kerosene lamp, we start digging a four-foot hole in my mother's grave. Well, I do the digging. Charlie smokes, swigs whiskey, and supervises. I use a straight spade to cut the outline of the grave and a layer of sod, placing large sections of grass off to the side. It's a balmy night, and in no time, I'm drenched in sweat, so I remove my shirt.

Car headlights sweep a section of the graveyard. I drop the shovel. Charlie waves a hand, relax. "Takes three hours to dig a three-by-eight six-footer," he says. "But four feet's enough." He places a jug of water near the Cross and says not to drink too much the once. He touches the Cross, nods, mumbles something to Lucy.

I want to dig deeper, afraid a dog might dig it up, but Charlie insists four's plenty. "Your mother always liked her space."

We hear a car horn in the distance, and I crouch behind a headstone.

"Relax," Charlie says. "There'll be cars now and then. Kenna's Hill's a main thoroughfare."

After shovelling for an hour, I want the old man to relieve me for a bit, but he looks so frail these past weeks, his skin blue and blotchy, that I can't bear to ask for help. It was all he could do to help me lift the heavy box off the truck. And I really don't mind the digging. The grief—that's another matter. I want it over and done with, so I work fast.

"Slow down," he says, face wrinkled with worry, "or you'll be the one in the box. And pitch the dirt farther from the hole so's you've got room nearby for the last few shovelfuls. Is the soil hard or moist?"

"Soil's firm, dry. Smells sorta sweet."

"Good. You won't have to worry about the sides caving in.

I lean for a moment on the shovel, watch him eyeing Lucy's grave before driving the heavy blade into the dry earth. In the steamy night air, I dig away thinking of what Arlene said that day we drove to the Brook. Thou shalt not kill means yourself or anyone else. And I wonder if I'd be doing what I'm doing if I were Catholic. "It's murder," she said. "No other word for it." In the end, I really didn't have a choice, one of those things a man's gotta do. All the same, I've been avoiding Arlene and her parents.

A siren sounds in the distance. "Too late for me," Charlie says and walks down the lane to scout around. When he comes back, I ask if he's seen anything.

"Ambulance."

I keep digging.

"Saw a headstone with White on it." He chuckles. "Gotta hand it to Old White, hell-bent on stealing the family business."

That jolts me, and I wish I were burying Bert White.

As the earth piles higher, I say I'm upset we're doing this so close to my birthday. He says the memory will be the perfect birthday gift each year. "No better time than your birthday for such an auspicious event. By the way," he says, "there's a gift for you in the print shop. Open it when I'm gone."

My birthday's a week away, but we celebrated a few nights ago at the house. The last supper, he called it. He's a fine chef. He invited Johnny over, and they cooked a beautiful chicken à la king. He insisted that we dress up. He wore his Sunday best and served us like a royal butler all evening, beginning with a little red wine. A wonderful meal, but I was miffed that he served Johnny first. For dessert Johnny baked a small blueberry coffee cake topped with crunchy cinnamon, my favourite. He stuck a lit candle in it, and they sang Happy Birthday. It was an evening I'll never forget. And I'll never forget that Johnny had no idea he was seeing Charlie for the last time.

I light a smoke, lean on the shovel again, and reflect on the limits of my love because my counterfeiting days will be numbered. The adventures of Robin Hood will end. I'll be like Robinson Crusoe, independent, free. Sonny's Auto won't be Charlie's Auto.

The digging is exhausting, and now I'm glad the hole will only be four feet. Now and then I take a break, drink from the water jug, or snatch my shirt and wipe the sweat from my face. Once as I'm catching my breath, I hear something stir in the nearby trees and stop digging. Charlie says not to worry, it's just the wind.

15

THE LAST SHOVELFUL. Charlie lowers the ladder, and I climb up. As I drag the pine box near the hole, he says to leave the ladder, we'll need it soon enough—he to get in the box, me to make certain there's no pulse or heartbeat.

"If the cyanide doesn't work, I'll pull a Lazarus and we'll try it again, a double dose. But it should be fine. If I come back from the dead," he jokes, "I'll tell you all about what's happening across the river."

He goes over the details again about Rosie and dropping the dough. "Check the texture of the bill. Cashiers can spot a fake bill just by feeling it." He asks if I have any last questions. Yeah, I say, and blurt one of Arlene's tongue twisters: Is there need to light a night light on a light night like tonight? He laughs and I say no questions, everything's in hand.

"Feel like I need a blindfold. Get the feeling I'm before a firing squad. Déjà vu! Another life, maybe. Doing the same sort of thing, in a way." He says he feels like he's being reborn. "One thing's for sure, I won't be comin' back as a banker."

We lean against a nearby headstone and smoke. I hear a car a ways off, then headlights wash the far side of the graveyard. I jump to attention. Charlie motions for me to relax and opens the whiskey bottle.

"I'll only have a quick swig, one for the road. Don't wanna be in the grave with a headache meeting your mother." He winks, cocks his head to the side. "Or have a bad dream." He's wearing his Harris tweed, taps ashes into the pocket, and reminds me to say my prayers each day. "The McCluskeys are a blessed clan. We've always responded to the divine impulse. Always give it free rein. A lot don't, son. We recognize miracles, however small: *Glory be to God for dappled things—for rose-moles all in stipple upon trout that swim.*" He looks up: "*For skies of couple-colour as a brinded cow*. God's silent smile is in all things.

The world is full of such miracles. But no one sees them. People have lost the power to see. They've become machines. Not the McCluskeys! We've always been grateful for providential guidance. Divine pointers, your grandfather used to say. People don't see God's creative presence anymore; they've lost the capacity to see visions. We've had no great spirits among us for a long time now. Be thankful every day, Sonny, and pray for this benighted generation."

He passes me the bottle, says I shouldn't drink till my eighteenth birthday, next Tuesday, but to have one while I'm waiting. We laugh, and I take a swig, tears stinging as I choke it down.

"I wanted to be around for your first swally. Happy birthday!" He reminds me not to forget the gift in the print shop.

It's a clear, starry night, and he looks at me admiring the stars and says, "What you're seeing up there is God." A wheezy chuckle. "Only person I always got along with." The Little Dipper leans toward the cemetery. He points. "Make a birthday wish, son, you'll be a man soon."

I stare at the stars, can't believe I'm going through with this. There's an uneasy silence, and I remember the Bible story of Abraham and Isaac he read to me when I was little. I wish this was the same thing, in reverse, and an angel of God will descend from the sky and stay my hand.

"Did you wish me a safe journey? My wish for you? Read that ledger carefully. It won't seem like much at first, but it's your lifeline."

He stamps out his cigarette. "When you fill in the grave, keep the earth loose around the pipe." He points to the breathing contraption he made. "So's I can push it up a few inches to signal if I'm not gone. If it all works out, come back and cut the pipe flush with the ground so's nobody will suspect anything. Hacksaw will do the trick. And put a few stones and weeds over it. Nuthin' special, no flowers or nuthin'. Leave no clues behind."

Before we wrap the rope around the coffin and lower it into the grave, I tell him it's time to get changed. Then I do the hardest thing I've ever done. I hurry to the truck and get the bag of clothes I'd stashed. "I'm not taking no for an answer," I say. He laughs, removes his jacket, sweater, and pants, and I help dress him in his grey flannel suit, shirt, and tie. I comb his hair a few times till it's just right, and I gotta say, he looks pretty spiffy. He says happy birthday again, gives me a bear hug, and says he hopes there'll be no tears . . . ever. "We're in eternity, Sonny, endless present."

"No tears."

He bear hugs me again, his voice shy as he says, "Promise me you won't let the family down, son. You've always been a good one to keep your promise . . ."

I turn away and look at the pile of earth.

"Promise me."

I lower my head, mumble yes.

"Thank you," he says and, releasing me from his grip, shakes the three morphine pills into his hand and pops them in his mouth. He takes a last swig of whiskey to wash them down and with a cockeyed grin says he'll miss his liquor for sure. With glassy eyes, he hands me the bottle.

"I need the morphine to counter the cyanide . . . 300 milligrams of KCN . . . potassium cyanide. Should only take a few minutes." His straining voice, barely a whisper. "If I twitch or hyperventilate, don't fret none, I won't feel anything. Only at the last few beats of the heart do you sense you're out of breath. Darkness comes quickly without panicked breathing as the soul departs the body."

He picks up the breathing contraption. "Be sure the pipe's a tad above ground, now," he says. "Just in case . . ." He sprinkles holy water Lucy always had around, removes his shoes and socks and orders me to do the same, we're now on hallowed ground. I do so, feel the earth cool beneath my feet. He climbs down the ladder and gets into the coffin. "The monks of old slept in their coffins," he says, flaps his arm. "Come closer." I lean over the grave. He tries to speak but has a coughing fit. Then, his voice low and scratchy, he says, "We're low on toilet paper."

He swallows the cyanide capsule, puts on the snorkel, lies down, and covers himself with the blanket we brought. His face is stoic. No indication he's jittery, even at the last minute. He folds his arms, my cue to remain silent and do my job. I take out the vial of olive oil he gave me, anoint his forehead, and pray what he'd asked: "Through this holy anointing, may the Lord in His love and mercy help you with the grace of the Holy Spirit. May the Lord Almighty, who opened your last door, open another one as full of joy and happiness."

"Amen," he mumbles.

I sit and wait. And wait. It seems forever for the cyanide to do its work. There's a sudden cry, a desperate gasp for breath, and I know he's gone.

16

I WALK TO THE HEAD OF THE GRAVE, MY MOTHER'S CROSS, AND SAY, "Well, it's forever now, faithful to the end." I light a cigarette, sit on a low tombstone, and get a jolt, imagining footsteps. Or maybe it's Charlie whispering something to Lucy. I watch for car headlights going by. After a while, a rustling in the bushes, panicked fear.

The billowing clouds remind me of waves breaking on the beach. Half an hour passes before I put on the stethoscope and listen for a heartbeat. None. I check his pulse. Nothing, though his wrist is warm. I take a flashlight from my pocket, open one of his eyes as instructed, and flash the light to see if his pupil will contract. Nothing.

"Charlie! Charlie!" I whisper and flinch, afraid he might respond. No answer. "Dad! Dad!" I call louder, knowing if he's still alive, that'll get his goat. Nothing. I check his pulse again, listen for a heartbeat. None. I touch his forehead softly, kiss him, make the sign of the Cross. Then I line up the snorkel pipe with the hole he'd made in the coffin cover, push it through, and close the lid. I climb the ladder and haul it up. After a minute I light one of the candles, open the Bible, and read the passage he'd marked:

> "*The Lord is my shepherd; I shall not want. He maketh me to lie down in green pastures: He leadeth me beside the still waters. He restoreth my soul: He leadeth me in the paths of righteousness for his name's sake.*"

I think it ironic that the old man would pick a Bible passage about righteousness, given his line of work. I grab the shovel and start covering him up. A spade of dirt for Charlie. A spade of dirt for Lucy. One spade of dirt after another. And another. It seems like forever covering him up, and I'm so tired I rest for half an hour. My muscles ache, and there's a blister on the inside of my thumb. I drink some water, and with arms like wet noodles I pitch shovelful after shovelful of dirt for what seems an eternity. When I finish, I pat the earth flat before spreading the sections of grass so it looks as it did before I dug it up.

I blow out the candle, make sure the snorkel pipe is about an inch above the earth, just in case. I put a few rocks around the pipe so it doesn't look like it's sticking out of the ground, remind myself to come back later and cut the pipe flush.

Then I light two taper candles and stick them on the grave. The flames flicker madly, like the wings of a trapped bird. As they settle down, I say my final farewell, kneel, and pray what he asked—that his guardian angel protect him on his long, dark journey across the river: Dear Lord Jesus who died for our miserable sins let him not be cast down but, in Your mercy, light his way to Your community of saints.

I blow out the candles and put them in the duffle bag. I'll keep them but never light them again—they're sacred now. I gather up his clothes, shoes, the lamp, whiskey bottle. I consider what I've just done and feel like a shipwrecked sailor.

I stand there staring at the grave, willing the pipe to move so he'll rise from the dead like the young cowboy in that movie he'd mentioned. Then, shock! What if he's in a coma? Racing mind, pounding heart, tears. I stand stock-still, out of breath, how he used to get all the time. I force myself to breathe slowly. After a while, the craziest thing, his strong arms are around me, that familiar bear hug. I feel calm and light. A strange sort of peace fills my heart and spreads like sunshine; and I know Charlie's okay and that I'll be okay too. A light rain begins to fall, and I watch grey, horn-shaped clouds drifting across the sky for ever so long.

It's almost three, the hour of the wolf, when I sling the duffle bag over my shoulder, grab the shovels and ladder, and head to the truck. A strong wind comes up, and the weather seems to change. In the distance, a dog barks. I sit behind the wheel and, before falling asleep, think about being free now to go my own way. When I wake, the grey dawn is coming on, but the sun won't show his head. I want to go back and check the grave, but I know it's over. He's gone.

I drive down Portugal Cove Road in thunder and hard rain. As the truck lurches up a hill toward home, lightning flashes and I see the Charlie's Auto sign in the distance. As I bounce down the dirt road, it flashes again and, in my exhausted state, I glimpse the Hand of God writing the words Sonny's Auto, my father's rattling laughter echoing in my mind. And I laugh too as I think about the old man's notion of eternity, how he'll be spending it with Lucy, and how he'd put one over on Father Almighty McCarthy and the powers that be.

17

IN MY JOURNAL I WRITE THE BURIAL DATE, Wednesday, August 23, then set the alarm and head to bed. I toss and turn, weaving images of Charlie's Auto, then Sonny's Auto, the gravesite (did I do the right thing? am I a murderer?), the print shop (how soon will I shut it down? will I survive without it?), Johnny (can I do what Charlie asked?), Arlene (her music, her religion, her motorcycle, her father) . . . until everything fades into a blur. I have two nightmares. In the first one, Johnny and Quinn find out about Rosie and threaten to call the police if I don't cut them in for fifty per cent. "Fifty per cent, McCluskey, or we'll squeal." Johnny keeps riffing, strumming his guitar.

In the second dream, a storm blows the roof off Charlie's Auto, rain floods the shop, and fake $20 bills blow around everywhere. The wind is so strong it blows everything away except for Charlie's large poster of Robin Hood, and a framed picture of Karl Marx, a gift from Mr. Crenshaw. Both hang above the pegboard. I wake, feel I've been hit by a truck and dragged for miles. I sit up in bed, say a prayer, go back to sleep.

In the middle of the night, the phone rings. Startled, I clutch the receiver, my feet hitting the cold floor. "Hello."

A deep, nasty voice says, "We need to talk. About Charlie. And I don't mean the Viet Cong." Dead silence. The voice is familiar but distant, the phone heavy.

"Who is this? Mr. Crenshaw?"

Click.

"Hello." I replace the phone, unclear who called, go back to bed.

When the grey light finally peeks through the curtains, I wake up an orphan, feeling what I felt when my mother died, sad and lonely. For months after her funeral, Charlie said that I told every visitor who came to the house and every stranger on the street my mother died. I was only five. I played games in which I was Lucy and nothing had happened. I asked Charlie repeatedly where my mother was, terrified that his answer would change. I remember being sick for a long time, constant headaches, upset stomach. I didn't know it then, but of course I was depressed.

I don't feel like it, but I say the Our Father lying in bed listening to my pounding pulse. Eventually, I get up, drag myself across the cold hardwood to the bathroom, wait outside for Charlie to finish his coughing, hawking, spitting, before realizing those sounds are gone forever. In the heavy silence I splash cold water on my face and look in the mirror. Those slightly flared ears seem pointier today, the circles under my eyes darker. But that old red hockey scar on the bridge of my nose doesn't look so bad.

I boil an egg, make toast. At the kitchen table I notice bread crumbs and a coffee stain on Charlie's placemat and can hardly eat, wish he were here reading from one of his Louis L'Amour books. The food tastes bland, might as well be eating paper. I think of the phone call. Did Mr. Crenshaw call? Was it someone else? Did I dream it? So tired I don't know, don't care.

After breakfast I get the hacksaw and drive to Mount Carmel Cemetery, hoping against hope to find the grave dug up and, like Jesus, Charlie's gone; he's pulled off his best prank yet and will show up just in time for my birthday. I park the car, head to the grave, and my heart sinks: everything's the same as I left it. I walk up and down the paved path making sure no one's around. Charlie was right, nobody ever comes here. I look at the gravesite and wish Johnny were here with me. Why did I feel jealous of Charlie's love for him? I'll never feel that way again.

I fall to my knees, shipwrecked again, call Charlie's name. No answer. And I know for certain I'll never hear my father's strained voice again. I kneel in silence, telling myself that Charlie has done what he wanted to do, and I've played my part, kept my promise. I get the hacksaw and carefully cut the pipe flush, go home, mope about the house, nap off and on till darkness falls.

18

SATURDAY MORNING AFTER BREAKFAST I HEAD TO THE PRINT SHOP TO OPEN Charlie's gifts. There are three. The first is a pocket watch owned by his grandfather. I recognize it immediately. The note reads: *Pass it on, son, when the time comes. Of course, no gift could be greater than the room you're standing in.*

There's a flask of whiskey in the desk drawer. The McCluskeys have been supporting the Jameson clan for centuries. I didn't bother to wrap it.

The other gift is large and rectangular, wrapped in newspaper. I tear it open: a wooden outdoor sign—SONNY'S AUTO. Note says: *Hang it up when the time comes.*

Happy birthday!
Love,
Dad

That really gets to me. At long last, the word Dad, the most important word in the world.

I pick up the ledger, a black, hardbound book, eight and a half by fourteen inches. I open it, remove a folded piece of paper. It's the will, dated and signed Charlie McCluskey and witnessed by Aunt Vivian.

LAST WILL AND TESTAMENT OF CHARLIE MCCLUSKEY. TO WHOM IT MAY CONCERN: I, CHARLES JOSEPH MCCLUSKEY, BEING OF SOUND MIND AND BODY DO HEREBY LEAVE ALL MY WORLDLY POSSESSIONS TO MY SON DAVID CHARLES "SONNY" MCCLUSKEY WITH THE PROVISO THAT MY HEIR EMPLOY AND CARE FOR MY "ADOPTED" SON, JOHNNY FABRELLA.

I'm not surprised at the proviso but find myself getting tense. Do I really want Johnny in the garage? I quickly relax, realizing he never shows up, hates work.

The will leaves a few things to Aunt Vivian and Uncle Ches.

I turn the page, begin reading.

CHARLIE'S COMMANDEMENTS

The only thing you'll need in this world besides what's in CHARLIE'S AUTO is in this ledger. Commit it to memory and burn it. I wrote things down as they came to me—rules mostly, like the Ten Commandments. Obey them. There's no particular order—my mind's a mess these days—but each thing is very important. So read everything twice. I did.

The rest of the ledger is in point form:

1. Thou shalt not tell. Keep the family secret. And keep my death secret. Never use the word death. Departure is a better word. Charlie's departure. Never let anyone hang around the shop except Johnny and keep the supply door locked when he's around. Plan each day, take out the supplies you need before he arrives. As you know, he's not a nosy person, but don't take any chances. He should never know about Rosie.

It's a long drive from Stephenville, but Aunt Vivian will come by now and then. As you know, she thinks I've gone to Toronto to see a specialist. I told her I rented a room there, no phone. She might call Uncle Ches, but he knows what to say. She won't snoop around the garage, she hates grease. And she never stays long, hates the city. Cousin Art won't show up. He's always fishing offshore. Besides, he thinks I'm crazy and wants nothing to do with me.

2. Never let a client in the garage. You know how it is. Just a reminder. Anyone getting a car fixed must leave, it's a matter of insurance. They can come back for their car. If they insist on staying, they can wait in the office. NEVER let anyone go down in the pit. It's always OFF LIMITS. Sign says EMPLOYEES ONLY.

3. Remember to keep holy the Lord's Day.

> 4. Never carry much money around. You're just a kid. Splashing money around will raise eyebrows. I stashed two hundred real 20s in the print shop in a burlap bag marked G for good money in case of an emergency. IN CASE—are you listening? You never know when you'll find yourself in a pinch. There's a list of bills to pay and people to help: Johnny's monthly allowance, Aunt Vivian, Mr. and Mrs. Bennett at the home, the Ricketts mortgage, etc.

There was another bag marked C for counterfeit with enough money till next spring, when I would begin working full-time in the garage. Charlie warned me to replace the money I spent as soon as possible. "Drop some dough now and then. You don't want to get rusty. I usually drop some every two months or so. Don't go any longer than that. You don't want to let the family down."

> 5. Keep Charlie's Auto Shop going. It's the family business. Hang on to it for dear life. That business is yours now—your life, your world, however humble.

My great-grandfather, David McCluskey, started Charlie's Auto. There's a collotype of him in the office hanging above Charlie's desk: stern-looking, full white beard, monocle, staring into eternity. A disciplined man of God, he spent his life working for the poor. I promise myself to honour his memory by getting into a routine. "Routines and rituals are good for a person," Charlie said, if I forgot a chore or slept in. "Make a schedule for your laundry, homework, dropping the dough, working in the garage, etc."

The dread of being alone drives me to the garage, where I stare at the old wooden sign that split into four pieces during a winter storm. Charlie couldn't part with it and hung it above the workbench: CHAR LIE'S AU TO.

The tools sit silently on the workbench, tools Charlie's eyes will never see again, his hands never touch. Next to his toolbox, a grease-stained paperback, *Education of a Wandering Man*. How often I'd chided Charlie for reading cowboy stories. He'd say, "Louis L'Amour had a lifelong love affair with learning, and so should you," reminding me that L'Amour left school at fifteen to roam the world. "You're older and you've only roamed around the Cove. Ha, ha!" I put the book in my back pocket.

The rusty steel door hulks in the shadow of the pit, Rosie and the old monster locked up behind. Pride in the good my family has been doing for generations battles a wave of loss that washes over me as I wonder again if this is my life, my world.

19

I PICK UP THE BOOK AGAIN.

> 6. THE GOLDEN RULE—You'll be tempted to let the cat out of the bag. It's hard to keep our little secret. But you must. You'll want to tell someone, believe me. DON'T! Watch your bobber, son, especially around girls. Remember Adam and Eve.

There's a section on drinking: "Keep an eye on booze or it will keep an eye on you. Too much drink doesn't mix with the business we're in."

Charlie loved his whiskey, but he was never drunk. He insisted I not start drinking till my eighteenth birthday and, as with everything in life, that I use constraint. "L'Amour says somewhere—hunger, thirst, and cold—man's first enemies, and no doubt his last. He should've added booze."

I'm reading a summary of things Charlie wants me to internalize when the telephone rings. Quinn.

"What's up, stunned arse? Comin' over to shoot hoops or you gonna play with yourself all day?"

I go to Quinn's place Saturdays to play one-on-one. I want to finish the ledger, but something tells me to get going. I remind myself to be normal, do the things I usually do, not raise any eyebrows. And every Saturday Quinn and I shoot hoops.

"On the way."

"Good! Can't wait to wipe you out, stunned arse." He hangs up.

We weren't always close. We got into a terrible row once shooting hoops, and he threatened me. I'm no pushover, and I don't back down from a fight. I grabbed him, twisted his arm behind his back, the way Charlie showed me. "I don't like threats," I said, "next time I'll break it." We've been best friends ever since. Charlie taught me to stand up for myself. Above all, he said, never let anyone threaten or bully you.

In a parking lot near his house, Quinn nailed a makeshift basket to a telephone pole where you can find him morning, noon, and night shooting hoops. Tall and wiry, he's a good basketball player, and I rarely beat him. Today, I miss almost every shot. I keep thinking of what Charlie said about finding a peaceful place for reflection and ask Quinn if he knows of a quiet spot.

"For grassin', Sugar Loaf." He swishes one. "For parkin', Signal Hill's perfect. Or you could stay overnight with Arlene at Butter Pot Park. Ha, ha."

I miss shot after shot. Quinn senses my melancholy, says, "You're worse than your usual stunned arse self today, McCluskey. Girl troubles?"

"Been thinking about Johnny. Not right he's out the Brook way all by his lonesome."

"Oh, he's fine. He's a lone wolf. Spends most of his time playing guitar, reading, and writing songs. He's in heaven, man. See him at practice with the Acid Test, he's fine."

"Told Arlene he wants to go to Vietnam, he's enlisting."

"So? He's a Yank. That's what Yanks do. Fight wars."

"It's a drag dual nationals have to register for the draft."

"Maybe the American military won't give a shit, him living way up here. Why should they care?"

"Says he's going, it's a family tradition, being a military man and all. Wouldn't feel right if he didn't go. His father was a soldier, his grandfather—"

"Oh, who cares?" Quinn makes a perfect jumpshot, grabs a second basketball. "Time for a round of knockout."

As we play, he says, "Speaking of knockout, how'd it go with Arlene at the Brook? Didja jump her?"

"Don't be ridiculous, she's a nice girl."

"Told Esther-Marie she's crazy about you. Said if you two tie the knot she'll get Charlie's Auto."

"What!" That throws me, and I lose control of the ball.

Quinn steals it, swishes another basket, and flashes his rabbity grin.

"She said that?"

"Yep. So Esther-Marie says."

That takes the wind out of my sails. I don't feel like playing anymore and tell him I have to get home.

"Stay for some lunch? Mom's been asking about you. Hasn't seen you at the bank lately."

"Gotta get home, work piling up at the garage."

"See you at school. Double date Saturday, before band practice? Thelma's."

"Sure, I'll talk to Arlene, letcha know."

"Great! Esther-Marie really likes Arlene. She's spending too much time in the water, startin' to look like a sculpin."

20

BACK HOME I GO ICE COLD. I'm about to run a counterfeiting operation. My mouth's dry, and there's an ugly sensation in my stomach as I read about paying my bills on time, avoiding debt.

> 7. A person with debt is a moron. You can't afford something, don't buy it.

Easy to say. Thank God for Rosie. It's a wonder Charlie's Auto made any money. He helped everyone. *We must help every person the good Lord sends our way. And He'll send them, believe me.* He hardly charged people for whatever he fixed; a valve needed cleaning, no problem; then he'd lube the chassis, free of charge.

He had a few things to say about Johnny and the Crenshaws.

> 8. Johnny helps everyone, and we must help Johnny. He's been a brother to you and a son to me. You know I think the world of him. Unfortunately, his uncle is a deadbeat. Harry Johnstone's never around and when he is he ticks off everyone he meets, except Bert White. Surprise, surprise.

It was his fondest wish that Johnny and I make a living at Charlie's Auto. "I know his heart's set on music, but there's no future in that. He can do music on the side."

And my father helped Johnny with his stuttering. When he visited, Charlie insisted on patience. "Never finish his sentences. And encourage his singing. He relaxes, has fun when he sings, never stutters."

Charlie's right, Johnny needs a Robin Hood. He's had it tough, father and mother dying, dropped out of school because of his stuttering—teased by classmates, given a hard time by teachers.

9. A word about his struggle with words: Isaiah 28:11. *For with stammering lips and another tongue will He speak to this people.* Stammering never held Moses back and shouldn't hold Johnny back either. As L'Amour says, "What a man wants to do he generally can do, if he wants to badly enough."

10. As for the Crenshaws, be careful around them. You've only seen Dr. Jekyll. He has a Hyde side. Pray you don't see it. Be careful in your dealings with him. He teaches you, so watch your bobber. You don't want to jeopardize your certification.

He likes to think we're good friends. We're not. We were partners of sorts and did a little business together. But like Dr. Jekyll and Dr. Lanyon, we had a falling-out. He threatened me. Nothing to concern yourself with. Just keep in mind that Crenshaw is a communist of the worst kind. He absolutely hates anyone who's rich. There's nothing wrong with money. Lots of good people have money. People get into trouble using it stupidly or hoarding it. You don't need seven pairs of shoes. Help the needy. Be a Robin Hood.

And I don't mean that all communists are bad. Some of the great saints were communists, but none of them murdered millions of people. Crenshaw is a devout Stalinist. Stalin killed over six million of his own people. And he's a big fan of Mao, whose Great Leap Forward caused the deadliest famine in history—50 million dead in five years. And there's that Vietnamese nut, Ho Chi Minh. Crenshaw thinks Johnny should fight for him. Uncle Ho has already executed half a million. Crenshaw admires these people. Hardly the gospel of Jesus Christ. Watch your bobber around him. And if he threatens you, strike back and strike hard. Don't hesitate. The less you have to do with the Crenshaws, the better.

In class, old Crenshaw always rants about how rich people have fancy lawyers and accountants who use loopholes to get more than their fair share. "They steal from the poor and give to the rich," he says. "And they want you to think they're the oppressed ones. The rich have stacked the deck against the poor since time immemorial. But the revolution is coming." In his classroom there's a Robin Hood poster with the caption: THE CLASS WHICH CONTROLS MATERIAL PRODUCTION CONTROLS MENTAL PRODUCTION. "Robin Hood and his band of Merry Men were early communists."

Charlie says Crenshaw's partly right about Karl Marx and he's right about the corporate welfare bums. "But only God, not ideology, can save us. He's wrong about communism, there's no place for God in Crenshaw's philosophy. But be kind to him. Poor soul's unhealthy, not long for this world. He has a lot on his plate: ill health, the Communist Party of Newfoundland, that crazy wife of his, other problems I'm not at liberty to talk about.

"Steer clear of Mrs. Crenshaw. Two kinds of crazy in this world, Sonny: the good kind of crazy—people like the guy going around with his wheelbarrow collecting bottles—and the bad kind of crazy—Mrs. Crenshaw. I know she has a Ph.D., coaches the wrestling team at the school, but she's a Jezebel. No young man should be left alone with her. She has a bolt loose."

And no young woman should be left alone with Randy Quinn. He melts at the sight of a pair of nylons. I remember our possible double date and want to telephone Arlene but decide against it. Her father might answer the phone. I can't bear listening to his laboured breathing, and I don't want to talk to him about possibly amalgamating the family businesses. I'll see her at school.

The ledger cautioned about doing my taxes on time, repeated the importance of not dropping dough twice at the same place and urged me to use only cash.

> 11. Keep the house clean. Don't live like a goat. Keep the print shop clean too. Avoid ink stains. Always wear your surgical gloves. Inky fingers are a dead giveaway. Keep the press spotless. One mistake in the print shop can lead to disaster. Burn all the leftover printing material in the wood stove. Make sure nobody's around when you do it.
>
> 12. Never feel sorry for yourself. That's a dead end. Many a life has been ruined by self-pity.
>
> 13. Read the Bible daily. As some wit once said, God writes straight with crooked lines. It's a great book. And keep your bowels open (eat lots of roughage—see below).

Each point in the ledger was clear, even though Charlie's mind was fading. There was a step-by-step outline for making counterfeit, advice about eating well, complete with menus, directions on cleaning and storing food, keeping an orderly house, wearing clean clothes. And there was a word on covering up his death.

> 14. I know you miss your Uncle Ches, he's a good man, and a great sailor. We've had our differences, but he's one of the best, another giver. He worked with me in the print shop for many years. When our father died, he went to Ontario. He wanted a change; he'd help the poor upalong. He set up a small print shop in Scarborough and volunteered at a halfway house nearby. He still helps there now and then. Your Uncle Ches is one of the best, a Robin Hood if there ever was one. Do as he says.

The note repeated what he'd already told me: my uncle was part of the family tradition and that Charlie had arranged with him to get a "legal" death certificate. When the time was right, I was to fly to Toronto for a few days, returning home with Charlie's empty but weighted coffin. Ches would make all the arrangements regarding the burial and call Aunt Vivian to drive in for the funeral, keep me company for a few days. I was to arrange for the music, "Amazing Grace" and "How Great Thou Art," which Johnny will sing. There'd be a brief church service. I was to wait for the call from Ches, fly up to be with Charlie during his "final hours," fly back with the coffin, cry and look sad at the funeral. *Keep on your mourner's face for a week or so, especially around Aunt Vivian.*

The ledger ended with a note:

> I'll miss you, son, miss your quiet nature. You're one of a kind. And I'll always love you. In this world and the next, which as you know, is just an extension of NOW. Most people don't have a clue about reincarnation and the transmigration of souls, but it's the truest thing you'll ever hear. Jesus taught about it when He was here, but the early church cut it out of the Bible. They thought it was too Eastern. One of the reasons I gave up the institutional church. No religion is an island, especially when the leaders get on with a lot of silliness about telling a man and his wife they can't be buried together.
>
> We'll meet again in another world. And in this world too while you're here. How's that, you ask? Well, every time you look in the

backyard at the birdfeeder I made for the blue jays, you'll think of me. Whenever you see a wrench, a broken-down car, a Jameson's whiskey bottle, a Camel cigarette, a greasy baseball cap. Death cannot touch that blessed cap, that cigarette, that bottle, that car, that wrench. We never die. Every time you see a western movie or read a Louis L'Amour book or pick up a power drill. Every time you hear a gravelly voice . . .

Don't be hard on yourself. The McCluskeys tend to be that way. Don't be. Life's a blink of an eye, as Johnny says. Be kind to him. Please. Everyone has a heavy load to carry, and everyone walks with a limp. It's just easier to notice in some people.

And don't worry about dying. It's no worse than stuttering. Ha, ha! As Louis says in *Last of a Breed*—"It is the measure of a man to die well. . . . When I die, remember that what you knew of me is with you always. What is buried is only the shell of what was. Do not regret the shell, but remember the man. Remember the father."

We're all going to die, son, and when it's God's will, so be it. Go forth and meet Him. The love of God frees us all.

Your loving father,

Charlie

P.S. So I'll be seeing you around—you'll know where and when. And I'll be seeing you on the other side too.

21

BEFORE THE TRADES SCHOOL OPENS, I MAKE A SIGN AND TAPE IT TO THE bathroom mirror: ALWAYS TAKE THE BUS. I remind myself to stick to last year's routine, act like nothing's changed even though my world will never be the same.

I make another sign saying *Open on Saturdays ONLY until I return from Toronto. Closed Sunday, the Lord's Day. Signed Charlie.* I don't want anyone to suspect anything, everything's normal at the McCluskey household. I take out my desk calendar, make lists of what to do. Pay every bill on time, get the groceries each Saturday, keep dentist appointment.

Yesterday I went to Thelma's, where Esther-Marie works part-time as a waitress. "Sonny, you look so sad," she said. "Is everything all right?"

I told her I was fine, a little worried about Johnny, that's all. Must remember to smile more.

I'll work the odd weeknight, Saturdays. While I can't put an arse in a cat like Charlie, I can handle most things that'll come my way.

The other day someone came to the office, loose muffler. Fixed it in jig time. No problem. Another time, an oil change. Had it done lickety-split.

I make a note to start dropping the dough soon. I'll need an evening in the print shop: *You don't want to get rusty*.

I think of Arlene White, pick up the phone to call her, change my mind. I lie on the sofa, recall what the ledger said about dating: You'll be getting serious about women soon. Find a sensible one. You're more likely to find someone like that at the hardware store than the dance floor. I met your mother out in BC on a tobacco farm. As L'Amour says in one of his books: Find a woman to walk beside you, not behind you. I like that girl Arlene you're seeing. She seems sensible, unlike her father. Her Aunt Laura was a fine woman and a close friend.

I browse through the ledger rereading bits here and there:

> Did I mention keeping the family business? It's been around a long time, ever since the McCluskeys gave up printing. Make your great-grandfather proud. Stick to your routines and rituals. Open the same time each day. Close the same time each evening. Charge everyone the same price. Keep holy the Sabbath. It's a day to stop worshipping our tools, to put them down and rest—a day of getting away from things, especially money and business.
>
> You'll get the blues now and then till you realize you're in eternity. Watch for His signs. It was a sign that sent me to the Anglican church. It's important to be alone occasionally, other than in the shop. Find a place with no distractions, a palace of nowhere, a place to sit still, think things through, make difficult decisions. You've heard me talk about how Jesus would find a quiet place to cast His care upon His Father. Do that, Sonny! There are lots of places in the Cove and the city. Find the right spot, be alert and open to what's happening. Listen for the unexpected. The silence will overwhelm you at first. God's voice is always overwhelming. You'll forget your cares and find yourself reincarnated—yes, born again—in the love of God.

That was my father's life, savouring the moment. I put the ledger down and go for a long walk on the beach recalling how often the old man urged me to live in the present rather than indulging in the illusionary future or worrying about the dead past. Once I told him I found that hard to do. He rolled his eyes, looked at me, gobsmacked. "Sonny," he croaked, "a dumb dog does it all day long."

He'd go off into the woods for hours. The world is full of noise, he'd say, clatter everywhere. Silence is a great luxury. The rich pay a fortune for it. They buy beautiful properties miles away from everything where there's no clatter. Here in the Cove, silence is waiting for us a mile down the road.

I put the ledger away and go for another long walk, try to collect my thoughts. There's so much to think about, so much worry. Suddenly, that strange sort of peace I experienced at the gravesite comes over me, and I feel better.

As I walk the wind shifts, and it rains so I pick up the pace. At home I take a shower and cook supper before finishing the ledger.

> 15. Don't curse and swear. Nothing worse than a foul mouth. If you have to say the F-word, say FUGG. And don't take the Lord's name in vain. Jesus died for us. That's why we're in eternity. You'll know what I mean when you start really listening to the silence.

I sit for a while thinking, then go to my desk, take out a fresh notebook, and begin a daily journal. I've never written a journal before, but I've read Robinson Crusoe's. And like his, I know no one will ever read mine. It'll be my silent companion, my man Friday. I remember Crusoe making a list of the pros and cons in his life, turn the page, draw a line down the middle, and write:

PRO	CON
Charlie would have died a miserable death in the hospital with me around watching him suffer. He didn't want that and neither did I. That's why I helped him to go on his terms. I should be happy he did it his way. He didn't want me to be sad.	Charlie is gone and I am partly responsible for his death and I must live with that guilt for the rest of my life.
Charlie prepared me for this moment making sure I have all the basic necessities looked after and more. I am a skilled mechanic and I know how to make money, good and bad.	I'm alone, cut off from the world. What if I get sick or Charlie's Auto comes on hard times? Or worse—I screw up at the shop.
Never forget that you're helping the less fortunate. As Charlie always said, your brain, your possessions, your bank account are only a twitch of fortune's string. And besides, why would I get caught? If I'm not greedy and do exactly what Charlie taught me to do, I won't get caught. Obey the golden rule: NEVER TELL ANYONE.	I'm a counterfeiter. If I get caught I could go to jail. Give it up. Be your own person, go your own way.

Charlie's philosophy is right. The rich will never help the poor. Be like him and do your little bit to change the world, day by day. Remember Robin of Locksley who was like Jesus. He was a great champion of the poor, like the McCluskeys. He was Charlie's hero, and he should be yours too. Honour Charlie's memory.	Making counterfeit is wrong and a crime. I should destroy the equipment and the money and get rid of everything in the print shop. Charlie's values are noble but the rich will always lord it over the poor. I'm just one person without the power to change anything.
Count your blessings! Have faith. Remember what Charlie said about feeling sorry for yourself. Most kids your age are trying to get away from home. You have your own home and no mortgage. You're 18 years old. Be a man not a mouse. You have been running most of the business ever since Charlie got sick. Continue to keep a journal like Robinson Crusoe. Record memories of your good times together. Find a girl. You're dating Arlene White. You like her a lot. Date her more. Ask her to go steady, maybe. As for being anxious, remember what Charlie said: Don't let that hold you back.	Living alone won't be easy. I'll miss Charlie more each day. Already I'm feeling terribly lonely and afraid. I'm only a kid. And I'm as anxious as Crusoe's parrot, Poll, when I'm uptight about things.

Before going to bed I read the list over a few times and add the following: *I'm scared.*

22

FOR NOW, IT'S BUSINESS AS USUAL, SO I HEAD TO THE PRINT SHOP. It's a day I've been dreading—making counterfeit for the first time without Charlie. When I'm finished, I'll drop dough for the first time without him too. Nerve-racking!

I bring the ledger, review Charlie's instructions, prepare for my first big test. When everything's ready, I put on my surgical gloves, take out two of Charlie's perfect $20 bills, and move to the camera, my mind so on fire about getting caught that I'm shaking. I breathe deeply, release the tension in my gut. Focus on the matter at hand, Sonny. Remember how Charlie went about it: alert, his face strained, all business. If you screw up, as Charlie said, you can always start from scratch.

I carefully position Charlie's old, scrupulously maintained Hasselblad to produce the sharpest possible image and photograph the fronts and backs of two crisp $20 bills. Then I move to the darkroom, develop the negatives, and prepare the light table to cover up the serial numbers before beginning the tasks of mixing inks and burning the plates. This takes a lot of time and care, and again my mind is a jumble of the ways I can get caught—Crenshaw, Quinn, Johnny, Arlene.

It's Saturday before I finish the job. Early morning, the room stinks of ink, which always reminds me of Charlie. I place the plate, raise the paper, start up Rosie, and watch her pick up water and ink with each spin. I cross my fingers, hold my breath, and wait for my first sheet of $20 bills. In jig time, my gut goes ice cold. There'll be no paper cutting and stacking today, the bills are too dark. I burned the plate too long. It's back to the drawing board before I can drop some dough and take care of Charlie's unfinished business. And speaking of unfinished business, Johnny has the blues.

He's in a tough spot: the military's been in his blood for generations. His father wanted him to be a soldier, and even though he's long gone, Johnny doesn't want to disappoint the Captain. I'll try talking him into settling down with his girl in Montreal. Arlene says that's my best bet, anything heavier will probably get his back up.

He called yesterday, asked me to drop by. "Hey, I didn't get my allowance this month, man. You said Charlie'd be back by now."

"I'll drop by with it."

"Gotta bad case of the blues, Sonny! And I don't mean the devil's music, little brother. I mean the real thing."

Scratch anyone's surface, you'll find unhappiness. Everyone pretends everything's okay, but it never is. Charlie always said that people walk around looking perfect in their new pyjamas, but deep down, everyone's a bit heart-broken, everyone walks with a limp, some more than others. That just about sums up Johnny.

I feel guilty about Johnny living out there all alone, his girlfriend a million miles away. No wonder he's often depressed. And his stuttering probably doesn't help. Thirty-five million people worldwide stutter. Quite the club! God knows how many of them are depressed. And what the McCluskeys are all about is helping hurt, lonely people—*where do they all come from*? It's easier to go without food than friendship: there's no poverty like loneliness.

I grab money from the safe, a loaf of bread, then head to Johnny's place.

The washed-out dirt road seems to have more potholes today. Johnny's uncle began fixing up their house when Johnny moved in, but he's wasting his money on such a dump. The sagging roof is half shingles, half tarpaper. And the house tilts.

As I pull into the driveway, he pokes his guitar through the second-storey window and plays the opening chords of "Johnny B. Goode." "Go, Johnny, go!" he screams. He always begins each concert with that song. "How 'bout that riff, man? Pretty good, huh?" He hits a final quavering chord, shows off his new Fender. "Better'n Robbie Robertson." Then he disappears.

"Play some real music," I yell. "Play Bob Dylan." He hates Bob Dylan.

He wears a tie-dyed T-shirt, his signature rawhide headband. Most weekends, he's at his house, practising. He says if it wasn't for music, he doesn't know what he'd do, it's what he lives for. I yell up again when the door opens.

He grabs the bread. "Well, if it ain't Charlie's Auto," he says, stuttering slightly. "C'mon in, man, great to have another house call, need my battery recharged. Whatja think of that Chuck Berry riff, man? Cool, huh?" He gives me a big hug, runs a hand through his long hair, and I see of one of those Greek heroes you read about.

I reach into my pocket. "Your allowance," I say, handing him a wad of money.

"It's great to see ya, little brother." He pockets the money, throws the bread on the counter.

I enter his dimly lit pad, pausing to adjust to the light. Posters of Chuck Berry, Uncle Sam, Che Guevara haphazardly plaster the walls. The living room is lined with shelves made of concrete blocks and pine boards, all filled with magazines, books, bric-a-brac, musical figurines. One shelf has a stand-up picture of his father in uniform, another of his Uncle Harry sitting on the porch step drinking a beer. There's a set of Harvard Classics he likes to quote from. On an end table, a tobacco tin with hashish. I warn him about leaving his dope around, he could get busted.

He shrugs, shakes out a piece of hash, puts it in a hookah, and flips open his Zippo. He takes a drag, holds his breath, looking as if he's swallowed something bitter. "Like that," he says, releasing the smoke. He stretches his long legs and closes his eyes as Country Joe and the Fish play in the background. "Guaranteed to stop stammering." He bursts out laughing. I can't tell if he's joking or serious.

"Hide that dope—jail time, you're caught with so much as a roach."

He says he'll hide it when I'm gone, but he won't. It's one of the things I don't like about Johnny. He lies.

There's a pause while he tokes, and I say that if he goes to Vietnam, he'll have to ditch the band.

"That'd be a drag, man. Real bummer."

The smell of smoke is pungent, foreign. He takes another drag, unable to hold back a burst of coughing.

"Have some, little brother" he says. "Puts hair on your chest."

I wave him off, I don't do dope.

"Don't knock it till you've tried it."

"Not my scene."

"You'll come around. Wanna *bee-ah*?" When he's stoned, he feigns a Yankee accent.

"Don't smoke pot, don't drink. You know that."

He hiccups, brushes away fragrant wisps from a nearby incense dish, and asks if I've been out with cousin *Ahh-lene* lately. "She's one in a million."

"Might ask her to a movie at the new theatre in the Avalon Mall."

"Miss my girl somethin' awful. Depressing. Talked to her last night, we're tying the knot. Wish I had the money to fly her down *he-ah*. Nuthin' worse than being poor, huh? I mean what's with money anyway. She wants to visit, just hop a plane. That's what the commies do. And we're tryna save the world from communism. What's that all about, huh?" His brow furrows. "Maybe the commies are right, the world's better off with their system."

"Mr. Crenshaw thinks so."

"Crenshaw! Asked him for a loan last week. He said sure if I'd make a *drop* for him in the city. Don't worry, little brother, I didn't. Good ol' Crenshaw! Says we should be able to use rocks for money." He cocks his head to one side. "Rocks! Why the hell not? *Excuse me, sir*, I'd like to pay for my groceries, here's a bag of rocks." He has a giggling fit, the way stoners do sometimes. "Old Crenshaw was here last week rapping about Plato. Couldn't shut him up. He's got Arlene reading *Das Kapital*."

I ask if he's read Charlie's favourite book, *Robinson Crusoe*.

"Read it last week when I was stoned. What's it about?"

"You read Louis L'Amour?"

"Cowboy stuff!" He laughs. "But read whatever you want, I say." Then his voice drops, and he asks if I'll do him a big favour. Can I lend him some dough?

"You just got your allowance." I reach for my wallet. He flicks his wrist, says, "I mean serious bread, man. Wanna buy a Gibson 335 guitar, like Chuck Berry's."

"How much?"

"A grand."

My eyes pop. "A grand!"

"Was gonna ask Charlie. He said to ask for anything, any time."

"Don't have that kind of dough, Johnny. Could lend you twenty, maybe."

He flicks his wrist again, says, "Forget it. You guys do too much for me as it is."

"Lemme think about it. I'll talk to Charlie. Gotta go. Got a job out CBS way."

He hands me a dollar. "Article on Jagger in that new magazine, *Rolling Stone*. Pick it up, will ya?"

"Sure thing." No sense arguing about taking money from Johnny.

SEPTEMBER

II

Speech is worth one coin,
but silence is worth two.

— The Talmud

23

I'M HAVING TROUBLE EATING, SLEEPING, EVEN COMMUNICATING. The other day at school I sat in the cafeteria with Quinn and Esther-Marie and didn't say a word. An intense loneliness dogs me. I just sat there smiling my fake smile. After they left for class, I walked to the library showing off my fake grin along the way. I hid in the stacks and read Louis L'Amour. Once I felt so down, I went to the bathroom and hid in a toilet stall for a long time. I don't know how long I sat there; when I showed up for class, everyone burst out laughing. There was the sound of scraping chairs, ruffling papers, thumping books. Everyone was packing up. Then the urgent shuffling of feet, class was over. Phillip Ryan and Gabby Gilchrist came by and asked me to go shoot hoops, but I lied that I had to study for a test.

At night I try to do my homework, but all I can think of is the long, lonely days at school, alone in the crowded hallways and walking up busy stairs. I pretend-smile so much my jaws are sore, want to crawl into a hole somewhere until this lonely feeling passes. At home I do nothing but play that Roy Orbison record "Only the Lonely." In a weird way, it cheers me up: *Only the lonely / Know the heartaches I've been through* . . .

Only time I'm normal is when I'm working in the garage. I'm at peace there fixing flats, charging batteries, replacing spark plugs, windshield wipers. Other times I'm condemned to no man's land, beset with doubts, and worries: Charlie, Crenshaw, Arlene, Johnny.

Another horrible dream. The Rickettses' old German shepherd, Bruno, digs up my parents' grave and drags Charlie's corpse to their property, where Mrs. Ricketts gives me a stern lecture about a proper burial for such a holy man.

I wake in a panic and can't get back to sleep, so I open *Robinson Crusoe*. I'm reading it again and enjoying it more than the first time around. I wish Charlie were here so he could read parts to me out loud, the way he used to at the kitchen table.

Each morning when my knees hit the cold floor, my first thoughts are that God will smile on him. As I pray, blurred thoughts whirl in my mind like Rosie's spinning cylinder leaving a bad imprint on a sheet of new bills.

The empty house bears Charlie's absence in every room but especially the kitchen, where we spent so much time together. I move around like a ghost, uneasy wherever I go, feeling Charlie's presence in everything I touch—his coffee mug, his chair. A current of heat rises in my throat at the sight of a whiskey bottle in the cupboard.

I'm so lonely I make him coffee, put it in his place, and talk to him. Strange, but it makes me feel better, especially when I say, "Drink up, Charlie, coffee's getting cold, we got work to do."

I leave his things undisturbed: brush in his shaving mug, razor on the sink. I pick up the brush, think of using it, put it back. I can't bear to enter his bedroom, but I peek inside. Tidy as usual, bed made, extra blanket folded neatly, western novel on the night table. Above the bed, a framed black and white photograph of them working on the tobacco farm. I shut the door, return to the heavy air of silence throughout the house, long for his rasping voice. I try to shake off my moodiness, but before I know it, I'm in the porch reaching for his garage-smelling shirt, catching my breath.

In the living room, I look at his bookshelf, sit in his chair, and think about the future. Can I carry on the family tradition? Part of me knows it's a good thing, taking from the rich and giving to the poor. A noble calling. It's right to sock it to the heartless rich, as Crenshaw says. Another part knows it's wrong, criminal activity. Do I really want to do what Charlie did all his life? Counterfeiting? Could I look myself in the mirror? I want to be the son Charlie raised me to be. *Promise me you'll care for the less fortunate, son.* I want to be loyal. But I want what's right for me, my own garage, and if I work hard, I'll have enough money to look after myself and others. I won't need Rosie. That's the future I see, not always looking over my shoulder, second-guessing myself, worrying all the time.

To stave off loneliness, I read the Bible. I love reading Charlie's favourite section: Jesus's Triumphant Entry into Jerusalem on an Ass. Or as Charlie put it, Jesus Moons the Romans.

I sit on the lumpy sofa, try to squeeze in some of the stuffing that's falling out. The living room has our big stone fireplace with the framed print of Robin Hood over it. I sit in Charlie's armchair by the tall, pine bookshelf, pluck out one of his Louis L'Amour books, open it, and a photograph falls out. It's an old Polaroid of me and Lucy when I was little. We're sitting under a Christmas tree. It's blurry, so I take a closer look and see that it's not us; it's Johnny Fabrella and his mother, Arlene's Aunt Laura. Why would Charlie have a photograph of Johnny and his mother tucked away? Must've come by at Christmas—always crowded at our place during the holidays. I replace the book, think of Johnny, an orphan at such a young age, living all alone out the Brook way. Then I realize that we're both in the same boat, we're both orphans now.

I light a fire, stare at the flames, think about my hand in Charlie's death: part obedient son, part murderer. I daydream about chucking it all in, making a stash of counterfeit and heading to Ontario to work with Uncle Ches, maybe. Carry on the family legacy there without any of the responsibilities. Is that being a coward? It would mean saying goodbye to my friends, the band, Arlene. And who would keep an eye on Johnny? The price I'll have to pay, maybe. You can't have everything in life. Only a fool thinks that.

I recall putting my father in the grave. It'll be a long, lonely night.

24

TODAY AT SCHOOL, QUINN RATTED OUT RYAN FOR STEALING FROM THE CANTEEN. Ryan told him he had a key, it was a student council perk, and gave him a bag of chips and a Pepsi. Of course, it was all BS. Quinn got quite a shock when the principal told him that nobody on the student council has a key to the canteen, Ryan was pulling his leg.

I got a kick out of that, but it seems the only thing that makes me happy these days is Arlene White's bright red hair and twisted smile. After class I meet her at the machine shop, and she says I look like something the cat dragged in; do I have the flu?

"My father's dying," I say. "He's in Toronto seeing a specialist."

"I'm so sorry, Sonny." She smiles her lopsided smile, rubs my shoulder, and says let's meet for lunch, after class in the cafeteria. During lunch she tries to cheer me up. When we finish eating, she says, "Lets go for a walk along the beach. We'll take the bike. I won't go fast, promise." She's the only girl in town who rides a motorcycle. She's tough but has a soft side too. And there's that beautiful voice. Charlie said to listen carefully to the voice of the woman I marry, make sure I like it because I'll be listening to it the rest of my life. No problem listening to Arlene's voice, especially when she sings, that's for sure.

We drive to the ferry terminal, park, look at the sailboats moving between Bell Island and Conception Bay.

"My Uncle Ches had a Snipe, fifteen-footer. He's a member of the Bowring Yacht Club. We used to sail back and forth. He taught me to sail."

"Sounds like fun. Did you race?"

"All the time. Usually finished first, thanks to Ches. He left me the boat when he went away. Quinn and I sail it, sometimes Johnny, but he's more trouble than he's worth. Not easy sailing a Snipe single-handed."

The six-mile-long island used to produce iron ore, but it closed two years ago. My Uncle Ches used to drop dough over there for Charlie. I'd go along with him for the ferry boat ride. I haven't seen much of him since he left, he comes home the odd Christmas.

Arlene laughs, says, "I hear there's no water over there, iron mine polluted everything. They ship water in from St. John's. Why would anyone live in a place where there's no water? Like living in the desert."

"Uncle Ches says the Germans torpedoed the loading dock during the Second World War. There's a memorial at Lance Cove. Ches took me there when I was little."

We watch the seagulls coming and going from The Clapper, a narrow, vertical column of rock near the coastline.

I point to it. "Ches said he saw a helicopter land there once."

"Impossible! Helicopter couldn't land on such a narrow strip."

I disagree. Uncle Ches is rarely wrong. Whenever I talk to him on the phone, he amazes me with his knowledge—he's a walking encyclopedia—but I don't say anything.

On the way home we stop at Thelma's for a hamburger and Coke. Then we go for a walk along the beach. She starts singing a new song that's out, "The Letter," by the Box Tops. Everyone at school's crazy about it. Think I'll buy the record, give it to her, maybe.

It's nice walking and talking, easy to be with her. Will I ask her to that movie at the new theatre in St. John's? *Would you like to go to a movie with me?* Johnny says those are the hardest words he ever spoke. Wonder if he has that problem with the girl he's marrying, Celine. Thank God I don't have to stay up nights worrying about stammering or Vietnam. He says he'll hear from the draft board any day now. Poor Johnny!

25

PARANOIA STRIKES DEEP / INTO YOUR LIFE IT WILL CREEP. Whenever I hear that song, my worry-meter starts ticking. The music has an eerie beat. It's always playing on Thelma's jukebox, and the Acid Test plays it sometimes. Paranoia strikes deep when I think of the cops finding out about Rosie or someone stealing my counterfeit and spending it around town. The McCluskey secret weighs heavy, like a burden on my shoulders.

Everyone these days is a suspect: Quinn, Mr. Crenshaw, the goofy guy across from me in auto mechanics who can't add two and two. Even Arlene. If someone close finds out about Rosie, will I be betrayed? Crenshaw might try to steal my counterfeit. And what if Quinn gets snoopy—he wants to be a cop—or Arlene suspects something? She asks about Charlie a lot. Worse, what if I mistakenly use a counterfeit bill on a date? Or . . . so many ways to get caught. Thank God Johnny doesn't like grease under his fingernails and hates real work. He hasn't been to the shop since Charlie's departure.

In a movie I watched the other night, one detective said to another, "People will slit their mother's throat for a buck. Prisons are full of such creeps." I recall the Good Book: The love of money is the root of all evil. Thank God Charlie didn't worship money. Just the opposite.

I've been a wreck since burying him, piercing headaches, nausea, burning stomach. Can't get a good night's sleep. I wake, a knot in my stomach, feeling like I've slept under a slab of cement, remind myself that I did what he wanted, not to feel guilty, be hard on myself. That makes me feel better, but it doesn't last. Some hours are nothing but a series of nervous, jerky moments.

Last Tuesday was my eighteenth birthday. If I were an American citizen, I'd be like Johnny, required by law to register for the draft. I hear Charlie say, "You're a man now. Next spring you'll get your auto mechanic certification. You can hang out your shingle: Sonny's Auto."

What will I do without him, especially if I screw up . . . in the garage, the print shop, dropping the dough? What if someone finds out about my double life? Two days ago, I mistakenly put some bad counterfeit bills for burning in the good money bag. I was in a sweat combing through the good bag till I found them.

I had another terrible dream last night. I'm in the print shop and can't find a way out. Johnny Fabrella and Comrade Crenshaw are with me. Johnny's wearing a Robin Hood outfit. Crenshaw's dressed as Karl Marx. They're smoking pot and offering me money—stacks of twenties. Johnny tells me if I show him how to operate Rosie, he'll let me sing in his band. I tell him I hate crowds, can't sing. He says no matter, he stutters. Country singer Mel Tillis is the worst stutterer in the world, and Bob Dylan and Leonard Cohen can't sing for beans. I say I don't know how to operate Rosie. He shrugs, says that's too bad, you could make a lot of money. When I woke, my pyjamas were soaking wet.

I stayed awake for hours; if only I had a time machine to go back to the graveyard and undo what I've done. Worst two words in the world: *if only*.

Thelma's is a cheerful buzz, teenagers at lunch, laughing, shouting. The cook yells, "Steak, medium rare, table three." Quinn points to a couple kissing in the booth next to us. As I look, he steals a french fry, says there's a rumour at the Trades School about me living alone. "What's with your ol' man, anyway? When's he coming back from Toronto?"

"He was home last weekend," I lie. I'll have to be alert, ask Aunt Vivian to come in one weekend, maybe, for company, say she's keeping an eye on me till Charlie gets back. That'll lower the temperature.

I'm about to scoot when a strange-looking man enters and gawks at everyone. He's about thirty, a stocky guy, tough-looking, wears a leather coat and a fedora, the kind Humphrey Bogart wears in the movies. It dawns on me that he might be an undercover cop. He looks my way. I pretend not to see him, finish my Coke, chat with Quinn, who notices I'm edgy.

"What's with the ants in the pants, McCluskey?" He turns, looks at the stranger. "You know that guy?"

The stocky guy removes his fedora, greasy hair swept back.

"Nope. You?"

"No. Looks like a creep."

The guy leaves after a few minutes without ordering any food. I'm happy I didn't hear *Paranoia strikes deep* on the jukebox while he was looking around. It was weird enough without the music.

I chat with Quinn about Johnny and the awful news out of Vietnam. "TV shows dead bodies everywhere," Quinn says. "It's a bloodbath, man. Johnny's an idiot. Can't believe he's signing up for that nightmare. It'll be the end of the Acid Test."

"We've gotta change his mind."

"Fat chance. He's a Yank. Yanks love war. Gotta go."

I listen to a couple arguing in the booth behind me before heading home, where I work on some routine maintenance before hitting the books: Mr. Anderson's corroded battery that Charlie left, Johnny's oil changes, filter replacements, brake inspections, tire rotations. Endless work. Charlie always worked ten hours a day, six days a week. Blue-collar jobs are never forty-hour weeks.

Muscles are really sore these days. You do a lot of stretching, bending, and twisting in a garage, especially when you work alone. Charlie urged me to avoid awkward positions. But what can you do when you're holding something by one hand and you need to reach behind for a tool with the other? And I'm working faster than I should to make up for lost time.

Muscles sore, but the headaches are fading, thank God. Still, I'm spending my days half asleep, my nights half awake.

26

NEXT DAY WHILE I'M FILLING UP THE OLD VAUXHALL VIVA AT WHITE'S ESSO, it dawns on me what Charlie meant by the mechanical bride. I'm squeezing the nozzle while admiring Arlene's slender means, looking forward to asking her to a movie. She's a strict Catholic, but I don't let that bother me, it takes all kinds. Framed in the big window lined with Pepsi bottles, she leans against the cash register. As I pump gas, she looks my way, and Charlie's words came roaring back: "One of these days you'll get serious about women. You'll get rid of your mechanical bride for a real model. Remember not to depend on her, trust nobody. Your wife should never know about the print shop. Nobody should know till the time comes to tell one of your kids, and only one. You tell two people anything in the Cove, you've told two hundred. As Louis L'Amour says, 'Tell nobody too much of your affairs and remember, in all dealings with men, or women, to keep one hand upon the door latch.'"

How could Charlie love my mother so much and not tell her about Rosie? Shouldn't the one you love know everything? I replace the nozzle, go inside. "How-D?"

She laughs.

I pay for the gas, and before I know it, the words are out of my mouth: "*Bonnie and Clyde*'s coming to town in a few weeks. Like to go?"

"Sure," she says. "Hear it's great." She feigns an English accent. "What time will you come 'round and knock me up?" That sly half-smile.

"Pick you up at eight, and don't be late."

"You're such a Clutzky," she says.

I tip the bib of my baseball cap the way Charlie always did. "Ma'am!"

There's a twinkle in her eye. I glance at the gas pump. No one waiting, so

I flirt a bit longer. As we talk, I see a notice on the wall behind her: WE DO NOT ACCEPT 20 DOLLAR BILLS. My heart jumps to my throat.

I say I'll see her Saturday night, hightail it outta there. In the car, my stomach knots, heart races. I grip the steering wheel. "Fugg!" Feel like Robinson Crusoe when he found Friday's footprint in the sand. WE DO NOT ACCEPT 20 DOLLAR BILLS. Are there cannibals on my turf too? Have to find out. Be cool, Sonny.

I go back inside and buy a package of gum. Arlene hands me the change, and I nonchalantly ask, "What's with the sign?"

She turns her brown eyes on me, hunches her shoulders. "Someone gave us a bad bill a few days ago. Probably a drifter. Daddy says if he catches him, he'll chop his hand off."

It takes an effort, but I growl, "Arrr!" and leave, listening to her high-pitched laughter.

27

CHARLIE WAS RIGHT ABOUT MRS. CRENSHAW: SHE HAS A BOLT LOOSE. She disappears for long periods, and Mr. Crenshaw has no idea where she goes. He announced one day in class that she was missing and asked everyone to keep an eye out for her. Arlene said she saw a tear in his eye. We all felt pretty bad for him. Phillip Ryan, our school president, says she's screwing around, she has a lover in Saint Pierre, a drug-dealing bodybuilder, Jean-Luc somebody or other, who does psychedelics. Ryan calls him the mean man with muscle. He's a stocky, bald man. First time I saw him up close, he was delivering a package at Johnny's. I was shocked. He has a scarred, pockmarked face, no eyebrows, and what looks like a swollen, red nose—the face of a heavy drinker.

Everyone at school is blown away by Mrs. Crenshaw's looks. She's a medium size with a sexy pageboy haircut, so black you want to keep looking at it. She's much younger than Crenshaw, only about thirty. When she smiles at you, you know it's fake, but your face gets hot. Look closely, you'll see lightly pigmented sideburns and a downy moustache which everyone says is the result of taking testosterone. She usually wears skin-tight black jeans and knee-high black boots. And she's never without her full-rabbit fur hat, her Moscow. Joey Skinner, the class Einstein, refers to her as the beautiful but wayward Mrs. Crenshaw. She coaches wrestling at Memorial University and the Trades School. She also promotes women's bodybuilding, a new thing these days. Last year she placed in the Miss Physique contest in the States. I've seen her perform, and I gotta say, she's a sight to behold.

Mr. Crenshaw's very proud of her, brags about her expensive tastes. Sometimes he invites her to class to promote bodybuilding and the wrestling club. And he invited us to a practice to see "her routine." She wore a heavy fur coat, and when she removed it, we were shocked to see a low-cut muscle suit. Her skin, she called it, and started posing.

Some of the boys, especially Billy Watson, think she's flirty and aggressive when posing. Quinn says he gets a boner every time she flexes her muscles.

For non-competitive posing she usually wears a black robe, which she removes before her routine. Underneath, a skimpy, two-piece black bikini, high heels, and a spray tan to make her body look leaner. Last visit, she posed for a few seconds while humming a song.

The band's dead set against her being part of the Pot Park Concert, but Johnny says that she's just singing background, lip-synching with Esther-Marie.

After she gave her little pep talk about joining the wrestling club, she urged us to consider bodybuilding. "Typical bodybuilding training is not easy," she said. "It usually involves training twice a day—approximately one hour of lifting and anywhere from thirty minutes to two hours of cardio. If I had time, I'd include my fitness routine performed to the *William Tell Overture*. It includes elements of dance, strength moves, and gymnastics.

"This pose is called the X-frame." She stood with her legs shoulder-width apart, raised her arms, and flexed her biceps to murmurs of amusement, a few embarrassed sighs. Someone at the back clapped and hooted.

"My favourite move is the pretzel push-up," she said. "It's my thirty-second finale. I'll do it for you sometime." She bowed, blew the class a kiss, and left.

"Now your minds are ready to focus," Mr. Crenshaw said. "Take out your *Manifestos*."

Ready to focus! Who could focus after that? Quinn must've been beside himself.

Old Crenshaw began reading *The Communist Manifesto*: "A spectre is haunting Europe—the spectre of communism . . ." Surprisingly, you could hear a pin drop.

Mr. Crenshaw and Charlie would talk for hours about Karl Marx, Robin of Locksley, and Jesus. Sometimes Johnny and I joined them but didn't say much. They'd quarrel about Christianity and communism, my father believing that communism would only work if there was a place for Jesus in the party. He thought you could keep the essentials of Marx on capitalism without the excesses of Stalin and state power. Crenshaw disagreed. Despite their many differences, Charlie thought Mr. Crenshaw was ahead of his time, and Crenshaw said the same of Charlie.

At the beginning of the school year, Crenshaw gives everyone a copy of *The Communist Manifesto*. He encourages us to read it everywhere: in bed, while eating, in the bathroom, even in the shower. He gives extra marks if he sees you reading it around school or in town. He teaches that modern history begins with the Russian revolution of 1917. He's always working himself into a lather about the exploitation of the proletariat. Not surprisingly, he's the leader of the Communist Party of Newfoundland. We wonder how he gets away with teaching about communism. Quinn says one day he'll get fired, sure as there's poop in a dead cat. But he's been teaching that way forever and plans to retire in a year or so. Then again, maybe his job is safe and he'll teach till he drops.

Crenshaw's an odd duck. At school, instead of marking tests and papers by writing comments, he uses rubber stampers. He's got a shoebox full of them with phrases such as THIS MAKES ABSOLUTELY NO SENSE and CAPITALIST PROPAGANDA and words like MORONIC and IDIOTIC. His favourite: THIS IS NUTS. "Stampers save tons of time," he says. "Students don't read comments anyway. They just look at the mark and throw the paper in the garbage."

He comes by tonight wearing a suit that looks second-hand, with a white shirt, the starched collar wrinkled with sweat. He sits, sips tea, strokes his bushy beard, his paisley tie. Those close-set, amber eyes don't miss a trick, especially in class.

I ask about my mechanics test. "Thought I knew every answer."

"You had a few screw-ups," he says.

"Really. Which ones?"

"We'll talk about it in my office. Heard from Charlie?" He places his cup and saucer on the leather ottoman in front of the sofa. He seems nervous, on tenterhooks. "How's he doing? When will he be back?"

"He's still pretty sick but should be back soon. Aunt Vivian's planning on visiting him. I'll probably go too."

"Ahead of his time, your father. Way ahead. Does he need anything?" He takes out a bloodstained handkerchief, wipes his runny nose and what looks like dried-up toothpaste. "Let me know," he says, the dirty handkerchief balled in his hand. "I mean it, comrade. Anything!" He coughs radio static from his chest. "You need anything, lad?"

"No." I say I'm making out okay, miss Charlie, but I'm holding up.

"You're always at school on time. That's good, comrade. Stick to your routine same as if Charlie was around. And you're doing well in your classes.

Mr. Graham says you read a lot of novels. Impressive! You can never read too many novels or too much history."

"Yeah, I really like *Robinson Crusoe*," I say. "It's about—"

"I know what it's about." He throws up a hand in frustration. "Imperialist propaganda, a capitalist textbook." He says to attend university after I graduate. "You'll go nowhere these days without a university degree. Review the curriculum, get a leg up." He asks if I'm sleeping well, eating properly.

"Oh yeah. Charlie left me a list of things—"

"Money," he interrupts, picking his beard nervously. "Did he leave a good lot of money till he gets back?" He opens the handkerchief again, wipes his runny nose, takes out a package of cigarettes, lights one slowly, mechanically.

"Yes, a little to tide me over," I say. "And I do everything on the list. He'll be proud of me when he gets back." I choke up.

"Now, now, everything will be fine," he says. "Your father's tough as nails. After treatment he'll be better than ever."

"Yeah," I say, my voice strangled, tense.

He takes a drag on his cigarette, grimaces, perks up. "Say, why don't you come by our place Sunday for dinner? Flo is back from Saint Pierre. She cooks her turkey special with all the fixin's. You're family, after all. Get to know Florence. You've seen her posing. Amazing, eh! She's thinking about entering the Miss Body Beautiful contest. She recently joined the World Women's Wrestling Association. She has a better physique than its founder, Mildred Burke. And she's a better wrestler than Mary Ellison, the Spider Lady. She won a bronze medal at the Alberta Freestyle Invitational last year. I was there. Should've won the silver. Nitwit referee made a dumb call. But poor Flo! Her first love is the theatre. She's a failed actress, alas. Couldn't remember her lines. I saw her in a play once—*Julius Caesar*, played Portia, muffed an important line. She was supposed to say *Think you, I am no stronger than my sex*. . . . It came out *Thank you, I am no stranger having sex*. . . . Oh dear!

"Will you come by? Sunday? Flo's learned a new twist with her pretzel push-up. Very amusing! I'll get her to pose for you. She has a new outfit, two, in fact. Costumes, she calls them. No end to her new outfits. I'm going broke buying her skin suits. She asked me the other day if I was jealous of her wearing such skimpy costumes. Jealous! Why would I be jealous? I said if it makes her happy, so be it. You know me, never one to complain, hmm. She can pose naked, for all I care. I'm a communist, not a prude."

I don't know what to say. Dinner's fine, but Mrs. Crenshaw posing?

"I won't be able to stay long. I have a test Monday, I'll have to eat and run."

There's always a chance she might not be there. Once we were invited for Sunday dinner and Mrs. Crenshaw had disappeared, went missing for a month. Mr. Crenshaw cooked dinner for us. It wasn't very good. Johnny says she probably went to Saint Pierre to get her testosterone shot from Jean-Luc (nudge, nudge, wink, wink); she's a free spirit. Poor old Crenshaw!

Next day I buy the *Daily News* to check about that counterfeit bill at White's Esso. I hope there's nothing in the paper. I need to drop some dough soon, and I'll be solo for the first time. Charlie warned me not to get rusty. And there are people out of work, children without food, patients without medicine, people who desperately need a Robin Hood. The paper has a pungent, inky smell. I think of Charlie and Rosie. I read about a St. John's lawyer standing trial on two counts of illegal possession of narcotics. Next page the glaring headline,

> **Police warn of fake money in circulation**
> PORTUGAL COVE—The RCMP reported yesterday that forged currency is circulating and notified the public, especially store owners, to be on high alert. A counterfeit $20 bill was used recently to purchase an item at a business in the Portugal Cove area. The public is advised to check $20 bills before cashing them. This counterfeit bill bears the serial number 0232515.

My stomach churns. I'm sure nobody has passed counterfeit in the Cove before. At least, Charlie didn't mention it. And he would know, he had his ear to the ground all the time. I breathe a sigh, happy the serial number doesn't match ours. But what if one of Charlie's bills finds its way here? I decide to lie low until things blow over. I'll wait till after the school holiday to start dropping dough. Too close for comfort right now.

Will I have to switch the type of bill I use if things get too hairy? Charlie showed me how to make $100 bills but urged me not to use them. I haven't made one, and I hope I never have to.

28

ONE NIGHT AT A TRADES SCHOOL SOCK HOP I'M ABOUT TO ASK HER TO DANCE when the DJ turns the music sky high; her shoulders slump and she mouths *Crazy*. She's wearing jeans, blue turtleneck pullover, rawhide headband. I think of the free spirits who flocked to San Francisco for the Summer of Love. I ask if she wants a Coke: she shouts above the music, ginger ale. We sip our drinks and watch people dancing to the loud music.

When someone lowers the lights, I take her hand, begin dancing to "The St. John's Waltz." We move clumsily at first, but when I put my arm around her waist, she pulls me closer. I squeeze her hand, and she rests her head on my shoulder as we sway back and forth to the music's slow rhythm. I like the smell of her hair, a strong, natural scent, the warmth of her body as she presses against me. It's so right, we're a perfect fit. I close my eyes, imagine slowly kissing her soft lips.

When the dance ends, we ride her bike to my place. We stand in the cool night air outside my house talking about school, teasing each other about the coming long weekend. Who's camping overnight? Am I? Is she? Will the folk group the Harmonies be there? Will Mrs. Crenshaw screw up?

She says good night and pecks my cheek. I'm disappointed with the kiss.

But since then, I meet her after a class or for lunch, carry her books to the cafeteria or on fine days a picnic table behind the carpentry shop. We've become inseparable; everyone calls us sweethearts. Mechanics class, I exchange places with Quinn to sit by her. Sometimes after school we ride her bike to Thelma's for her favourite, a chocolate sundae, and talk about bikes and cars.

Several times, knowing her father isn't home, we make snacks, play records, or watch TV at her place. Her mother, a tall, sinewy woman with grey, close-cropped hair, a bright sheen to it, is usually around. She has false teeth, stern eyes, and sometimes breathes with a slight whistling sound. She's severe-looking, always seems preoccupied. Sometimes she watches a soap opera with us, periodically criticizing the risqué way an actress is dressed. "Good Lord! That's some mother's child." Awkward sidelong glances.

I'm afraid of Mrs. White. She's a light year away from my memory of Lucy. Around five she says, "You'd better say goodbye to your friend, Arlene. Your father will be home for supper soon." Her mother never calls me Sonny, always "your friend." Would your friend like a cup of tea? Would your friend like the volume turned up on the TV?

One afternoon as we chat about our fathers, I remind Arlene that Charlie's sickness is from lead poisoning working in the garage. "He's stubborn, refuses to wear a mask. I always wear one. Our course in health and safety stresses the importance of masks and proper ventilation in garages. Does your father wear one?"

"No."

Knowing she's a devout Catholic, I say Charlie studied to be an Anglican priest when he was young, he wanted to change the world, be a Robin Hood.

She doesn't think the Robin Hood philosophy would go over too well in her church. "I don't think Father McCarthy's big on stealing."

"But Jesus was a radical, He tried to turn everything around, change the social order, whatever it takes, even revolution. We should help, using our God-given gifts to—"

"I've more important things on my mind than Robin Hood," she says. She's worried about her father's drinking. Her mother's always bugging him to go to AA. "He drinks every day." Her voice cracks. "Sometimes he drinks at work." She says her mother's beside herself with worry. "She's thinking about leaving him." She pauses, clears her throat. "I'm thinking about leaving both of them, hopping on my racer and heading out west."

To take her mind off family, I mention the long weekend. She asks if I'll drive her to Butter Pot. Can I take her tent? "Band's playing, come rain or shine." She can't wait to do her rendition of "By the Time I Get to Phoenix."

"Practising every day."

"Sure," I say, "I'll drive you." Anything to avoid that café racer.

I spend the next few days getting up to speed on Charlie's charities. Easy work, but delicate. I keep good records, don't want to make any mistakes. Everything has to be done exactly as Charlie said.

Today after school I get a lift home on Arlene's racer. We stop at Thelma's for a hamburger and Coke, then go for a walk along the beach, seagulls soaring overhead. It's pleasant till she brings up amalgamating the garages.

"Be perfect, don'tcha think?"

"No." She might as well have slapped me in the face. "Forget it, it'll never happen."

"Why not? Daddy says we'll build a new place between White's and Charlie's Auto. We'll get all the traffic coming and going to Bell Island. Like being on a freeway exit. We'll handle the gas and convenience store, you'll do the repairs. Makes perfect sense, doesn't it?"

"No."

"Sonny, I need to speak confidentially. May I?"

"Certainly." Is she trying another tack?

"White's Esso is in financial trouble. We have to sell, which Daddy will never do, or amalgamate or find some other way . . ." Her voice catches. "Or we'll be on the street."

That puck to the face again. I think of what Esther-Marie said: If she gets Sonny, she gets the garage.

"I think Daddy's right about joining the garages."

Silence.

"If we amalgamate, everyone wins. Solve his money problems, might stop drinking."

More silence.

"Well?"

"Well, what?"

"Dont'cha agree?"

"No."

"But it makes perfect sense, Sonny—"

"Makes no sense. Charlie's Auto will be Sonny's Auto, and that's that. There'll be no—"

"Amalgamation doesn't mean you won't have Sonny's Auto. It's just a name."

"More than a name. It's my life, the family business, all I ever want. Besides, gas stations are a dying business. I don't want to be a gas station."

"But this isn't just about a gas station, White's Esso. I truly believe it'd be best for both businesses if you let Daddy decide—"

"Arlene, my father decides what goes on at Charlie's Auto, not *your* father."

She grabs her helmet, and it looks like she'll throw it at me.

On the way home, she drives so fast I'm afraid we'll have an accident. I yell to slow down.

"Hold on tighter," she shouts. "Don't touch my boobs."

29

CRENSHAW SMOKES, SIPS TEA, SAYS IN A LOW VOICE THAT HE'S "having a little problem."

"With my school work?"

"No. As I said, we'll discuss that in my office." He looks sullen, slumps forward. "It's my motorcycle," he says suddenly, as if he's changed his mind about what he really wants to say. "Could I drop by with it?"

"Bring it to the garage any time."

He has a 1960 blue and white Honda Benly Super Short. Not the most impressive machine, only fifteen horsepower, but it has a few pluses.

"Bloody bike chain. Charlie lets me use his tools."

"Bring it in, I'll see to it," I say. "I'm in the shop Saturdays." I don't want him in the garage.

"I'll do it, Sonny. I'll pay for oil, grease, that sort of thing." He stops suddenly, puts a hand on his heart. "Water . . . a glass of water, please." He reaches inside his pocket, removes a small vial of pills. I race to the kitchen, get a glass of water. He takes a pill, sighs, leans back on the couch. "Nitroglycerine," he says. "Be dead long ago without the good old nitro."

"More water?"

"No. Be fine in a minute. Just need the garage to fix the bike chain."

He doesn't own a car, just the Honda. You see him scooting around wearing his Maple Leafs helmet. He's a big Leafs fan.

He catches his breath, asks if I'm still dating Arlene White. "I like that gal, she has a brain."

"Yes."

"Good for you," he says. "A witty gal, that one. She's read the *Manifesto* twice, you know. And *Das Kapital* got her wires hummin'. You've read it?"

"Parts," I lie.

"I loaned her Gibbon's *Decline and Fall* and Trotsky's *History of the Russian Revolution*. Hang on to her, comrade. She's a reader." He chortles. "Most of the class can't read See Jane run, See Dick run."

Nervous laughter.

"Really knows her onions, that one. She's reading *The Adventures of Robin Hood* and a book on that cult, the Sullivanians? Says it's the same book. Two cults." He snorts. "Don't tell Charlie that."

"She has me reading *Middlemarch*."

He leans forward. "Sonny," he says in a low voice, "I'd like to ask a little favour of you."

"Anything, Mr. Crenshaw."

He looks around blankly. "Well, your dad and I are very close, as you know. Partners and all. Comrades."

I recall Charlie telling me not to trust him, but I'm curious and say, "You're one of his Merry Men, Mr. Crenshaw. My father thinks the world of you."

He looks away. "Humph! Think the world of him." A brief silence as he rubs his forehead, asks in a trembling voice if I'm aware that Charlie lends him money now and then.

"No. But my father's a generous man, helps many people, he's a real Christian."

He rubs his forehead again, humphs and gives me a long stare. "I never borrow much, fifty here, a hundred there."

My jaw drops. "That's a lot of money, Mr. Crenshaw." I recall the ledger: *Watch your bobber.*

"You see, Sonny, I have a little problem . . ." His voice a whisper again. "Can I share it with you? . . . My little problem. In confidence?"

I say my lips are sealed. "I won't be like the monk who ratted out Robin Hood."

He arches an eyebrow, looks at the floor, and says, "You see, Sonny, I have a little gambling problem. It's not serious, mind you. A minor problem. I lose a little money now and then betting at cards. As a result, I occasionally find myself in need of a little loan to tide me over during my emergency, if you know what I mean. Whenever I borrow from Charlie, I give it back next payday. And that would be Friday next. Charlie always helps me out. What's money between comrades? It's only paper. Which, as you know from my classes, is precisely what money is. Nothing but paper! Anyone can make it. Our currency could be rocks if we wanted." Scornful laughter.

The ledger! Charlie hasn't mentioned this. Is it true? I ask how much he needs. He looks at the floor again, says a hundred will do the trick nicely.

"Whew! That's a fair amount of money, sir."

"Well, yes." His voice grows shrill. "Yes, it is. Truth to tell, I could use a lot more. I'm flat broke."

I take a firm stand, say I don't have that kind of money. "I'm sorry. I—"

"Well, *you* might not have that kind of money, but *Charlie* does. I know that for a fact, young man." He wipes his nose, spits into his handkerchief, arches an eyebrow again. "I know all about that *anonymous* donation to the Ricketts family. And I know he gives Johnny money each month and—"

"But a hundred dollars, sir! That's a lot of money."

"But I always pay it back, you see. Always! And I know Charlie has lots of money. He said he can get money any time, day or night." His eyes pierce mine. "And you did say he left you some money to tide you over while he's away. Payday is Friday next." His voice is childlike, pleading. "I could call Charlie, if you prefer."

"I'll see what I can do, sir," I say. "Charlie might call tonight. He put extra money in my bank account. If he says okay, I'll bring the money to school tomorrow. I'll need to go to the bank, of course." That isn't true, but I don't want him thinking I keep money around. He sounds desperate.

"Oh, that would be fine, just fine, Sonny." Thrilled now and showing it. "Charlie always tides me over," he says, coughing radio static again.

"I'll drop an envelope on your desk after lunch."

"Thank you, lad, thank you. Charlie will approve. We're comrades, after all." He points a finger at me. "And Sonny, not a word."

"My lips are sealed, sir."

"Wouldn't want this getting back to Mrs. Crenshaw. She's a Baptist."

"Your secret is safe with me."

He gets up, says thanks for the tea and the loan, he'll return the money on payday, not to worry.

"That's fine, Mr. Crenshaw, no hurry if Charlie approves."

"Is the shop open? I'll fix that loose chain and be gone." He pats his coat pocket and says, "Never mind, I have a key."

"A key!" That rocks me. "To the garage?" My heart's a jackhammer.

"Charlie gave me one ages ago." He pats his pocket again.

When Charlie was around, he used to spend a lot of time in the garage. He's an excellent mechanic. Did Charlie give him a key?

I follow him to the garage. "I'll let you in and close up."

He says he hates being rubbernecked. "Go back to the house, Sonny. I'll turn off the lights and lock up. Only be a minute."

As I leave, he says that I can borrow the history from Arlene. He means the Trotsky book. "See you on Sunday, comrade. Six. Don't be late, hmm. Mrs. Crenshaw can't abide tardiness."

"Sunday at six." I head to the house and stand sentinel at the kitchen window until the garage lights go out. True to his word, he's gone in about ten minutes. I race to the garage and check it out. All seems in order. I open the print shop, look around. Everything's fine there too. I glance at the old monster standing silently in the shadows and swear to God I hear it groan. There's a garbage bag of discarded counterfeit for burning. I look at the bag and think of Crusoe finding a drawer full of money on board the doomed ship. *What art thou good for? Thou art not worth to me—no, not the taking off the ground* . . . I take a last good look, go to the hiding place where the good money bag is stashed, and count out five twenties to pay for Mr. Crenshaw's gambling debt.

30

TODAY I WORK FLAT OUT AT THE GARAGE. It helps me feel closer to Charlie. It's like he's there working alongside me. I catch his gravelly voice now and then: *Sonny, the monkey wrench, please . . . Sonny, where's my ratchet set*? And whenever I make a mistake, his loud, cackling laughter: *You son of a monk*!

He was right; we'll be together forever. Nothing will change that, even going my own way.

Johnny calls, asks if I need any help at the garage. He doesn't want any money, just wants to help me out. "You looked really beat the last time I saw you, little brother."

I laugh. "I'll pay you, c'mon over. Doing a brake job, can use your help."

"Be there right away, I'll make spaghetti for supper. Can sure use the money. Gotta get that Gibson 335, man."

"Johnny, how many guitars you got?"

Laughter. "I love you, little brother." *Click*.

He's right, I'm dog-tired. Last time I was this bushed I left the garage door unlocked. I look around: oil changes, tire repairs, dead battery with the charger on the fritz. I replace spark plugs in one car, then another.

Note to self: Remember to buy more spark plugs at Canadian Tire.

I decide to leave Mr. Walsh's Volkswagen until after supper—brake jobs take time—and work on Mr. Bailey's Dodge Dart. I love that slant six engine: 145 horsepower with its larger carburetor and revised camshaft. The slant six is one of the most bulletproof engines ever made. And though it's powerful, it still gets over thirty miles to the gallon. I've heard of slant sixes getting over 300,000 miles without removing the tappet cover once.

Now and then I look up something in Charlie's book of words, as he called it. *Hawkins' Mechanical Dictionary* comes in handy in the shop. As the subtitle says, it's a cyclopedia of words, terms, phrases, and data used in the mechanic arts, trades, and sciences, and was first published in 1909. I thumb through it, mulling over weird words like twitter bit (the tip of a countersink that accommodates the screw head). As Charlie always said, no harm in hanging around words. It even contains a passage on Printing and the Printing Press, some of which Charlie has underlined. But there's nothing on counterfeiting. The spine of Charlie's copy is thumb-worn, the covers greasy with all the use over the years.

Note to self: Buy a new copy of *Hawkins' Mechanical Dictionary*. Charge it to Charlie's account. Ha, ha.

Another migraine today. I spent half the night fretting about the stocky guy who came into Thelma's. Was he a cop?

I'm sticking to my schedules, abiding by the ledger, which I read over again last night. So far, no mistakes. I hope I never make any. Like Charlie says, it doesn't take much. One little screw-up and *kaboom*! Down come the dominoes.

I'd like to invite a friend or two from school over but don't think it's a good idea to have anyone in the house. I'll meet them at school and Thelma's instead.

I can't stop thinking about Johnny and his girlfriend. I'd hate to be stuck in one place and my girl in another. In a way he too is like Robinson Crusoe on his island. And the war news gets worse and worse. The TV showed bombs dropping on villages.

Charlie showed him how to do it. I showed him how to do it. I was sure he knew what he was doing. Big mistake, I screwed up. Charlie said the only thing wrong with screwing up is refusing to admit it. We all screw up, he said. Be a man, not a mouse about it. Own up!

Actually, it was a double screw-up. I'm not supposed to do difficult work. Charlie: Don't take on tricky jobs without your certification. Stick to the simple stuff: oil changes, tires, batteries. And keep a close eye on Johnny.

We were fixing the brakes on Mr. Walsh's Volkswagen Bug, and I asked Johnny to take over the job while I did a tune-up. Mistake number one.

Johnny thought the grinding sound was caused by worn-out brake shoes. I told him the problem was a faulty drum. He finished the job, took it for a drive, and said he had to go make supper. I checked the brake pedal, and it didn't feel right. But the grinding sound was gone, so I convinced myself it was fine. Mistake number two.

I was tired and in a hurry. I should've seen Johnny's mistake, started again from scratch.

Luckily, Mr. Walsh is a good friend of Charlie's and didn't make a fuss. When he brought the car back, I replaced the faulty drum and added more brake fluid and grease to reduce the friction. I said there was no charge. He insisted on paying.

After he left, I was really upset. It rocked my confidence, I gotta say. On the way back to the house, I thought about what I'd done, or rather, failed to do—inspect Johnny's work carefully. How often Charlie said, "Not exactly kissing cousins: speed and fatigue."

Johnny apologized for the mistake and promised it would never happen again. "I know I'm lousy in the garage, man. I'm sorry."

I chided myself and made a mental note: If Johnny's gonna make a living at the garage, as Charlie wanted, I'll have to look a lot closer at his work from now on.

31

A FEW WEEKS AFTER CHARLIE DIED, I'm cleaning up the garage one Saturday when I hear wheels on the crushed stone in the driveway. I peek out the side window and my heart stops. A cop car. A stern-looking man gets out, walks to the office door, and knocks. He's tall, brush cut, beaky nose, and there's no mistaking the yellow stripes on the sides of his pants. A Mountie. I steady myself, take a deep breath, answer the door.

"You open?" the Mountie asks. He has a worm-like scar on his chin.

"Yep." A piano-wire knot in my gut.

"Wasn't sure you were open, bein' Saturday and all."

Charlie lectured me once about dealing with the law: "Say nuthin'. *Watch your P's and Q's!*"

"Drove over a dirt road out the Brook way. Muffler's loose. Rattling like hell. Illegal to drive with a damaged muffler, you know."

"You might have a leak," I say. "Exhaust leaks can cause a rattling sound." I yank the garage door chain, guide the car over the pit. He gets out, whistles, and says, "Pretty clean ship you got here." He points to the pictures above the pegboard. On one side, the bushy-bearded Karl Marx with the quote: *The rich will do anything for the poor except get off their backs.* On the other side, Robin Hood and his Merry Men with the caption: *Fight for those who can't fight for themselves. If that makes you an outlaw, so be it.* Cop laughs, nods at the Marx picture. "That your granddad? Looks like a hippie." I smile, go down the steps, look at his muffler, and see the problem right away, loose bracket, badly corroded. I turn to get a new bracket from the parts drawer and run smack dab into him.

"Whoa!" he says, "Sorry about that." Before I can tell him to leave, he crouches, looks around, and says this sure is quite a bunker I have down here.

He points to the steel door. "That where the bodies are buried?" A spurt of choking laughter.

My heart jumps. "Where we keep our supplies: batteries, brake shoes, mufflers—"

"Hey, Churchill didn't have a bunker this good. Holy cow! This is somethin'!" He whistles sharply. "Whew! What is it, six feet? I'm five eleven. You must be five eight. How do you—"

I point to a riser near the back wall. "I stand on that box." I'm nervous as a long-tailed cat in a roomful of rocking chairs but careful not to look at the steel door.

Cop cocks his head, asks why the pit's so deep. "Most of 'em are only about four feet. That right?"

"My father likes it this deep," I say. "He's tall as you. Easy for him to work."

He points a nicotine-stained finger. "Must be a pain moving that box around all the time. You could fill it in with slab-on-grade. Bring it up a foot or so. Wouldn't mind giving you a hand. Built a few houses in my time."

"Oh no, that's fine, I'm used to the box now. It's fine."

He says if I change my mind, just call the station. "You know where the office is, end of the Cove near the ferry. What the kids call the Hup and Down. Race their cars there every Saturday night. Drives me crazy. I'm not there, leave a message."

He follows me up the steps babbling about the cold weather, he's from out west, BC, Newfoundland weather's a drag. He's a talker, as Quinn would say.

"Hop in the car," I say. "Only take a second to change the bracket, no charge. Just a bracket, happy to help out."

"Really? Wow! Thanks. Thanks so much." He extends a callused hand. "Mitchell! Corporal Charlie Mitchell."

My heart pounds as I shake his hand, hasn't beat this hard since the night I buried Charlie. I head into the pit, grab a new bracket, replace the old one.

"Thanks again," he says when I return. "Don't forget. Slab-on-grade." He winks, nods. "Bring it up a foot."

I nod back, wave goodbye, lower the garage door as he backs out. Whine of the motor, tires crunching stone, and he's gone. Relieved, I close my eyes. Inside, I fall against the wall, scared stiff, my head spinning, Charlie's rattling laughter the loudest I've ever heard. But I'm not laughing, I'm hyperventilating. *That where the bodies are buried*?

Charlie! His name's *Charlie*. Fugg! What're the odds! I look around the garage. It's sparkling clean, everything in its place, unlike most garages, which are cluttered, chaotic. Charlie insisted on a well-organized workplace. I wonder about the cop, afraid I've been discovered. Is it a set-up? Blood pounding in my neck. "Maybe I should give this up, Charlie," I say, as if we're chatting while cleaning up the shop. "Maybe I can't face what's ahead." Then I remember what he wrote in the ledger about holding on to the family business. This is my world now, however humble, my body shaking, a spring coiled somewhere tight in my chest. And for a moment the sickening sorrow of it all makes me think I'll go mad.

When I get hold of myself, I recall the things Robinson Crusoe salvaged from the shipwreck, how he held on to them for dear life: "Two guns, one axe, three cutlasses, one saw, three Dutch cheeses . . ." I look at Charlie's soiled boots on the floor, the greasy cap he wore tipped ever so slightly, his dirty overalls hanging on a nail in the corner. I look around the shop: screwdrivers, wrenches, ratchets and sockets, pliers. I see what Charlie saw every day, feel his presence: jack stands, oil caddy, battery charger, engine hoist. On a side wall, hooks with hammers, wrenches, various saws; in front of it, a large workbench with an iron vise at one end, at the other, drills, cans of drill bits. In a sunlit corner, a band saw. And I know in my heart that the meaning of my life is in front of me—this shop. I look at the pictures of Karl Marx and Robin Hood: "I'll hold on to the shop, Charlie, I promise. You can count on me." And I make up my mind then and there to hold on for dear life to every last thing in the place. And I think of Rosie, Charlie's state-of-the-art printer hidden behind the steel door, and I promise I'll hold on to her for dear life too.

32

SAW A BRIGHT RED CAFÉ RACER TODAY IN ST. JOHN'S WHILE PICKING UP PARTS. It looked nicer than Arlene's, but I won't tell her that. It was parked next to a 1965 Mustang convertible. A beauty night-mist blue two-door with bucket seats and chrome-styled steel wheels. A new Mustang costs over $2,000; it's a car I dream about owning. Maybe I'll be lucky, find one that's beat up, can bring back to life at Charlie's Auto. Sure be nice to pick up Arlene White in a Mustang convertible and drive to the A&W for a milkshake. Now that's something worth dreaming about.

I'm daydreaming about the long weekend too. It's getting close. Everyone's going to the Pot Park party to hear Johnny Fabrella and the Acid Test.

And what I'm dreaming about most is hanging out my shingle. I got two tests back today, 95 in automotive math fundamentals and 98 in history, which isn't hard if you write a few sentences about the evils of capitalism and the exploitation of the working class. Mr. Crenshaw might ask a question about the reign of Ramses II or the Ptolemaic Dynasty, but if you mention the inequality of the economic system and the exploitation of workers, you'll get an A. Crenshaw's been asking about Charlie. I hope he doesn't get too snoopy.

I can't wait to drop some dough, get Charlie's charity work up to date and go my own way, be like Robinson Crusoe—independent, free. It's always uppermost in my mind, what I want most in life. I just have to decide if Arlene will be part of that dream.

Aunt Vivian pushes through the door with one hand, an ice cream cone in the other, beside herself that Charlie left me alone. "That man, that man," she hollers and licks her cone. "Rocks in his head, leavin' a youngster like you all alone." She's a heavy-set woman, and her boobs slosh under her thin shirt as she walks about inspecting the place with her piercing blue eyes. "Humph!

Pretty tidy," she says, "I'm impressed. You looking after Johnny? Giving him lotsa work at the garage?"

"Yes, but he rarely comes."

She laughs. "Johnny and work, not exactly kissin' cousins." She nudges me toward the kitchen. "Get the peeler out, let's put on a big pot of stew before I catches the train."

I help her gather what she needs as she continues her harangue about Charlie, but I know it's all bluster. "Told me he'd be back in a few days." She snickers, showing her stained, uneven teeth. "Few days, my ass!"

"He's pretty sick, Aunt Vivian. And I just turned eighteen, I'm not a baby."

She throws her arms around me and squeezes hard. "If I was closer, I'd come by every day, but I hates the drive, hates the city."

"I'm fine, Aunt Viv. Really, I am."

"Promise you'll eat proper."

"I will. I do."

"And if you needs anything, any little thing, you call me, do y'hear! Only a phone call away, y'know. And y'knows you're welcome to come to Stephenville any time you feels like it. Door's always open." She gives me another big hug, takes a giant step back, and beams. "Look at you. Sure, you're as handsome as paint. You're all McCluskey, you are." She forces a $10 bill into my hand. "For the Butter Pot weekend." She's so kind, Aunt Vivian.

33

CONCEPTION BAY SOUTH IS ABOUT FOURTEEN MILES FROM PORTUGAL COVE. There are various communities along the coastline. The ledger lists nine towns where Charlie dropped dough over the years, places like Topsail, Manuels, Foxtrap, Kelligrews, and Upper Gullies. Before heading out, I review Charlie's records—nine months since he dropped dough out there. The last places, Manuels Mall, gas stations in Kelligrews and Seal Cove, all starred indicating they're excellent drop-off locations.

No news of the counterfeit twenty cashed in the Cove, and nothing came of the Mountie who wanted his muffler checked. I cross my fingers, that's the end of it. I can't lie low forever, need to take care of Charlie's charities and get on with a normal life, so I head straight to the hiding place, remove the bag of counterfeit bills, put five twenties in each pocket, and hit the road.

First stop, the Esso station on the highway. I'll have breakfast, exchange a twenty, gas up with another twenty. Return trip I'll have my favourite, a hot turkey sandwich, at the overpass Irving using the last fake bill. All in all, I'll swap $200, come home with a clean chunk of change.

It's a beautiful fall day, cool but sunny, and I enjoy the drive until about halfway, when the sunshine changes to misty rain. I stop at the Manuels Mall, where I window-shop at several stores, mostly clothing, but there's a kiosk, The Smoke Shop, and a small booth, Chocolate Heaven. There's also a drugstore. Easy money, as Charlie would say. I'll drop a few twenties and head to the next town.

I hit The Smoke Shop first. Charlie and I always dropped money without a hitch, but near the kiosk, my heart's thrumming in my ears. Jitters, excitement—a new thrill. Maybe because it's my first time without Charlie.

A short woman with rouged cheeks smiles. "May I help you?"

I smile back. "Pack of Camels, please." She passes me the cigarettes, asks if I'd like matches. "No . . . yes, please." I hand her a twenty. She gives me the change, says thanks. I leave, my heart bursting through my chest. I think of Bonnie and Clyde—an intense rush—and the first time I saw Arlene in a bathing suit.

I walk the mall in a trance, my shoes squeaking, then head outside for a cigarette before hitting Chocolate Heaven. Nervous as hell, I light up, inhale slowly, trying to calm my nerves, think of Charlie, his chain-smoking. I people-watch, try to pull myself together. Suddenly, I burst out laughing. An older man wearing a greasy cap, slightly tipped—the way Charlie wore his—stares at me. *Paranoia starts to creep*. Settle down, Sonny, this is serious business. Charlie's voice echoes: *Nuthin' out of the ordinary, son. Never tip your hand.*

I finish my cigarette, stroll to Chocolate Heaven. I order a milkshake, change my mind, ask for chocolate ice cream, change again, order vanilla. The clean-cut teenager serving me hardly looks my way. He scoops ice cream from a bucket into a cone, hands it to me. I order a Mars bar. Another twenty, another thrill, but nothing like the rush at The Smoke Shop. The kid hands me the change without a word. It always startles me how involved people are with themselves. I reach for the money, knock over a box of straws, apologize, pocket the change, and pick up the straws.

At the drugstore, I look for a copy of *Rolling Stone*. The clerk says it'll be out next month. I remove a copy of *Popular Mechanics*, my favourite magazine. I thumb through the Automobiles and Driving section, turn to the Regular Features, and read a brief letter to the editor on using a fire extinguisher. At the checkout, I purchase the magazine. Again, the clerk doesn't look at me.

Half the counterfeit spent, I head to the car feeling pretty good, stash the clean money in a grocery bag under the passenger seat. Next stop, a mom-and-pop gas station, Shanahan's Golden Eagle. I'll buy a bag of chips, a Coke. Inside, an old woman with sunken cheeks sits behind the counter knitting.

She looks up, says, "Grand day! God's glory is upon us t'day."

"Beautiful day." I saunter toward the cooler, grab a Coke, a bag of chips.

The old woman talks about the weather. "Looks like a cold winter, worst in years. Dogberry trees is full. Bad sign. Lotsa dogberries, lotsa snow."

I put the Coke and chips on the counter.

"My, but you're some handsome young fella," she says. "What's your name?"

"Sonny."

"Sonny! Now that's a lovely name. Sure, any word with the sun into it is beautiful."

"This your place?"

She says she and her husband, Walter, have owned it since they were married, nigh forty year ago now.

"How's business?"

She frowns, shakes her head. "Bit slow lately. I spec it'll pick up nigh Christmas."

Her forehead wrinkles. She asks if that's it, just a bag of chips and a Coke? I take out my wallet, something tells me not to use a fake bill.

"Does ye want any gas? Gas is how we makes most of our money 'ere."

"Filled up this morning."

She nods, says sulkily, "Oh!" opens the cash register.

I pay with a real $1 bill, scoop up the change, and leave. In the car, I hear Charlie saying how proud he is, I'm one of Robin's Merry Men for sure. I don't know if I am or not, but it feels good. I know that kind old lady doesn't cheat anyone, want to go back, give her some money. No! That would be tipping your hand.

I use up all but two twenties in Kelligrews, Upper Gullies, Seal Cove, stash the clean money, and decide to drop a twenty in Chamberlains, saving the last bill for supper at the Irving station. In Chamberlains, I stop at Ed's Mini Mart to buy some groceries. Two men wearing stocking caps are in heated conversation when I walk in. The place smells of Camel cigarettes, reminds me of Charlie. The man behind the counter has a blemished face, looks unhealthy. "I'll kill the bastard if I finds out it's he." I cock my ear, pick up bread, milk, eggs, and head to the counter.

"But 'ow can ye find that out?" the man being served says. "If it's 'e?"

"Well, the two times he was here he just looked dodgy to me, is all. Can't be one hundred per cent sure, now, it were a while back. Bought gas and groceries, wore that ol' jacket."

Paranoia starts to creep. Could they be talking about Charlie?

"Is 'e from 'round 'ere?"

"A townie, I spec. Drove a tow truck."

My heart almost comes through my throat. I freeze. Charlie? Get hold of yourself, Sonny. They could be talking about anyone. Still, I want to return the groceries and hightail it out of there, but it's too late, the food's on the counter, owner's ringing in my order. I'm nervous, fumble my wallet, it falls to the floor.

"Mind you don't drop them eggs, now, sonny." For one long, horrible second I think the owner knows my name. He hems and haws, says, "That'll be a dollar and two cents." I thumb my wallet for a real bill, but I used my last good dollar at the mom-and-pop, only two bad twenties left. I pass him one, he hands me the change. I swallow hard and get out of there.

On the way to the car, dark clouds gather and a cool wind begins blowing. I'm scared witless, want to go back to the store, get that fake twenty. I drive off thinking about what was said back there. Is Charlie still alive? Relax. Those men weren't talking about Charlie. Still, I make a note: check Charlie's records when you get home.

A few miles and I calm down, convince myself there's nothing to worry about. I'll never be back at that store again. I'll never use the tow truck for a drop in Conception Bay South, never go back to Chamberlains.

Back at the print shop before storing the clean money, I put aside an amount for the charities and take out Charlie's notebook. Good records, I remind myself, keep good records. Then I open the notebook and write:

October 25, 1967 (CBS Drop)

TCH Esso: 1 breakfast: 1.10
Topsail Golden Eagle: 4 gals of gas @ .29 per gallon = 1.16
The Smoke Shop (Manuels Mall) 1 package of cigarettes: 32 cents
Chocolate Heaven (Manuels Mall) 1 ice cream cone: 15 cents . . .

I double-check each amount. Next to Ed's Mini Mart I write NEVER AGAIN. When I add everything up, the total spend is $9.13. The net is $190.87. Not a bad haul, I hear Charlie sing out. All in a day's work!

34

THE BAND SENT ME TO CONVINCE JOHNNY NOT TO ENLIST ON HIS OWN. He registered for the draft, so I won't come on strong.

He's outside, feeding a stray ginger cat when I arrive.

"*Rolling Stone* magazine's not out till next month," I say.

"Good to see you, little brother." He passes me the tiniest, frailest cat you've ever seen. She's missing a leg. "Isn't she the cutest little thing? Musta got caught in a trap. Lotsa trapping out this way. Poor little thing! I'm saving up to get her a prosthetic."

"I'll help."

"Thanks, man. I call her Ginger." He kisses her, pets her, gently places her by a milk bowl. We head inside, and he asks if I'd like something to eat. "Got some leftover risotto."

"No thanks."

We go to the living room, where he picks up a paperback and looks at me with glazed eyes. He speaks haltingly. "Reading *The Red Badge of Courage*. For my rendezvous with Uncle Sam, my civic duty. Red for war, yellow for cowardice. Hero wants red so he can cover up his yellow. Poor kids! Join the army to find glory. Heartbreaking . . ."

"You don't have to go to Vietnam, Johnny. You're not a coward if you don't—"

"Yeah, I am. Gotta go. Can't go AWOL."

"They banned that book."

"Yeah. You know what that cat Crane had going for him: the closer the writer gets to life, the better he becomes.

"Charlie told me Stephen Crane was nowhere near those battles. He worked from the photos."

"Well, the photos worked, man. Got my attention. Put me in the scene."

"You know you can hold off the draft for four years with a student deferment. It's called a 2-S."

"Forget it. Gotta go."

"You heard Crenshaw, over eleven thousand soldiers killed so far."

"Yeah, old Crenshaw enjoys that sort of thing." He flips through a few pages of the book:

In the eastern sky, there was a yellow patch like a rug laid for the feet of the coming sun; and against it, black and pattern-like, loomed the gigantic figure of the colonel on a gigantic horse.

He looks at me, runs a hand through his hair, and reads silently. Then he closes the book. "Give my left nut to write like that, McCluskey."

"It's well-written." But he's not listening, he's crying.

"Think you could kill someone, Sonny?"

"No." But as Charlie often said, if a man doesn't have God in his corner, he can be made to do anything. *Auschwitz.*

"Old man did some killin', World War II, Korea. Why, Sonny? Can you answer me that?"

"No."

"He'd be disappointed in me, huh? His cowardly son, unable to kill someone. Not doin' what a man's gotta do."

"Everyone's different, Johnny. We're not all meant to be soldiers."

"Just wanna play music, man. What about you, Sonny?"

"Just wanna garage. And I want you to be part of it, Johnny. Charlie wants you—"

"No place for me in that world, man."

"Sure there is, if you spend time at the garage. Charlie says—"

"Thinkin' about changin' the name of the band to the Acidheads. You ever dropped acid, little brother?"

I gulp.

"Should try it. Dissolves the ego. It's replaced by an abiding love of all things. Endless tenderness, big love. The tiniest thing becomes special, a flower, an ant. Total immersion in the present. Nirvana now! No worries about the crazy future. No worries about being a coward."

"You're not a coward, Johnny."

"Yeah, I am. Everyone is deep down. I couldn't live with myself if I didn't serve. I'll peel potatoes, carry a stretcher, some damned thing, but I gotta go. For the old man as much as myself. That make sense, Sonny?"

"Guess so." But it didn't make a lick of sense. If I were in his shoes, I wouldn't go.

"Old man was army. His old man, marine. Military's in the blood." Tears stream down his face, and I see Arlene. "Just wanna play some music, man, that's all. Don't wanna kill anyone." He wipes his eyes, says he's sorry. And I wish Charlie was around to cheer him up. Charlie could do that when you were down. Johnny lights a cigarette, and the strangest thing, the tilt of his head, the way he squints at the flame, for a second he looks the spit of Charlie.

"Got a buddy in Manhattan, just drafted—Vito Rossi. Tunnel rat over there. Says Vietnam smells like raw sewage all the time." He lowers his eyes. "His father has the boot franchise for the war. Huh! The boot franchise! Sending your kid off to get shot for that." He shakes his head. "Boot franchise! Somethin' else, man."

He walks to the stereo, turns it off, picks up his guitar, flashes the candy-apple red finish. "Bought a new Fender Jazzmaster. Cool, huh?"

Someone knocks, speaks with a French accent: "Special delivery for Monsieur Fabrella!" Johnny jumps off the couch, takes out his wallet, races to the door. Chatter with the delivery man. "I'll get the rest of the money, Jean-Luc. Need a few more days, that's all." Then muffled talk, something about Saint Pierre, and the Frenchman says he has to split, Flo's waiting for her package.

Flo? Mrs. Crenshaw?

Johnny comes back with a package and puts it in the freezer. He looks worried. I ask if everything's okay.

"Fine. Money problems, that's all." He flashes the Fender again. "Who doesn't have money problems, man?"

"That's why you should work more at the garage."

"Hungry, Sonny? Could make you somethin'. Want one of my special sandwiches?"

"Already ate. Johnny, the band members asked me to talk you outta signing up. You go to Vietnam, it'll mean the end of the Acid Test."

"I go to Vietnam every time Celine hangs up the phone." He sighs. "Ever think about the future, Sonny? I don't mean tomorrow. I mean the end. That's the real reason I wanna go to Nam, to face the end, put my life on forty-five rpm, get it over with, do what we're all here for anyway. I know it sounds depressing, but . . . ever feel like that?"

He's upset, so I don't say anything. Silence is the best way sometimes.

"Miss my girlfriend somethin' terrible!" He removes his wallet again, pulls out a photograph. Celine looks like Twiggy: big eyes, long lashes, short hair, miniskirt.

"Move to Montreal, why don'tcha? Learn to speak French, maybe. Become a Frenchy."

"Or maybe just learn to speak. Thank God for hash. No problem tokin' and singin'."

"But your speech is getting better," I say.

He reminds me that Charlie paid for a speech pathologist in the city. "Big help, man. Good ol' Charlie! Yeah, it's better." He walks toward the fridge, stops as if he's changed his mind about something, and says, his voice breaking, "A cold fish, my old man. His father was worse. Mother told me Nonno Fabrella was the coldest person she'd ever met. But the old man was a good provider, if nuthin' else. He tried, I'll give the guy that, gave it his best shot. But he was no Charlie McCluskey, man. Word still trips me up . . . *Father*."

I pass back the photo. "She's cute." He puts it in his wallet, gets up.

"I'm crazy about her. Wanna be with her all the time, breathe the air she breathes. Oh, we're tying the knot, all right."

"Charlie'll get you a ticket to get her down here."

"Can't take any more money. Charlie pays for everything around here. No. Can't be always asking for loans, man."

"Bet she misses you a lot too, huh?"

"Love to see her, man. I'll get her here. I'm saving up. Miss her? You betcha. There's nothing more beautiful than a girl who gets excited about things, holds things close to her heart. I love that about Celine. She has her own interests, lives by her own rules, she's going to be a nurse. And she's not clingy."

"Lotsa work at the garage. Charlie—"

"Charlie helps everyone. Saw him give Uncle Harry fifty bucks once. Harry said he was broke, no money for groceries. Charlie took out his wallet and handed him a pineapple. Your father's a saint, man. Bona fide! And I know he doesn't have the bucks deluxe, not just running a garage. Wish I could do more for him."

Some Saturdays, when Johnny isn't sleeping fifteen hours straight, he calls and invites us over. He's a great cook, knows more about it than Charlie, who was excellent himself.

"Hell no, I won't go!" He picks up an acoustic guitar. "Vietnam! Helluva long way to go to get shot." He strums his guitar. "Asian hellhole!" He smirks. "I can't join the resisters, the ones who think with their legs, as the Captain said."

"You go to Vietnam, it'll mean the end of the Acid Test."

"I go to Vietnam every time Celine hangs up the phone."

I get up, repeat that there's work at the garage. "Come by."

He says he can sure use the dough, goes to the fridge, takes out a Dixie cup. "Got the munchies, man." He shakes his head. "The boot franchise!" He scoops ice cream, shakes his head again. "The Dixie cup franchise!"

"It'll be okay, Johnny."

He shushes me. "It'll never be okay. Never!" Dismisses me with a flick of his hand, sits down, doesn't say anything for what seems like a small eternity. I stand there looking at him with a sinking heart. But I don't mind the silence. Eternity is a place I'm getting used to.

35

WHEN I PICK HER UP I HAVE THE HEEBIE-JEEBIES. There's a lot on my mind. Nervous? As my communications instructor, Mr. Graham, is fond of saying, That's an understatement. I'm really uptight about the fake bill in the Cove. What if there's more counterfeit around? And I'm uptight about what that geezer in Chamberlains said. And every now and then I think about Charlie not telling my mother about Rosie. It makes no sense to love someone and not share something like that. I'd want my wife to know about Rosie, about everything, no secrets between us. I mean, isn't that the meaning of love? And if Charlie wouldn't tell her about Rosie, were there other things he didn't tell her? Things he didn't tell *me* about?

During the first part of the movie, my mind's like a blue-ass fly hopping on hot rocks: Was Charlie buried deep enough? Will Johnny go to Vietnam? Will I screw up in the garage again? Should I really give up the family legacy, go my own way? Will another $20 bill wind up in the Cove? I want desperately to ask Arlene again about that notice. Are the cops involved? Maybe I should ask Quinn. But talking will lead to questions, so I'll clam up. I'm in one helluva sweat, though, and hoping she won't notice.

When I do take in the movie, I think about the McCluskeys. I mean, here are Bonnie and Clyde looting banks, stores, and gas stations all over the place and thinking they can get away with it. Unlike my family, they're selfish. They're not helping anyone, giving to the poor. They aren't like John Dillinger or Robin Hood, Prince of Thieves, that's for sure.

How disappointed Charlie would be. I get fidgety remembering what he said about counterfeiting, that it's not stealing if you help others, level the playing field. His words come back: "We're good thieves, fighting the corrupt rich. That's the opposite of stealing. Robin Hood wasn't greedy. He was like Jesus, turned things upside down, made a better world. Never be ashamed of Robin of Locksley. The world needs more Robin Hoods."

Halloween, when he'd dress up as the Prince of Thieves, I'd tag along as Little John, Crenshaw as Karl Marx. We'd give hampers at the doors and say, "A gift from the Merry Men of Sherwood Forest." We'd get some pretty weird looks, but Charlie insisted our costumes were more appropriate than witches and goblins, Halloween's the time to turn things upside down. "No better time in the calendar," he said. "All Hallows Eve."

Thinking of all this makes me edgy, so I concentrate on the movie. After a while I want to hold Arlene's hand, feel as excited as when I cashed my first counterfeit bill, my heart galloping. I sneak a glance her way, can't bring myself to do it.

A little later, I notice my hand resting on hers, which is on her thigh. She doesn't move it away, silently rests her head against my shoulder. Things are looking good till I think of her father chopping off the hand of the guy who cashed the counterfeit bill. Then I'm in a sweat again.

After the longest time, I squeeze her hand. She squeezes back. I feel like doing jumping jacks in the aisle. Then our fingers interlace and stay that way, which puts me in a real quandary because now I'd like to kiss her. It's dark in there, so I'll just lean over, give her a smooch, maybe. But I don't have the courage. I just sit there praying my hand doesn't get sweaty.

Then my mind shifts again to dropping dough—the many causes to look after—and I miss the ending. I know Bonnie and Clyde get riddled with bullets but hope Arlene doesn't ask about it.

We drive to the A&W, order whistle dogs and root beer. I ask if she's read *Robinson Crusoe*. She says she loved it but wishes Man Friday, the native Crusoe rescued from the tribe of cannibals, were a woman. "Wouldn't that be more interesting? More like Adam and Eve." That crazy, crooked smile.

"I don't think so."

"Be more romantic, don'tcha think? If it was us, you'd climb coconut trees, bring back the best of the bunch. You'd race barefoot across the sand catching little fishes or gathering strange birds' eggs. Oh, how romantic!" She flashes a mock surprise, sticks out her tongue, and laughs. "At sunset we'd lie by the water listening to the waves, feasting on the fruit you'd gathered."

I tell her to write that down, it's pretty good. "You could write a female Robinson Crusoe novel, maybe."

"I'd call it *The Life and Romantic Adventures of Robyn Rousseau.*" She squints, that crooked smile again.

"My dad wanted to write a novel, a western about my mother." Suddenly I'm upset, turn, and roll down my window.

We sit there eating, and I wonder about that counterfeit bill again. Was it Charlie's? Arlene asks if something's wrong.

"No."

"My goodness, you were a bundle of nerves during the movie, on the edge of your seat the whole time—"

"It's my father . . ."

"Your father's so good to everyone. Unlike mine." She reaches over and strokes my hair. "You love him a lot, huh?"

"Uh huh. But he's such a walking contradiction."

"Oh?"

"He's a good person and all, but he has some weird notions. Sometimes I think he's right, sometimes I don't." I describe his belief in reincarnation and the transmigration of souls. "And he believes we're living in eternity right now, we're here forever. And dharma and karma—"

"My goodness!" Arlene interrupts. "Sounds pretty complicated. Catholic teaching—"

"And he believes in a thing called situational ethics, that there are times when it's okay to lie or cheat or steal—"

"Really? That doesn't sound right. You mean like Bonnie and Clyde?" She leans closer, her lively eyes wide open.

"No. More like Robin Hood. He says it's okay for a mother to steal food for her hungry children."

"Sounds sensible to me, I'd steal to feed my kids. Who wouldn't?"

I slurp my root beer, she laughs, and I laugh at her laughing.

"Charlie used to say if the variables are right a person can be made to do anything."

"Used to say?"

I cover my tracks. "I mean before he went to Toronto."

She says she's not crazy about Charlie's philosophy. "It's a bit like brainwashing, indoctrination. I'd never teach my kid that stuff. And Robin Hood and his Merry Men were probably a cult. You heard of the Sullivanians, that cult? Same thing."

"Robin Hood and his Merry Men weren't a cult. If you're calling changing the world to help the poor brainwashing, so be it. Count me in."

"How do you count cows?" she quips. "With a cowculator."

That cracks me up. She has that way about her. She'll break the tension, stop you from getting too serious.

36

OUT OF THE BLUE SHE SAYS, "Would you like to play the whispering game?"

"The what?"

"The whispering game. It's fun. I call it Whispering Sweet Nothings. Makes you concentrate. For a while you only whisper. Sometimes you listen to nothing." Her forehead wrinkles. "Let's try it, okay?"

"Sure."

"So, how's school going?" she whispers.

"Pardon?" I can hardly hear her, lean closer.

"How's school going?" her breath hot on my ear.

"Fine," I whisper.

"Just fine?"

"Watson's class is pretty good."

"Yeah, but he's a male chauvinist. And that voice—"

"Voice?"

"Nothing grates more than an out-of-tune violin." We giggle. She whispers, "Anything else?"

"No."

"What one book would you bring to a deserted island?"

"*Robinson Crusoe*." I laugh. "No, my favourite, *Dr. Jekyll and Mr. Hyde*. You?"

"A book on boat building." She sticks out her tongue.

Silence. A shudder races through me. I'm used to stretches of silence working at the shop, but this isn't that kind. This is nervous silence. I'm about to say something when she whispers, "Aren't you going to say something else?"

"So, how's school going?" I whisper.

"Pretty good, I'm really enjoying *Robinson Crusoe*."

We burst out laughing. Whispering is a bit weird, but fun.

"I like that Crusoe keeps a journal," I say.

"I keep a diary. Everyone needs a place to keep secrets."

"Secrets?"

"Yeah, everyone has secrets."

No kidding, I think.

More nervous silence, she says, "I'm getting all A's in math." Her brown eyes sparkle.

"You like Comrade Crenshaw's history class? He's at the house a lot talking about—who else?—Karl Marx."

"All old Crenshaw ever talks about."

"Johnny says he loves the Doctor Club. They talk a lot about communism."

"The principal sometimes calls Crenshaw to his office for not following the curriculum. There's a rumour they're writing him up. He'll probably get fired. He stamped the word *nitwit* all over Betty Murphy's term paper." She stifles a laugh. "Some students say he's pushing drugs, but he's a kind old soul. I like him, and I love history." She pauses, sits up. There's a painful silence. "You really think it was okay for Bonnie and Clyde to rob banks?"

"You think it's okay for banks to rip people off?"

"Banks play by the rules. Bonnie and Clyde didn't play by the rules."

"Whose rules? Banks write their own rules, and politicians write the loopholes."

"But look what happened to them in the end. They had a date with destiny. Would you want your life to end like that?"

She snookers me there, so I don't say anything.

More nervous silence.

"Bonnie knows deep down that what she's doing is wrong. It's her conscience eating at her. Father McCarthy says you're doomed without a conscience. That's why I loved *A Man for All Seasons*. Thomas More had—"

"But banks rip people off. The rich have been robbing the poor forever. Even small convenience stores gouge people. Double the price for a loaf of bread? C'mon!"

She says it's still wrong to steal, two wrongs don't make a right. Another long silence and she whispers, "They deserved their date with destiny."

"Would've been a better movie if they gave the money to the poor. Like John Dillinger."

She stares off into space, something on her mind. I don't say anything, figure she'll say what she's thinking if she wants to.

She's silent awhile longer, then says, "Sometimes whispering sweet nothings I say a sour something."

"Sour something?"

"Here's one: my father has money problems . . . and he's an alcoholic."

"Arlene, I'm so sorry—"

"He has congestive heart failure and suffers from anxiety. My mother thinks that's why he drinks so much. I think Mother's the reason he drinks so much. They scream at each other all the time. Sometimes he throws things. He has anxiety attacks. It isn't pretty, especially when he's drinking."

I don't know what to say, reach over, touch her hand.

She shrugs, snaps the radio dial. That's a trait she has if she's troubled: she can shut down, turn away.

"Let's listen to some music. We can stop whispering now."

She turns on the radio, says, "How'd you like whispering sweet nothings?"

"Okay. Different, for sure."

"It's like when the lights go out in a snowstorm and you light candles. Like sitting by the fire in the dark hearing the snap, crackle. Very romantic."

We finish our whistle dogs, and she changes the station, her breasts lifting, head to the side. She looks stunning. She finds the country channel, her favourite.

"By the Time I Get to Phoenix" comes on. She hums along, flubs, "By the time I make Albuquirkie . . ."

I ask if she'd like to drive up to Signal Hill. Which is a way of asking if she'd like to go parking. Which is a way of asking to go necking.

"Sure, I'd love to go parking." She stifles a laugh.

When we arrive at Signal Hill, she points to the city lights, feigns her English accent and says, "If you marry me, *dahling*, all this will be yours one day." We burst out laughing. "Heard that in an old movie."

A heavy silence seeps in, so I turn on the radio. We listen to music and stare at the city lights, and I try to get up the gumption to kiss her. Just as I'm about to, she leans over, strokes my hair, and whispers, "Hold your breath, Sonny." Then she kisses me. And when we get a good rhythm going, a freight train couldn't stop us.

37

"WE NEED TO TALK. About Charlie . . . and Johnny."

A shiver runs up my spine. That deep, nasty voice. The words jolt me, words I heard on the phone the night I buried Charlie. It wasn't a dream. I stop cold.

"Follow me."

I head down the narrow hallway, climb the steps to his office. The door creaks open. He kicks it shut. "We don't want to be disturbed. Sit."

The office contains a cluttered oak desk, a huge, framed picture of Karl Marx hanging on the wall behind it, floor-to-ceiling shelves on either side stacked with books. Piles of magazines spread out on a faded Persian rug, lopsided towers of books here and there. He removes a binder from a chair, locks the door.

"When's your father expected back?"

"Dunno. He's quite sick, seeing a specialist."

"We have a little problem, hmm."

"I thought I got everything right on my last test."

"It's not about your test." He kicks a book aside, walks to his desk, draws the curtains. He's in a foul mood, looks different, hungover. He removes a flask of whiskey and a glass from his briefcase, unscrews the flask. I think of Dr. Jekyll's potion. "I'll come right to the point, lad. You know your father's a member of the Doctor Club. Bona fide. We don't just discuss philosophy. We deal in . . . hmm . . . pharmaceuticals."

I'm shocked. "Charlie . . . drugs? I don't believe it. I—"

"There's a lot you don't know about our precious Mother Teresa." He downs the whiskey, replaces the cap. Quinn's right, he has a nasty side.

"Charlie's not the pillar of the community he appears to be. We all have our secrets, boy. You know one of mine, why I need a little loan from time to time."

"Mr. Crenshaw, there must be some mistake—"

"No mistake, lad. Johnny's in serious trouble with the Club. In the past, your father always bailed him out. Money's never a problem with Charlie. That's a fact. Unlike Johnny, facts don't lie."

Silence. I sit there, dazed, getting angry. Is this true?

"You find this difficult, I know. But we'll keep it our little secret, hmm? Wouldn't want to sully Charlie's reputation, now, would we? Your father did a little more than fix up old cars for the poor—"

"Mr. Crenshaw, this can't be right. There's some mistake. I know my father wouldn't—"

"No mistake, I said!"

A puck to the face. I'm stunned.

"And why am I telling you this little family secret, lad? Because your Johnny boy's in serious trouble. He tells lies, you know. White lies, black lies, and a few other shades. Point is, he owes money, a rather tidy little sum, I'm afraid."

"Money?"

"He works for the Doctor Club from time to time—ahem—as I say, in the pharmaceutical business. Owes the Club over two thousand dollars and—"

"Two thousand dollars! Mr. Crenshaw, that's a lot of money."

"Jean-Luc isn't happy. Manfred isn't happy. I'm not happy. Appears he purchased a few guitars, among other things, with the money owed. We've given him a deadline."

"Mr. Crenshaw, this doesn't involve me. I don't . . . I'm Johnny's friend, but—"

"Involves your father, lad. Get hold of him. Johnny's buggered now, needs help. What's the Good Book say about your brother's keeper, hmm?"

"But we're a small business, we don't have money to—"

"When he was in his cups one evening, Charlie told me he can get money any time. *Any amount*, he said. Ergo, there's money somewhere. *Find it*."

I clam up, something twisting in my stomach.

"Doctor Club's not to be messed with, boy." He's spitting sparks now. "Jean-Luc's a perfectly ghastly man. He was owed money by a Frenchman a few years back, top-notch soccer player from Paris. The man was given a deadline. When he didn't pay, the fool woke up one morning without a foot, severed from the ankle. Kind of Jean-Luc to use anaesthetic, hmm? Heaven forbid anything should happen to your bandleader. Is Johnny left-handed or right-handed?"

A chill races through me. He repeats the question.

"Right-handed."

"Good. Jean-Luc wouldn't want to make that kind of mistake. Does he fingerpick? He'll be a phantom picker if he doesn't come up with the money by the deadline."

Something inside me begins to shake, my blood freezes. I think of *Dr. Jekyll and Mr. Hyde* again. He's worse than Mr. Hyde. I stare at the floor, not daring to breathe.

He looks my way with his narrow glance. "And who knows what might happen to you, hmm? Young lad living all alone . . . accidents happen."

I'm glued to the chair, my mind blank.

"Look, you're Charlie's son and I'll look out for you, believe me. But I can only protect you for so long, Sonny. And there's only one way to help Johnny, come up with that money."

He walks to a bookshelf, removes a thick Bible with a sturdy cover. "Now, what about that deadline, hmm?" He looks at his desk calendar, scribbles. "Let's say a week after Remembrance Day, shall we? More than sufficient time. Monday, November 20. D-Day! Instead of Patton, you can expect Jean-Luc, hmm. If Johnny doesn't pay up by then . . . well, that will be most unfortunate." He continues, his tone nastier. "Florence needs a few new outfits, wants to travel to New York, possibly London. Must keep her happy."

He opens the Bible to a hollowed-out section. "Smuggler's Bible." He smirks. "Hollowed be thy name." He removes scrunched-up paper from the hole. "A note Charlie got some time ago. Poor Charlie! Not long for this world." He flips the ball of paper on the floor, passes me the Bible.

"Put the dough in there, two thou, return it to my office before the deadline. Johnny wouldn't manage too well on his Fender with a missing hand, I shouldn't think. Different kind of fender-bender than you're used to, hmm?" He smirks again, hair prickling on my neck. November twentieth, then, Monday after school. I trust everything will go tickety-boo. But you know me, I'm never one to complain." He hovers over me, whispers, "The Doctor Club is not to be toyed with, Sonny," turns and leaves.

I sit there stunned, holding the fake Bible, staring at the ball of paper on the floor.

I know you've been avoiding me, McCluskey, ergo, this note. If you think I'll take NO for an answer, you're sadly mistaken. Little late for a change of heart, Charlie. I'm holding all the cards, my man, includ-

ing the jokers. It's completely up to you whether I spill the beans about our little club. Now wouldn't that be nice, your little boy finding out his old man's in the drug trade. I need the money by this weekend, Sunday evening at the latest. Florence has a pick-up in Saint Pierre. If you don't make the deadline, I assure you Sonny will know all about you by Monday morning. And if you think I won't tell him, well, once again, my man, you're sadly mistaken.

A grand, no later than Sunday. Place the money inside the Bible and drop it at the house.

You say you work for the poor. We're all poor, Charlie. And there's nobody poorer than yours truly. I owe Jean-Luc $5,000, the Communist Party considerably more, and Florence who knows how much. So put on your Robin Hood hat, man, and do your bit for the poor.

I'll pay it back. That's a promise. I've paid you back with dirty money before. I'm sure you'll take it again. What we do with Jean-Luc and Manfred is nobody's business. It might be against this country's laws, but it's morally right to stick it to the corrupt capitalists even if a few people get hurt along the way. It's warfare, Charlie. Class warfare: The robes ye weave, another wears; / The arms ye forge, another bears.

I turn the page over. It's blank. I check the hollowed-out Bible. Nothing. My mind races, trying to take it all in. Dirty money? I sit there mute and immobilized.

38

SEPTEMBER 1659, ROBINSON CRUSOE WROTE IN HIS JOURNAL: *I, poor miserable Robinson Crusoe, being shipwrecked during a dreadful storm in the offing, came on shore on this dismal, unfortunate island which I called "The Island of Despair," all the rest of the ship's company being drowned, and I myself almost dead.*

And so it is with me after that meeting with Crenshaw. I might as well be shipwrecked on a deserted island. Was Crenshaw telling the truth? Or is he up to something? Maybe he's trying to get money from me while Charlie's away. Whether it's true or not, I can't let him think I'm a pushover, let him get away with threatening me. I recall Charlie's advice: *If anyone threatens you, strike back and strike hard.* Time to make a move.

I believe what he's saying about Johnny. Johnny's capable of drug dealing. But Charlie? No way. But what if it's true? Are there other secrets? Other counterfeits?

Dejected, I turn to my refuge—reading—and Louis L'Amour's *Son of a Wanted Man*. It takes me longer than usual to read a chapter. I stop when I come to a dog-eared page or a whiskey stain. But instead of tears, there's anger.

Son of a Wanted Man is about a bandit named Ben Curry who wants to give his secret outlaw kingdom to his adopted son, Mike, who knows all the tricks of the trade, but he's never broken the law. I think of Charlie handing me the print shop, and getting caught by the law, and I know the time has come. My Robin Hood days are over.

Charlie and Johnny are on my mind all day at the garage, so I quit work early to scout out a quiet place to be alone, a palace of nowhere, to collect my thoughts.

Should I tell Arlene about Johnny? If I tell her, I'll have to say everything: Charlie, Crenshaw, the Doctor Club. How will I strike back at Crenshaw?

There's a light drizzle in the Cove, but St. John's is clear and sunny. I look up at the sky—blue eternity, Charlie called it. I drive to Virginia Waters, a wooded trail along a river that snakes toward Pleasantville, which used to be Fort Pepperrell, the American military base where Johnny's father was stationed. I wish the Captain didn't have such a hold on Johnny.

There are several quiet spots along the river, but people are trout fishing, so I head home.

En route I remember a spot on the Indian Meal Line where Charlie and I picked blueberries. I drive there and park the car on the side of the road near a trail. I walk for about a mile and come to a small, rocky meadow lined with late-blooming flowers and a few sparse trees. *Be alert, something precious will be given to you here.* I look at the blue sky, but I'm really antsy, so I sit on an old tree stump, keep an eye out for a rabbit or a fox, maybe.

After a while I close my eyes, think about Charlie, the fun we had berry-picking nearby, the good times in the garage, then the possibility that he's involved with the Doctor Club. I think about Crenshaw's threats and get angry. Whether it's true or not, I can't let him get away with this. I ponder awhile about getting back at Crenshaw. And what if it's true about Johnny? How's he going to pay back the money he owes? He's always broke.

I think of Arlene. Will things work out? Johnny's tying the knot, I might have to cut the cord. Time for a sheet of paper: the pros and cons.

If it works out, I'll break Charlie's golden rule, tell her about Rosie, tell her it's temporary till I go my own way. She'll accept that. I can't keep her in the dark the way Charlie did with Lucy. It'd be nice to have help burning the plates, the darkroom, even dropping the dough.

A light wind comes up, warms my skin, gently combs my hair. I sit there breathing slowly, knowing that this is it, my precious palace of nowhere. No distractions. This is where I'll come when I get the blues, when I get anxious and paranoid, when I want to be reminded that I'm in eternity.

OCTOBER

III

An idea upon which attention is peculiarly concentrated is an idea which tends to realize itself.

— Charles Baudouin

39

FOR HER SEVENTEENTH BIRTHDAY I PLACE A FLAPPER HAT ON HER HEAD AND give her a gift-wrapped, illustrated edition of *The Merry Adventures of Robin Hood*. I peck her cheek as she cracks chewing gum, takes the present, heavy as a phone book. "Happy Birthday, sweet seventeen. Happy every day! as the Chinese say."

"Goodness me! What a nice surprise!" Her brown eyes brighten as she undoes the wrapping. "Thank you." She affects her British accent: "*How fabulous, dahling. Kiss me. Kiss me as if it were the last time.*" I break into laughter, peck her cheek again. She straightens the flapper hat, pirouettes, points to the pegboard tool organizer and folding bench. "Ta-dah! Everything in its place," she says. "Proud of me?" She's not a tidy person.

I nod. "Everything in its place."

It's late afternoon, we're in the machine shop. I've been helping with her part-time job: cleaning the lathes and drill presses, arranging tools for the week's classes.

For some reason she seems slimmer today. She leans on the bench, that lopsided grin on her face, her eyes oddly focused on me. And for a split second, she looks like her Aunt Laura. Perhaps it's the flapper hat.

She's flipping through the book when she sees Mr. Russell, the vice-principal, walking by the open doorway. She pushes me down, keeping a hand on my head. "Only designated students are allowed in the shop after school."

She's wearing blue jeans, ink marks on the knees, the gold zipper winks. She taps my head—stay down—whispers she got a hundred on her last test. I tell her she's one smart cookie, but she brushes aside the compliment; it's not smart, she just stays with the problems longer, *that's all*.

She taps my head again—okay to get up now. She sticks out her tongue, fingers the gilded edge of the Robin Hood book. "This is beautifully bound. Too beautiful for a thief."

"Depends how you look at it. To me he's a hero. In the sixteenth century, Robin Hood became part of the May Day celebrations."

She laughs. "Comrade Crenshaw would love that." She removes her hat, twists her ponytail into a bun, spikes it with a mechanical pencil. "Johnny gave me a birthday gift."

"Oh?" I perk up. "Lemme guess, a Chuck Berry album."

"A book." She chuckles.

"Robin Hood?"

She pokes me. "*The Great American Song Book*. Country music and lyrics for a hundred songs. He wants me to sing 'I'll Never Find Another You' at the Butter Pot concert. It's by Sonny McCluskey. Oops! I mean Sonny James." She giggles, sings, "*There's a new world somewhere* . . ."

I reach my hand around her waist, fingers touching the tight skin above her sharp hip bone.

"*Sonny*!" she slaps my hand, meaning *not here*. "*And I'll be there someday* . . ."

I notice her shoes, Oxford penny loafers, a shiny new penny in each slit. "You have penny loafers. With pennies—"

"For luck," she says.

"Nobody puts pennies in loafers anymore."

"I do. I'm somebody."

The shoes are polished, but the toes are scuffed.

"Always wear them in the shop. Why I get hundreds. Baseball player has a rabbit foot. I've got penny loafers."

"Think those milling machines are safe? They look pretty old. Some kid could get a bad cut."

"You're the only kid who comes in here, Sonny . . . *I'll pee right there beside you*," she flubs, "*whenever I get the flu / That's why I'll always need another you*."

I laugh, snake my hand around her waist again.

Outside the lab window, the sun is going down. Soft, yellowish-red light. I want to kiss her, grab her hand, race outside and stare at the sky until the sun disappears. I point to the window.

"The golden hour!" she says.

"Looking forward to the long weekend at Butter Pot Park?"

"What long weekend?" She pokes me, whispers, "I could never camp overnight with you around."

"Arrr! Never say never," I whisper.

She's about to laugh when I cover her lips with mine. Her breath smells of peppermint.

"I'd love to camp with you overnight."

"Would you really? In your heart of hearts?" she whispers, throwing her arms around me.

"Yes. Yes," I whisper harder. "In my heart of hearts."

I'm in class arguing with Crenshaw that communism is collapsing. "It's just a matter of time before Russia and China become democratic," I say.

He looks at me steadily. "Capitalism turns everything into commodities, including human beings. That's degrading."

You're degrading, I want to say.

"FDR taught us how to rein in capitalism," Ryan says.

"FDR didn't stop the rich from believing that taxation is theft and the common good does not exist." He says that deep down FDR was a communist but not a good one.

The bell rings, he says we'll take this up next class. "Sonny, I'd like to talk to you about your last test."

Another threat. Well, two can play that game. I wait till everyone's gone, but Crenshaw walks away. He's starting to get on my nerves. I must make a move, can't let him get the upper hand. If you let someone get away with threatening you, you'll be under his thumb the rest of your life. That's not going to happen. I know what to do.

I decide to get Crenshaw out of our lives by dropping some pot in his desk and telling Quinn about it. Quinn hates his guts and will rat him out. I know it's wrong, Crenshaw will lose his job, but I don't care. Maybe this is one of those times when two wrongs do make a right. Crenshaw's had it coming for a long time. I need him out of my life and Johnny's life.

I drive to Johnny's and tell him straight out that I want some dope. Shrieks of laughter.

"You're kiddin', right?"

"No."

"Really? You're serious? What kinda dope? Getcha whatever you want, little brother."

"Marijuana."

"Well, I'll be! Sonny McCluskey's gonna do some Mary Jane. Get it by tomorrow, if you'd like. Good shit, but it'll cost. How much you want?"

"Enough for a few joints."

"Consider it done, rolled and all. Wow, man! I knew you'd see the light one day. Welcome to the club, little brother."

I hope he doesn't mean the Doctor Club.

Then I go shoot hoops with Quinn.

As we play, I ask Quinn if he really thinks the Crenshaws do LSD.

"Definitely!" he says. "And he does cocaine too. God knows what she does with that Jean-Luc character when she's in Saint Pierre. Hard drugs, I'm sure. My dad says the Crenshaws shouldn't be teachers, they're not fit."

I tell him that I was early for class yesterday and saw Crenshaw putting dope in his desk.

"I think it was dope."

"Really?" Quinn says. "You should've reported it to the administration. That's a criminal offence."

I say I'm not 100% sure. "It looked like weed. Tiny plastic bag. Wasn't much if it was dope."

"You can get jail time for a roach, McCluskey."

"Didn't check his desk. Pretty sure it wasn't tea. And he keeps booze in his briefcase."

Quinn swishes a shot. "If it's dope he put in his desk, Crenshaw's days are numbered in this town."

40

BUTTER POT PARK IS ABOUT TWENTY MILES FROM ST. JOHN'S, off the Trans-Canada Highway. It has acres of woods, great hiking trails where you can disappear with your girl. The place is full of beavers, and the odd squirrel skitters about. But as Arlene says, no wolves, snakes, or politicians. There are numerous campsites, each with a picnic table and fireplace—great spot to pitch a tent.

Friday, we pack Johnny's guitars in the trunk of the Vauxhall Viva, tie our tents to the top, and Arlene, Johnny, and I drive out. Quinn and Esther-Marie have gone ahead with the musical equipment in his Volkswagen van. It's a beautiful day, blue skies smilin' at me, as the song says.

At the concert site we set up in record time, thanks to the students I hired to put up a huge tarp for the band in case it rains. It's surprisingly warm for October. Afterwards, in a big open area where the stage is, about a hundred couples gather drinking wine and beer, passing around sandwiches. Everyone feels good. The Harmonies play folk music for a while. They're pretty good, but you can feel the excitement in the air waiting for Johnny Fabrella and the Acid Test.

The crowd gets bigger just before Johnny opens the show with his Chuck Berry riff and "Johnny B. Goode," crouching on stage and mimicking Chuck Berry's famous duckwalk with his new Gibson 335 guitar. "Cool guitar," someone yells, "just like Chuck Berry's." Johnny's stoned, in his element. Like everyone, I'm amazed at his fingerpicking, smooth as silk. And he always adds something new to every song. It's mind-blowing watching him burn up the stage. He's a born musician, he'll never be a mechanic. And I look at him now in a different light, buoyed up, proud, he's family. Charlie was right, he's come a long way.

One of the stagehands gives me the thumbs-up, meaning the sound system and blue spotlight are working fine. All around me, wafting clouds of pot, cheerful voices. Happy long-haired kids flash peace signs, hand around a jug of wine. A flower child wearing a headband, tie-dyed shirt, yells, "Play 'Handsome Johnny,' handsome Johnny!" Loud cheers. Someone else shouts, "Go, Johnny, go." The crowd goes nuts, everyone grinning ear to ear. The long-haired guy in front of me takes off his shirt, sweat rolls down his back. He spins around, offers me his joint. I wave him off. He turns back, screams, "Go, Johnny, go."

Johnny finishes, salutes, bows flamboyantly, and wows the crowd again with his version of "The Letter" by the Box Tops. Everyone goes wild. As he plays, he bounces all over the stage in a sparkling, sequined jumpsuit, knee-high boots, and silver cape. The girls scream as if he's Mick Jagger. He pumps his fist, eyes flashing, cape and bright red hair flapping behind him as he lunges here and there with the microphone stand: *My baby, just-a wrote me a letter*.

Everyone has goosebumps, the crowd alive, joining in, swaying to every beat. It's a great vibe. I'm so happy to be here, so happy for my big brother.

Suddenly, a stray dog appears, running around the stage. It's spotted, stubby tail, spindly legs. The stage manager tries to catch it. Johnny stops him, crouches down, whispers, and the dog comes to him. Everyone cheers. He pets and kisses it, lifts it up. "Anyone here own this little cutie?"

A gangly blonde charges the stage shouting, "That's Pebbles. He's mine."

Johnny leans down and passes her the dog.

More cheering and hooting.

Then Arlene calms everyone down with her rendition of "By the Time I Get to Phoenix." When she finishes, she raises the microphone, everyone screams. She purses her lips, her eyes are on fire. "Welcome to Butter Pot Park!"

The couple next to me yell, "Sunny! Sunny!" Suddenly, a hundred voices chanting my name.

She taps her fingers against her thigh. "I'd like to slow things down a little with a number called 'Sunny.'" A roar from the crowd. She's braless, wearing Levis, a tie-dyed T-shirt, fringed suede jacket. She moves around the stage like a cat.

I blush when she looks at me and sings, "Thank you for the smile upon your face."

The final number is "Wild Thing," and Johnny announces that he has a big surprise for everyone. "Wanna introduce a new entertainer this evening. Mrs. Florence Crenshaw—Flo—will be singing background with Esther-Marie." A thrill ripples through the crowd as she comes on stage.

"Wild thing, you make my heart sing," Johnny sings, and the crowd hoots and whistles. It's hard to tell if Mrs. Crenshaw is singing or lip-synching. She looks different, glassy-eyed, high. Halfway through the song, she removes her fur coat. She's wearing a black turtleneck sweater and pants that make her look tall, black boots. She steps away from Esther-Marie, begins dancing, slowly moving her hips, snapping her fingers. Now and then she stops dancing and begins muscle pumping, flexing, and posing. Some people gasp in embarrassment, others hoot as she waltzes toward Johnny, arms outstretched like she's sleepwalking. She stops suddenly, her face wild, and does her famous pretzel push-up. When she finishes, the crowd clamours for more: "Encore! Encore!" Johnny starts the song again while Mrs. Crenshaw returns to her place and sings background.

After the concert, people storm the stage to congratulate Johnny and the band. When things settle down, I set up a table with sandwiches and pop, which the band wolfs down. As they chat, I joke with the stage crew, help pack up the equipment, cart it to Quinn's van.

When we finish, Arlene says she's cold, and we head back to her tent for a jacket. Then we go for a stroll, she nestling close to me. We walk slowly over the scurrying leaves along the trail to Butter Pot Hill staring at a sickle moon. When we arrive at the hill, we're suddenly kissing, her tongue teasing mine. We hold each other for a long time in the gentle breeze, and I recall dancing to "The St. John's Waltz."

"You were great tonight," I whisper. "I had goosebumps during 'By the Time I Get to Phoenix.' And Esther-Marie did great backup."

"It felt so good up there," she whispers. "Do you think they liked my flub—When I'm six foot four?"

"I sure did, very witty."

She shakes her head, wets her lips with her tongue. We continue walking, staring at the yellowish-red sunset and what seem like rain clouds in the distance.

I say, "Keep at it, you could make it in the world of rock and roll."

"Johnny wants me to do a solo when we cut our first album. I'd love to make it in the music world. We'll see." She chuckles. "Course, my backup plan is small engine repairs."

"I only have Plan A: Sonny's Auto."

"You know, Sonny, you'd make a fine teacher. You should think about it. Maybe down the road you could teach at the Trades School. You'd make a great automotive mechanic instructor."

"Don't wanna be a teacher, I know what I want."

"Just a suggestion." She asks what I thought of Mrs. Crenshaw's performance, rolls her eyes.

"Was she really singing up there?"

"No. Johnny's favour to old Crenshaw. Flo fancies herself an actress, God knows what else." She slips her arm around my waist, and we walk back to the main campsite, where couples are sitting around a fire drinking and singing songs. She shares a beer with Quinn and Esther-Marie, and we join in the singing.

41

LATER, A WIND COMES UP AND LIGHT RAIN FALLS. A rumble of thunder as we race back to her tent. We crawl inside, cuddle and kiss, listening to the rain, me inhaling her hair's natural scent. Nearby, a lonely stretch of beach leads to Big Otter Pond. I hear the water lapping against the rocks, and for some reason it reminds me of the night I buried Charlie. Arlene senses something, asks what's wrong.

"Nothing," I say, "guy rope's flapping." I unzip the door, pretend to fix it. Back inside, Arlene's in her sleeping bag, clothes in a pile. A bubble develops in my stomach. "I'm chilly, wet."

She unzips her bag. "Warm in here." She pats the bag. "Slip out of those wet clothes and come whisper sweet nothings." A burst of excitement pulses through me. Inside the bag, I pull her close as she cups her hand behind my neck, nibbles my earlobe, then bites. "That's how the Eskimos do it," she says.

I bite her neck. "That's how the Newfoundlanders do it."

She laughs, squeezes so hard I feel bone, rolls on top of me. She's strong, agile, and for a second, I think of saying she should be on the wrestling team but don't break the mood.

She sighs, the length of her throbbing against me, whispers, "You're the Sonnyshine of my life."

I stroke her hair. She shudders.

"You took a big chance wearing no bra tonight," I whisper.

She laughs. I echo the laughter, her hair brushing my face, kiss her cheek, feel her lips on my neck, hard nipples against my chest.

"You're so perfect," I say. She whimpers, her body stiffening, as if in shock.

She presses hard against me. "*Here*!"

"Here?"

Too late. I lean up, fall back, she on top, her weight a feather duvet. Writhing, gasping . . . little moans. Then animal breaths, roaring breaths, a frantic wildness as we spin out of control, my heart pulsing against her, blood pounding. Then a perfect rhythm, I'm sure I'll die and go straight to heaven. Then all's still, neither time nor place, as I slip into eternity.

We lie there awhile, dizzy with love, listening to each other's ragged breathing, heat radiating from our bodies.

I'm sure she's fallen asleep when she whispers, "Oh, Sonny!" in a way I've never heard my name before. "Oh, Sonny . . ."

I lie motionless, the breath coming out of me, listening to the soft sound of water lapping, faint music. In the distance a whirring sound like Rosie's spinning cylinder. Then all's quiet again except for the water lapping against the rocks.

A long silence. She turns on her side and falls asleep.

I look at her and wonder about being in love. She sounded sad after making love. And what is love? Did Charlie love Lucy? Why the secrets? I think of Mrs. Crenshaw and wonder if she loves Mr. Crenshaw or if she's in love with Jean-Luc. Is that why she's always going to Saint Pierre? She was stoned at the concert. I saw Johnny give her a pill backstage. And does Johnny really love Celine? What does anyone know about love anyway?

My mind races to what Crenshaw said about Johnny, his threats. In the stillness I feel a headache coming on. I listen to the trees cracking, consider our future. I can never be honest about the person I really am—someone who's helped his father die, someone who runs a counterfeiting operation. . . . I drift in and out of sleep, angry about Crenshaw's threats, angry that what he said about Johnny is probably true. Now there's a sour something. Vietnam won't be the death of Handsome Johnny. Drugs will. Finally, I conk out.

In the wee hours, a car door slams shut. Then other sounds: a snap, a hiss, footsteps, and the tent door unzips. Johnny pops his head in, says in a stage whisper, "Florence? Mrs. Crenshaw! Jean-Luc bring the dope?"

"Wrong tent," I whisper.

"Oops! Can't find my tent." He disappears.

Later, the door unzips again. Johnny: "Can't find my tent, man." He crashes at our feet.

"Take my sleeping bag." But it's too late, he's out for the count.

In the morning, we crawl over Johnny, walk to the restrooms to wash up, brush our teeth. On the way back, she's cranky, says my hair is messy and my shirt looks dirty.

There's a spectacular, apple-juice sunrise as we take a brisk walk up Butter Pot Hill. "Love the golden autumn sunlight," I say and point to the graceful birches and maple lining the trail, glorious reds, yellows, oranges.

"Strange how deeply colours affect you." She sounds depressed, falls silent. I wonder if she's upset about having sex.

At the top of the hill, we stop and breathe in the cool, clear air. I ask if she's feeling okay.

"Feeling fine, Sonny," she says harshly. "You should amalgamate the garages. Stupid not to."

I don't say anything. We stroll back to the campsite, start packing the car. In no time she has the tent down and rolls it up just as Johnny returns from the washroom.

"Perfect timing!" I say.

He looks at me with bloodshot eyes. "They loved Mrs. Crenshaw. Knew they would. She's somethin' else."

"Gave them quite a rush," I say.

"There was a cop at the concert, undercover. Mrs. Crenshaw spotted him. Why are the undercover ones always easiest to spot? Wonder if he's looking for me. Special delivery of my draft card, maybe." He yawns. "Let's hit the road."

I put his new guitar in the trunk, can't find his old one. "Where's your other guitar, Johnny?"

"Gave it to a hippie-friend after the concert, Miles Cantwell, lives out the Brook way."

"What!" Arlene says. "Your acoustic guitar?"

"He's joining a band. It's an old, second-hand. Got two acoustics, Miles needs one."

Arlene glares at him. "Get it back, Johnny. That guitar was expensive." But she knows he won't.

We pile into my Vauxhall, and Johnny passes out in the back seat. On the drive, Arlene is unusually quiet, despondent. "You sang beautifully last night," I say.

"I don't see why you're so against joining the garages," she says.

"Arlene, I don't want to talk about this anymore."

She folds her arms and looks away.

Johnny wakes and says we should've brought food for everyone, sandwiches, at least.

"People were hungry after the concert. Next year I'll make sure there's a chip wagon out there."

Then he rants about Mrs. Crenshaw's hot, hot moves all the way to town.

42

Next day I have a splitting headache, but I invite Arlene over and we watch a movie called *What He Knew*. It's set in the '50s in Quebec, about a guy who got away with murder. He's a bit fidgety at times but leads a normal life: married, kids, a factory job, church every Sunday. He shows up at work on time each day, does his job well, is polite and friendly. Nobody suspects he's a killer.

I think of my double life. The murderer looks like he won't get caught even though he's carrying a heavy load. One night he's listening to the radio and hears that the cops arrested someone for the murder he committed. He gets uptight about someone taking the rap for his crime. The penalty for murder is execution—the electric chair. He gets ornery all the time, forgets things, argues with his wife and kids, is late for work. He starts drinking. His wife worries there's something terribly wrong, wants him to see a doctor.

He becomes so crazy with guilt about the innocent man getting executed that he goes to confession. That's when I learn about a thing called the seal of the confessional, because what some people confess can put the priest in a difficult situation. Arlene explains that whatever is said in the confessional box, even if it's murder, must be kept secret. The priest takes a vow not to tell anyone's sins.

"Is that why Robin Hood's men killed the monk who betrayed Robin Hood's presence to the Sheriff of Nottingham?"

"No! That wasn't confession. That was what we call *murder*, and Robin Hood's men needed to *go to confession*." She rolls her eyes.

I remember going to church with my mother occasionally, but I never went to confession. And Charlie never mentioned confession, so I'm not sure if Anglicans have it. I ask what happens in confession. "Do you just say your name and the crime you committed?"

She laughs, says most people don't commit crimes: they sin, usually little sins like being jealous or mean, hurting someone's feelings. Venial, she calls them.

"Like saying you'd amalgamate the garages, regardless of what I think."

"It's what *I think*, and it's hardly a sin, Sonny. It's a business decision."

"Not to me."

We're silent for a while, then she says that confession is one of the seven sacraments, and I ask, "What's a sacrament?"

"Pretty simple. A sacrament is an outward sign of God's grace." She explains that the penitent goes inside a dark confessional box, blesses herself, and tells her sins.

"Hold on," I say, "doesn't the priest see you?"

"No, you're in the dark the whole time. There are two types of sins, venial, the little ones, and mortal. The mortal ones are called the deadly sins. An example of a mortal sin is murder. A venial sin is something small like stealing candy from a store or—"

"Scaring the hell outta me on your motorcycle."

"Yeah."

"And what about what we did last night? Was that a sin?"

"Yes, sex outside marriage is a sin."

"Is it deadly? A mortal sin?"

"Yes. I shouldn't have done it."

"Then why did you?"

"The flesh is weak." She lowers her head and sighs. "That's why we need confession, to ask forgiveness."

"You mean you regret what you did?"

"Sort of. I broke a rule."

I ask what if you steal something big, like a lot of money. What kind of sin is that? She says that'd be a mortal sin too.

"What happens after you confess your sins?"

"The priest blesses you, gives absolution. That means you're washed clean from your sins. He then gives you penance, usually something easy like saying three Hail Marys and an Our Father. You make an Act of Contrition and leave. I always feel a bit lighter afterwards." She says it's all in her catechism, I can borrow it if I want. "It's all there, step by step." She's excited now. "You should go sometime, join the church, maybe. It's good to be reminded of your weaknesses, examine your conscience each day."

It sounds like hocus-pocus to me, but I like the idea of confessing in the dark to someone who'll never know you, never tell anyone what you said.

"Your mother was a Catholic." She's sitting up now, excited again.

"You pressuring me?"

"Your father's Anglican, that's almost Catholic. My parents think you should—"

"Forget it, not joining any church. Read the Bible, that's good enough for me."

When the movie ends, she repeats that I should go to confession. "Get rid of all your sins," she teases. "They must be piling up by now." I remind her that I'm not Catholic; she says that doesn't matter, the church is more ecumenical these days, she'll introduce me to her priest, Father McCarthy.

I tell her I'm not interested, but if I decide to go, I'll meet him in the dark.

43

I'M LOOKING OUT THE BEDROOM WINDOW at the birdfeeder Charlie made for the blue jays, and his ghost comes roaring back, laughing to beat the band. So does my headache. But this time it isn't guilt about Charlie. It's Arlene. Deep down I know it's over. I have to be honest with myself. It can't work. She deserves to know everything. Then I recall what Johnny said about Celine: I want to breathe the air she breathes. I can't fool myself. Some nights I lose sleep thinking about how complicated it all is. The other day she said she'd like to work at Charlie's Auto, it'll help with her mechanics course. "I might even teach you a thing or two." I doubt that.

Then there's the amalgamation question. I can't have that.

I'm so confused. At times I think I'll tell her about Charlie and Rosie, ask her to tie the knot. Other times I feel like calling it quits, don't even want to talk on the phone.

And what if I do tell her about Rosie? I don't think she'll accept "right over might" as a very good defence. She won't want to be with a criminal, Robin Hood or no Robin Hood. She's too straight and too Catholic to accept what I'm doing. What sensible person would?

When I raced the Snipe in Conception Bay with Uncle Ches, he taught me about sailing to weather. That's when your boat turns toward the source of the wind. You become unbalanced and pull the tiller to windward to counteract the effect. If you're racing, there's a magical moment when you pull the sheets tight for maximum speed, but not too tight, or you'll capsize. It's a balancing act. It's where I am with Arlene. Decision time. I'm sailing to weather.

Best to cut my losses, otherwise it'll get harder to move on. I don't want to wind up like the person in that song she sings, "Walkin' After Midnight," searchin' for *me*. I'll tell her soon, after Johnny ties the knot, end of the month.

I gave Johnny money for Celine's ticket, said it was a loan from Charlie. He can pay it back by working at the garage if he sticks around. Celine wants him to move to Montreal.

Celine's mother and Aunt Yvette are coming for the wedding. Arlene's excited, wants to decorate Johnny's living room for the ceremony. I said we'd need a lot of decorations to cover up that mess. She poked me. "Be nice." The reception is at Fong's Chinese Restaurant in the Cove. Johnny loves Chinese food. Deep down I'm happy for him. As it says in the Book of Genesis, it's not good to be alone. We're all hoping he'll go back to Montreal with Celine, forget Vietnam. It'll mean the end of the band, but so be it. His life's more important than a rock band.

Thinking about their happiness makes me feel miserable, so I go to my desk, take out a piece of paper, draw a line down the middle, and write PRO on one side and CON on the other. I wonder what Charlie would do, recall that he wouldn't trust Lucy with his secrets.

PRO	CON
She's fun, we have a lot in common, especially mechanics. She's trying to get her father to open a small engine repair shop.	She agrees with her father about amalgamating the two garages.
She's clear about her goals, loves music and motorcycles.	She never mentions my goal, my only one.
She's very honest, speaks her mind. Would make a good mate: intelligent, talented, kind, has Christian values. I should try to make it work.	I have to end it. She deserves someone who can be totally honest with her. I can't tell her about Rosie and Charlie. She can be very critical. She even bugs me about my hair and the way I dress. Wants me to convert to Catholicism. (No way.)

I mull over how crazy everything is, what a mess I'm in, and all I can manage to write is her name:

Arlene! Arlene. Arr. Arrrr!

Next morning, I spot an envelope sticking out of the mailbox. No name on it, just the words *My baby just-a wrote me a letter*.

I grab it, take off like a rocket for the school bus, but she's not there. I sit alone at the back, my heart thudding, tear open the envelope:

Dear Sonny,

I feel the need to communicate with you. I have not stopped thinking about you. You were in my thoughts all night. I'll never forget our weekend at Butter Pot. I know what happened is something we shouldn't have done. I blame myself, not you.

I'm not unhappy about the time we spent together, I just wish it had been a little different, that's all. I'm happy about the things you said, and I can't get you out of my mind, your eyes, your lips, that cute scar on your nose, your smile. It surprises me how much it has come to mean to me after such a short time.

You tell me I should follow my dream of becoming a singer. Oh, how much that means to me! And my dream of being a mechanic too—I can do both. You say that all will be well, and though I worry day and night about my father's problems, I believe it. You're right, I shouldn't be afraid of life's music. For me this has been one of life's better experiences. The future will take care of itself. It always does. Do you know that Crispian St. Peters song:

But I've got a feeling
Yeah, down in my shoes
I said way down in my shoes

I look out the bus window, recall what Esther-Marie told Quinn: If she gets Sonny, she gets the garage.

I was hoping that by not speaking with you on the phone last night, I'd be able to concentrate much better on the physics book I'm reading. No such luck! Instead, I found myself thinking of you the whole time and getting nothing done. I'd be reading about whenever speeds are comparable to the speed of light (they no longer add up as simply as they did in Newton's world), and I'd find myself staring into space, reliving our time in the tent together. It was a mistake, and I apologize.

But I know that I'm very fortunate that you've come into my life, Sonny. You've added colour to an ordinary life. The sun shines brighter, good food tastes better, the rain falls more intensely. A bubble of excitement for living exists within me, something I've never known. Every-

thing seems possible. Even a taste for Bob Dylan's music. Well, maybe not everything.

I want to share all my experiences with you—tell you what I'm doing with our basement—reshaping it to give it a French look (Frenchifying it . . . is that a word?), and about all sorts of trivial things which make up my life (and probably wouldn't interest you anyway). You've made me feel beautiful and cherished, something I haven't felt for a long, long time, and rarely in such an easy and comfortable way. I'll keep that feeling inside me and it will enrich both my happy and sad moments. Thank you.

Arlene

P.S. Oh God! What am I going to do? I can't stop thinking of you, and to be honest, I don't want to stop thinking of you.

No word about Sonny's Auto. Lots about her dreams, nothing about mine. I'm sad, but I lift the paper and breathe in deeply, the faintest hint of her hair stronger with each breath.

44

I LOOK OUT THE KITCHEN WINDOW. Crenshaw's snooping around the garage, peeking in the side window. He seems to be talking to someone nearby, rounds the corner with a man wearing a leather jacket—Jean-Luc or someone just like him. He's broad-shouldered, looks like a bodybuilder. Crenshaw looks toward the house; I open the window and call his name just as they mount his bike. I watch them speed off, feel marooned. Trouble brewing. He's up to something, must keep a close eye on him.

I inspect the print shop. Everything's in order. I look around the garage, find a Black and Decker electric grinder near my power tools, recognize the CTT stamp right away: College of Trades and Technology. It's clear. Crenshaw and Jean-Luc planted it. They're trying to frame me for taking the tool. I grab the grinder and head to the school.

After I've returned the power tool, I meet Crenshaw in the parking lot. He looks stoned sitting sidesaddle on his Honda Benly, nobody around. It's a cold, grey afternoon, light rain falling. It seems colder, lonelier, looking at him staring off into space, strands of hair and Maple Leafs scarf blowing in the watery wind. His crooked, bumpy nose is blue, pupils dilated, a thin, white film on his upper lip. He wears a shabby Harris tweed jacket, like Charlie's, under an oilskin poncho. A Leafs helmet dangles from the bike's handlebars.

I say hello. He jumps, startled, says sorry. "Didn't notice you. I was reflecting on Heisenberg's uncertainty principle. You know it?"

"No. Mr. Crenshaw, I know you put the school grinder—"

"Simple idea, really, anyone could have thought of it. The position and velocity of an object cannot be measured exactly, even in theory." He says that it's oddly like Karl Marx. "The ultimate constitution of matter cannot be reduced to conceptual terms. Ergo, logically speaking, there's nothing there that we can *objectively* know." He puts on his helmet. "Perhaps religion is not the opium of the people after all. Perhaps it's materialism."

He's ignoring me, and I get angry, ask again why he put the school grinder in Charlie's Auto.

He smirks. "Why, to grind you down, lad."

"You're trying to frame me. Little insurance, so I'll come up with the money Johnny owes the Doctor Club."

"I wouldn't say *frame*, exactly, lad. To quote Jean-Luc, a warning shot across your bow." A sneer in his voice. "Not likely you'll graduate if school property is found in your garage."

I tell him the Doctor Club will get the money. "Not all at once, maybe, but they'll get the full amount."

He kick-starts the bike. He calls the Honda *The Rhonda*, and when he starts it, he always sings that Beach Boys tune: *Help me Rhonda, Help, help me, Rhonda*. The bike won't start. After a few heftier tries, he shrugs, shouts over his shoulder, "This is very non-Rhonda-*ness*."

He keeps trying, singing above the wind, "Clock's ticking, lad. D-Day's only a few weeks away."

"You'll get your money."

He cackles, pats the handlebars, shouts above the rattle, "You think the Hegelian ontological argument is a sound one?" More cackling, radio static from his chest. He knows I don't know, knows there's only one thing on my mind, enjoys teasing.

The engine starts. He snaps his chinstrap and heads off, his blue and white scarf flapping in the wind.

The fat is in the fire. Old Man White wants a meeting Saturday about "joining forces." I say I'm busy. He insists. "Charlie makes all the decisions, he's in Toronto." He asks when he'll be back. I say I'm not sure, he's seeing a specialist.

"Come by anyway," he says. "You'll soon make the decisions at Charlie's Auto. Let's talk."

I don't want to raise eyebrows, say I have plans with Arlene Saturday, it's Halloween, I'll see him then.

"Wonderful! Just wonderful," he says. "Lots to talk about, Sonny. Money to be made. Big meeting, young man. Big business meeting."

I tell Arlene I'm not meeting with her father, I'll put it off. She says that'd be rude.

"Halloween I'm dressing up as Robin Hood, knocking on doors out the Brook way, giving out groceries. Could use your help."

"I'll dress up as Maid Marian."

"That would be cool. Ver-ry cool!

45

ONE SATURDAY MORNING I GET THE FRIGHT OF MY LIFE WHEN I LEAVE THE office and find the garage open. Arlene's dressed in her blue Esso overalls, shirt sleeves rolled above her elbows, deftly rearranging the tools on the pegboard. Her hair is pulled back in a ponytail, and she's wearing my greasy baseball cap.

"What are you doing here?" I shout.

She grabs a push broom, removes the mask. "What's it look like? Cleaning up. Toldja I wanna help out."

"Thought you liked things sloppy," I say sarcastically.

She glares at me, eyebrows tightly knitted.

"The place is spic and span. Always clean."

She thought she'd come over, help out on her day off. "Thought I'd be your Girl Friday, like Man Friday in *Robinson Crusoe*."

"How'd you get in here?" I shout louder, about to blow a fuse.

She points to the office door. "It was open."

"For employees only. You're supposed to come to the office. Sign says Employees Only."

"But I want to be an employee." Her crooked smile's not so cute now.

"Fugg!" I yell. "You're not allowed to just barge in here. I don't want anyone in the shop without my permission. You can't just—"

"Sheez! Don't get your pee hot. It's just an auto repair shop, for crying out loud. It's not Fort Knox. I know a little about small engine repairs." She ambles toward me, stopping by the pit, craning her neck to get a better view.

My heart sinks. "Insurance!" I catch my breath. "Insurance policy. You're not covered. If anything happened, the business would be in jeopardy. I'd never get insured again. I'd lose the business."

"Well, just put me on the insurance policy." She shrugs, says peevishly, "Simple! Just add Arlene White, Soprano." She hums, starts down the steps to the pit.

"Stop!"

She keeps walking. "Wow! What a cool spot. Wow! Cool!"

"You can't go down there!" Hoping I haven't left anything out for the wood stove. Once I left a bag of bills that failed the ink test. I usually keep everything behind the steel door.

"Why not?" she calls out. "Just an old pit."

"Get up here!" I race down, pull her arm. I'm really torqued now. For the first time in a long while, an anger fit's coming on.

"What's behind that old door?"

"Nothing. Just supplies." I lead her up the steps, and it dawns on me—Bert White: *Don't let her do Old Man White's bidding.*

I holler, "Is this your father's idea?"

"No, it's not my father's idea. For the love of God, Sonny, what's wrong with you? I thought you were a really sweet guy. I thought we were going steady."

"I don't want you in the garage. Period!"

A brief pause. She walks away, yelling, "Oh, I get it. You're jealous. You don't want girls knowing as much as guys about fixing cars—"

"That's ridiculous. Why are you so upset?"

"I'm not upset!" She shuts her eyes. "You're the one who's upset. I know a little about repairs. As much as my father."

I want to say that's not much but bite my tongue. "I don't want my girl mucking around in the garage like some grease monkey, that's all. I used a gallon of turpentine last week to clean the grease spots off—"

"Oh, Sonny." She sidles over, and I calm down at the touch of her hand on my hair. She kisses my cheek, whispers, "Can't I help sometimes? I wield a mean hammer, and I've worked with Mr. Hammond at the school. I can't put an arse in a cat, mind you, but I'm getting better and better at small engine repairs—lawn mowers, generators, chainsaws, any small engine. Mr. Hammond says I'm a born mechanic. I fixed my uncle's Harley-Davidson last week."

"Arlene—"

"There was black smoke coming out of the exhaust." She's excited now and showing it. "Knew right away it was the carburetor. It was backfiring, hard to start, so I pulled it apart and cleaned it. I love working on machines." She sticks out her tongue. "Oh, Sonny, I just want to help, that's all."

"Sure. Lots of ways to help," I whisper. I need to buy time. "There's ordering parts, bookkeeping, and—"

"Chauvinist!" she shrieks, veins popping, eyes radiating fury. She yanks off my cap, flings it to the floor, and storms off.

I look out the window at her madly kick-starting her bike. I pick up the cap, return it to the worktable, annoyed and anxious about keeping someone so headstrong out of Charlie's Auto.

46

WE DON'T SPEAK FOR A WEEK. She avoids me at school, doesn't take my calls. I miss her terribly. Like Johnny says, I yearn to breathe the air she breathes. I blame myself for the breakup, but in my heart, I know it's her fault. Maybe now's the time to go my own way. Quinn tells me that Esther-Marie says she's ripping mad, she had no idea I was such a chauvinist. He suggests patching things up, pronto.

"How?" I ask.

"Sex usually works."

"Get serious, Quinn. We're not having sex."

"She'd like to be a civil engineer. Be civil. Call her up, say you're sorry."

I take Quinn's advice, call, and say I'm sorry for being such a jerk. Arlene says she's sorry too, she was way out of line going to the garage without my permission, she'll tell her confessor she's guilty of her first break and enter. Ha, ha! I say she can help out around the garage once in a while. "But there are a few rules, for safety and such."

"Perfectly reasonable," she says. "Oh, Sonny, I want to help, that's all."

That night we go to Thelma's for dinner and afterwards stroll along the beach. We talk about our fathers, agree we're both living with a lot of pressure. When I kiss her good night, she says, "I see a bright future for us, Sonnyshine."

One day while I'm cleaning out the big oak desk in the office, I notice a slight crack between the side of the desk and the filing cabinet. My eye drifts toward something in the gap. I pull out the desk and withdraw a ledger like the one Charlie left. This one, though, is partially burned. It looks like he attempted to destroy it but changed his mind. I open it, most of the pages are ripped out. A minute later I begin reading what's left.

January 1, 1959
DEAR GOD BLESS THESE WORDS AND ALL WHO READ THEM

I hope this diary helps me understand a little about the life God gave me. Lucy has been dead five years now, but she's on my mind every day. For the longest while my life was a succession of dream-messages and prophecies, of packing up and moving on. Until I met Lucy and settled down. Not a day goes by I don't think of her and remember the good times we had. We were born for each other. Two hearts beating as one. Like the song says, you'll never know dear how much I love you.

I put the book down, close my eyes, and see Charlie kissing my mother as he helps her dry the dishes. A few minutes later I begin reading again.

She left me a beautiful gift in Sonny—another way she's here with me, in eternity. Praise God! Every day I see him I see her and thank God. Sonny is such a good boy. He warms the cockles of my heart. And he's been such a good friend to Johnny.

He'll be ten this year, and even though these past years haven't been the best years of my life, I thank God for giving me a son when I was forty years old. God has been as good to me as He was to Abraham. And Sonny's taking a real interest in the auto shop. It's such fun showing him how to take an engine apart and put it back together again. And he loves the toolbox I gave him. I pray to God I live long enough to see him handle the business on his own, the day I can see the sign SONNY'S AUTO replace mine. It's a good business and a happy way to make a living.

I rifle through half-torn, half-burnt pages.

January 10, 1959
DEAR GOD BLESS THESE WORDS AND ALL WHO READ THEM

Death is just a doorway. In a book called The Walking Drum *one of Louis L'Amour's characters says I do not expect to be remembered . . . only enjoyed. Now that's perfect. Just perfect! I'll tell that to Sonny.*

That hits me a ton, reminds me I'm living in eternity, so I read it again.

We're just supposed to enjoy each other, live in the moment. Isn't that living forever? In the seminary I studied Emerson, who said write it on your heart, that every day is the best day of the year. That's the secret to living in eternity. Yet the closer I get to the end, the more I do think about it. The doc told me to think about it. He says I have to get a few tests done.

In the garage today Sonny handed me a carburetor he fixed and said the bowl was clean, but it needed a new gasket. He said he'd love to have his own auto shop someday. Moved me to tears. I love him so much. I hope he grows up to be a McCluskey rebel. I plan to raise him so he'll be like Robin Hood. Robin's motto: Steal from the rich and give to the poor. My kind of hero. And a smart one.

I put the ledger down again. It's like a message in a bottle. My heart stops when I read how I warmed the cockles of his heart. And I agree with what he said about Robin Hood, I'm proud of him for helping the poor.

The diary goes on about how he's been spitting up blood, about people in the Cove and whatnot. I read the rest slowly, hanging on every word. As I close the ledger—the remainder is pretty badly burned—I fumble the book and notice some writing at the back. I flip to the end and read:

March 6, 1961
DEAR GOD BLESS THESE WORDS AND ALL WHO READ THEM

A Double Life
A Novel by Charlie McCluskey

I met Lucy while picking tobacco in British Columbia. We moved east and I built a little brick bungalow in Portugal Cove, Newfoundland. Lucy is tall with shiny brown eyes, and she has thin limbs. I like that in a woman. I fell in love with those big brown eyes. And if you'd seen the way she worked, you'd have fallen for her too. She was wearing a broad-brimmed straw hat that first day I saw her, and every time she stood up to stretch her lean body I thought I was staring at the sun. Lucy looked like a model, with no makeup, of course. She never wore makeup. She never needed any. She had a rounded jawline and an attractive, straight-edged nose. I like that in a woman too. And her skin, where it appeared from underneath that Army Surplus shirt she always wore, was bronze-coloured from the burning sun. As the song says, you'll never know dear how much I love you.

Some thirty feet from the bungalow is a garage with a sign out front that says CHARLIE'S AUTO. I built that garage with my bare hands. The garage has everything you need to repair and paint a car or truck. It has two bays. One of the bays has a six-foot pit. Along one of the walls there's a rusting steel door which leads to a print shop, where I keep some very important equipment, including a machine I call Rosie. Rosie spits out money—$20 bills mostly. But once in a while she delivers a crisp $100 bill, which I keep hidden in the sole of my shoe until it burns so bad I have to spend it. My name is Charlie, and I lead a double life.

The remaining pages are badly charred. I think of Crusoe gathering cargo from his shipwreck: *For sudden joys like griefs, confound at first.* A few sentences are clear: *As I've told you time and again, nobody will know Johnny is our son. I owe the Doctor Club some money, but I'll provide for him, rest assured. I'll make sure he always has work at the garage. I'll put it in the will.* Then awkward phrases, almost indecipherable handwriting:

> *yu mst kno yu mean the wrld t me Lra my lfe menless withot yu. Dont wan live withut yu.*

The rest of the page is so badly burned I make out only a few partially scrawled letters toward the bottom of the page . . . *yo r sistr wnt evr mn wh t yu . . . to me. N vr.*

I stare at the words trying to decipher them. Your sister? Lucy? Did Lra mean Laura? I ponder the words awhile. *Your sister won't ever mean what you do to me. Never.* Is that what he'd written? My heart sinks. There's no getting around it. Charlie had been in love with Arlene's Aunt Laura, Johnny's mother. Johnny, my half-brother? My chest tightens as I close the charred book.

After a while I read the part about my mother again before placing the ledger in the desk drawer with the other one. I think of Charlie two-timing Lucy with her sister, and I'm angry but grateful for the truth.

I think of Johnny again and remember the Polaroid Christmas photograph that dropped out of the L'Amour book. It makes sense now. No wonder Charlie favoured Johnny so much. Arlene was right, we all have our secrets. The energy drains out of me, and a dizziness rises as I see the birthday photograph of Lucy and me in the garage, the old black and white one of them working on the tobacco farm. It was faded, taken from a distance, so I couldn't make out much facial detail. They were in profile laughing, horsing around, Lucy wearing sunglasses, a sundress.

I go to his bedroom and look at it for a while, then lie down on the sofa, close my eyes, and see my mother in her broad-brimmed straw hat picking tobacco. I hold her image for a long time before thinking about how Charlie had deceived her, and I miss her more than ever.

I fall asleep, and when I wake, I think for some reason of the time Charlie changed a fake $100 bill at the bank. "Biggest thrill of my life—socking it to the bankers. Just slipped that C-note in the Royal Bank deposit bag and bingo, a hundred per cent profit! Now that's the real acid test for dropping dough. But I wouldn't recommend it. Ha, ha."

I miss my mother so much and feel so sorry for her that I want to do something to hurt Charlie. How can I honour his memory now? I take a long walk and decide I need to do something to cheer up, a challenge, something exciting. I put on my overalls and go to the print shop, intent on doing something I've wanted to do for a long time, something Charlie told me to never do. I crank up old Rosie and begin making my first $100 bill.

47

BANKING DAY. Unlike Charlie, I don't put the counterfeit in my shoe. I slip the fake C-note into the deposit bag and drive to the Royal Bank in St. John's. I'm nervous but thrilled, same as I was the first time I cashed a counterfeit bill.

The bank is busy today, three tellers, each with a lineup. I pick one, stand behind a hunched old man who's just finishing, when I notice Mrs. Quinn at the next teller. I usually get served by her, but not today.

"Hello, Sonny," she says. "Can I help you?"

"I'm fine, Mrs. Quinn, I'll wait."

"I'm free, Sonny. Do you have your deposit book?"

Fugg. I consider bolting when she says, "Haven't seen you at the house lately, Sonny."

"Pretty busy at the garage."

"How's your father?"

"Feeling better, thanks. Should be home soon." I gulp, hand her the deposit bag with the counterfeit.

"Looks like Charlie's Auto's pretty busy these days." She counts the money, signs my receipt book, and says to stay for lunch next time I come to shoot hoops.

"Sure thing, Mrs. Quinn." I smile, take the deposit bag, and leave. Outside the bank, I know I shouldn't, but I start running.

48

IT'S HALLOWEEN, THE "BIG BUSINESS MEETING" WITH MR. WHITE. I hope he doesn't ruin my date. I'll be polite but firm. Before driving to White's Esso, I head to Mount Carmel Cemetery to check the gravesite. I park the car and walk to the metal Cross marked Lucy Byrne McCluskey. Nearby, a few juncos make a row and disappear. No activity at the site. I kneel by the grave, red and gold maple leaves whirling about, ask Lucy to keep an eye on me, tell her I'm angry with Charlie, lonely and afraid.

Listen to the silence. Suddenly, that strange peace I felt the night I buried him.

A blue jay lands on a rusty Cross—a hint of eternity stealing through my day. Such a beautiful bird—white-faced with its unique blue crest, cool black collar around its throat. It hops, blue-black iridescence, and sings—soft clicks and whirs—liquid, high notes reminding me of whispering sweet nothings with Arlene. Blue jays usually make a terrible ruckus. Not today. The song doesn't last. The little guy flies away, leaving a tiny feather behind. I ask Lucy to keep an eye on me and leave.

Mr. White's face is bright as a new penny as he straightens his floppy bow tie. He always looks so uncomfortable in his shirt and tie. He fancies himself a mechanic, but he's all business. His mouth is fixed in a permanent grin as if he's meant to be forever smiling. He's clean-shaven, has hair that's pin-straight, slicked back with a side part. Looks like he used some garage grease to give it a high gloss. There's a cold sore in the corner of his mouth.

He says he's glad I've come. "How's Johnny? Martha's been asking for him. We're all worried about him. Is he working at the garage these days?"

"No."

He says he'll get straight to the point. "Have a seat."

I smell alcohol.

"The Whites and the McCluskeys should form one business, we'll build one big service station, catch the ferry traffic coming and going. Big money to be made."

He says I'll be in charge of Charlie's Auto soon. "And who knows what's in store for you and Arlene, eh?" He has a coughing fit. "We team up, we'll make twice the money." He pounds his fist into his hand. "We simply can't lose if we team up."

"Mr. White, my father—"

"I know, your father's adamantly opposed." He says I'm young, not fixed in my ways, it's an offer I can't refuse. "What do you say, my boy? Fifty-fifty! We'll make a bundle. I was *Cove Business News* businessman of the year in '64."

"Mr. White, my father makes the business decisions—"

"Arlene tells me he's gone away." He's sorry to hear about his health. "Serious, is it? You'll make the decisions soon, my boy. You'll be the boss. You're what, now? Eighteen? Nineteen?" He belches again.

I turn away, can't bear his asthmatic panting.

"What is it?" he says in a high, cranky voice. "Johnny? You're worried about Johnny? He's Martha's nephew. He can come work for us. Johnny's family."

"It's not Johnny."

"Then what? You want a bigger cut? Let me think about it. Meanwhile, you think on it too, Sonny. It's a perfect fit, young man, and one day this joint venture will be all yours. Will you think about it?"

I say yes, shake his rough hand, and head to the store. When I arrive, Arlene's sitting behind the counter reading *Time Magazine*. The notice about $20 bills is still posted. She flashes a picture of a group of doctors in an operating room. "There's a surgeon in South Africa planning to do the world's first heart transplant." She picks up a wrench—Charlie stealing through my day—leans on the cash register, sticks out her tongue. "Would you like me to walk you home?"

"My place for lunch? Leftover pizza, Coke. Then we'll dress up, deliver hampers out the Brook way."

"Sure thing."

At the house, we sit on the couch eating pizza. She asks if Charlie will be coming home soon.

"Charlie might never come home."

Silence.

She asks about my meeting with her father.

"Same old, same old. Wants to team up."

"Well, you probably would make more money and—"

"Arlene, we've discussed this."

Longer silence. She's squirrelly, leans in, wipes sauce from my chin, pecks my cheek. I think it's beginning to dawn on her that I'll never team up with White's Esso. Charlie's Auto will be Sonny's Auto, and that's that.

"Been talking to my Uncle Ches. Charlie might have to stay upalong for another while. More tests."

She raises her hands, palms outward. "I worry about my father too." She narrows her eyes, says in a thin little voice, "He's drinking more. Mother says his heart's getting worse. Maybe he'll get a transplant." There's a catch in her voice. I put my arm around her. "He's becoming so difficult. If he doesn't go to AA, she doesn't know what she'll do. She's threatening to leave him again."

"It'll be okay, Arlene," I whisper. "Everything will be fine. Don't worry."

"Oh, I worry," she says. "I worry morning, noon, and night. One of these days I'm gonna hop on my bike and just go, go, go."

Hiccuping sobs. She sings off-key: "*Think I'll go out to Alberta . . .*"

More tears, I feel the prick of shame on my face for never asking about her difficult father. I hold her eyes but don't say a word.

49

WE GET JOHNNY'S PLACE READY FOR THE WEDDING. I buy new towels, linen, for the guests. Quinn fills the cupboards with groceries. Johnny finds a few cans of paint, and we spruce up the place as best we can. Arlene snags a couch, kitchen table, and chairs from the St. Vincent de Paul Society. We cover every ugly spot with streamers, pictures, posters.

I rent Johnny a new tuxedo and shoes from The Model Shop in St. John's. When he puts on the tux, Arlene says he's the cat's meow, should dress up more often. Quinn feels he looks great too, done up like a twenty-dollar piss-pot.

I examine Johnny's face and see Arlene, none of Charlie's features.

Over the doorway we hang a huge banner: CONGRATULATIONS MR. AND MRS. GIOVANNI FABRELLA. BUONA FORTUNA!

It's Saturday, the day of the wedding, and the old house is so cold I can see my breath.

Although we worked hard to tidy up, it's still an ugly house and smells strange, the scent of mould, damp everywhere. I look around at the chairs and tables we borrowed from the school cafeteria and set up in the living room. A couple dressed like Antony and Cleopatra warm themselves at the fireplace. They look like they're auditioning for a B-grade horror movie. Cleopatra has towering black hair, red lipstick, and cat-eye makeup. She keeps stroking a black cat.

Quinn whispers, "All the hippies from Eden Farm on the Bauline Line were invited." I look around at the long, scruffy hair, headbands, and grungy bell-bottom jeans held up by wide leather belts.

A woman with a sallow, wizened face wearing granny glasses and carrying a hemp bag offers me a joint. "Cool, babe," she says when I refuse. She flashes a peace sign. "Do your own thing."

Johnny's Uncle Harry looks pretty shoddy: bloodshot eyes, overgrown hair, skinny as a beanpole. He shakes everyone's hand and asks if they want a drink. The hippies do their best to turn him on, but no luck, he's sticking to his Captain Morgan.

Mr. and Mrs. White are off in the corner sipping wine. The woman with the hemp bag offers them a joint. Their eyes pop as they move away from her.

Arlene and I and Mr. and Mrs. Crenshaw are the only ones there from the Trades School. Johnny says he wants to relax, doesn't trust having establishment types around. He doesn't mind Mr. Crenshaw "because he's a communist." Old Crenshaw downs Scotch after Scotch and is a bit tipsy from the get-go. I'm about to join him when he offers a drink to Jean-Luc, from Saint Pierre.

Celine is pretty with fiery black eyes. She has a small, heart-shaped face and long, wavy hair. She's always smiling, and it makes her face glow. She wears a turquoise dress with a V neckline, Johnny, his tuxedo. They look elegant standing together, arm in arm, chatting with Celine's mother and her sister, Yvette. Monique, their mother, is a small, darkish woman with a half-plucked moustache and a gap between her front teeth. She wears a mangy fur coat. Yvette is pudgy-faced with a shock of white hair.

As I join them, Monique is thanking Johnny for the plane tickets. Johnny says Charlie paid for them and pats my shoulder.

"Is he here? I want to thank him."

"He's in Toronto," I say. "He sent a telegram."

"You must give me his address. It was so kind." She turns to Johnny. "Will you be coming to Montreal? They're saving the Expo pavilions and opening an exhibition called Man and His World. We'll take you there."

"For sure Johnny will come," Yvette says, "to join the resisters."

"The jury's out on that," Johnny says.

"Jury?" Monique says. "There is some trial or something?"

"No, he means he hasn't made up his mind yet," I say.

"Whew! That's good, no trial."

Johnny grins, turns to leave. "I have a country to serve."

When he's out of earshot, Yvette turns frosty, says to her sister, "Don't worry, for sure we'll get him to Montreal." She leaves, flirts with Mr. Crenshaw.

I help Quinn set up the stereo system.

"Who the hell's gonna dance?" Quinn says. "Freezin' in here."

I head toward the fireplace to warm up, notice Mrs. Crenshaw and Jean-Luc cuddled in a corner sharing a joint. I'm shocked when they hold hands.

Arlene appears, holding a beer. "Do communists believe in free love?" she asks.

There's booze everywhere and what looks like hash brownies. Johnny keeps shouting, "Gonna be one helluva *pahty*. Plates of brownies *ova heah*, buckets of *beah ova theah*." And there's wine, champagne, and hard liquor on the buffet table, which is lined with breads, cold cuts, and salads. I try one of the sandwiches. It tastes hard because they've been laid out too long.

"Ladies and gentlemen, your attention, please!" booms a man with an Afro and full beard. He wears a rawhide headband like Johnny's and a faded khaki trench coat, the type you see in British war movies.

"Who's he?" I ask Arlene.

"Name's Moss or Ross. Johnny calls him the *Reverend* Manfred. He's doing the ceremony."

I recall seeing him once at Johnny's, but he was leaving, so we didn't speak. Uncle Harry said he's a pusher, "owns a commune somewhere."

The Reverend Manfred gathers the guests. "Hear ye! Hear ye! As a bona fide Justice of the Peace for the city of St. John's, I will now commence the wedding ceremony." He puts on a pair of John Lennon glasses and calls Johnny and Celine from the kitchen. Quinn places a record on the stereo: "Here Comes the Bride."

The Reverend Manfred places a crown of daises on Celine's head and kisses her on each cheek. "You're one far-out chick," he says and places a string of love beads around Johnny's neck. Johnny nods, flashes a peace sign.

"Far out, man," Reverend Manfred says in a beautiful bass voice. He rants about the Vietnam War, says that Johnny should head to Montreal with his beautiful bride. Then he booms, "Celine and Johnny, repeat after me: I promise to be a true companion and remain a lifelong friend by this wedlock." After they repeat the vow, Manfred says, "I now pronounce you man and wife. You may kiss the bride." Everyone claps and cheers. Cleopatra throws confetti. Johnny takes Celine's hands, steps back, and beams at her.

"Kiss the bride," Yvette shouts. "Vite! Vite! We're all froze to death."

Manfred passes them a piece of paper to sign. "Upon witnessing, I will file your marriage certificate at city hall." He hands the paper to Antony and Cleopatra to sign. Then he shakes a bottle of champagne, pops the cork, and sprays the room. Cheering and squealing! Everyone claps and lines up to say congratulations while Manfred and Yvette mill about sipping and pouring champagne. Manfred flashes the peace sign and kisses everyone, male and female, on the lips. "Peace," he says after each kiss.

Mr. White waves and comes toward me. To avoid him, I head outside to get a breath of fresh air. A Halloween skeleton holding a tray of brownies greets me at the kitchen entrance. Outside, a tall, raven-haired beauty in a flower-patterned shirt and corduroy pants smokes a hash pipe. I compliment her on her beautiful hair. "Wow, thanks!" she says, offers me the hash pipe.

I shake my head. "I'm allergic to pot."

"Wow, bummer, man."

She says she's from "The Farm" and I should come by sometime. It's on the Bauline Line. "A happening place."

I return to a living room of music and laughter. A young woman wearing hip-huggers and ankle bells wanders from guest to guest with the tray of brownies. "Time to get high, babe."

I shiver as I look around the cold, dilapidated house at the collection of oddballs, this bizarre gathering. Then I spot the bride on her tippytoes, reaching up to stroke Johnny's hair, and my heart melts. I envy him, and I wonder if Arlene envies her. And it suddenly dawns on me that he's my flesh and blood and nobody has made a toast. I take out the telegram I prepared, grab a glass, tap it with a fork: "Ladies and gentlemen, your attention please!"

I remove an envelope from my suit pocket. "Ladies and gentlemen, a telegram from my father: I'm so sorry I could not be with you on this auspicious occasion. I am so happy for you, Johnny and Celine, and wish I was there to witness your special day. Johnny, you have found an excellent wife. Be good to her and always listen to her. Lucy used to say I never listen, or something like that."

Loud laughter.

"Remember what the Good Book says, 'An excellent wife is far more precious than jewels.' May God bless you both, and I hope to see you soon."

Everyone claps and cheers.

"And Charlie sent you the perfect wedding gift." I wave the envelope. "Some dough."

"Hear! Hear!" Reverend Manfred shouts. "Please raise your glasses to the newlyweds."

Everyone cheers again.

I follow with a toast to the groom. "Johnny, you've been a brother to me . . ." There's a catch in my throat. "And I hope Celine will be a sister. Welcome to the family."

More cheers.

Monique makes a lovely toast to the bride. "And we hope to see you both in Montreal very soon so Johnny can start learning to speak French."

Cheers.

The toasting finished, Quinn, who's unusually grave during the ceremony, nudges me, lowers his voice, and says, "Well, he's tied the knot. Vietnam doesn't matter, that's it for the band, man."

"We'll see. Celine wants him to stay in Canada."

"Fat chance." He looks around. "Can you believe all these hippies, Sonny? Like something out of *The Twilight Zone*."

Crenshaw happens by and lifts his glass.

After a while, everyone complains about the cold, and Johnny suggests we pick up the booze and head down to Fong's for the reception. The words are hardly out of his mouth and the house empties. On the way, Arlene asks why they didn't have a best man and maid of honour. "And was that a real marriage certificate those hippies witnessed?"

"Beats me! All in all, a pretty lousy ceremony."

"It's a sin," Arlene says. "They should've had a church wedding. It's more dignified."

50

AT FONG'S, WING LUNG, THE OWNER, STAGGERS OUT FROM THE KITCHEN holding a raw chicken which smells buttery. "Ahhh, Johnny, happy evy day," he says excitedly. "Happy evy day!"

The restaurant is a long, rectangular room, crowded tables in the middle, booths along the side walls. Wing Lung places the CLOSED sign in the window and helps us push back the tables and chairs to create a dance floor. Quinn sets up the stereo, puts on a Chuck Berry record. Arlene turns up the volume, kicks off her shoes, and she and Johnny sing along: *Go, go*! *Go Johnny go*! Arlene's a whirling dervish burning up the floor.

The raven-haired beauty and another hippie take my hands and we start dancing to "I'm a Believer" next to Mrs. Crenshaw and Jean-Luc, who are out of sync doing the twist.

"Move to the groove, baby," Quinn shouts to Wing Lung, who's doing the mashed potato.

During the break, Johnny looks for Manfred. "Where's the Rev?" he keeps asking. "Where's Manfred?"

Arlene and I pull a few tables together forming a long row, and Yvette and her sister help Wing Lung bring out plate after plate of chicken balls, fried rice, chop suey, and chow mein. The hippies are ravenous and gorge themselves.

When Mr. Crenshaw is in his cups, he points to Johnny and says, "Marriage! Another opiate of the people."

"They look very happy," I say.

"Love is blind." He lets out a little chuckle. "Lovers don't see reality, which is to say, reality is not always to be desired." He nods toward Johnny, who's heading out back with Manfred, Mrs. Crenshaw, and Jean-Luc. "Time's running out for the Fender-bender. . . . I'm fond of the young man—he's talented as all get-out but seems unable to decide on a direction in life. Music or the military?" He snorts. "He'll drown, I'm afraid, in what Kierkegaard calls *the sea of possibility*." He taps my shoulder, strokes his beard, and asks if he might speak with me *privately*. I follow him to the front door, and we step outside. He doesn't mince words. "Time's almost up," he says. "Got the money, lad?"

"Next week," I say. "You said November twentieth."

He nurses his Scotch. "Monday next. And, oh, Sonny, I need another loan. Florence would like to go to Saint Pierre to take a French course. Just a hundred dollars. I'm sure you can manage. I'll return it next payday."

I want to ask about repaying the money I'd already loaned him but bite my tongue.

I'm taken aback, say I'll check with Charlie when he calls over the weekend.

"He'll say where the money is," he says drunkenly. "He'll lend me the money. Always does. He's a good comrade, understands it's just paper, could be rocks or the bark from trees." He swirls his Scotch, snorts. "In the bronze age they used axe blades. Charlie says you could make your own, for that matter."

That throws me, but I don't flinch.

"You have a number for him?"

"He calls me, doesn't want anyone to have his number. You know how private he is."

He leans toward me, whispers, "Put the hundred for Florence in the Bible with the rest."

"Mr. Crenshaw, I don't think I can do that. I'm having enough trouble trying to find—"

"I noticed your grades are slipping, boy."

"Grades slipping? I got 95 on my last mechanics test."

"Clerical error, I'm afraid. The grade was 59. I've corrected the record with the administration. You need a 60 per cent average to graduate. Pity if you missed it by a few points, lad."

"Mr. Crenshaw, I've had enough of your threats—"

"Spunky, eh!" He leans toward me. "Chip off the old block, hmm?" He leaves, calls over his shoulder, "Monday, the twentieth, D-Day!"

Back inside, I realize I haven't congratulated Johnny, so I head out back. As I arrive, Manfred is passing around a joint, saying, "Every gram a measured gram, Jean-Luc." The Frenchman pats Johnny's back: I notice he's missing a finger. "Crenshaw says you've done the other deal. Bring the dough to Eden Farm."

Another deal? I turn quickly, walk back inside, and talk to Quinn. Celine passes by. I hug her, wish her *bonne chance*. She thanks me for the plane ticket, and we talk about Johnny and Vietnam. Suddenly, she becomes sullen, whispers, "He received his marching papers today. Reporting to Fort Dix in New Jersey for basic training. They make it sound so official. *From the President of the United States. To Monsieur Giovanni Battista Fabrella*." I hug her again, ask if there's anything I can do, just let me know. I have some savings, could help. She sighs. "Might take you up on that, Sonny. *Merci*." Silent tears as she says life is so unfair. "The day of our wedding! *Mon dieu*! Please don't say anything." She wipes her eyes, says she's so worried, she wants Johnny to come to Montreal with her. "But he's stubborn, that one, says it's his civic duty to sign up, his father would be proud of him." More tears. "There are so many *resisters* in Montreal now, thousands of *resisters*." She asks if I'll talk to him, convince him to come to Montreal. I say I will, of course I will. As she walks away, I think of Arlene living alone in Montreal.

At four in the morning, the bride and groom say goodbye. Manfred leaves with his arm around Yvette. Mrs. Crenshaw and Jean-Luc are nowhere in sight. Mr. Crenshaw has passed out in a chair by the food. We wake him and listen to a drunken rant about the evils of capitalism. "The pursuit of capital is a pathological disorder, chaining our species to the dark and dungy walls of Plato's cave." He's still ranting as we send him off in a cab.

Then I walk Arlene back to her place. On the way she says, "When I get married, I'm having a Catholic wedding. No hippies! No pot! No one from Eden Farm." I want to tell her that's something we'll never have to worry about but decide to leave it for another time.

NOVEMBER

IV

There will come a time when you believe
everything is finished; that will be the beginning.

— Louis L'Amour

51

D-DAY FAST APPROACHING. Johnny won't have the money. A hopeless case. I'll have to give him the dough; there's no other way.

Every morning now the air is crisp, the potholes are icy, and windshields are frosted over. Scraping time again. Soon noses will be runny, cheeks will be red and raw. I'll be swamped changing tires for winter.

Saturday morning, I drive to Duckworth Street and walk to the war memorial for the annual parade and ceremony. Charlie and I always went. It's windy and cold, people hunching along, wearing caps and gloves, pulling their winter coats tighter.

I stand on Water Street and watch the parade, stamping my feet to keep warm, trying not to imagine Johnny crawling through the jungle.

The parade stops. I hope the speeches are short. Toward the end, a bitter wind comes up, whipping the flags and blowing a sea cadet's hat into the street. A bugler plays taps, an air cadet reads the poem "In Flanders Fields," which Mr. Graham had us memorize. Graham hates poetry, says he's forced to teach "that bloody war poem every year." Most of the time he teaches basic writing skills. I like the poem, except for one line: "Take up our quarrel with the foe." In class I said, "The war's over, why aren't we talking of peace with our enemies? Mr. Crenshaw says World War I was supposed to be the war to end all wars."

"Fat chance!" Graham said. "There's been more blood than ever."

"Mr. Crenshaw calls patriotism the big lie," I said.

"Mr. Crenshaw is a communist."

I suggested that *Take up our quarrel with the foe* be replaced with *Peace, goodwill toward men*. "Wouldn't that be more Christian?"

Graham gave me a dirty look and said those words wouldn't fit the rhythm. He told me to count the syllables. "Way too many syllables for the beat of the poem, McCluskey." I asked how we were ever going to stop war if we kept talking about quarrelling with the foe. "It's just a poem, McCluskey," he said. "You don't have to take it so seriously." A poem about a war that killed millions and I shouldn't take it seriously?

I ask why we don't have white poppies or doves on Remembrance Day to promote peace.

"You're *way too serious*, McCluskey," Graham said. And then the bell rang, and he told us to take out our composition books. "Thank God that's over for another year."

I eat at the kitchen table, the tinny clatter of my knife and fork on the plate echoing in the empty room, reminding me of those first few lonely days without Charlie. After a while his voice comes back through the years talking about the futility of war. I go to the bookshelf, take down his book of war poems, and read his favourite, "Dulce et Decorum est." The effect is soothing, makes me feel secure, like a hand-knitted sweater from Nonia in St. John's. It's the best meal since his departure. Afterwards, I turn on the TV.

Several soldiers, a little older than my classmates, laugh and horse around. One leans against a bunker. Another washes himself. Others at picnic tables swat mosquitoes, rub on insect repellent.

An announcer says the soldiers are with a helicopter unit in South Vietnam: "*These brave kids—the oldest is twenty-one—nicknamed their unit the Hawks. We're in a war zone covering over thirty thousand square miles in South Vietnam.*"

I remember Johnny asking if I'd kill someone, look at the TV, and my stomach falls to the floor. Some of those soldiers will be dead tomorrow, others the next day, others in another war years from now. And on and on. I think of Johnny's Manhattan friend, the tunnel rat, whose father has the boot franchise.

Helicopters land, take off. A solitary, helmeted soldier holding a rifle stares flatly off in the distance. You can tell he's a country lad. He looks terrified.

An aerial shot of a bloodied Vietnamese boy running. Then there's an extreme close-up of the boy screaming in pain.

I recall Mr. Crenshaw saying patriotism can be twisted into a big lie. "Permanent" would be a better word—a permanent lie. How can people be conned into this useless fighting? In the ledger Charlie wrote: *The rich just run the flag up the pole to sucker people into war.* Johnny's words return: the boot franchise, the Dixie cup franchise. The rich get richer.

I stare at the screen, close my eyes. Tears stream down Johnny's face—Arlene's face. I see ten-year-old boys and girls carrying rifles, drilling with hastily raised militias—children slaughtered for a lie: *Take up our quarrel with the foe*. I turn it off.

52

"IS THERE SOMEONE ELSE?" she says.

Remembrance Day ends with a bang. We're on the phone, I've just whispered a sour something: It's over.

"I've thought the whole thing out. It won't work, the two of us, I'm sorry."

"There's someone else." Her voice catches. "You can tell me, I'm a big girl—"

"There's nobody else, Arlene. It's just that . . ."

"That what?" her voice shrill, perturbed.

"We have different values, that's all." Stay firm, Sonny. Hold your ground. "Look, I've given it a lot of thought, even written down the pros and cons. It won't work, it—"

"Different values?" she interrupts. "What are you talking about? We have the same values, we—"

"No. You deserve someone better, someone who's perfectly honest with you."

"Perfectly honest?" her voice harsher. "You're not honest with me?"

"Not a hundred per cent, no."

"I don't know what you mean."

"There are things about me you don't wanna know."

"Look, Sonny, we all have problems. Nobody's perfect."

"No, I mean things about my family." My skin prickles, a ripple of fear.

"Look, I know Charlie's a bit weird, but we can work things out—"

"No, I don't mean Charlie. I . . . I can't go into this on the phone." Staticky silence. "Or ever."

"What? What are you talking about? Was it the night at Butter Pot? Is that it? I shouldn't have pressured you—"

"No, it's got nothing to do with Butter Pot."

"Then what? What is it? I have a right to know."

"It's just that I don't think it'll work out between us, that's all."

Piercing silence. "Why the hell not?"

"Look, I'm in a really tough situation here—"

She sighs. "Oh, is that what you call our relationship, a situation?" She hangs up.

I call her right back.

"I'm sorry, Arlene."

"Forget it, Sonny. You've always said you wanna do your own thing."

"I hope we can be friends."

"Friends!" She says something about the plans she's made for us, but the line gets staticky and I can't make out what she's saying. She hangs up.

I want to call her back again but stay firm, put down the phone. I sit on the edge of the bed, fold my arms, try to collect my thoughts, pick up the phone again, drop it. I head to the kitchen cabinet for the flask of Jameson's and pour a stiff drink. I shouldn't be doing this, belt it back, pour another.

No easy way to break up, but as the song says, "It's over, it's over, it's over."

53

I'M THUMBING THROUGH HER COPY OF *MIDDLEMARCH*, unable to concentrate, wanting to call her back, thinking about driving to her place, when the phone rings. Uncle Ches. He's brief. "Come right away. There's a direct flight to Toronto tomorrow noon. I've booked you a seat, meet you at the airport."

I say thanks, tell him I'll be there, lie on the bed thinking about the night in the tent with Arlene. After a while I grab my coat and head out the door. Halfway to her place, I turn around and come back. It's over.

Next day, I'm excited and nervous. I've never been on a plane before, never been outside Newfoundland. The flight goes smoothly. I sit next to a puffy old woman who's going out west to see her grandchildren.

At arrivals in Toronto, I scan the crowd for Uncle Ches's bald head. He doesn't look anything like my father, lamb-chop sideburns, brush moustache. He's the same height as Charlie but heavy-set, chunky, and jowly. Steel-rimmed spectacles, bulging eyes. He looks funny; Charlie always looked serious.

He hugs me, says, "Your father was a wonderful man." In the car, he asks if I've been to the yacht club lately. "Racing the Snipe?"

"Now and then."

"Remember what Charlie always said, 'Trim your sails to the eternal winds.' That's the only race that counts, boy. Our only hope."

I want to talk about Crenshaw, Johnny, but I'm not sure how to bring any of it up. Maybe later. I try to pay for my plane ticket; he won't hear of it, gives me cash to spend during my visit. "Take it," he says, "don't argue with me. I can be more stubborn than Charlie."

Later, at a Leafs hockey game, he says if I'd like to come to Toronto and start over, don't hesitate. Long silence. I know he's speaking a sort of code, asking if I want to give up Rosie. "Good friend, Steve Bannerman, runs Steve's Service Station, could get you a job there, no problem."

I say thanks, I'll think about it. Now that it's over with Arlene, I just might take him up on it. For the first time, a new life seems possible. It would be good to move on, without Charlie, without Arlene.

That night I lie awake thinking of my future, ridding myself of the chains of Charlie's Auto. I imagine what it would be like working in Toronto with Uncle Ches. If I can't manage a new life with Sonny's Auto, Steve's Service Station will do. And for the first time since that strange sort of peace I felt after burying Charlie, I feel light, free, ready to move on. I fall asleep, dream about it, wake in the middle of the night secure in the knowledge that I won't spend my life the way Charlie did.

Next day, Ches shows me the halfway house where he volunteers. I help him deliver clock radios to six guests and a new colour TV to the common room. He introduces me to everyone. All very interesting, especially Chapman (who goes only by that name), a wizened eighty-year-old who'd swindled a widow out of $10,000.

A few days later, I head back with Charlie's coffin. Ches has arranged everything. Barrett's funeral hearse will meet me at the St. John's airport. "I gave strict instructions for a closed casket. I've sealed it shut. I called the church and asked that the body be interred the day after you arrive. There'll be a brief ceremony at Barrett's chapel."

At the Toronto airport he passes me an envelope containing the official death certificate and cause of death papers. "Give these to the funeral director when you get home," he says. "God bless you, Sonny. Everything should run smoothly. You have my number. Call me if there's a problem." He hugs me, presses a $20 bill in my hand, says, "God made this money, the fresh air too—"

"For His children's use," I say. "He never made the difference between rich and poor."

He smiles. "Right over might." He winks, says goodbye.

On the flight home, all I think about is Arlene.

54

"WAS GRACE THAT TAUGHT MY HEART TO FEAR / AND GRACE, MY FEARS relieved . . ."

I'm not sure Johnny will finish singing. He's crying during the entire hymn. I try not to cry but can't help it, more tears for Johnny than Charlie.

After the hymn, the vicar, Reverend Newton, a bearded man with long, unkempt hair, introduces himself and says, "Welcome to the celebration of the life of Charles McCluskey. Charlie has gone to be with his beloved wife, Lucy, and his saviour, Jesus Christ . . ." He thanks God for Charlie's life, reads from scripture, and concludes with a blessing: "Rest in peace. I now hand the deceased over to the care of God."

The vicar's assistant, an acne-faced blond, reads a prayer for those who mourn and a prayer of readiness to live in eternity.

I'd asked Johnny to get Arlene to sing Charlie's favourite hymn, "How Great Thou Art." Johnny picks his guitar, and Arlene sings beautifully, which brings tears to Aunt Vivian's eyes. I can't look at Arlene, and I can't look at Johnny either: my brother, drug dealer for the Doctor Club.

At the gravesite, I stare at the empty coffin being lowered into the ground. Only Sonny McCluskey knows the truth. And the truth will stay with me alone. I've done my father's bidding, kept my promise. I look around the small, overgrown cemetery, stare at the coffin, and think of the road ahead.

The ceremony lasts about fifteen minutes. Reverend Newton wears a black cassock, white surplice, and purple stole. He casts earth upon the coffin and sprinkles holy water. He then reads from the Bible: "I am the resurrection and the life . . ."

Afterwards, the priest shakes my hand and says he's sorry for my loss. I thank him, glad it's finally over.

Johnny cries, hugs me hard. “Great man, Sonny. We’ll miss him. . . . Won’t be the same without Charlie.” He’s stuttering more than usual.

Quinn and Esther-Marie come over and hug me, both teary-eyed. Esther-Marie says, “Arlene’s feeling really down. Says she’s leaving town.”

“Heading to Alberta, maybe,” Quinn says.

“I’ll talk to her,” I say. “Thanks for coming.”

Crenshaw approaches, says he’s sorry for my troubles. “See you Monday, my office, bring the Bible.” He catches Johnny, whispers something.

Everyone’s invited to the house for sandwiches, tea, and coffee. As they leave, Aunt Vivian tells Arlene that she sang like an angel and begins sobbing. I thank Arlene for singing. She doesn’t look at me, turns and walks away.

“What a dear, dear man Charlie was,” Aunt Vivian says. I tell her I’ll catch up in a minute, need to be alone with Charlie. I stare at the mound of dirt, feel guilty about the empty coffin, but glad it’s over, thankful I don’t have to deceive Arlene about Rosie.

My thoughts turn to Johnny. He’ll have to get out of Dodge.

I look at the coffin. In the end, Charlie got the last laugh on Father McCarthy, who has no idea where Charlie really is.

I reach in my pocket, take out the flask of whiskey I brought for a toast.

“Here’s to you, Charlie! I love you, but I’ll never be you. I’ll live my own life.”

I screw the top on the flask, throw it in the grave, hear it clatter off the coffin. I’ve made my choice, taken my stand. From now on I’ll never listen to Charlie or anyone else.

I catch up with Aunt Vivian, who hugs me, asks if I’m okay. I say I’m fine, but I’m not. Then I remember what Arlene said about keeping a diary, that everyone has secrets. If only she knew the half of it. And speaking of half, half-brother’s a secret I’d prefer not to keep, but there’s a dead man’s “good” name to consider.

On the way home, we pass Arlene mounting her motorcycle. I wave. She gives me the cold shoulder again. *Vroom*!

When we get home, Aunt Vivian says she’ll stay a few days before catching the train back to Stephenville. She wants to “rest her weary bones a spell.” She’ll keep me company, cook a few good meals. “I’ll tell ya some wunnerful stories about Charlie. Such a dear man. Did you know he met your mother on a tobacco farm out in BC?”

Ches calls, asks me to write an obituary. "Your last official act," he says. "Keep it simple, put it in the *Daily News*."

This is what I came up with:

> **Portugal Cove**—Charles Joseph McCluskey died November 12 at his brother's home in Scarborough, Ontario. He had been unconscious for several hours and the end came peacefully. He suffered from lead poisoning which his doctor said caused anemia, kidney and brain damage. The long-time owner of Charlie's Auto, he was well-known for his kindness to everyone he met. His motto: I treat every car like my car.
>
> He loved playing Robin Hood at Halloween, knocking on doors and giving out free, well-stocked hampers. He was often referred to as the Mother Teresa of the Cove.
>
> Charlie was an avid reader and sharp of wit and tongue. He enjoyed western movies, berry picking, and playing darts at the Legion. And he loved solitude, cherished time in the woods. His credo: Live in the moment.
>
> He is survived by his son Charles (Sonny), his sister Vivian, brother Ches, and close family friend Johnny Fabrella. He was buried at St. John's Anglican Cemetery.

I read it over the phone to Ches, who said it was mighty fine, would I write his when the time comes.

55

PANIC IN THE PRINT SHOP! I check the business journal where I record each counterfeit transaction. Something doesn't add up. I double-check, count the stacks of money again, look on the floor, crawl under the machine, shake the burlap bag, turn it inside out. There's a $200 discrepancy, $200 missing from the counterfeit bag. Either that or I've made a terrible mistake. That's possible, I'm exhausted lately; the other day I left the steel door unlocked.

I'm worried sick, do another full sweep of the place, dump the counterfeit bag, recheck it. I even check the plate-making station, the press. Nothing. Did I accidentally burn $200 with the bad bills? Mix things up? I comb through my record book, try to calm down, but my heart races, my fear confirmed. There's counterfeit money missing.

More bad news: Crenshaw called. Johnny hasn't come up with the money for Jean-Luc and the Doctor Club, clock's ticking. "We're preparing the anaesthetic." *Click.*

I want to tell Johnny about Rosie. But he can't be trusted, lies too much. And it doesn't matter, he's been ordered to report to Fort Dix a week after his twenty-second birthday. As if finding out on his wedding day wasn't bad enough. He has to take a physical, fill out forms, and report in two weeks.

Time to vamoose, he told me, meaning Vietnam's his only way to escape the Doctor Club. He'll have to split if he doesn't want to lose a hand. Celine's out at the Brook with him, a little honeymoon, before heading to the States.

"It'll be a short-lived honeymoon," Quinn said. "His number's up. Poor fella! Kiss the band goodbye."

Celine called last night, beside herself. "Please talk to Johnny," she says.

"Every day Jean-Luc and Manfred are here looking for him. Some honeymoon! Hippies at the house all hours of the day and night. Can hardly breathe with so much pot." She breaks down crying. "It's like a bad trip. There's some drug trade going on all the time. Please, Sonny, talk to him. He loves you. He'll listen to you. I want to go back to Montreal. With Johnny. With my husband. I'm so sad. This is not the life I want. We might as well be in a foxhole." Tears. "He's so beautiful, you know. He's a poet. Wrote me a song, 'I Dream of Celine.'" More tears.

"I'll talk to him."

I run into him at Canadian Tire and we chat, but it's no good. "Can't go to Montreal, man," he says. "Heavy shit goin' on with the Doctor Club."

He tells me the fighting has started in Dak To. "Bloodiest battle of the war. They'll slaughter thousands of our troops. Johnson's an idiot. He speaks with 'a forked tongue.'" So does Johnny. His forked tongue got him involved with the Doctor Club.

"My father was alive, I'd have reported to Fort Dix long ago."

"Go straight to Montreal, Johnny, join the resisters. Settle down with Celine, start a new life. Isn't that why you got married?"

He eyes me intensely. "I'll live in Montreal after the war, maybe, become a Frenchman. For now, it's Fort Dix with my comrades-in-arms."

I tell him he's crazy. "Charlie'd say you're all a pack of fools."

He shrugs, says a man's gotta do . . .

I wouldn't go, come hell or high water, and he shouldn't either. Charlie wouldn't want us to.

It's late November, the afternoon light grows greyer. It gets dark earlier. In the mornings, the ground is frozen.

Keeping the records up to date at the shop is a drag. It's the businessman's curse, doing the books. There's nothing worse on God's earth. Just when you're pooped from a hard day's work, record keeping. And I still don't know what happened to the $200 that went missing. It keeps gnawing at me.

Another call last night from Jean-Luc. "Time's up," he said. "I've ordered a manual for our lying friend: one hundred simple lessons for one-handed guitar players." *Click.*

They've called Johnny too, and I told him to put them off until I can find the money he owes. I give Johnny some work, try to take his mind off the Doctor Club. The outside of the garage looks shabby, paint chipped, peeling, so I buy brushes and paint and give him strict instructions not to smoke dope.

"If you need anything, come to the office."

He nods, flashes a peace sign, but in no time, I find him in the garage, spaced out, staring at the poster of Robin Hood.

I ask why he's in the garage. "You know the rule, nobody in the garage without me. Could lose my insurance."

He grins, scratches his head. "Your old man was a Robin Hood, man." As he backs lazily toward the door, he points to the picture. "That's Charlie, man! Robin Hood."

Second day, he's stoned again, but his work's meticulous, so I don't say anything. After he leaves, I find a joint by the garage. I'm upset and next day confront him.

"Johnny, you can't work here if you're gonna smoke weed on the property. We could get arrested. Yesterday I found a joint—"

"Musta fell outta my pocket, man." He snorts. "Ahh, who's gonna know?"

"That's not the point. You're pretty loose with your dope, Johnny. You're gonna get caught. At least find a decent hiding place. Jail time if the cops find so much as a roach."

"Awright! Awright!" he says. "Don't be such a ninny. I'll hide it under a rock or somethin'." He turns away. "Depressed these days! Weed keeps my mind off the war, man."

That throws me, so I let it drop.

56

SUNDAY MORNING, I WAKE TO THE PHONE RINGING.

"It's D-Day! Doctor Club met to check the surgical equipment. Seems we're short on anaesthetic. Pity!" *Click.*

I'll give Johnny the money to split town. Crenshaw said he owes over two grand. I'm wondering about the exact amount when the phone rings again. It's him.

"Military police at your door?" I ask softly.

He's sobbing. "They . . . they drugged me. Said it was a warning, shades of things to come. And . . ." Loud groans. "Ripped out one of my fingernails. Threatened to cut my hand off."

"Johnny, listen—"

"I was walking home, next thing I know I'm pinned to a car and thrown inside. They wore masks. Said Jean-Luc sent them. Thugs!"

More sobbing. "They said if I miss the deadline, there'll be no anaesthetic."

He's desperate. Will I drive him to Eden to meet Manfred, to drop off some of the money he owes? Harry disappeared with the car.

"Johnny, I know you're drug-dealing. I know you owe at least two grand."

"No drugs involved, man." He owes Manfred some money, that's all. "Please, Sonny, will you drive me? Please."

"I know what's going on, Johnny. How much you owe the Doctor Club? I can help. What's the exact amount?"

"Dunno. Hundreds."

"The truth, Johnny."

"Thousand."

"The truth!"

"Two thou and change. Bought guitars, new costume—"

"You've gotta stop lying to people, man. Sell those guitars."

"Already tried. No takers. Only have about two hundred dollars. Will they chop my hand off?" Hiccup-sobbing.

"Listen to me, Johnny. I'll be there shortly. I'll bring half the money. Call Manfred, tell him you'll have the other half in a few weeks. Hear me? That'll buy you time to beat it. You can join the resisters in Montreal."

"No! Vietnam's my only way out." His voice sounds weak, plaintive.

I say I'm on the way, tell him again to call Manfred, and head to the print shop to take $1,000 from the four Charlie left me in case of an emergency.

As we drive to the Bauline Line, I hand him a wad of money. He counts it, says he'll repay every cent. "I'm writing a song that'll be at the top of the charts, will make a bundle."

"We'll work that out down the road, Johnny. Tell Manfred and Jean-Luc you have a friend who's sending the rest. That'll keep them at bay till you high-tail it outta here."

"Thanks, little brother." He reaches over, hugs me, starts crying.

"Drug pushing's a dead end, Johnny."

"No drug pushin' where I'm goin'."

"Lotsa dope in Vietnam. You could get a dishonourable discharge, wind up in the cooker."

We park the car on the side of the road and hike an unused ski trail toward Eden Farm. It's windy as hell and raining off and on. I'm not dressed for this little jaunt, light windbreaker, Hush Puppies. Johnny's got an umbrella, raincoat. The trail is mucky, fallen trees and branches, water trickling everywhere. There's a stale smell from the marshy earth. In no time my Hush Puppies are soaking wet. Lucky for Johnny he's wearing boots.

"Hope I can find the place," he says. "Only been here once."

Another lie.

"Have you seen the log house? Beautifully built, Manfred's good with his hands." He takes off his raincoat, insists I wear it, then races on, his bright red hair streaming behind him.

We hike for about a mile, climbing over fallen trees and stumps, scratched by flying branches, the cold autumn rain chilling me to the bone.

After a while I shout, "How much farther? Feet are killing me."

"Almost there, c'mon!" He's moving fast, well ahead now. "It's here," he calls from the woods. "See smoke."

I hurry toward him; sure enough, there's smoke in the distance. He stands waiting, sweat and rain running down his face. The cold has nipped his cheeks red.

"Be quiet," he says. "Manfred has a rifle. Don't spook him."

"Just my luck. Try to help, take a bullet for my troubles."

We jog toward the smoke, stopping to catch our breath. About ten minutes later, a small opening; nestled amidst trees, a log house. Johnny's right, it's impressive. A two-storey with covered porch, long picture window in front.

"Logs are hand-hewn oak," Johnny whispers.

"C'mon, let's get this over with. I'm freezing."

We creep toward the window and peek inside, me shivering to death, Johnny babbling about the hand-hewn logs. On the far wall is a huge fireplace, a raging fire in the hearth. Standing near the fire is a tall, naked woman—the raven-haired beauty who'd offered me the hash pipe at the wedding. She's back-on: straight, slender legs slightly apart, pulling a section of her hair and pinning it with a side comb, fire glowing on her back and buttocks.

In the firelight she looks a little older than I am, loopy earrings, pearls around her throat. I've never seen a naked woman. In the tent, Arlene was naked but it was dark.

Shocked silence.

Johnny tugs at my sleeve.

"Just a minute."

He tugs harder, points over my shoulder as Manfred appears, the Frenchman at his side. Manfred introduces Jean-Luc, who shakes my hand, says, "*Bonjour*." He's wearing a T-shirt even though it's freezing out. He has beefy biceps. Manfred's wearing the same rawhide headband and faded khaki trench coat he wore at the wedding. He looks stoned.

"Johnny, be good!" Manfred flashes a peace sign. "Thought you might've been the pigs. They snoop around sometimes." He invites us inside. Johnny says no, withdraws the wad of bills from his pocket. "Gotta split."

"Every gram a measured gram," Manfred says.

"How's Celine?" Jean-Luc says. "Nice to see we have a French connection." He smirks.

"She's going back to Montreal soon," Johnny says.

"Have a friend in Montreal," Jean-Luc says. "Always looking for pretty girls. Pays them well for their services."

Johnny flinches. "Celine has a job."

"Just asking. Can get you work there too."

"Uncle Sam call yet?" Manfred asks. "It's a sick war, man. Bummer of a war." He peels the bills from the wad, counting them, turns to Jean-Luc. "It's half, man."

"I'll have the rest at the end of the month," Johnny says. "Getting a loan from a friend in New York."

I clench my fist. "I'll vouch for him."

"That's cool," Manfred says. "Say hi to Celine for me."

"Maybe after the war you'll become a Québécois," Jean-Luc says.

Manfred says, "Yvette asked me to come to Montreal." He gun-muzzles his index finger, taps Johnny's wrist. "Get the rest of the dough by the end of the month."

Jean-Luc shakes Johnny's hand. "Firm grip, man. Very firm." He sneers, flashes a peace sign, gives Johnny a joint, and we head out.

We're back at the car in jig time, Johnny well ahead again. He rolls down the window and lights the joint. "You're the best, Sonny. I owe you, man. I'll pay back every cent, I promise."

How's he going to repay $1,000? Might as well be a million.

He tokes, says, "Hell, I'll go to Vietnam, the Captain would be proud."

"They'll come after you for the money."

"Good luck to 'em. Won't give those crooks another cent."

I sit freezing in the dull afternoon light waiting for him to finish smoking, wondering if I should tell him the Captain's not his real father. I'm feeling empty and weak as I watch a drifting black cloud chase another. It's that same stunned feeling you get when you've been hit in the face by a hockey puck.

"Dunno what's gonna happen to those poor people out the Brook way when I'm gone. Will they have enough heat this winter? Enough food? Give my allowance to them, will you, Sonny?"

I think of the causes Charlie helped, the anonymous donations he made to people like Mr. and Mrs. Ricketts. It'll be hard to tell them all there'll be no more money. Then I think of Lucy and Laura, and my mind goes blank. I sit there shivering, turn on the heater.

"The hippie world's not for me," Johnny says. "Peaceniks, but not enough music in their lives. Gotta have music, man, morning, noon, and night. Couldn't live at Eden Farm."

I look at the grey sky. "Start packin' your things, makin' a quick getaway."

He stares at me wide-eyed, says he couldn't ask for a better friend. "You're a real brother, you know that, little brother?"

I stare at him, say, "There's something I need to tell you."

Long pause as we look at each other.

A clownish grin. "What?" he says, giggling in his stoned way.

"Nothin," I say. "Forget it." I pull the car onto the highway and speed back to town.

57

IT'S EARLY MORNING. I'm in the print shop looking for the bad counterfeit to burn when terror rises in my throat. I'm like one dead or stupefied, as Crusoe would say. The good money bag is missing, the remaining $3,000, my emergency money.

The counterfeit bag is where I left it. But the good bag? I count the fake money, still $200 missing from last week.

My throat tightens, roof of my mouth feels shellacked. I ransack the place. Brain going in a thousand different directions, feel weak, shaky. Bag must be here. Where? Race to the office, check the safe, there by mistake? No. Heart racing. Go to the hiding place. Not there. Run to the house. Upstairs. Charlie's bedroom. Sometimes he'd count there, put it under his bed. Nothing. Sweat rolling down my neck. Hyperventilating now. Deep breaths. The stove. Did I burn it? Where is it? Need water. Stolen. Fugg! Must be. Who? Arlene the only person around. Her father's money problems! No. Impossible . . .

Who? Johnny? No. Crenshaw? A desperate man. Yes, Crenshaw!

I count the counterfeit again. Heart still pounding. Gotta be a mix-up. Only $200 is missing from last week. Really sweating now. All gone. The remaining money Charlie left me.

What about Arlene when we had the blow-up? She only went to the pit once. Too righteous.

I sit in a chair, try to slow my breathing, get another glass of water.

Johnny was in the garage, but too spaced out, just stared at the Robin Hood poster.

Crenshaw! Been snooping around. Who else but Crenshaw? He has a key to the garage, but the print shop? Does he even know there's a print shop?

Unless . . . unless Charlie told him about it. No! Charlie would've put that in the ledger.

Maybe old Crenshaw dipped into the counterfeit bag too, why my record book is off. And is that where the White's Esso counterfeit came from? Crenshaw? But that serial number's different. Maybe Charlie told Crenshaw something. He's threatened me, ordered me to find money for Johnny, was pushy about a loan, knew about Charlie's anonymous donation to the Ricketts family, pushy about that too. He'd only need a few minutes to bolt with the bag. Could've stolen it last night, any night. Must be him.

He was anxious asking for another loan for Mrs. Crenshaw. And there's his poor health, needs money, maybe, for his nitroglycerine, other medicine. Charlie said he'd drop dead one day of a heart attack.

Dizzy now, lightheaded, heart bursting through my chest, and I'm sure I'll drop dead of a heart attack before old Crenshaw.

58

I WATCH SHEETS OF BAD BILLS CRUMPLE IN THE FIREPLACE, STARE AT THE yellow flame, feel the heat on my face, rain battering the roof. Money to burn, Charlie would say.

Loud knocking on the door. My heart jumps. I look through the peephole. Arlene! What the hell's she doing here? Ten o'clock. I stare at the wood stove, will I let her in? More knocking. Hide the garbage bag in the kitchen, tell her you're finishing an overdue assignment, you'll see her in the morning. I open the door. Gusting rain all day, the smell of earth in the air. She's soaking wet, panting like she's run a mile.

"Arlene! What's up?" A clap of rain drumming against the window.

She gives me a sharp look. "Ain'tcha gonna invite me in?" She's jittery as a squirrel.

I wave her to the fireplace, grab a towel from the bathroom. She looks different when I return, standing in the flicker of the firelight, wet hair all snaky curls, and I want to wrap my arms around her. "Is everything all right? Finishing an overdue assignment."

"That can wait. I'm pregnant."

"What!" A double take, she's looking down, nodding. My stomach caves. She's saying this to get back at me.

"I'm not a piss-prophet, Sonny, but it's been over forty days." Her voice rising in distress. "Forty days and forty nights."

I'm stunned, don't want to hear this. "Fugg!"

"I'll second that motion, Mr. Chairman." She sits up straight, wide-eyed.

My heart races, same as when I discovered the missing money. "You sure? I mean, how can you be certain? We only did it once, Arlene."

Holding back tears: "Last time I checked, Sherlock, once is more than enough." She looks miserable. "Well, Sonny?"

Silence. An emptiness like no other.

"I don't know what to say." My mind's blank.

Her jaw drops. "But of course you know what to say."

"Fugg! You sure? One hundred per cent!"

"I don't need a carpenter to hammer a nail. Been six weeks since my last period. The rabbit died, McCluskey."

I shrug, don't know what she means.

"A euphemism."

I shrug again.

"A nice-ism. Code for something." She throws her hands in the air. "Long story." Her eyes narrow. "About pregnancy." She sighs, shoulders sag. "Years ago, 'the rabbit died' was a phrase for a positive pregnancy test. Used to inject a woman's urine into a female rabbit. If the woman was pregnant, the hormone jolt caused the rabbit's ovaries to enlarge. Common misconception at the time that the rabbit would die if the woman was pregnant. Called the AZ test."

"Oh."

"Yeah. Crazy, huh? Well, the rabbit died, Sonny. Didn't feel like eating a while back, thought something was wrong. It was weird. I felt like throwing up at the mention of food, knew something was out of whack. Then boom! I was starving and I just knew. I said Arlene, you're cooking for two from now on, baby. Pardon the pun."

I smell smoke from the wood stove, have to get rid of her. "Quite a shock, can we talk in the morning? Let's meet at Milt's Place at seven." Milt's is a popular restaurant with a cheap buffet breakfast.

She folds her arms, stands stone-faced. "Well, aren't you gonna tell me how you feel?"

"I'm shocked, Arlene. I don't know what to say."

"Don't know what to say? Well, are you happy? Sad? We're having a baby, Sonny—"

"Yeah."

"*Yeah*? That's all you can say. *Yeah*."

I close my eyes, feel my body jerk slightly.

"What is it with guys?" she says breathlessly. "You, Charlie, Quinn, my father . . ."

"Whataya mean?"

"You're all the same."

I'm afraid to speak. "Whataya mean?"

"Whataya mean?" she repeats snidely. "That's exactly what I mean."

"Arlene, I-I—"

"You know something . . . I should be having this baby with someone who's decent and kind . . . someone like Johnny. Not you. You just don't get it."

"Get what?"

"Ughh!" She jumps up. "How did I ever fall for you!" She storms out.

"Seven o'clock, Milt's!" I shout. "Arlene!" She doesn't look back.

I finish burning the trash from the print shop. Money to burn, and like Crusoe, nowhere to spend it. I stare at the fire, think of Arlene, what to say in the morning. A baby? I'm eighteen, she's seventeen, just kids.

Her parents flash through my mind. I consider running away, making some counterfeit and hitting the road. I could drive across the island with Johnny, catch the morning boat to Nova Scotia, meet Uncle Ches in Toronto. I watch the flames dance wildly, think of the night I buried Charlie, wonder what he'd say. Nothing in the ledger about knocking someone up.

On my deserted island again. I lie back on the hard floor and think of Crusoe making a list, the good and bad of his situation, weighing both sides like debtor and creditor. I do the same, the pros and cons. Too hard to do in my head, so I go to my desk for pen and paper.

59

I SHOW UP AT MILT'S AT SEVEN. It's a small, bright place with L-shaped diner booths. Near the entrance is a wooden counter with a pot containing a plastic flamingo, which Arlene always pats. I walk to a booth behind two truckers. A skinny blonde, face dotted with blue pimples, walks by carrying a tray of breakfast platters, a pot of coffee.

I'm barely seated when Arlene walks in. She looks tense as a piano wire, hair pulled back in a ponytail. She's wearing her racer jacket, bell-bottom jeans. My blood jumps as she drops her books on the table and slides into the booth.

"The rabbit definitely died, McCluskey. I'm pregnant." Her eyes dance. "My periods are weird, but I'm sure. Like my math tests, one hundred per cent!"

I meet her anger with silence, sad and happy at the same time. I love babies, but pregnancy? Last thing I want. We're not even dating anymore. I don't want to be a father. I'm not even sure how I feel about my own father anymore.

"You look sad," she says. "Are you sad or happy?"

"Both, I guess." I've heard students mocking girls who got pregnant. I never feel that way. Charlie's influence, I guess. At Christmas he'd remind me that Jesus was illegitimate. "Best bastard the world ever had, king of bastards."

"I told Mother. She told Daddy. Daddy wants to talk to you. Mother thinks it best if I don't see you for a while."

"Your parents are straight out of *Father Knows Best*."

"Mommy and Daddy may be old school, Sonny, but they have my best interest at heart. And I learned a long time ago that you don't fight Daddy, because you won't win. When Daddy sets his mind to something, that's it. That's why we need a plan."

"Father knows best."

"For God's sake, Sonny, my parents are upset. They're only being sensible. You're eighteen years old—"

"Yeah, and I have my own business, my own house. I can look after myself . . . and you and the baby."

She turns aside. "I told Daddy I'd talk to you about Charlie's Auto."

"You what? You said what?"

"Well, that's what you told me. On Halloween. You said down the road, maybe, if we tie the knot—"

"Fugg! I didn't mean that literally."

"Whatta you mean you didn't mean it *literally*? You meant it *metaphorically*?" She gives me a sharp look. "I'm all ears, Sonny."

"Fugg! You shouldn't have said that."

"Okay, I'm sorry. Thought it'd be a good idea, way of smoothing the waters."

"Smoothing the waters! Fugg! Don't bring up Charlie's Auto again with your father. Ever!"

Her voice catches. "I'm sorry." She opens her purse, pretends to be looking for something. "What do you think Charlie would've said?"

"He'd be happy, say you'll have a little helper in the garage soon. The way I was for him. And he'd help us in every way. Cripes! You brought up the garage with your old man."

"Okay, I said I was sorry, okay?"

"I don't wanna give him any ideas. Charlie's Auto's not for sale."

"Look, Sonny, I know you're the kinda person who plays by your own rules, but Mommy and Daddy only want what's best for me. For us. For me, you, and the baby. And they knew your father was very sick—"

"And you shouldn't have mentioned my father's health. That's private. None of their business."

"Okay. I'm sorry, all right. God! Can we please, please talk about what really matters?"

The blonde with blue pimples appears, fills our water glasses, passes us menus. I order coffee and toast, Arlene says tea.

I drink my coffee and think of Mr. White in his three-piece suit, dry-cleaned Arrow shirt. *Businessman of the Year*.

Arlene says she has two important questions she wants me to answer with a simple yes or no. "Question number one: Do you want the baby?"

"Yeah, guess so."

"*Guess so*? Cripes! Yes or no, Sonny!" She's spitting sparks. "It's your child we're talking about. Flesh and blood."

"Yes, if it's the only option."

"*Only option*? Yes, it's the only option, Sonny."

"Then maybe, yeah."

"Good. Now we're getting somewhere. Question number two: Will you marry me?"

"Marry? What?" That throws me for a loop. I fall silent.

"Yes or no, Sonny?" Her voice is stern. "We don't have to get married tomorrow or next year. I just want to know if that's in the cards for us down the road. Us and the baby. The child needs a father. *Yes or no*?"

"Dunno. Lots to think about. . . . Guess so, maybe."

"*Yes or no*?"

She has me on the ropes.

"Down the road, maybe, yeah."

"Good! Now we need a plan." She looks anxiously around. "Daddy says you should always have a plan."

Plan! I glance at the black print along the thick edge of her textbook: SONNY & ARLENE. "We don't need a plan." The idea nags at me like a loose tooth. "I've been up all night thinking, Arlene. What about . . . an abortion? I know a girl who went to Toronto—"

"Out of the question!" Her eyes pop.

"Why?"

"It's a criminal offence, Sonny. I could get two years in jail. Life imprisonment for the doctor. Besides—"

"Besides what?"

"Sonny, I'm Catholic."

Silence.

"I'm a practising Catholic."

"So?"

"Cripes, you really are a dumbo." She puts her face in her hands, undoes her ponytail, runs her fingers through her hair, and shakes her head. "Oh, Sonny, Sonny." Her voice is tinny, childish. "I'm having this baby, Sonny. With or without you." She slices a hand across her throat. "*Capiche*?"

There's a long pause, and she says that her parents want to see me.

"I don't want to—"

"Well, they want to see you, to talk about us, the baby. Please don't make this any harder than it is. Let's not risk everything."

"Risk everything? Whatta you mean? You'd put your parents ahead of my feelings for you?"

"I don't have to, Sonny. Please! Please say you'll see them."

The waitress arrives with our orders. Arlene says thank you, on second thought she'll have some toast, a little peanut butter.

"What about putting the baby up for adoption?"

Her eyes are laser beams. She puts milk in her tea, stirs to beat the band.

"I know your father. He doesn't want to talk about us or the baby. He only wants to talk about one thing. I don't wanna talk to him."

"Sonny!" She snatches my toast, bites hard into it. "This is about a little more than merging businesses."

"Plenty of couples get along without family involved. We're not in India, where parents arrange everything."

She bolts upright and says that not meeting with her parents is out of the question. She repeats the importance of coming up with a plan, when to meet, what to say. "I know Daddy. Unless you impress him, unless you convince him we care about each other and want to settle down, he'll just laugh and say, Humph! Young love. We'll raise the baby. That child will be a White."

"No way!"

She says she'll tell her parents I'm coming by, that'll please them. "It'll mean you're responsible. Say we plan to get married down the road, ask their permission. They'll like that. Say you'll run Charlie's Auto full-time when you get your papers in the spring. I'll help—"

"No!" I slouch in the booth. "Don't want to open that door. He'll go on and on with all that old bullshit about teaming up—"

"Well, what do you want to do?" Face rigid, eyes defiant. "Tell him we're moving into the Salvation Army?"

"I want to do what normal people do. Look your father in the eye and ask for your hand, maybe, if that's what I decide. That's it. Nothing more. Nothing about teaming up. I want to be a man, not a mouse. Tell him I have deep feelings for the baby . . . us—"

"And when he says you can't live on love—because that's what he'll say, Sonny—what will you answer?"

"I'll tell him I'll provide for you and the baby. I have Charlie's Auto. For God's sake, Arlene. I'll sell newspapers if I have to, dig ditches—"

"Sell newspapers!" She winces, her mouth twisting faintly to the side. "I can imagine what Daddy would say to that. Charlie's raised you with some weird notions."

"Leave my father out of this. You've said enough about Charlie."

There are tears in her eyes as she throws her half-eaten toast on the plate. "Cripes! Why don't you play by the rules?" She snatches her books, races off in a huff.

I pick up my knife, push the toast around the plate. A sudden twinge of nausea spreads from my stomach to my mouth, takes my breath. I drop the knife. The queasiness passes as suddenly as it came. The waitress arrives with Arlene's toast. I say thanks and go pay the bill.

60

THE NEXT MORNING THE PHONE RINGS AT SIX. "Get your pants on. We're going for a bike ride."

"I'm not getting on that thing while you're in a bad mood."

"I'm not in a bad mood. We're going to Milt's. C'mon, I'm starving."

I brush my teeth, hurry into my clothes, race outside. She's at the house in jig time.

She hands me a tiny stuffed tiger. "My first toy," she says. "Put it in your pocket. For the baby."

On the way to Milt's, she yells over her shoulder, "It's not about us anymore, Sonny. All about the baby now."

At Milt's she orders two lumberjack breakfasts, says, "Eat up, you're gonna need it. We got a kid to raise."

I laugh. Is she trying a new tack? Gotta hand it to her, she's got grit.

As we wait for the food, she says again that the baby's the priority now. "And if we're having the little guy, he'll need a mother and father. Right?"

I don't say anything, look around.

"Right, Sonny?"

"I'm sorry about yesterday at Milt's. I was frustrated, upset about meeting your parents, they intimidate me."

"It's okay, I understand. I wasn't at my best either."

Silence.

"Do you think it'll be a boy or a girl?"

"Dunno."

"Guess. What would you like?"

"A healthy baby."

"Me too."

"You really think we should marry because you're pregnant?"

"No. It's not the best reason. But it's a good reason."

We sit there in awkward silence, me thinking of what I like most about her, her boldness, but not wanting to dwell on it. I feel eyes on me, look for the waitress. A chubby guy sets the lumberjack platters before us.

"You okay?" she says.

"Yeah, guess so."

She smiles, reaches over, and squeezes my hand. "Everything's gonna be fine, Mr. McClutzky. How are you at changing diapers?"

I burst out laughing. "You sure have a way about you, Arlene."

61

THAT EVENING ON THE PHONE I SAY I'M SORRY AGAIN.

She says she's sorry too, not to worry, our love is strong. She quotes our favourite song: "You make me feel like a natural woman."

"And if I make you happy, I don't need to do more."

"Look, we'll work it out," she says. "We just have to convince my parents that we're serious, mature. Then everything will be fine. Just be nice and polite. And don't forget what I told you about Daddy, he'll fight tooth and nail if you challenge him. And he'll win, he always wins. Let's go over our plan."

"And your mother?"

"She's upset, she can be very stern. Just be polite. Tell her you love me, the baby, that we have a plan. You'll run the garage—"

"Will you be there?"

"They want to see you alone. They insisted. I said yes. Daddy might have an attack if I'm there." She says he might be drinking, best not to rattle him. "I won't be far, don't worry, everything'll be fine. Don't upset him, that's all. If he starts breathing quickly through his mouth, sharp breaths, that's the sign of an attack. Don't say anything. Mother will know what to do. He'll rest till it passes. You might have to leave, come back later."

Good grief! Daniel entering the lion's den.

"And say something about baptizing the baby. They'll insist on—"

"I don't know about that."

"Well, at least hint at it. Can you do that, at least? Hint at it." She moans, says to come by Thursday around seven, when her father's in the den. "I'll answer the doorbell, invite you in, tell Daddy you'd like to see him."

Then she'll disappear around the corner, linger in the hallway while I talk to her parents. She anticipates the possible questions they'll ask, and we discuss how I'll answer them. She reminds me to be forceful about looking after the baby. Baby! The word sounds so strange to me. We broke up, and now we're going to be parents together.

"We'll meet afterwards, behind the garage," she says. "I'll be just outside in the hall listening. Don't worry, deep down Daddy is very easygoing. Just don't mention anything about selling newspapers or digging ditches. And don't say fugg, for God's sake. He'll throw you out. Stand tall, pull your shoulders back. And don't scrunch up your eyes when you get serious. You look kinda goofy when you squint."

"Thanks for the vote of confidence."

That night I can't sleep. I have terrible headaches, get up and make coffee, walk the floor. Another plan. I curse myself for agreeing to Charlie's plan, wish he was around to talk about Arlene, Johnny, Crenshaw, the baby, this new life Arlene and I have created. Then I think of my mother, and I'm glad he's not here. I finish my coffee, go back to bed, my mind racing about being a father. I'm eighteen years old. I don't want to be a father. I need a father.

I can't sleep, have a terrible headache, get up and make more coffee, walk the floor, agonizing over Arlene's pregnancy. How could I be so stupid? Should I bring up adoption again?

Arlene says she'll stay home till the baby's born, then she'll move in with me. Is that a good idea? Will I be able to make enough money at the garage to get by? Will I have to dip into the counterfeit? Should I, given what's happened? Should I go back with her just for the baby's sake? Do we need to get married? I thought it was over. It's all so woolly. Should I tell her about my father, the counterfeiting operation, Johnny?

I fall asleep, dream I tell Johnny he's my half-brother; he lunges at me with a hand like Captain Hook. I jolt awake and worry about him being in tow with people like Manfred and Jean-Luc. How could someone so smart get involved with a bunch of creepy drug dealers? I recall Charlie saying your friends are a mirror.

I pace the floor in a sweat about the missing $3,000. It had to be Crenshaw. Who else? No other way it could've gone missing. How to approach him? Such a delicate matter. No way around it, I have to confront him, it's inevitable. I'll have to find words that let him say he took the money without revealing I'm a counterfeiter. Even though I'm angry with Charlie, I wish he were around, he'd know how to handle it.

I get up, take a shower, curse myself for not wearing a condom. I put on Charlie's old bathrobe. That makes me feel better. I pace the floor. Eventually, as the soft grey light seeps through the bedroom blinds, I lie on the couch and fall asleep.

Next day I don't eat, I'm groggy during mechanics class. Crenshaw says he'd like to see me afterwards, some news from the Doctor Club.

The thought of meeting Mr. and Mrs. White churns my stomach. I don't like them. He's gross, she's a cold fish. In-laws! Outlaws, more like it. His constant panting, coughing gives me the willies. And he wants the garage. My garage! And it's a safe bet he'll use his daughter to try and get it. How did I get in such a mess?

When I ring the Whites' doorbell that evening, my heart pounds. I'm heartily scared, as Crusoe would say. I clench a fist, which I often do when I'm edgy, shift my weight uncomfortably. My mouth's dry, as if I've eaten sawdust. *Please God, help me get through this.*

62

MR. WHITE CAN BE FRIENDLY ENOUGH, BUT I'M USUALLY AFRAID OF HIM, the way I am with Mr. Russell, our vice-principal. Perhaps it's the way he dresses, so formal, or the sound of his voice, so harsh. He likes to play the bigwig. I hope he doesn't have one of those attacks.

One of our first dates, I was in the kitchen making sandwiches (Arlene had gone to the bathroom), and Mr. White came by. He rubbed his hands together, belched, and said, "Sonny! Sonny McCluskey," an edge to his voice. I said hello. "I've always admired your father. Fine businessman." I could tell right away he didn't mean it, they were just empty words.

Arlene takes me to his office. He's sitting at his big rolltop desk fondling a plastic trophy, his pride and joy, a man carrying a briefcase. The plaque reads: Businessman of the Year. The desktop is higgledy-piggledy, littered with loose papers, stacks of file folders. On one side, piled high, boxes marked Esso Invoices, on the other a stack marked Esso Receipts.

Mr. White wears a crisp white shirt, a thin layer of flesh spilling over the collar. As always, he's wearing his floppy, black bow tie. His pants are pulled up, exposing tartan socks. He's holding a copy of the *Cove Business News*.

Arlene says I'd like to speak with him, winks, and leaves. I straighten, pull my shoulders back.

Mr. White goes to the doorway and calls out, "Martha! Martha, come here, please. Sonny's arrived." He walks back and forth, snapping his fingers.

Mrs. White appears, wearing a thick hairnet, printed housecoat. Her eyes are haggard. Lips pursed, arms folded tightly, holding in her rage. She stares at me with a cold glare.

"Sonny would like to speak to us," Mr. White says in a thin voice, his neck thrust forward.

I half-smile, behind the smile, trepidation. "I . . . I've come to talk about Arlene—"

"Arlene?" Mrs. White interrupts, a grating tone.

"Arlene and me." I fall silent.

"And you?" A sneer. "And? Anyone else?"

I get what she's driving at. "And the baby."

"Ah, yes . . . *the baby*." An uneasy pause. She lets out a scornful sigh. Another fierce glare, her harsh tone sinking in. "Well, her father and I are disappointed, to say the least. I thought Protestants were the ones who knew all about birth control—"

"Now, now, Martha!" Mr. White says. "Let's hear what the boy has to say." He wheezes, short of breath.

She shoots a glance his way, fists on her hips. "What he has to say, Bertram, is that he's knocked up our daughter."

Shock!

"Martha! We agreed—"

"Fine, Bertram! I'll put my two cents in, and you handle this."

I grind my teeth, angry, frightened. Another nervous pause. "Well?" Mrs. White says, false teeth bared, face reddening.

I catch my breath. "Well, I've come to propose to Arlene. We want to get married."

"Young man, I am profoundly shocked. I simply cannot believe that you would allow my daughter—"

"Now, Martha," Mr. White says. "We agreed that—"

"We agreed that you'd handle this, Bertram. And you're not doing a very good job." She pauses, mouth twitching.

I repeat that Arlene and I want to get married.

A solemn, earnest nod, then Mrs. White harrumphs. "Marriage! You mean a shotgun wedding." She spins, rushes out of the room.

Voices from the hallway. Arlene: "You've rattled him, Mommy. He'll have an attack." Mrs. White: "I simply don't care. I've had it with him."

Mr. White stares my way with a hangdog look, scurries to his desk, his mouth hanging open. As usual, I can smell alcohol on his breath, a sickly sweet scent.

"She'll come around, Sonny. It's been traumatic for all of us. Martha actually told me she'd love to have grandchildren. She's hoping for a boy and girl, a gentleman's family."

He spins his swivel chair, sits down with a grunt. "We'll just have to make the best of a bad situation. Arlene is always one to handle things properly. And what is it they say? Everything always works out fine in the end. For my part, I'm happy that you and Arlene are considering marriage."

He burps, asks if I'd like a cup of coffee, something to eat.

"No, thank you."

More voices from the hallway: "We've discussed this, Arlene. The answer is no, capital N, capital O."

I grind my teeth again.

Mr. White places his hands behind his head, stretches, says every dark cloud has a silver lining.

"Sir?"

"Well, that settles the amalgamation question, eh?"

"Sir?" I can't believe he's bringing this up now.

"When you and Arlene get married—she wants to get married—we'll be one big happy family. Have you thought about my offer?" He wheezes, bends over, catches his breath. "As I've said, I've been after your father for years. Sorry to hear he passed away. How are you getting by?"

Before I answer, he continues, "For years I've wanted him to join forces. Years! Build a new place by the ferry terminal, catch all the traffic, one stop for everything. You're in charge of Charlie's Auto now, Sonny. We'll team up, make twice the money. Your father kept putting me off. But you, you're a young man, you see the future, not fixed in the old ways. Whatta you say, young man? We'll make a bundle. Have a seat. Have a seat."

I say thanks, sit in the chair next to him. This is not at all what I expected. It's clear the Old Man is more concerned about amalgamating the garages than his daughter's pregnancy, and he's using her—them—as leverage.

"My father was opposed to teaming up with anyone, and I agree with him."

"We'll see about that. You'll do as your told. Hmph! Young kid living alone—"

"Is that a threat? I don't take kindly to threats."

"Call it what you will. I just don't think someone your age, living alone, should make business decisions. Someone older—"

"Johnny lives alone."

"Johnny's a grown man. Old enough to die for his country."

"So am I."

There's a pause, the corners of his mouth turn down, bottom lip pouts. I tell him I'll talk to my Aunt Vivian, but I doubt she'll change my mind, the family business goes back generations. He grunts, and I say, "Mr. White, I came here to talk about Arlene and me, asking for her hand, the baby's future, not about our garages."

His clean-shaven face tightens, and he moans, eyes half-closed. "The last time we spoke about this, and just now, you said it was a family business." He snaps his fingers. "If you marry my daughter, that's what we'll be, Sonny. Family! Why not have one business? Team up. Build a fine new garage. One big happy family!" He leans forward, red-faced, out of breath, waiting for me to agree.

From the hallway, Mrs. White shouting, "I don't care! Good night, Arlene!"

I shudder, inhale deeply. "It was my father's garage. It's been in the family—"

"Family's family. You can keep the name . . . Charlie's Auto. Is it the name that bothers you?"

"Changing your name is one thing, changing your business another."

"We'll make a lot of money." He wipes sweat from his forehead with the back of his hand.

"Mr. White, gas stations are a dying business."

He looks shaken, pulls back with a sour face, stares stonily into space. His tone turns harsh. "And just what do you plan to live on, eh?"

"The garage—my garage—and my father left some money." He knows exactly how we plan to live, with money from the will and help from the Whites. Arlene will move in with me after the baby's born. "Mr. White, your daughter and I love each other—"

"You can't live on love." He speaks calmly, patiently, his bright blue eyes blinking rapidly as he spins his swivel chair, his sagging shoulders back-on to me.

"I have the garage. I plan to run Charlie's Auto full-time in the spring, take care of your daughter and the baby." I come on strong, the way I'd said I would, an ear cocked for Arlene lurking in the hallway. "And my father's money should last a while."

Mr. White flinches as if from a blaze of light. He spins in his chair again, looks directly at me, sneers. "Good grief! Are you working *now*?"

"Part-time at the garage. I work Saturdays, some days after school, evenings if I don't have much homework. I have some savings, and my father left everything to me—"

"Harrumph! Savings!" His twisted expression reminds me of Mr. Andrews, the no-nonsense school bursar. He bends double, has a coughing fit without covering his mouth. "I hear you calling my daughter letters. L, Y, K, M. . . . What's that all about?"

I laugh, say that's a joke, a play on her nickname, Ar. "I call her Whitey sometimes."

"Nicknames, eh!" Again, a sneer.

I feel like a fool. I've come to talk about marrying his daughter and wind up explaining nicknames.

"And what does Arlene call you?"

"Oh, she calls me Sonny. McClutzky, sometimes, if she's mad at me."

He stifles a snicker. "Arlene says you'll get by looking after the baby, I doubt it."

"Well, we're hoping you and Mrs. White will help out. Until we get on our feet."

A sneeze, a sneer. He mumbles something.

"Sir?" I say, looking at his pin-straight hair.

His thin voice becomes a squeak. "You have money, you say. How much money?"

That throws me. I say enough, until I'm working full-time at the garage.

Arlene appears in the doorway. "Daddy, you okay?"

"Fine, darling. I'm fine."

"You sure?"

"Yes, sweetheart, I'm fine. Sonny and I are almost finished."

Arlene looks my way, smiles, and disappears.

"You're a Protestant?" Mr. White says out of the blue.

"Yes, sir. Well, sort of Protestant, my mother was Catholic. My father was Anglican, but he didn't practise. He was a preacher for a while in his younger days."

"Strike two," he mutters. "Do you attend Sunday church?"

"No, but I read the Bible."

"Like all good Protestants, eh!"

Thinking I'll impress him, I mention that my father was big on creating a just society, treating the downtrodden fairly. "He believed Jesus was the original Robin Hood, turning things upside down, looking out for the poor. Levelling the playing field, he called it."

"Who's on second?" Mr. White murmurs. His eyes blink rapidly as he drums his fingers on the desk.

Angry, I scramble to my feet, choke back the words *Fugg off*, recall Arlene saying he'd chop the hand off the guy who cashed the fake $20 bill. He bends double again, coughs. I wonder if he has lead poisoning.

He asks how I'm doing at school.

"I'm doing fine, graduating this spring."

He asks if I like sports. I say I like basketball, shoot hoops with my friend Quinn, who's pretty good, plays in the city league.

"What do you like besides sports?"

"Reading, mostly, when I'm not in the shop. I like being alone. And with Arlene, of course. I like *Robinson Crusoe*. And I like movies. Last week we saw *West Side Story*. It's about two young lovers—"

"I know what it's about," he says angrily. "How are you doing in mathematics?"

"Okay, I get B's most of the time."

"B's!" He swivels away from me again, arranges papers on his desk. I look at his sagging shoulders, the back of his wrinkled neck.

"Mrs. White and I think it best if you don't see our daughter for a while," he says emphatically, still back-on.

"Don't see her?" The words rock me.

His voice rises an octave. "Her mother and I are not happy with the situation, think it best you don't see her for a while."

"What?" It's a punch in the throat.

"Good night, young man," Mr. White says coldly, making a sort of grunt.

"But you don't understand, sir. Arlene and I—"

"I said good night." He swivels around, clutches the newspaper, rolls it, and glares, his cheeks flushing red.

"No! Good night? What do you mean? Doesn't Arlene get any say in this?"

"No, she does not."

"I get it." I'm ripping mad now. "This is about amalgamating the garages. This is Dr. Jekyll and Mr. Hyde."

"Dr. Jekyll and Mr. Hyde?" He twists his face, over-pronounces the words.

"Only it's Dr. Jekyll and Mr. White."

He jumps from his seat as if a spring has been sprung. "Listen, you little prick, you knocked up my daughter." Boiling mad now. "I'll have you before the law. Christ!" He flings the newspaper at me. "Get the hell out of my house. And never come back. You hear?"

Startled, I jump up, hear myself say, "Oh, fuck off! Who the hell do you think you are! You're a loser, Mr. White, a fucking loser. Chrissakes, you can't even run a fucking little gas station." I race from the house, head to the back of the garage, light a cigarette, and wait for Arlene.

Why do I smoke these things? I really don't enjoy smoking. . . . What would Charlie say about what just happened?

Light rain falls. I pull up my windbreaker collar as wind whines through the garage eaves. Where is she? Why is she taking so long? As I smoke, I hear Charlie laughing. "You put him in his place, Sonny. That old McCluskey left hook. That's my boy!"

I wish Arlene would hurry. I want her so badly, to whisper in my ear that everything's okay. The plan! I say to myself, the stupid plan. Why'd he get on with that old BS about teaming up?

About ten minutes pass. A wave of nausea, I feel like vomiting, think of Arlene obeying her parents, not taking a harder line. So unlike her. Her parents are a mess. It's all so messy. I miss her wit right now. What's taking her?

A sudden thunderclap. The rain falls harder. I move to the corner of the garage where there's more protection and smoke, listening to the dripping from the eaves. I love the rain. As a little boy I'd look out my bedroom window at the many shapes it made on the glass. At times I'd even talk to it. I loved lying in bed listening to its pitter-patter on the roof. Sometimes with the rain pelting the window, thunder rolling in the distance, I'd fall into a deep sleep.

I finish my cigarette, throw the butt away. I only enjoyed smoking with Charlie. I wait for Arlene, rain from the overhang dripping on me now and then, but I don't mind. I notice a small bird nestled under the eave, wonder how long he'll stay there, whisper a sweet nothing: "If you're going to eat, you'll have to get wet."

Arlene doesn't show. I walk to the car in the driving rain. At home I'm still dripping wet, need a towel, but head straight for the phone.

Mrs. White answers. "She's asleep."

"I'll come by tomorrow."

"Don't, I'll call the police." She hangs up.

63

NEXT DAY AFTER CLASS I FEEL SICK. I march down the long corridor and head home, thinking about the confrontation with the Whites, happy that I'd stood up to them. At least I'm not a mouse. At home, to lift my spirits, I take a flask of whiskey Charlie kept hidden in the cupboard. I walk and walk, now and then taking a swig. If anyone stops me, asks where I'm going, I'll say I'm going where my girl goes after school, Thelma's. As I walk, I wonder what we'll do now that Mr. and Mrs. White aren't in our corner. I wish Charlie were here, I need him now. I chug more whiskey, throat stinging. My heart pounds, head feels like it will explode.

When I reach Thelma's, I buy a Coke, sit down in a booth, slowly sip my drink. I feel nauseous, want to pray. I hear Charlie saying grace: *For what we are about to receive, make us truly grateful, Lord. And keep us ever mindful of those who have not.* I close my eyes. Pinpoints of light, like the time I was hit by a puck. I cross my arms on the table, rest my head, think of the long, lonely road I have to walk without Arlene. The nausea worsens, dry mouth. I breathe slowly, in-out, in-out, fall asleep.

The voice sounds distant. I lift my head groggily. The face looks oddly familiar. For a second I think it's Arlene, then Quinn, finally realize it's Esther-Marie. She's wearing her waitress uniform. She touches my shoulder. "You okay, Sonny? You don't look too good."

Shouldn't I be dating Esther-Marie? "You're so kind and caring."

"You've been drinking. You smell like a distillery."

"Will you go out with me?"

She laughs. "You're drunk, Sonny. You're going steady with Arlene."

I'm dizzy, sick to my stomach. "What?" For a second, I'm not sure where I am, think I'm dreaming, feel down and out.

"You okay?" Esther-Marie says. "You look really pale." She touches my forehead. "Think you have a fever."

Dazed, I say, "Just want my own garage. That too much to ask?" I look at Esther-Marie's short hair, thin lips, feel like I'm seeing her through the wrong end of a telescope. I retch, lean over, and throw up.

64

THE NEXT EVENING, ARLENE IS WAITING ON THE FRONT STEP. After telling Mr. White to fugg off, I thought she'd never speak to me again. I invite her in, go get her a Coke.

She's sitting on the couch when I return. "I'm so sorry," she whispers. I can hardly hear, so I sit by her. She puts her arms around me.

"Was he serious about staying away from you?"

She nods. "But my parents know that when push comes to shove, I'll shove hard. Sonny, I'm so sorry I left you alone with them. I was so worried about his health. I thought it best. . . . It was a terrible mistake. Please forgive me—"

"I told him to—"

"Yeah, I know."

"Your mother's really upset."

"Yeah. We talked. I told Mommy and Daddy we're going to continue seeing each other. I told them I love you and we're having our baby and getting married and that's that. We're getting married, at some point, aren't we, Sonny?"

I throw my arms around her and squeeze so hard she screams.

I pull back, say I'm sorry. "I didn't hurt the baby, did I?"

"You kidding? He's a McCluskey, through and through. All brawn, no brain." She laughs, whispers, "I can't stop thinking of you."

I kiss her on the lips.

She squeezes me. "I can't move in here yet. They'd disown me. But I'm coming over here every day. I'll cook you some really fine food—my specialty is lasagna—and I'll help out in the garage." She stops whispering. "I love you, Sonny McClutzky."

I throw my arms around her again, my life jacket for the raging sea I'm in.

"Can I keep helping in the garage? I wanna be a full partner, Sonny."

I hug her, kiss her. "Yes, on one condition. You can work in the office, the garage, but not that greasy pit. Promise? Dangerous down there, a car could fall and—"

"Okay, okay, I won't go down in your precious pit. I promise."

We kiss again, she whispers, "Thank God, Sonny, thought I lost you." We stretch out on the couch, hold each other tight, and fall asleep. It's hours before we wake, more rested than I've felt in a long time.

I make hot dogs, open Cokes, and we stuff ourselves. When we finish, she rubs her tummy, says she craves ice cream. "I think little junior likes ice cream."

I go to the freezer, call out vanilla or chocolate?

"Just a second. . . . He wants chocolate."

I bring back a tub of chocolate ice cream, a bowl, spoon.

"Oh, a gallon tub!" She beams. "Thirty-two scoops in a gallon tub."

"Fill yer boots," I say.

That night I write in my diary: As the other song says, *It's not over*. But little do I know there's bad news on the doorstep and our love is about to experience a trial by fire.

DECEMBER

V

We crucify ourselves between two thieves:
regret for yesterday and fear of tomorrow.

— Fulton Oursler

65

"THE COPS CAME BY YOUR HOUSE?"

"Harry said they took my hookah." Stuttering, irritable moaning.

"I warned you about hiding your pot. Time to bolt, Johnny. I'll drive you to the boat."

He says no, too far, 500 miles of rough road. "I'll take the bus or train, need a ticket."

"You kiddin' me? Cops will be all over those places. And it's the Bullet. Takes a whole day to cross the island. Bus isn't much better. You're out of time, Johnny. Cops on your tail, Doctor Club knockin' on the door." I say we'll leave at sunrise, gotta be back by early tomorrow., backlog of work at Charlie's Auto. Truth to tell, I'm worried to death about the missing money, anxious to confront Crenshaw. I need to stay put right now, but he's desperate.

He kicks the sofa, says he's changed his mind, won't go, he's not afraid anymore.

"Reality check, Johnny, the cops came by your house. Your uncle said they took your hookah. Get outta here. Get to the border."

"Maybe I can—"

"They're looking for Manfred too, and Jean-Luc, who want the rest of their money. You're in a deep hole, Johnny. It's now or never, man."

"You're right. Could wind up in the slammer." He says he'll go to Fort Dix, where he'll be safe. "Funny choice, huh? Vietnam or prison." He squints. "I guess a man's gotta do . . ."

"You don't have to go to Vietnam, Johnny."

He laughs. "I'm in Vietnam, man, in so many ways. I'm headed to where I already am."

He says he'll say goodbye to Celine, ask her to find a nice place in Montreal. He'll settle there after the war, become a Frenchy, start a new life. "Maybe I can learn to speak one language right."

I don't want to do this, but it's his hour of need. And he looks pathetic. I remember Charlie asking for help, Charlie always at my ear.

"Long drive, Johnny, one end of the island to the other. We'll leave at daybreak. It's December, bound to hit bad weather, Newfoundland, not New York."

He wipes his eyes, says he doesn't want to go to jail. "Gotta give up drugs. It's a nowhere trip."

I shake my head.

Nervous silence. "Daybreak it is," he says.

He wants to take his car. I insist we take my Vauxhall, a better car with studded tires.

"Your car's a target. Cops'll be looking for it. I'll come by suppertime, pick you up. I'll ask Quinn to help with the driving. You can both sleep at my place tonight."

I head back to the house, go to the safe, get a hundred bucks from the charity envelope, go to the print shop, and crank up Rosie, time to replenish the good money bag, drop some dough on the road. Turn on the press. Lift the paper. Place the plate, watch it pick up water and ink with each spin. In a few minutes, hundreds of images of our glorious queen. God save the queen!

I call Quinn, ask him to come.

"You nuts?" he says. "Lost your marbles? He's in trouble with the law. And I ain't haulin' my ass from here to Port aux Basques for Fabrella or nobody else, no-how. Forget it, man."

I beg him, but he won't budge. "Whyn't you ask Arlene? You can go parking in Terra Nova on the way back." He hangs up.

66

JUST AFTER DAYBREAK, I PUT A BOX OF EIGHT-TRACKS IN THE CAR, and we set out for Port aux Basques. Near the overpass, dark clouds gather, and it rains. A bad omen? We stop for coffee and muffins at a Golden Eagle station and Johnny brings up Mrs. Crenshaw. "Think she's crazy?"

"She's okay."

"Okay? Okay! That all you can say? Man, she's dynamite. You see the posing she did during 'Wild Thing' at the Pot Park concert? Don't know how I kept control of myself. Man, oh man! Foxy Florence! Gonna be a big draw for the Acid Test. Big, big draw. Could be all the rage—posing during hot numbers. Think we'll make *Ed Sullivan*."

"Forget it, he banned The Doors 'cause they wouldn't cut 'Girl we couldn't get much higher.'"

"Still, it's cutting edge, man. I'm on to a new thing *heah*. Foxy Florence, yeah!"

I remind him that she's married, he's married, and I plan to marry.

"Think she loves old Crenshaw?"

"Guess so."

"Don't think so, be shocked if she and old Crenshaw are rolling in the hay."

I say that's none of our business.

"Wouldn't mind wrestling her, think I could pin her? She's really strong. Pinned Harding twice."

I don't say anything.

"You know you only have to pin your opponent for two seconds, right?"

"Yeah, she's strong, Johnny. Could probably pin Mad Dog Vachon."

"Oh, she's strong, all right. She's a tiger."

I repeat that she's a married woman.

He pouts, jolts upright in his seat. "After the war, when I get the band going again, I'm hoping she'll join us on a cross-Canada tour. I phoned her before I left, asked if she'd be interested, said she could be an equal partner. Told me she'd think about it. I'm sure she just needs a little nudge. She has such a sexy voice, don'tcha think? Sultry."

"She has a deep voice."

"Deep? You kiddin' me? Deep? I'll say. Could probably teach her a few tunes. She's good-looking, huh? Could be a movie star. Think she'll join the tour? I mean, you know, pose during the really hot numbers. What a turn-on! She's hot stuff, man, we'd sell out every gig."

"Doubt Crenshaw'll want his wife travelling across the country posing with a rock band."

"You never know," he says. "You never know what lurks in the shadows, my friend. They don't strike me as a happy couple."

"They're very happy."

"Course, there's Jean-Luc, zee beeg Frenchy." He drums his fingers on the table, shakes his head. "Yip, think I'd give her a good go on the old wrestling mat. All-in wrestling."

I repeat that they're a happy couple.

"Think you could pin her? Think ol' Crenshaw has?"

I don't answer. He waves a hand in exasperation, says he'd call her again when he gets to the States. "I've written her a letter, in my backpack, no time to drop it off, mind bringing it to her?"

I say sure, happy to.

"You know, she's a really kind person. She loaned me bread to buy a new amp, over a hundred bucks. Very kind. I mean, a hundred bucks, that's a lotta dough, man. She's got a heart of gold." He drums his fingers again. "And a body of steel."

Back in the car we smoke cigarettes, chat, and listen to music all the way to Gander, where we stop for lunch at a Chinese restaurant called The Asian Cafe. Johnny goes inside to get a table; I jog to a drugstore to drop some dough.

When I get back, Johnny's talking to the owner, Mr. Fang.

"Ahh, welcome." Mr. Fang shakes my hand vigorously. Chubby face, a funny-looking lump on his forehead. "Good buffet today. Cheap. Follow me." He tugs my arm, motions toward the buffet table, points to the steaming pans of food. "Specialty. Asian Cafe buffet!" He pats my back, smiles. The restaurant is a small room with crowded tables. We fill our plates, sit by a window, and wolf down our food. When it's time to pay, I decide to drop a fake twenty. Before ringing in our order, Mr. Fang takes out a pair of thick-lensed glasses, puts them on, and holds my twenty-dollar bill up to the light. This sinks my very soul within me, as Crusoe would say.

"A good bill," he says, eyes bulging. "Once in while, get a bad one." He examines my twenty more closely. "Very good. This is fine. Good watermark. Very good."

I'm in a sweat, think I've passed him a bad bill, but mistakenly given him a clean one from the drugstore. Fang says he hasn't seen many bad bills lately, takes a twenty from the cash register, shows a matching watermark.

My blood jumps. I tell him we have to catch the next boat at Port aux Basques. I'm a bundle of nerves, can't wait to bolt, but ask when he's last had a bad bill. He screws up his face as if smelling something foul. "No bad bills lately. Once, maybe twice since I open. I always check. Better safe than sorry." He hands me change and a discount coupon for our next meal. Johnny says it was a great buffet, and we hightail it out of there.

As we drive, I mention the draft dodgers in Montreal. "Why don't you chuck in the towel? Join 'em, become a resister. Been thinking about them the last while, and it's rocked me some, I gotta say. I admire them."

"You'd be a draft dodger? Helluva thing."

"Dunno. Guess you'd have to be in their shoes. Just thinking . . . about freedom, I guess."

"And he's fighting for Canada, he's fighting for France," he sings, strumming an imaginary guitar. "He's fighting for the USA." He rolls down his window, lights a joint, and listens to music before nodding off.

67

WE PASS SNOWY FIELDS, DISTANT, DIMLY LIT HOUSES. I'm anxious about Arlene and me, want to stop, get pen and paper, write down the pros and cons of making it with her. CON: She'll drop me if I tell her about Rosie. I'm a criminal. PRO: We're having a child. We should stay together. Work it out, somehow. PRO: Go my own way. Talk Arlene into joining me after the baby is born. A new town, new life. Work for Uncle Ches, maybe. She's not crazy about her home life. Get away from her crazy parents. CON: What about the house? Charlie's Auto? The print shop? PRO: Get rid of everything, start fresh. CON . . .

It gets twisted in my head. I decide to figure it out later on the back of a napkin.

The Trans-Canada Highway is clear, a few snowy patches. As we near Deer Lake, there's a beautiful orange-juice sunset, and Johnny wakes but dozes off again. He snores just as it starts snowing hard. I rouse him, ask if he'll stay awake, keep an eye out for moose, but it's useless, he's out for the count. I turn on the radio, CBC.

"We're in for some west coast weather," the announcer says. "Freezing rain for Port aux Basques, a wind warning for the Wreckhouse area." He goes on about Wreckhouse being the windiest place on earth before giving the moose report: "There's a moose a-loose in the Curling area. Drive carefully! Don't wanna hit that big fella." Next, a commentary on draft dodgers in Canada. I look at Johnny, listen intently, keep a keen eye on the road. I want to stop to eat, decide I'll get to the boat with time to spare, grab a sandwich there.

We drive west past endless white land. The snow gets thicker, and I pray we won't get caught in a storm. Suddenly, I tense, the car swerving on black ice, veering from one side of the road to the other, wind whipping across the windshield.

Johnny snaps awake. "The hell's—?"

"Black ice!"

I grip the steering wheel, hold my breath, helpless as the car comes to a stop in a snowbank.

"You okay?"

"Yeah." Johnny moans.

I put the car in neutral.

We get out and push through blinding drifts of snow till we free the front wheels. Johnny scrapes the snow and ice from the back window with his bare hands. We stare at each other, stunned.

"Go, go," I tease. "Go, Johnny, go." He flinches, gives me the finger. He's freezing, cheeks and the tip of his nose raw.

We climb back inside. Johnny says, "Freezin' out *theah*. Dunno what's worse, drivin' through a snowstorm in Newfoundland or crawlin' around Vietnam."

I look up. No separation between sky and road, just a blank movie screen. I run the defroster for a few minutes before inching onto the highway.

Near Corner Brook we stop at an Esso station for coffee. The owner, an abrupt, muscular man with the deepest eye sockets I've ever seen, warns of heavy snow. "You'll make the ferry okay, slow down going through Wreckhouse!"

On the road again, I clutch the steering wheel and lean forward, looking past the wipers at millions of snowflakes spinning toward us. Through the snow, I glimpse a ski hill. Oh, to be sliding now, then going for hot chocolate.

Johnny nods, dozes off. I remember when he broke down crying, imagine him crawling around the Vietnamese jungle. I fear for him, what he has to face, and I don't want to let him go. It dawns on me that I should tell him who he really is, change his mind about going to Fort Dix, keep him safe. But I can't bring myself to do it.

When he wakes, he plays music, fingers drumming the dash, head bobbing, driving me crazy. I stare straight ahead, turn my thoughts to Arlene. In my mind's eye I picture her in that cute little flapper hat, want her to look like that forever, wonder if we'll have a boy or a girl.

We arrive at the ferry terminal, hug, and say goodbye. I open my wallet, take out five good twenties, and Johnny blushes. "For you," I say.

"Wow, man! You're an angel. Just like Charlie. Thanks so much." He chokes up, says he'll pay it back, pay everything back, once the band's together again after the war. "Once we make the big time. And we will, Sonny."

"Forget it. Good luck."

He hugs me, says, "You think I'm doing the right thing, Sonny? Going to war for Uncle Sam. Am I a coward if I don't go? I mean, the old man—"

Tough choice. I think of the Doctor Club. "You're torn, Johnny, between your heart and head. Glad I'm not in your shoes."

"You're such a good friend, Sonny. Charlie, too. Don't know what I'd do without you."

I want to blurt out that we're brothers but can't. Want to see his reaction, hear what he says, know how he feels. But it's something I can't bring myself to do.

"You know, Arlene couldn't ask for a better guy." He chokes up again, says he almost forgot, withdraws an envelope from his backpack. "For crazy Mrs. Crenshaw? Thanks."

The letter piques my curiosity, but I don't say anything, it's none of my business.

We say goodbye again, he thanks me for the dough. "I'll write to you from the jungle."

For a second, a little part of me wants to go with him, begin a new life, forget all my mistakes, lies, deceptions, tell him the truth about everything, spend time with my own blood. But I want to get back to Arlene as fast as I can. And there's that little matter of missing money.

I get in the car and head out the highway, where I book a motel room for the night. At the restaurant I order a hot turkey sandwich and coffee. As I eat, I write down the pros and cons of staying with Arlene. It's not difficult this time. I don't want to have the life that Charlie had, deceiving Lucy, and decide I'll tell the truth about everything, take my chances. One thing's for sure, I'll find out how strong our love is.

Next day, for 500 miles Arlene is all I think about, except for now and then when I stop to drop some dough.

68

I ARRIVE HOME BUSHED, BUY TWO A&W BURGERS AND FRIES, GORGE MYSELF, and sleep the sleep of the dead. I have a terrible dream. Mrs. Crenshaw keeps trying to pull my face off. "Ugly mask. Take it off," she keeps saying. "You're a phony. Phony mask." I tell her that it isn't a mask, it's my real face, when Mr. Fang from The Asian Cafe appears, shouting, "Nooo, it's counterfeit. Take it off, take it off now." Quinn pops on the scene, laughing, "We gotcha, McCluskey. Gotcher number, man. Phony baloney!"

Next day around noon, Arlene comes by. We snack and go to the garage. I've decided this is the day I'll show her the pit, tell her we'll have no secrets from now on.

I'm impressed with her work. She really knows engine repairs. Crenshaw's dropped off his motorcycle, and she knows instantly that the problem is an uncharged battery and a poorly lubricated chain.

"Chains should be well-lubricated and pulled to proper tension. Should sag between three-quarters and one and a quarter inches between sprockets. Crenshaw's not riding his bike enough. Ride it twenty miles a week or charge it after each run."

In jig time the engine's revving. I give her the thumbs-up. She grins, sticks out her tongue.

Later, she removes a headlight while I go to the office to get a work order form. When I come back, I tell her I have a surprise, there's something I'd like to show her. I open the steel door, turn on the light. The place stinks of ink. I watch Arlene closely as she begins examining Rosie.

She walks past the paper cutter, the light table, toward the photography room. "Sonny, what is all this?" Her lips quiver, she looks as if she'll burst into tears.

"A family secret I want you to know about. It's been the family business for generations."

She laughs. Her voice catches. "Family secret?" She lets out a choking moan. "Some kind of printing business?"

"Yes, we've been helping the poor for generations. Charlie was a Robin Hood, his father too. Goes way back."

She walks around Rosie, picks up a sheet of twenties. "The money-printing business?" She walks toward the darkroom, drops the sheet of twenties on the floor.

"I can explain—"

"Oh my, my!"

"Arlene—"

"*Counterfeiting*?" Tears of shock. She starts shaking. "You're a *counterfeiter*?" Her voice distant.

"Arlene, I can explain . . ."

Stony silence, her face rigid. She sinks to the floor.

"There's a simple explanation, Arlene." But I know there isn't, not for her. Explaining is a dead end.

"Good God, Sonny, you're using *counterfeit*? How long's this been going on?" Her voice is hoarse, cracked, her face distorted, pale, eyes lively as a trapped mouse.

"Well, not very long," I lie. "Just use it to help the poor, level the playing field a bit, you know. The way Charlie used to. . . . It's not for me, for charity and Charlie—"

"Oh my God!" Her lips quiver again. She points a jittery finger at the counterfeit, lets out a deep sigh.

I realize I've made a terrible mistake, ask her to promise she'll keep it secret.

"Promise? Promise! Promise you . . ." She closes her eyes as if in pain, stands up, falls back, and leans on Rosie. "Cripes! Why didn't you just hijack a Brinks truck? Be a lot less hassle." A panicky flutter as she stares at the printer. Her face goes white again, looks like she might faint. She walks away, stumbles, and I move to catch her. Her hand shoots straight up. "No! No, please don't touch me. *Puh-leeze*!" Crestfallen, she walks away.

I stand there for a long time. An hour? Two? I can't say. Shipwrecked again, I feel a heaviness that could last forever. Hammering heartbeat and the vertigo I had at Thelma's. I switch off the light, go back upstairs, walk around the shop in a daze, rearranging tools. I do this for some time. An hour? Two hours? Three? Until I throw up. After cleaning up the vomit, I go back to the house. Around two in the morning, I take a shower. Will Arlene report me to the cops? Will she tell her parents? Will she ever see me again? I lie in bed, eyes closed, breathing deeply, praying the nausea will go away. Eventually it does, but I don't sleep a wink all night.

69

IT'S UNCOMFORTABLE SITTING IN THE BACK PEW WEARING ONE OF CHARLIE'S old suits, baggy pants, coat hanging slack, trying to straighten his oversized necktie. The church is small, simple. A huge wooden Cross behind the pulpit, a table nearby with bread and wine. Off to the side, a small organ, the coffin with flowers on top in the aisle.

In the front pew, someone is standing, beckoning Mr. Russell, who heads that way. They chat, and he points in my direction, waving frantically. I look around. Me? Russell walks to the back and asks me to sit next to Mrs. Crenshaw. An usher with sunken eyes and bushy eyebrows humps ahead of me, pointing with a silver cane to the front pew where Mrs. Crenshaw sits alone, dabbing her eyes with a handkerchief. I slide in next to her, kiss her cheek, say I'm sorry. She nods, reaches in her purse for a pill.

The whole school is at the funeral. Mrs. Crenshaw has insisted on a service at the Baptist Church. The place is packed. I notice quite a few people Charlie had helped over the years, Robin Hood people, people Mr. Crenshaw knew too. The Cove is a tiny place.

"I want you to sit here," she says. "Charlie and Vlad were partners, like family." I smell liquor on her breath. "Family should sit up front."

She's dyed her hair lighter than usual. Even her eyebrows seem lighter. She wears a black dress, hair drawn tight in a bun, first time I've seen it like that. There's that sickly stench of perfume. She's holding her rabbit hat, twisting it as she leans toward me, whispering, "I heard from Johnny. Called me before he left town, asked if I'd like to join his band on a cross-Canada tour after the war." I remember Johnny's letter. "The band wants me to pose for a few numbers. *Prendre une pose*, Jean-Luc calls it. I'd rather pose for 'Wild Thing' than *The Manifesto*, that's for sure. Vlad used to have me pose while he read.

Bo-ring!" She tenses, seems to flex her muscles. "Johnny offered me an equal partnership." She hiccups, starts crying, little squeaks. "I've never had an equal partnership in anything in my life, not even with Vlad." Her shoulders jump as she squeaks. Quick little jerks. "I've always had a secret yen for the stage, you know. Might be my big chance." She turns toward the coffin, breaks down crying again, her eye makeup running. I whisper that everything will be fine. She nods her head, mutters, "No, it won't."

I look at the coffin and think of my hand in Crenshaw's death, the Doctor Club, Johnny.

I wasn't in class when it happened, the day I wanted to ask about the missing money. Ryan and Gilchrist filled me in.

Ryan: "He came to class with a big box and started packing his things. He said it was his last class, he'd been fired. We were all in shock. He looked around as if searching for someone, said we'd know why soon enough, unless *the rat* had already told us."

Gilchrist: "Nobody said a word. We just sat there watching him packing up. It was sad."

Ryan: "Someone said later that Mr. Russell found dope in his desk."

Gilchrist: "Before leaving, he started working up a sweat ranting about the have-nots."

Ryan: "Then his hand went to his chest, and he let out an almighty groan. It was scary, loudest sound I've ever heard. Frightened the life outta Marjorie Kean."

Gilchrist: "Then he leaned on his desk and asked if someone would get him a glass of water. Tracey raced to the sink, but it was too late. He collapsed."

Ryan: "Hardy ran to the principal's office, and Tracey went to first aid for Mr. Barnes, who was in our classroom in a jiffy. Barnes called Crenshaw's name a few times—James, James—then checked his pulse. When there was no answer, he started pushing hard and fast on Crenshaw's chest and doing mouth-to-mouth. Now and then he'd cock his head and listen while feeling Crenshaw's chest. I don't know much about hearts attacks, but after a while I knew he was gone."

Gilchrist: "Barnes stood up; I could see his lips were bruised. He started shaking, and someone called out, "Oh my God, is he dead?' And suddenly everyone was crying."

Ryan: "Hardy showed up with Russell, who told us class was dismissed, we could go home. Some of us wanted to stay in case old Crenshaw came to and needed something, but Russell said he'd take care of everything, please go home."

For days it was all anyone talked about. "It'll be horrible not having Old Crenshaw around," Ryan kept saying. "Never a dull moment in his classes."

"Unlike Graham," Gilchrist said and reminded us that Crenshaw always donated money to the poor.

Esther-Marie couldn't stop crying. "We'll miss seeing him scooting around town on his Honda," she said. "Arlene says his bike is still at her garage."

I wanted to say I won't miss him threatening Johnny and me, working with the Doctor Club. But I just flashed my fake grin and agreed.

We wait forever for the minister. He finally appears wearing a large-sleeved, black gown. The service is long and sad with too much singing and continual bellowing of *Amens* and *Hallelujahs*. And the smell of candle wax is constant. Mrs. Crenshaw is pale, tearful throughout, which forces my tears to well up. At one point she begins whimpering. I want to put my arm around her but don't.

The minister delivers a sermon about family, loved ones, and community. *How sad a day it is, but how beautiful too, to be here celebrating the life of Vladimir James Crenshaw, who did so much for our town.*

My thoughts turn to Arlene, but I'm too tired to think. I drift off till the minister's voice jolts me awake. He's shouting about the last days, how we'll all be raised up like Lazarus. I think of my part in Charlie's burial, and a wave of loss washes over me.

When the minister finishes, Ryan makes a brief speech about how kind Mr. Crenshaw was, how much he cared about the poor, how clear he was about why Newfoundland was a have-not province. "Free market?" Ryan shakes a fist and mimics old Crenshaw. "Free kiss-my-ass market!" The students laugh and shout *Amen*! *Hallelujah*! Mrs. Crenshaw starts whimpering again. Someone yells, "But he wasn't one to complain." Ryan continues his mimicry: "Now, at the risk of offending some of your bourgeois values . . . are you listening, class? *Class*! Now, that's the little word the rich want you to forget." More laughter, *hallelujahs*. Ryan looks at Mrs. Crenshaw. "Your husband knew the value of the little things: helping with the wrestling team, managing the equipment, driving the van to tournaments."

Someone shouts, "Paying for lunch."

Hallelujah! *Amen*!

"Mr. Crenshaw wanted us to create a just society," Ryan says. "He taught that class struggle is of *our own making* and it's *our responsibility* to change. As he said time and again, things don't have to be the way they are. We'll miss him and be forever in his debt."

More *amens*, loud applause.

Mrs. Crenshaw leans my way, mutters, "*Pfft*! He'll be forever in my debt, I can tell you that."

After the graveyard ceremony, Mrs. Crenshaw invites me back to her house for a little celebration of Vlad's life. "Just the two of us," she says as Quinn approaches. I don't really want to go.

Quinn pulls me aside, says we need to talk. "Meet me at Thelma's at noon. Mounties came by my place, asked a ton of questions about Johnny."

I tell him I feel really bad about Crenshaw's death.

"The Crenshaws are weirdos," he says. "Johnny better make a move. Ball's in his court."

"He split," I say. I can't believe he's not upset about Crenshaw's death.

"I'm not sticking my neck out for him or anyone else. His uncle said they raided the house. I think he's dealing drugs. They took his hookah. Can you believe that, Sonny? Johnny? A pusher?"

I said I could. "He probably needed the money. And people do a lot worse for a lot less."

70

"I CAN'T STAY VERY LONG, MRS. CRENSHAW."

She smiles in her fake way, takes my coat, says sit in the living room, her tone surprisingly harsh. She looks the way she did at the concert, high, maybe. She doesn't seem to be upset. I tell her I'm so sorry for her troubles.

"*Pfft*! Been waiting for his heart attack for years. Would you like a drink?" she asks, doesn't wait for a response. "Of course you would. You'll have a whiskey, *neat*."

I don't know what neat means. "I'd love a Coke."

"You'll have something a little stronger than *that*. Times like this I'm partial to mescaline." She takes a yellowish green pill from her coat pocket, pops it into her mouth, and swallows. "You look like a pretty big boy to me. Shot of whiskey, it is. For Vladdy. Bad . . . bad Vlad!"

I say I don't drink alcohol, but she's at the liquor cabinet pouring drinks, calling out, "What'd you think of the church service?"

"Very solemn."

"Solemn, schmolemn." She scowls, waltzes over with two tulip-shaped glasses, and passes me one. The mixture of liquor and perfume makes me queasy.

"I always drink it neat. Shame to poison good whiskey with mix." Her wild eyes scare me. Mescaline? She clinks my glass. "Here's to Vlad!" She gulps. "What do you think of Johnny Fabrella?"

"He's a nice guy," I say. "Very talented."

"*Pfft*! Talented, schmalented. He's a smooth operator, I'll give him that. I think he has the hots for me. Has he ever said anything about me? You know, gossiped."

I say no, he's not that kind of guy. "He's a married man, Mrs. Crenshaw."

"Not that kind of guy. Bullshit! He's as horny as a dog with two dicks. Had to tie him down at the Pot Park Concert."

She sits next to me and says in a sad voice, "It's me has the gambling problem, not Vlad. He had the drug problem. Only it isn't just gambling. Other problems too . . . money. Debt! Why he needed your help." She flushes red.

I almost choke on my drink. "You . . . you know about that? Mr. Crenshaw told you about the money I loaned him?"

"My dear young man, I know everything there is to know about Jimmy Crenshaw, including his drugs—legal and illegal. Unfortunately, he knew nothing about me." She pauses, her shoulders jump, sharp spasms.

I feel bad for her, ask if she'd like a glass of water.

"Who's gonna pay for my makeup and costumes now?" It looks like she's holding back tears.

I look at the door, tell her I have to leave, I have a test tomorrow.

"I needed money, Jean-Luc needed money, he needed money . . . for *the party*. . . . Let's have a party!" She throws her hands in the air.

She grabs her purse, pulls out an envelope. "Want to know how desperate he was, read that." She drops the envelope in my lap. I open it and read:

Dear Madame Crenshaw:

As head of the Bolshevik Party of Moscow I write to express my sincere condolences on the recent passing of your husband, Comrade Vladimir J. Crenshaw. We appreciate the noble work your late husband did on behalf of the Newfoundland Communist Party (NCP). Unfortunately, it is with deep regret that I must inform you that the Party will no longer pay Mr. Crenshaw's annual stipend of 2010 rubles (2000 $Cdn).

Once again, please accept our sincere condolences on your husband's passing.

Kind regards,

Comrade Viktor Popov Kusnetzov

"Comrade Viktor Popov Who Bit Your Cock Off!" Mrs. Crenshaw says sarcastically. "*Pfft*! Prick! Cutting us off like that." She twirls her index finger. "*Let's have a party*."

I'm frightened, want to bolt. What a mess she's in. What a mess I'm in.

She asks if I want another drink and, before I can answer, if I like drugs.

"I don't do drugs."

"*Pfft*! Everyone does drugs."

Her voice catches as she says, "Some little bastard planted that dope in Vladdy's desk. He'd never bring dope to school. Whiskey, but not dope. Any idea who'd do that?"

"No, Mrs. Crenshaw, I don't do dope." I try to think of another excuse to leave.

"*Pfft*! Everyone at the Trades School does dope. Keep your ear to the ground at school. There's a reward in it for you. Doctor Club means to find who did it."

"I'll let you know if I hear anything. Mrs. Crenshaw, I really have to go and study." I get up to leave.

"Please stay a few more minutes. . . . So sad to die like that." She sniffles. "You like dancing?" She ambles to the stereo and plays "Release Me." She turns, stretches her hands out. "Dance?"

I sit frozen on the couch. I'm really uptight about the Doctor Club finding out who planted the dope in Crenshaw's desk and startled about her gambling problem and Mr. Crenshaw's drug problem.

"To live a lie would be a sin . . ." she sings, waltzes my way, and yanks me off the couch, Dean Martin's voice filling the room:

Her lips, they're warm while yours are cold
Release me and darling let me go.

We dance. The light from the window casts long shadows on the floor as we prance about. It's kind of eerie. And I'm choking on her cheap perfume. I do my best to follow her awkward steps. Now and then she sways back and forth, pulling me with her, squeezing so hard I almost cry out. When the song ends, she just stands there holding me tight, sobbing.

"I owe Jean-Luc money too. . . . Christ, Vlad! He says he'll break my fingers, one by one." More sobbing. I don't know what to say or do. She has such a grip on me I'd need a crowbar to pry myself loose.

"You okay, Mrs. Crenshaw?" No answer. Between sobs she whispers something in my ear, but I can't make out what it is. Sounds like she wants money. Then she sways back and forth, loses her balance, and we both topple to the floor. She leans back, mascara running, lips trembling, and squeezes my arm. "You have nice muscle." Her ferrety eyes are wide open. I look away, feel like I'm in a Hitchcock movie.

"My, but you are *strong*." She squeezes my arm again. "Such muscle!"

I say it's from working at the garage. I consider grabbing my coat and leaving but don't want to be rude.

"You should come out for my wrestling team." She moves her mouth close to my ear. "I need more money." She wrenches my arm and twists it, putting pressure on my shoulder. It feels like an electric shock.

"Ow! You're hurting me."

"*Pfft*! That's called *The Armbar*." She flips both of us upward so that we're sitting, she behind me. Then she grabs my elbow, pulls it up and backward toward her, bends my wrist, and forces the open palm of my hand into her chest. My wrist hurts so much I scream.

"That's called *Barely Legal*. When can you get more cash?"

I beg her to let go. "Please, Mrs. Crenshaw. Please!"

"You think on that while I get out of these widow's weeds." She stands up, says, "You're a lot stronger than Vladdy. He was a wimp when it came to the *Barely Legal* hold."

I hobble to the couch, feel like I've been in a car crash. I look at the door, consider leaving again. My hand aches so much I'm sure it'll fall off. There's no fooling myself, she's dead serious about the money. The words of the ledger come back to me: *No young man should be left alone with her. She has a bolt loose.*

When she returns, I gasp. She's in her bodybuilding outfit, flings the missing money bag at my feet, and begins posing. "Don't know how much is there. Count it!"

I stare at the letter "G" on the burlap bag, open it, and count out $54 and change. I almost swallow my Adam's apple. "Mrs. Crenshaw, you . . . where's the rest of the money?"

"*Pfft*!" She shrugs, continues posing.

"You spent almost three thousand dollars? That was money my father left for me," I cry. "I—"

She shushes me. "Vlad said Charlie had loads of dough. He has his ways of getting it, Vlad said. His *secret* ways."

"What do you mean his secret ways, Mrs. Crenshaw? We run a small garage, some years we barely make ends meet."

"Well, you'd better find out *his ways*," she says hastily. "I need money, you hear me? And if you think my *Barely Legal* hold is painful, I can show you my *Bite the Dragon* move. That's *not* legal. Pressure's all on the neck and spine. A wrestler from Saskatchewan died from it last year."

"Money? You need money? How . . . how much, Mrs. Crenshaw?"

She kicks the burlap bag. “Fill that thing up again. That’ll do for a while.”

I gag, sit farther back on the couch. “Mrs. Crenshaw, I don’t have that kind of money, believe me—”

“Listen, you little grease monkey . . .” She moves toward me. “Christ, I mean business here . . . Vlad said Charlie has tons of dough. Get it!” she hisses. “Go find it. You hear me? You know the chokehold? Jean-Luc told me to give you a taste of coming attractions if you don’t cough up the money. Hope I don’t have to use my chokehold—”

“I’ll look tonight,” I say. “I’ll try and find the money.”

“Good boy!” she says, puckers her lips, and blows a kiss.

She walks to the closet, removes my coat, and flings it at me. “Have the money by Thursday,” she says. “I need to be in Saint Pierre Friday night to see Jean-Luc.”

“I’ll try,” I say, and leave, cradling my wrist, grateful that Mr. Crenshaw had only taken $200 of the fake money. That’s all I need, crazy Mrs. Crenshaw dropping my counterfeit dough all over town.

71

I'M AT THELMA'S WITH QUINN.

"Mounties asked a ton of questions," he says. "I told them everything I knew. Everything. Like I said, wasn't sticking my neck out for Johnny Fabrella or anyone else. He's a pusher, isn't he?"

"Dunno." My breath quickens. The next thing he says floors me.

"I took my father's advice about the incident at the bank."

"Incident at the bank? Father's advice? What incident?" My heart skips a beat.

"Mother says she doesn't know where the counterfeit came from, thinks it might've been in your deposit bag, but doesn't wanna make a fuss. Father said to ignore her, she's too emotional, if the Mounties questioned me to tell the truth, so I did."

"You told the Mounties I cashed counterfeit at the bank?" Charlie was right, you can't trust a cop's son.

"Not exactly. I said my mother received a counterfeit hundred-dollar bill, thought it might've come from you."

"Same thing, Quinn."

"Where the hell'd you get a counterfeit bill, McCluskey?"

"Who knows? Lotsa business at the garage lately. Counterfeit cashed at White's Esso a while back."

"I'm quitting the band," he says as we walk outside. "It won't work without Johnny. And there's too much shit goin' on. And too much work. Gonna focus on basketball."

"I know how you can stay in the band and do half the work," I say.

"How?"

"Chop off a hand."

He gives me a weird look. “I’m quitting.”

“Me too, garage is a full-time job now.”

“You heard from Johnny?” he asks.

I don’t answer, don’t look at him. “Don’t mention anything else about me to the cops. This time I will break your arm.”

He points a finger at me, shakes it. “Just try it.”

I clench my fist. Pressure builds inside my chest until it feels like I can’t breathe, and then pain shoots through my wrist as my fist hits his jawbone. Did I break a finger? His eyes water as he clutches his face. I don’t care. I throw another punch, catch his cheek. My arm feels like it’s ripping from my shoulder.

I shove him. He stumbles back, still holding his face, blood oozing between his fingers.

“Screw you, McCluskey!” I can barely make out the words from behind his hand. He turns and bolts.

I stand there, silent, alone.

72

LATE THAT NIGHT, THE PHONE RINGS.

"I'm running the show from now on."

He doesn't say who it is, but the accent is French. Jean-Luc.

"Doctor Club wants the rest of Johnny's money. Cough it up by next week."

Silence.

"Clear?"

"Yes."

"There'll be no more warnings. *Comprendez*?"

Click.

At timed intervals the phone rings throughout the night. I don't pick up, cover my ears with the pillow to drown it out, but I can still hear it cutting through the silence.

73

SHE COMES TO THE HOUSE AROUND SEVEN IN THE MORNING AND POUNDS on the door. I let her in; she says she'll stay with me, but there are three conditions. One: Give up making counterfeit immediately. Get rid of Rosie and never make another bad bill. I say okay. It's part of my overall plan anyway, just a matter of when. Two: I want you to convert to Catholicism. This would never have happened if you were going to Mass every Sunday. Three: Talk to Father McCarthy about turning myself in to the police. "That's a sensible first step," she says. "He'll give you good advice."

"Father Almighty McCarthy!"

"Father McCarthy's a fine man, he'll know what to do." She says I'm in one helluva predicament, it won't hurt to talk to someone besides her. "Unless you want to go straight to the police."

The police are out of the question, and I tell her so. She says she can't live with a criminal, makes me promise to talk to Father McCarthy. "You don't have to see him face to face, you can talk to him in the confessional, in the dark. He won't know it's you."

I have no intention of giving up Rosie right away, Johnny could be back tomorrow looking for more money. And I'm being threatened by Mrs. Crenshaw and Jean-Luc. I might have to skip town too. But the baby? I'm between a rock and a hard place, need to buy time, think things through. And I need to keep her quiet, so I agree to go.

"Good! I'll go too. Confession is every Saturday evening at the church. You'll feel a lot lighter after you've confessed, I always do. Just tell the priest the truth."

She gives me her catechism to review what I need to say in the confession box and says my mother would be proud of me.

I kneel in the darkness, clenched hands resting on the shelf below the grille. A small wooden door slides open. I lean toward it and say, "Bless me, Father, for I have sinned . . . I've committed a terrible sin, Father."

"That's fine, my son," a low voice whispers, "we're all prodigals. Continue."

"Are you Father McCarthy?"

"Yes."

From the shadows I barely make out his raw face, a few wisps of hair on a bald head. I say I'm nervous, I suffer from anxiety.

"We all have weaknesses."

I confess several invented sins—Arlene advised to say I had a lot of bad thoughts—and then ask about the seal of the confessional.

He says, "Don't you know that? Priests won't reveal what they hear during confession, even under threat of their own death or that of others. If a priest breaks the secrecy of the confessional, he's automatically excommunicated from the Church. Anything you confess will be forever sealed."

I take a deep breath and say that I'm a thief, I steal money.

"You must make every effort to return what you've stolen. You can repay the money anonymously, over time, but you must make reparations—"

"But you don't understand, Father. I don't steal money. I make money. I'm a counterfeiter. That's how I steal. But I'm a good thief, like Robin Hood. I have a job, give the money to the poor, and—"

"A counterfeiter! You must stop doing that. Counterfeiting is stealing, it's a grave sin, and a serious crime with a severe penalty. You could go to jail for a long time."

"Should I turn myself in to the police?"

"That'd be a good start. How long have you been counterfeiting?"

I say about a year, don't mention Charlie did it all his life, it's not Charlie's confession.

"Have you stolen . . . I mean, made much counterfeit money?"

That's easy because of my records. "Five thousand dollars," I say. "And I've used around a thousand, charities mostly, another thousand for my brother, who's in trouble."

A long silence.

"Aren't you upset, Father?"

"No. This is my job. Forgiving sins. No different than laying bricks or driving a truck. No, I'm not upset. Concerned . . . for you."

I say that makes me feel better than I've felt in a long time.

"Good. That means you have a conscience. Anyone else know of this?"

"Just my girlfriend, she wants me to go to the police. She says they'll go easier on me if I turn myself in."

"Sensible girl. Yes, go to the police, tell them what you've been up to. They'll take it from there. I'm sure the court will go easy on you if you turn yourself in." He pauses, asks if I have any other sins to confess, questions.

I want to ask why a Protestant can't be buried in a Catholic graveyard but decide I'd better not. "No questions, Father."

"Make an Act of Contrition and pray the rosary for your penance."

I'm stunned. It seems an awfully small penalty for stealing so much money. I muddle through the Act of Contrition, say thanks. As I'm leaving, he says, "Don't be too hard on yourself. You sound like a young man. Things will work out. You have your whole life ahead of you."

I thank him again, recall what Charlie wrote in the ledger about the McCluskeys being hard on themselves—a small piece of eternity again, light as a butterfly. Before leaving, I decide to take advantage of the seal of the confessional and ask about something that's been bugging me since Charlie died.

"Father, one other question. If a man takes his own life, instead of dying a painful death in a lonely hospital, is that a sin?"

"The Church honours life from cradle to grave."

"What if someone helps him? The man dying in the hospital. I mean, what if someone buries him after he takes his own life? Is that a sin?"

"Where's the sin in that? That's a corporal work of mercy, burying the dead."

I say goodbye.

"Good luck, be sure to say your daily prayers," he whispers, and the small wooden door scrapes shut.

As I leave the church, I don't feel all washed clean, as Arlene calls it, and I certainly don't feel the way she does afterwards—lighter. But I do feel a little different than when I walked in—heavier, maybe. Still shipwrecked.

74

"SONNY MCCLUSKEY TO THE MAIN OFFICE, PLEASE. *Sonny McCluskey, the main office*." Next day, I get the shock of my life when two RCMP officers show up at school. The principal calls my name on the crackling PA and introduces me to a tall Mountie with rock-hewn features and broad shoulders who smiles and says he'd like to ask me a few questions, we can use the vice-principal's office.

There's a heavy snowfall outside the window. Mr. Taylor, the maintenance man, is shovelling snow off the front steps. Mrs. Henry, the skinny secretary and school gossip, pretends to be busy, looks up from her typewriter at the falling snow. She turns her pointed face my way. "Looks like a white Christmas!" she says. And to my surprise adds, "But not an Arlene White Christmas." I frown. She flashes an accusing stare, lowers her head, hits a few typewriter keys.

The tall policeman nods past her, grins, removes his cap, and places it under his armpit. He has short grey hair, parted razor-sharp.

"After you," the Mountie says, pointing to Mr. Russell's office as another Mountie, baby-faced, wearing a Klondike fur cap, joins us. His face is strained as he speaks with his friend. He removes his cap. He has the kind of haircut that looks like someone put a bowl over his head.

They introduce themselves as Corporal Evans and Sergeant Kennedy of the St. John's RCMP detachment. They waste no time asking questions about Charlie. Where is he? When will he be back?"

"He died last month."

"Sorry to hear that," Evans says. Sergeant Kennedy says he's sorry too. Evans takes out a notebook. "Was he out of province before his death?"

"Back and forth to Toronto seeing a specialist." I clench my fist, shift my weight uncomfortably.

"A specialist?" the Klondike cap, Kennedy, says. He slumps in his chair, cracks his fingers.

"About his health," I say. "For tests and treatment. He died of lead poisoning."

"Who's his family doctor?"

"Didn't have one. My father was very stubborn about doctors, hated hospitals."

Corporal Evans takes out a sketch, asks if it looks like Charlie.

I stifle a laugh. "Looks like Count Dracula."

Evans laughs, Kennedy gives me a stern look, picks some lint off his jacket, drops it on the floor.

Evans, writing in his notebook: "Have an address for the Toronto specialist?"

"No. My father was a private person."

"Know the doctor's name?" Evans says. "The specialist?"

"Think it's Warren. Williams, maybe," I lie. "No, can't remember." I consider giving Uncle Ches's name but decide against it. I'm getting edgy remembering what Charlie said about talking to cops: *Watch your P's and Q's.*

Kennedy says, "You deposited a hundred-dollar bill at the Royal Bank recently. Were you aware it was counterfeit?"

"First I knew, my friend Quinn mentioned it."

"And that would be Mrs. Quinn's son, Randall. She works at the bank."

"Yeah."

"Any idea where it came from?"

"No. Lotsa business at the garage lately. Oil changes, muffler jobs, out-of-town, mostly—"

"Counterfeit circulating in CBS. You get customers from out there?"

"Sometimes."

Silence.

"Am I being arrested?"

Kennedy laughs. "No. But please keep detailed records of all transactions from now on. Check your cash carefully. Your father ever get a bad bill?"

"No." Wish I hadn't sounded so sure, quickly add, "Dunno. Don't think so."

I must look sad, because Sergeant Kennedy puts his hand on my shoulder and says, "Don't worry, son. We're not saying you did anything wrong."

That makes me sadder. He pats my shoulder, hands me his cop card. "That's all, son. Let us know if you recall his doctor's name."

They murmur to each other, then Evans says, "Know a young man Johnny Fabrella? Plays in a local band called the Acid Test."

"Official name's Giovanni, Giovanni Battista Fabrella," Kennedy says. "Moved here from New York few years back."

"Yeah, I know him."

"Like to talk to him. You be seeing him?"

"Dunno," I say, again shifting uncomfortably. "He lives out the Brook way, near the Indian Meal Line. Don't see him much."

"He a friend of your father's?"

"My dad helped him out, gave him work now and then at the garage."

Evans stands up, says in a soft tone, "Mmm hmm, you see him around, contact us." He adds almost as an afterthought, "Know a Jean-Luc Gaudet? From Saint Pierre. Hangs out at a hippie place called Eden Farm on the Bauline Line."

"No."

Sergeant Kennedy fingers his fur hat. "Ever been to Eden Farm?"

"No."

"We'll be in touch, Sonny."

They say thanks and leave.

In the hallway, students cluster outside the main office asking what's going on. The place is buzzing, cops are at the school. From down the hall, a loud voice: "Is someone being arrested?" A shout from the throng: "They're questioning Sonny McCluskey." Another shout: "Is he in trouble?"

After class, I meet Arlene by her locker, tell her the police questioned me about Charlie and Johnny. I say I covered for them; she turns pale.

"Why didn't you tell the truth? Turn yourself in, they'll go easy on you." Her brow furrows in concentration. "That was the perfect time to tell everything. You told me; you told the priest—"

"Arlene, I'd never betray my father, what he stood for. I couldn't. And Johnny's my friend, your cousin, and—"

"He's a pusher." Her eyes widen, fingers clench her skirt. "You're not going to tell the police, are you? If you don't, you can colour me gone, Sonny. I mean it. They're going to find out, just a matter of time."

"I might be a thief, Arlene, but I'm no Judas."

"And what about the baby? You considered that? Leaving your child fatherless?"

"I'll be there for the baby, you know that."

She shrugs, half-laughs. A glare of defiance. "You're gonna wind up in the slammer, Sonny. With Robin Hood, John Dillinger, and all the other thieves." She lets out a disappointed sigh. Before walking away, she says in a faint, thin voice, "And it'll serve you right."

75

BACK HOME, I REMEMBER JOHNNY'S LETTER. I know it's wrong to read someone's mail, but after what I've been through with Mrs. Crenshaw, I open the envelope:

Dear Florence,

Thank you so much for considering joining the Acid Test to pose during our cross-Canada tour. Unfortunately, it might be a while. I'm taking a little detour through the States. But I want you to know I meant every word about an equal partnership. I don't know how I kept control of myself on the stage the night you posed during "Wild Thing" at the Pot Park concert. You're a powerful performer.

As you read this letter, I'm on my way to Fort Dix to see Uncle Sam. When the war is over (and there's talk it will end soon), I'll get the tour going right away. I hope you'll be able to come on short notice but realize that will depend on Mr. Crenshaw's health. If he keeps using hard drugs the way he does, he won't be around much longer, so that might be a moot point. I know it's none of my business, Florence, but you really should consider leaving Mr. Crenshaw. He'll only drag you down. Just some friendly advice, take it or leave it.

I want to apologize for not paying back the money I owe you for the new amp I bought. Thanks again. I hoped to have the loan repaid by now, but as you know, Mr. Crenshaw didn't pay me the money I was owed for the deal he and Manfred and I did in St. John's. That was a lot of money I was owed—a lot more than I paid for the amp. Mr. Crenshaw said that the Party was in trouble financially and I'd have to wait. Well, I can't wait any longer, which is why I'm writing you. Sonny is driving me to the boat tomorrow, so if possible, I'd like to get my money by then. I need it to tide me over. Just give me a call and I'll come by for it. If that's not possible, I understand, but I'm really strapped for cash and would appreciate it if you'd send the money soon to Celine's address in Montreal: Celine Moreau, 4398 Rue Rachel, Montreal, Quebec. She'll get the money to me. Thanks.

As you know, your husband and I (and Manfred) got the money illegally, so if it's not paid back, there's nothing I can do about that. I can't go to the police—which I wouldn't do anyway. I only hope that, unlike Mr. Crenshaw, you are a person of integrity, and will feel compelled to send me what I am owed, less the loan for the amp, of course ($149.50). If there's no way you can find the money (I know Mr. Crenshaw is constantly broke), maybe we can make some sort of arrangement for you to repay it "in kind" while you're posing on tour with the Acid Test.

I wish you the best of luck with Mr. Crenshaw. I know what a difficult situation you're in and will need all the luck you can get. Keep a song in your heart.

All the best,

Johnny

Fugg! Even Mrs. Crenshaw is involved with the Doctor Club. They're all pushers. And it sounds like Mr. Crenshaw pushed more than his fair share.

76

I DON'T TALK TO ARLENE FOR DAYS. At school we chat, but she's distant with me. One morning toward the end of the week, there's a knock on the door. I open it, nobody there. An envelope marked *Sonny* sticks out of the mailbox. Arlene's handwriting. I wait till I'm on the school bus before reading it. I sit alone at the back, my heart thudding, as I tear open the envelope:

Dear Sonny,

Don't worry, your secret is safe with me. You're the father of my child, after all. Nothing will ever change that, so your secret is as safe with me as with a priest in confession. I only hope you do the right thing. If you turn yourself in it will be a lot easier on you than if you're caught. We all have a date with destiny, Sonny. I just don't want mine to be yours. So, colour me gone.

You believe you're a Robin Hood, that it's okay to cheat the lousy bankers, but I believe that two wrongs don't make a right no matter how you look at it. I know. I know. Like Charlie and Comrade Crenshaw, you think you're making the little changes that will turn the world upside down. But I don't agree with your brainwashed notions. I don't want to be part of some insane fantasy where you're going around trying to save the world. Call me naive if you want, but right is right and wrong is wrong.

I guess it comes down to this, Sonny. I can't live with a thief, even a good thief.

I love you, but I can't live like this. Who can? I know you think you can get away with it and what you're doing is right, it's what Charlie taught you, but I think it's warped.

It breaks my heart to write these last few words, but you leave me no choice. Goodbye, Sonny, I'll always love you, but I can't stay with you.

Arlene

77

AFTER READING THE LETTER, I KNOW THE JIG'S UP. Any day now and I'll have to get out of Dodge. I call Ches, tell him everything, ask his advice.

"Unfortunately, your only way out is *in*. Turn yourself in, Sonny. Sooner or later, the Doctor Club will cut off your hand. Fess up before the cops catch all of you. You can come here and start over, but the RCMP will find you, they always get their man. It'll be easier if you go to the police. You're just a kid, court will be lenient." He chuckles, says in a cracked voice, "Look at the bright side, if you wind up in Kingston, you'll have a regular visitor."

I know he's right. I can't let Arlene go, and everything is closing in on me. The cops seem to have a bead on Charlie. It's just a matter of time before they learn the truth about Rosie. Looks like they know about Johnny and Manfred and the drug dealers at Eden Farm. Soon the son of a wanted man will be a wanted man. And crazy Mrs. Crenshaw and Jean-Luc will put the squeeze on me for money till the day I die. How often do they think I can fill up that burlap bag with thousands of dollars? I'm trapped. Maybe Charlie was right after all about karma. What goes around comes around.

I call Arlene, tell her I'm going to the police.

"Thank goodness! It's the right thing to do, Sonny. I'm so happy. I've been praying you would. It's the smart thing, too. They'll go easier on you for turning yourself in."

There's a deep silence, and I say, "I can't live without you, Arlene. Feel awful about screwing up my life."

"Look, I admire you for turning yourself in. I know I've been tough on you, Sonny, but hang in there. You'll make something of yourself. Everything will work out. George Eliot says it's never too late to be what you might have been."

"All I want is you and the baby and Sonny's Auto."

"Trust me, everything will work out, hang tough."

I walk home, burn all the records, the ledgers, the remaining counterfeit. Then I drive to the RCMP headquarters in the Cove, Ches's cracked voice ringing in my ears.

When I arrive, a uniformed police officer is putting up an artificial Christmas tree. A German shepherd is curled up in the corner. The dog perks up when I enter, ears twitching. I recognize Corporal Mitchell's ruddy face, that thin, worm-like scar down his chin.

He says Merry Christmas, introduces an older Mountie typing away at his desk, who looks up, smiles. Then he introduces the dog. "Rupert's on loan from the St. John's detachment. Sergeant Reynolds is teaching him to sniff out drugs. It's the new thing in Europe—K-9 units. It'll be standard fare here in a few years." He puts on one of those voices people use talking to babies. "Rupie's ahead of his time, aren'tcha, wittle fella? Yes, you are. He's such a good wittle fella, aren'tcha, boy?" Rupert growls, paws a toy. Mitchell points to a chair, says, "Have a seat. Be with you in a minute."

I look around anxiously. Will he arrest me right away? Put me in a cell? I'm guilty of a serious crime. I'll be punished, feel weak, empty. I'm about to go against everything Charlie taught me, everything the McCluskeys stood for.

The office is small: two desks by a large window, file cabinet, Xerox copier against the wall, coffee table and chairs for guests, kitchenette. A hallway leads to another room. A jail cell? A chill runs through me.

I close my eyes, see the print shop, the garage, the house. What will happen to everything if I go to jail? What will happen to me? I try to sum up my life in a word. Counterfeiter? Mechanic? Loyal son? Certainly not that. Shipwrecked sailor, more like it.

"Would you like a coffee?" Mitchell says.

"No." Who is this person? What does he really care about me?

"You look worried. Somethin' on your mind? Here to help."

I look at the Canadian flag in the corner, above it a framed picture of a moustached Mountie hanging on the wall. He's formally dressed, the red serge, stetson hat.

Mitchell blinks, eyes the picture. "Big chief!" He chuckles.

I think of leaving the police station, the province, the country. I could be at Fort Dix by tomorrow, take Johnny's way out, sign up for the war. Do they take Canadians? I think of Charlie, Rosie, Mrs. Crenshaw, and Jean-Luc . . . feel sick. "Is there a washroom around?"

"Down the hall. Take your time."

Inside, I splash my face with cold water, look in the mirror. *Oh, Sonny*! Arlene: *Sunny, one so true*. I'm in the washroom so long Mitchell calls out, "You okay?"

"Fine. Be right out." Splash my face again, think of Grandfather McCluskey, the years and years of hard work.

"Sure you don't want a coffee? Tea?"

"No." I return to my seat, put my head in my hands, think about placing the blame where it belongs, Charlie, even though there's a trail of my fake bills across the island. But deep down I don't feel right saying it's all Charlie's fault. That's a betrayal. I'm not a Judas. And I believe in my heart that Charlie was partly right, trying to make a difference in this crazy, one-sided world. Who am I to judge?

I tell Mitchell I've come to turn myself in. "I'm a counterfeiter."

Silence. Mitchell runs a hand through his brush cut. "Seriously?" he says. "You serious?"

After I spill the beans, he says, "Holy cow! Like something out of a movie. Wow!" He sounds like a kid in junior high. "City detachment thought someone was up to something shady. Counterfeiting, huh? Wow! You're just a whippersnapper, remind me of my cousin Benny. How old are you?"

"Eighteen." He doesn't believe me.

He whistles, says he remembers me, I'm the kid from Charlie's Auto who fixed his muffler, *for free*. Have I done that slab-on-grade he recommended?

"No."

He grins. "This is big stuff. Seen a documentary last year about counterfeiters." He shakes his head, whistles, says we should look at the place where the funny money's made. "We'll take my car. No need to raise eyebrows." He winks, grabs his cap. "Let's take Rupert. He's friendly, goes everywhere with me, stays at the house." Rupert looks up, barks. Mitchell says he's a little hyper, pats him and scratches his head. "Such a good wittle boy, Wupie!"

He puts Rupert in the back seat, points to the front. I get in, wonder what Quinn and his father will say about me being a jailbird.

Mitchell has the sharp smell of Old Spice. He starts the car. "You're in a heap of trouble, son," he says. And we drive to Charlie's Auto.

78

ON THE WAY I ASK IF THE LAW MIGHT GO EASY ON ME FOR TURNING MYSELF in. He purses his lips, cocks his head to one side. "Hard to say. You're young, eighteen." He whistles. "Court might take that into consideration. Course, could get a tough judge."

I ask if he thinks I'll go straight to jail.

"Hard to say. Might let you go home. If there's an opening at the Whitbourne Youth Correctional Centre, you could go there over Christmas. If there's a trial, things could drag out." Then he asks about Charlie. "According to the chief, he's a person of interest."

I say Charlie died, and a shadow passes across his face.

"Gosh, sorry to hear that." He touches my shoulder. "My dad died when I was about your age."

We pull the car into the driveway, and Rupert starts growling and barking like crazy.

"Easy, boy!" Corporal Mitchell says. "Settle down. Easy, boy!"

But Rupert doesn't settle down. When Mitchell opens the back door, the dog bolts to the side of the garage and begins barking his fool head off. Tail wagging frantically, Rupert paces back and forth, circles, then hovers over a large rock, sniffing feverishly. As we run to the dog, Mitchell says, "Ten to one he's found something. What you got, boy? What Rupie got? Good wittle boy!" He's more excited than old Rupert.

My heart sinks as I remember chastising Johnny for toking on the job. Rupert jumps up and down, snapping excitedly at the rock until Mitchell lifts it, removes a plastic bag. "Good boy! Good boy!" Mitchell pats him. He reaches inside his pocket, gives Rupert a biscuit. "That's a good boy!" I shouldn't have told Johnny to hide dope when he was stoned. The officer opens the plastic bag, pushes back his cap, and says, "Well yippie yi yo ki yay! Whatta we have here?" He removes a joint from the bag. "Well, if this isn't your lucky day, son."

"That's not mine," I blurt. "Someone painted the garage a while back. He was stoned. Musta been his. Musta put it there—"

"It's on your property, son. 'Fraid that makes it yours."

"But it's not!" I shout. "I don't smoke dope. It's not mine."

"It's yours till proven otherwise in a court of law." He puts the bag in his pocket. "Now, let's have a look at that funny money you make."

Dejected, I lead him inside the garage. He keeps shaking his head. "Holy cow, this is somethin' else. You're just a young whippersnapper, for cryin' out loud."

In the pit I open the steel door and show him everything. He's like a child at Christmas. Rupert appears out of nowhere, jumps excitedly. Mitchell gives him another biscuit, says settle down, be a good boy.

"Man, this is quite the little operation you got here. What's that?" Pointing to the old monster in the shadows. "Must weigh a ton."

I snap to a sort of attention. "That's the monster. Early printing press, my great-grandfather's. Used to print the *St. John's Gazette* way back when."

"So, you been in the printing business for a while, huh?" He laughs. "Whatta you gonna do with it?"

"Dunno. Like to save it, family memento. Been around a long time. Meant a lot to my father."

He says he'll keep it for me if I get a jail sentence, which is possible, now that I face two charges, counterfeiting and illegal possession of narcotics. "I've got a pretty big garage." He's sure he'll fit it in, loves antiques.

I recall Charlie's last wish, save the old monster, get pissed about Johnny being so stupid with his dope.

"I'll hold it for you. Mind if I tinker with it? Get it up and running?"

I say thanks, not really listening.

He saunters to the old monster, runs his hand over it. "Man, this thing's somethin' else." Shaking his head, wandering back my way. "You run this operation all by yourself? And you been doing this *how long*?"

"Coupla months. My father ran it for a few years before he got sick."

"Like I said, he's been on our radar. Whew! How much money you printed since he left? Anyone else involved?"

"Not much. A few grand. Started a few months ago." I don't see any need to mention the Crenshaws, Manfred, Jean-Luc. "No one else involved."

"Whew! A lone ranger!" He whistles, points to the closet in the corner. "That your darkroom? Cool. I know a bit about this stuff. From the documentary I saw."

He moves to the printer tray, picks up a sheet of twenties. "Well, looky here!" He flinches.

My heart sinks. A spoiled sheet I'd forgotten to burn. I cringe. How could I be so stupid? I almost laugh. That's a question I don't need to ask myself. Not after murdering my father, getting Arlene pregnant, joining Johnny and the drug trade, counterfeiting . . . a long list.

Mitchell's eyes bug out when he holds the sheet of twenties up to the light. "Holy mackerel! Isn't that what you guys say around here? Whew! What an operation! Who'd have thought there'd be something like this going on in the Cove? I mean, Toronto, yes. Montreal, Vancouver, you betcha! But *the Cove*? This is somethin' else, man. And your father's been at it how long? Few years, you say?"

"Coupla years, maybe. Don't know, exactly."

He asks me to start up the machine, show how it works.

"Don't really feel like it. Takes time." Other things on my mind.

"Okey doke."

He smiles politely. I ask again if he thinks I'll go to jail.

He shrugs, closes his eyes, and that shadow passes over his face again. He says the courts will probably go easy on me for spilling the beans, the dope might be another matter. "Hard to say. Tough one. Depends on precedent, the judge you get. Some judges are death on drugs. Pray you don't get Adams. You don't want to go up in front of The Beak."

"The Beak?"

"Not the sweetest chocolate in the box. A judge I would *not* recommend."

I ask if I'm being arrested.

"'Fraid so. There a phone around? Need Constable Noble to come by with the car, a camera."

I ask if I can call my girl.

"Sure. I'll have another look around." He says that when Noble comes, he'll take a few photos and a statement, make the formal arrest. "Meanwhile, be a good idea to consult a lawyer. Some good lawyers in the city. Check the yellow pages. Hear Harrington's good."

He takes off his cap, runs a hand through his hair. "Wow! This is really somethin'!" He tells me to make my call, he'll just mosey around. He whistles, says he can't wait for Constable Noble to see all this. "Whew! Just like in the movies. Holy cow!"

79

THE WALLS OF THE SMALL, DAMP CELL ARE CLOSER THAN I'D EVER IMAGINED. One minute I dream of being with Arlene and the baby living a normal life in the Cove, the next I'm opening Sonny's Auto, hope rising, only to be smothered by my guilt about Crenshaw's death and the guard's distant steps near my cell, or the grate of the key in the lock. Then all is cement walls and iron bars, my daydreaming fades to reality, and I'm depressed, helpless. Again and again, I come back to the same question: Why did I let this happen?

Once a day I'm permitted half an hour in the exercise yard, a gravel square with not a tree or flower in sight. Yesterday from the lazy, blurred voices, an inmate asked if I wanted some dope. He had a five o'clock shadow, black circles under his eyes. "Can cop a joint or two for the right price."

I thought of the last and only time I got dope from someone. Poor Crenshaw! I shook my head and walked away. Last thing I need, another drug charge.

In my cell I remember the dark days alone in the house after Charlie died: emptiness. I stir my coffee and remember how Charlie stirred his. I look at the coffee mug and talk to him. But unlike before, it doesn't make me feel better. I move around my tiny cell like a ghost, a stranger to myself.

Arlene and Esther-Marie's visit makes things worse. We meet in a small room, four straight-backed chairs around a wooden table, a box of Kleenex in the centre. There's a guard standing in the corner.

Arlene strokes my hair. "You okay?"

"No touching!" the guard growls. "You can give him a hug on the way out."

There's an awkward silence before Esther-Marie asks how I am.

"Okay, food's lousy. Anyone heard from Johnny?"

Dead silence.

"We brought you some food," Arlene says, "snacks mostly."

Esther-Marie says that Quinn was shocked. "Counterfeiting! Whew!"

"Everyone makes mistakes," Arlene says sharply.

They also bring books, magazines, a deck of cards. They give me a big lift, but when they leave, I long to go too, get dizzy, throw up in the toilet. I lie on the bed shifting uneasily, staring at the flaking ceiling: raging rapids, winter blizzard, ocean foam. . . . Eventually I open a copy of *Jekyll and Hyde*. Thank God for reading, my refuge, and my only one.

"Because you turned yourself in, there's no trial." My lawyer, a big, broad-shouldered man with crow's feet at the corners of his eyes, says he's been appointed to act for me. "You're a charitable case, McCluskey. Not the only one at Her Majesty's Penitentiary." He hands me his card: James H. Foster, Attorney, says he'll try to get the drug charge dropped.

"Hope so."

"We'll see. Depends on the Crown."

"That wasn't my dope, I've never done drugs."

"As I said, we'll see, depends on the Crown." He's tense, crabby, says jail might be temporary. I'll be transferred to Whitbourne if space is available. "You plead guilty, probably get a lesser sentence for the funny money. But because of the unusual circumstances, a teenager running a counterfeiting operation, the judge wants a hearing to go over the evidence."

It's the worst time of my life—torturous days, nightmarish nights. The small cell is cold, damp, smelly. Cement walls, steel bars, paint peeling on the stained ceiling. Rusty sink and toilet. I lie on the single bed, a thin, uncomfortable mattress, no pillow. The guard says, "Thin mattress, easier to find contraband." He's a sympathetic, obese man with almost no neck. The blanket's thin too, makes me itch. Only good thing about the place, I don't have to share it. The mattress smells of pee, there's a poop stain on the toilet seat. Cell hasn't been cleaned since the last guy left. Thankfully, you're allowed to wear denim jeans and a plain shirt, not stripes.

Before lights out, I read the Bible, but there's a rat scratching inside a wall. I make a mental picture of the PROS and CONS of my situation but quit right away. It's hopeless, can't keep anything straight. A long, sleepless night, an eternity waiting for dawn. And not Charlie's idea of eternity.

In the morning around seven, the rattle of the guard's keys. Breakfast is always the same: a plastic tray containing cereal, milk, burnt toast, a pat of butter. Today there's something on my plate that looks like wet chalk. Sausage? Lunch is usually two hot dogs or a hamburger, supper two small fish patties or pasta. Where's Johnny when you need a good meal? I try eating the bland cereal, drink a little milk, open the Bible, take my mind off things reading about Joseph and the many-coloured coat.

The guy in the next cell shouts, "Same shit every day, man. You'll get used to it. What's your name, man?"

"Sonny."

"Rick. Welcome to the Ritz. Food's better in the cafeteria. Only eat supper there. Steak once a month, ain't bad." He's silent, then yodels, is silent again, then says, "Keep an eye out for Fitzgerald. Fitzy's got a permanent boner." Yodelling again.

During the day I read and write in my journal. At night I'm overcome by dizziness, dry mouth. I sleep an hour or so, wake with a splitting headache, wanting to vomit. My days half asleep again, nights half awake.

My lawyer shows up, says I might get bail, but the dull days linger, and before I know it, Christmas arrives. Guard says, "Bad timing, man. Nuthin' happens around here at Christmas. But cheer up, tasty meal comin'." That evening he brings me a turkey dinner on a military tray, but I can't eat, swallow some mashed potatoes, a little cranberry sauce. I've never been so depressed in my life, not even after Charlie's death.

80

PERIODICALLY, I'M ALLOWED A TELEPHONE CALL, THINK OF AUNT VIVIAN, decide against it. What'll I say? Hi Aunt Viv, I'm a jailbird. Embarrassed, I put it off, indefinitely.

I call Arlene. We chat for the allotted time. She visits when she's allowed. She says she'll stand by me no matter what. Last phone call she asks what I think about calling the baby Charlie if it's a boy, Lucy if it's a girl. That brings a lump to my throat.

Boxing Day, she arrives with my mail. "Letter postmarked USA," she says. "Johnny got his gun." I tear it open:

December 5, 1967
Dear Sonny,

Well, here I am in the Vietnam jungle, making war, not love. And it's sad, man.

The bus ride to my unit was blocked with soldiers and Vietnamese farmers. There were chickens clucking up and down the aisle and under the seats all the way. One young woman held a clucking chicken in one arm and a howling infant in the other. Poor soul! The highlight of the trip was the magnificent view of the rice paddies. Stunningly beautiful! I plan to write a song about them: In the Mekong Delta where bamboo wheels work by water buffalo yellow and green rice fields stretch for miles. . . . They blew me away, man. But always there's the sound of choppers overhead, and Vietnamese soldiers everywhere. They all look like little kids to me. It's so sad, really. It got me down something awful.

Well, Sonny, this will be my first Christmas in hell. I'm writing from the jungle where it's unbearably hot. Most days it's so humid my uniform gets soaked right through. And the insects are gross, worse than the heat. Yesterday I was bitten by the biggest ant I've ever seen. It's a jungle war, Sonny, and the news is grim. The well-armed Viet Cong have snipers in every tree, and they can survive for weeks on a bowl of rice. We gotta have our steak and fries, man, and that means hauling around a ton of crap.

The enemy, as they're called—they're human beings with families just like us—have mines and booby traps everywhere. Yesterday we carried a stretcher through the remains of a shelled village, ruins of bombed trees everywhere. There were dead bodies all around, and the immense silence was broken now and then by the wailing of voices coming from the few huts that escaped the shelling. We chased the poor Vietnamese out of their huts and set the straw on fire. The army thinks it's good to deny the Viet Cong shelter. Of course, it only turns the locals against us. Later we rescued a soldier who had his foot blown off, carried him on a stretcher for over a mile of dangerous terrain. Took hours. This in a place where you gain a mile by walking two, always knee deep in muck and mire. It's always a hard slog. I spend most of my time carrying a stretcher through the swamp dreaming of getting back to camp for a decent meal. Sore feet and damned short rations, as Crane would say. One of the other stretcher-bearers took a bullet to the shoulder yesterday and was flown out. Maybe I'll get my red badge soon and get out of here too.

The Viet Cong attack in ambushes and escape through a sophisticated network of tunnels. They're like ants. We'll never beat these guys. They know how to fight. They're tougher and better organized than we thought. And they don't play by Queensberry rules, man. Just finding them is a nightmare. So our military drops napalm to burn away the leaves of the trees, destroying the beautiful jungles here. It blows my mind. Sometimes they wipe out the villagers too. Ground troops use flamethrowers. I've seen kids running and yelling, ripping their clothes off. Morale is really low in my unit. There's so much frustration, many take drugs. It's hashish heaven down here, man. One upside, anyway. Keeps me from thinking about the coward that I really am.

But enough about me! How are you, Sonny? How's Arlene? Quinn? Esther-Marie? Everybody. How's Comrade Crenshaw? Mrs.

Crenshaw? I'm ashamed to say some nights I dream about Foxy Florence more than Celine. I'm looking forward to getting back home and starting up the band again for that cross-Canada tour. Thinking of the band gets me through many a day. If you see Florence around, tell her the tour is my first order of business when I get back.

I gotta say I miss you all very much. More than I thought. Nothing like a war zone to focus the mind, man, make you realize what's important in life.

Gotta go! Mortar fire in the distance, bullets whistling overhead. I can hear a chopper not far off. Any minute now our new Sarge (the previous one was killed by sniper fire two days ago) will signal to make tracks.

I don't know when you'll get this letter. They said it'd take a month or so because of the war and all. Tell everyone I was asking about them, Sonny. And be kind to everyone. Life's a blink of an eye, man, especially around here. Lose someone all the time. And remember to play some music every day. I write a few lyrics when I get a break from the swamp. Keep a song in your heart, man. Precious little music here in the jungle. And I miss it something awful.

Your friend,
Johnny

81

THAT NEXT DAY I ANSWER JOHNNY'S LETTER:

December 27, 1967
Dear Johnny,

There's no simple way to say this other than to say it. You're my brother. That's right. Your father is my father—Charlie. He had an affair with your mother. The result was Johnny Fabrella, who's really Johnny McCluskey. Charlie would say you're like Jesus, a bastard. He and your mother kept everything secret to their graves. The Captain didn't know.

So there you have it, Johnny. No wonder Arlene thinks we look alike. And no wonder we got along so well all these years. Blood's thicker than water, as they say. I've known about this for some time but for personal reasons couldn't tell you. Another story for another time. I'm writing to you from jail (part of the other story).

Johnny, you should finish up with that crazy war because the last thing your real father would've wanted for you is Vietnam. Captain Fabrella thought otherwise, I know, but Charlie hated war and everything it stands for. He called it a racket. Don't feel guilty about living up to your father's expectations anymore. He wasn't your real father anyway.

I apologize for not telling you this before you left. It drove me crazy not telling you the truth. I wanted more than anything in the world to stop you from leaving, but I couldn't. I had my reasons and will explain when next we meet. And anyway, I suspect you still would've wanted to honour Captain Fabrella's wishes.

I hope you don't hate me for all this and that when we meet again we'll still be good friends. I miss you, big brother. I mean that.

That's all for now, Johnny. I hear the guard coming down the hall, and I'm almost out of paper anyway. Oh, I forgot to mention old Crenshaw died. I'll write you a longer letter with all the news soon.

Your brother,
Sonny

P.S. I'm really looking forward to seeing you again, so don't get shot, you crazy bastard.

JANUARY 1968

VI

In trouble to be troubled, is to have your trouble doubled.

— Daniel Defoe

82

JUST AFTER CHRISTMAS MY CROTCHETY LAWYER SHOWS UP, SAYS HE GOT A meeting with the Crown to discuss bail. "Highly unusual, but Jenkins would like you to come along. If it goes well, you could get out."

"Jenkins?"

"The Crown prosecutor. He'd like to meet you. His father grew up in an orphanage. I told him you were an orphan."

"You what?"

"Believe me, it'll work in our favour." Excited now, he says, "I know you're an adult, don't consider yourself an orphan, but technically, you are. Agree with Jenkins if he mentions it. Arthur has a real soft spot for widows and orphans. Just say both your parents died, you're living alone. That's all he needs to hear. Remember, we're trying to avoid the max."

"The max?"

A flicker of a scowl. "The maximum sentence for counterfeiting: twelve years. You'd have to serve time in Kingston."

I shut my eyes, see the Vietnamese kids yelling, ripping off their burning clothes.

"Don't worry, it's my first case, I don't plan to lose. And Jenkins has a big heart, especially for young offenders." His voice rises. "He'll get the Crown to recommend a light sentence."

"How light?"

"Trying for two years less a day. You can serve it here. Right now, I'm plea bargaining, trying to get the drug charge dropped. Not easy getting hold of people Christmastime. Oh, by the way, a Mr. Bertram White offered to put up bail money, if necessary."

When I hear that, I want to remain in jail, say I'd just as soon stay put.

"Dr. Jekyll!" I mutter.

"What?"

"Nuthin'. Forget about bail."

"Won't hurt to get to know Mr. Jenkins a little. Might go easier on you. Let your shirttail hang out, mess up your hair a bit, try to look a little depressed." For the first time in weeks, I burst out laughing. *Look a little depressed.*

At the Crown's office, my lawyer says I'm young, never been in trouble with the law, I'm extremely sorry for what I've done, will never do it again. "And I'm convinced that marijuana belonged to a Johnny Fabrella, now residing in the United States. My client hired him to paint his garage."

Mr. Jenkins seems nice enough, but he looks a bit like Frankenstein's monster: huge forehead with hair combed flat on the top of his head. All he needs is the bolt through his neck. He's the oddest-looking duck, I gotta say. But he puts me at ease right away. I guess he can see I'm nervous. He offers me a Coke, says in a hollow voice, "Relax, we're here to help you, young man."

Foster smiles, even though Jenkins sounds sad and looks sullen.

They talk gobbledygook for a while, then Jenkins pats my shoulder, asks how I'm being treated at Her Majesty's. "How was Christmas dinner? I'm told they serve quite a nice meal Christmas Day." I'm not sure if he's poking fun, stare at his big forehead, say it's a pretty good meal, but don't mention I threw up most of Christmas Day and that the jail cell smells like a sewer. He riffles a few papers, says he was informed that I have no parents. "You are without mother and father? Correct?"

I say yes, turn away. Thinking of Charlie and Lucy upsets me. I guess I'm overtired, and the memory of being without them at Christmas hits me hard.

The prosecutor says it's a tough world, children need parents to keep them on the straight and narrow. He passes Foster a box of Kleenex, nods my way. I take a few tissues, blow my nose, say I'm sorry, I hadn't meant to get upset.

"Don't feel sorry, son," Mr. Jenkins says. "We all make mistakes in life, even the best of us." He frowns, looks at Foster. "Isn't that right, Foster?" My lawyer's head jerks backward as if avoiding a punch. More mumbo-jumbo, and it looks like I might get bail until Jenkins says the word *ineligible*, but not to worry, my hearing to go over the evidence is only a day or two away.

"How soon till sentencing, you think?" Foster asks.

Jenkins snorts. "The big day! Everyone always wants to know the big day. Hard to say, really. Depends on how long the hearing is. Judge Roberts can be a stickler. A week or so, maybe." Then he turns my way. "How are you doing, young man? They treating you well? Need anything?"

I shake my head, say everything's fine, I'm being treated okay.

The meeting with the Crown lasts about half an hour, and I'm taken back to jail. Before I leave, Jenkins hands me a copy of *Tom Sawyer* and says it's a book every young man should read. Foster makes a big fuss about getting such a wonderful gift, but I just say thanks and we leave.

83

THE HEARING DATE KEEPS CHANGING AND I SPEND THE TWELVE DAYS OF Christmas in jail. After Old Christmas Day there are several more delays, the hearing doesn't begin until mid-January. It's pretty boring. I spend my time sleeping, walking in the yard, and reading. I try writing Aunt Vivian. That's not easy. Eventually I'll find the right words. I talk to Rick in the next cell about Newfoundlanders in the First World War. He's fanatical about the battle of Beaumont Hamel. Every day in the yard: "Of the eight hundred Newfoundlanders who went into battle that morning, only sixty-eight were able to answer the roll call the next day. More than seven hundred killed, wounded, or missing." He lent me several books on the Newfoundland Regiment, the Battle of the Somme, and the Gallipoli Campaign, and he quizzes me on them daily.

Foster says not to worry about the long delay, that'll work in my favour. I ask why. He grins, says, "Yours is not to reason why," suggests I write up a few words to say in case the judge asks. "Nothing heavy. Something simple, show a little remorse, that sort of thing."

"This is *in camera*, Mr. Jenkins," Judge Roberts says, "speak your mind." He's a stuffy-looking, bristle-haired man, flushed complexion, a harsh tone of voice.

Finally! the hearing. It lasts much longer than expected because of constant interruptions by His Honour. We are in his chambers, a library with red leather chairs, a large, birch desk. My lawyer and Jenkins sit with the judge discussing my case. I'm on a bench off to the side looking at the shiny gavel on the judge's desk.

"Irrelevant!" the judge says, irritable now. "This meeting is not about sentencing, it's merely to review the evidence."

I go out of my mind listening to the prosecutor expanding on this little point and that little point, a constant staccato of yes, Your Honour, no, Your Honour. His Honour drives me crazy asking for more information about printing counterfeit—where did the paper come from? The ink? Most of the time I just close my eyes and block everything. It's like some horrible dream.

I'm daydreaming about the baby when Judge Roberts says, "Very well, gentlemen, there's agreement on the statement of facts and recommendation for sentencing." He bangs the gavel. "Meeting adjourned."

84

ARLENE SHOWS UP WITH A TELEGRAM FROM THE STATES. "Been checking Johnny's mail," she says. "This one's from the US Army, addressed to Harry, who hasn't been around for weeks. Neighbour says he went to Labrador." She passes me the yellow paper, looks at the floor to hide her feelings:

WESTERN UNION
TELEGRAM
WU AGENT SAM
1125A PST 06 JAN 68
MDW Army WSH A
3 XV GOVT PD Washington DC 15 Jan 68
(Don't phone. Deliver only)

Mr. Harold Johnstone
P.O. Box 17, Brook Road
Portugal Cove, Newfoundland

ON BEHALF OF THE DEPARTMENT OF THE UNITED STATES ARMY IT IS MY DUTY TO INFORM YOU THAT YOUR NEPHEW PRIVATE GIOVANNI BATTISTA FABRELLA, UNITED STATES ARMY, IS PRESUMED TO HAVE BEEN KILLED IN ACTION. THIS PRESUMPTION WAS MADE AS PER THE PROVISIONS OF THE MISSING PERSONS ACT ON 14 JANUARY 68. MY SINCERE SYMPATHY TO YOU AND YOUR FAMILY. YOUR NEPHEW DIED SERVING HIS COUNTRY. IF I CAN BE OF ANY ASSISTANCE WHATSOEVER, PLEASE DO NOT HESITATE TO

CONTACT ME. ON BEHALF OF THE UNITED STATES ARMY PLEASE ACCEPT MY SINCEREST SYMPATHY.

WILLIAM M. O'REILLY JR.,
COMMANDER OF ARMY PERSONNEL.

I look at the date. Tears burn my eyes. He died before he got my letter. I hand back the telegram. "Go. Please."

She turns and leaves. "I'm so sorry, Sonny," she says. And I know by the crack in her voice that she's crying.

Back in the cell, I keep asking myself who's the real coward. Certainly not Johnny. I didn't tell him the truth about who he is, about everything. I could've saved his life, maybe. And my father's life. I might as well be in jail for murder. I'm responsible for two. And how can I ever be a decent father to my own child? Who am I if not a coward and a murderer? How many times do I ask myself why? Why didn't I tell him? Maybe I am Charlie's son after all.

85

THE BIG DAY FINALLY ARRIVES. I'm like someone in a Louis L'Amour novel, sitting in the prisoner's dock, my hands cuffed waiting for sentencing. I wish I had my coat to cover them, no lookin' good in handcuffs. I feel ridiculous, ashamed, hope the photographer for the *Daily News* isn't here. I can hear Quinn now: "How you gonna shoot hoops with those things on?" And they're not on right, no space between metal and skin, so my wrists chafe. I sit there, shoulders hunched, a stranger to myself, thinking of my life again, trying to sum it up in a word. This time there's only one. Prisoner.

The words PRESUMED TO HAVE BEEN KILLED IN ACTION pop in my head. Maybe Johnny's not dead. Maybe he's hiding in the jungle somewhere. Who am I kidding? The US Army doesn't make those kinds of mistakes. Then Old Crenshaw haunts me. Nothing will take the edge off my guilt.

I look over my shoulder. Arlene sits by her father. No Mrs. White. Mr. White's reading a newspaper. He looks my way, a firm nod. I don't know if the nod means I'm in your corner or it serves you right. They're a few rows back. Arlene's wearing a long brown coat and the flapper hat I gave her. She sees me turn around, holds up a hand, and wiggles her fingers. Then she pats her stomach and mouths the word *Charlie*. It's good knowing that despite everything she's by my side. Lot of girls would've left me. I think of my mother, how loyal she'd been to my father, think of his two-timing, block it.

I notice people Charlie helped over the years, look at Arlene again, remember her saying not to worry about Charlie's Auto. "If worst comes to worse, Daddy will look after the place till you get out."

I glance at Mr. White, get edgy. "I'll have to think about that, talk to Uncle Ches."

Foster leans over, says cheer up, it's going to be a great day. "Prosecution's dropping the drug charge, and the judge agrees. Recommendation from the Crown will keep you out of Kingston. Everything's going to be fine, just fine." He winks. "I've talked to Jenkins, I'm confident you'll get a light sentence—one to two years. Recommending two years less a day." He whispers, "With good behaviour, you'll be out in a year. Don't worry, we have a very sympathetic judge. Thank God we didn't get The Beak. Judge Roberts believes in giving young offenders a second chance, and you turned yourself in, that bodes well." He pats my arm. Somehow, I don't share his optimism. "Under two years and you'll be able to serve your sentence at Hump."

"Hump?"

"HMP: Her Majesty's Penitentiary, your current residence, 89 Forest Road."

"And if it's over two years?"

He pauses. "Like I told you, over two years, the federal pen, Kingston. Two years less a day, you serve your sentence at Hump. Might serve it at Whitbourne." He pats my arm again. "Don't worry. Everything's going to be just fine." He clears his throat, unpacks his leather briefcase, his skin pulled so tight you can see veins by his temples.

86

JUDGE ROBERTS BURSTS INTO THE ROOM, BLACK ROBE WITH SCARLET FACING down the front flying every which way.

The bailiff calls, "All rise!"

The judge bangs the gavel. "Court's in session." I think of *Ironside* and *Perry Mason*—lawyers and judges bickering: *Objection*! *Sustained*! *Objection*! *Overruled*! When he's seated, the judge says, "The defendant will please rise for sentencing."

Foster says, "Judge might ask if you've anything to say before he passes sentence. Keep it simple. Say you're sorry, you won't do it again, and sit down."

I nod. He says to put on my sad face. "Bite your fingernails."

"Young man," the judge says, "you've admitted guilt to a serious crime, making and passing counterfeit. This crime carries a maximum sentence of twelve years in prison. Counterfeiting violates the very core of our society. Without a legitimate currency, worse, when fake money is mixed with legitimate tender, the very fabric of our democracy is in danger of being shredded." He says that throughout history most countries had the death penalty for passing counterfeit. "The Dutch boiled counterfeiters alive." He pauses for effect.

"I don't know if you understand, young man, that your heinous trade could seriously undermine, even ruin, our economy. Thankfully, counterfeiting has been kept at a minimum here. Nonetheless, we cannot understate the seriousness of this egregious crime. Before I pass sentence, do you have anything to say for yourself?"

"Yes, Your Honour." I take out the little speech I prepared the night before. I thought about showing it to my lawyer but decided against it. I'd put a lot of thought into it and didn't want to change anything. I decided not to mention Mrs. Crenshaw and the Doctor Club.

I wrote something that I truly believe and want to say publicly whether my lawyer likes it or not. I stand up, clear my throat, and read.

"Your Honour, my father always taught me that the world is an unfair place, a place where the rich get richer, and the poor get poorer. Rich people have lawyers and accountants to find loopholes so they can make more money. Might makes right and much craves more, my father always said."

Under the table, a gentle tap from Foster's foot.

"The rich get richer while the average person works from paycheque to paycheque." Then I use Mr. Crenshaw's favourite example. "Even government employees have indexed pensions and golden retirement parachutes. Not so the have-nots—the working class who corrupt politicians rip off."

A firmer tap.

"When I was a little boy, Your Honour, my father read me the story of Robin Hood and His Merry Men. Growing up, Robin of Locksley was my hero, and I guess he still is. Like him, I've always tried to be a good thief. And while you might view my actions as criminal, Your Honour, I assure you my motives were always pure—what I did, I did to help the poor, to level the playing field, to make our troubled world a more equal place for all. Thank you, Your Honour."

I sit down, look over my shoulder. Arlene looks disappointed. But I'm proud of my little speech, and I know Charlie would have been proud too.

Foster leans in and whispers, "Judge Roberts is a public employee."

87

THE JUDGE HARRUMPHS, TUGS AT HIS ROBE. "Robin Hood! A fairy tale. Cinderella." He steeples his fingers and sighs. "I'll say this for you, young man, I admire your pluck." He scribbles something and says, "Now, because you informed the police of your criminality, because you came to them of your own volition, and because of your young age—and I'm told you're soon to be a father (he rolls his eyes)—I'm rendering less than the maximum sentence, twelve years."

Foster nudges me with his elbow, winks.

"Notwithstanding the aforementioned confession on your part, because of the imminent threat to the social order, and with a view toward deterring others who might follow foolishly in your footsteps, I am not accepting the Crown's recommendation of two years less a day."

I turn to Foster.

Judge Roberts takes a deep breath, scratches his neck. "I am compelled rather to hereby sentence you to three years in federal prison, less time served, to commence immediately at the maximum-security facility in Kingston, Ontario."

My heart flutters. Short quick breaths, sweaty hands. Foster stares straight ahead, shoulders sagging. The judge slams the gavel and adjourns the court. As he departs, I peek over my shoulder at Arlene. She's crying but waves, mouths the words *I love you*. Mr. White has a dreamy look, still plotting a way to get Charlie's Auto.

I turn to Foster, who shakes his head. "Now, that's a shocker. Didn't see that coming. But you didn't do yourself any favours with that little speech of yours. Good thief!" He spits the words. "You know what an oxymoron is?"

I shrug, think he's calling me a moron.

"There's no such thing as a good thief." Foster, angry and showing it, groans, puts a hand on his forehead. "Moral of the story: never let a client speak."

I turn again, Arlene's head is down.

"Don't worry," Foster says. "We'll have you out in two years, with good behaviour." He squints. I fold my arms, drop my head.

The security guard taps my shoulder and leads me through the exit door to a police car. Back in jail, I learn I'll be leaving for Kingston on the morning flight.

In my cell I lie down, close my eyes. I'm back on my desert island again, only this time it's Kingston. I chide myself for writing that speech, should've shown it to my lawyer. Pride goeth before a fall, Charlie always said.

I'm exhausted, unable to sleep. Three years in the federal pen. Three years! I wish Foster hadn't said anything about the judge being sympathetic. People shouldn't say things like that. He raised my hopes. I start crying, but it's a dry cry. My tears are all gone.

I think of Arlene, the baby. Whose eyes will he have, nose, mouth? Three years before I hold the li'l guy, three whole years before I play with him. It's a kind of death. I block all thought of it, have another dry cry.

I lie there thinking about what goes on in prison, stories I've heard, movies, block that too. I can look after myself. Then I feel awful about not being there for the baby, not telling the truth about burying Charlie, Crenshaw's death . . . leaving it so late to tell Johnny he's my half-brother, not exposing the Doctor Club . . . the mess I've made of my life . . . when Charlie's ghost comes roaring in: *Never feel sorry for yourself. That's a dead end.*

I open the Bible and begin reading. After a few pages, I wonder if they have a library at the Kingston penitentiary. I figure they must have some sort of library. I'll study history, literature, mathematics, science. I'll follow the university curriculum just as Crenshaw advised. I plan then and there to get a university degree. I'm sure they'll allow me to have some of my own books in prison: *Robinson Crusoe* and *The Education of a Wandering Man*. I'll even bring *Middlemarch*. And I'll read *Dr. Jekyll and Mr. Hyde* again and all of Louis L'Amour's books, maybe.

I tell myself there'll be lots of time to read and study, that's for sure. And who knows what else? Write a novel, maybe . . . a western that was started a long time ago by an old friend of mine. I already know the opening and how it should turn out: *I met my Lucy while picking tobacco in British Columbia. We moved east, and I built a little brick bungalow in Portugal Cove, Newfoundland.*

Acknowledgements

This is a work of fiction, and all the characters are imagined.

While writing this novel, help came from many quarters:

I am extremely grateful to my editor, Cat London, who patiently helped me confront my many missteps. I have learned so much from her editing and from our correspondence. She provided the kind of assistance of which writers dream.

My agent, Michael Levine, has kept the faith with me since first reading the manuscript.

My publisher, Jerry Cranford, believed in this book from the beginning. Thanks for your confidence and patience. Thanks also to Margo and Garry Cranford for their prudent editing in the final, galley stages.

My friend Larry Mathews, a great champion of Newfoundland writers, spent many hours editing and discussing the novel with me and provided numerous insightful recommendations. I cannot express to him sufficiently my gratitude.

Thanks to Sheldon and Dawn Currie, who gave the first draft of the manuscript a detailed, critical reading. You are a constant source of encouragement and enlightenment.

Anne Emery, thank you for reading an early draft of the manuscript and offering advice. Your intelligence helped shape this book.

Ian Colford has read much of my writing over the years and has been very generous with his time and expertise.

My Sunday-morning brothers, Gordon Rodgers and Ed Kavanagh, are a constant source of knowledge and support. I am especially grateful to Ed, who edited several drafts of the manuscript and provided valuable advice and suggestions.

Alex W. MacLeod addressed more than a few flaws and provided friendship and moral support.

Libby Creelman, Ramona Dearing, Bethany Gibson, Jane Warren, thank you so much for supporting my writing. I am in your debt.

Michael Oliver was always eager to share his considerable poetic talent and perceptive commentaries.

To my children, Rachel, Beth, John-Paul, Sarah, thanks for your abiding love and support.

Thanks to my brothers: Bill for reminding me daily of the importance of rewriting; George for his encouragement and advice on several legal issues in the novel; Michael for his help and sense of humour; Chuck for his enthusiastic support.

My nephew Andrew, the new writer in the family, is always upbeat and encouraging. Keep writing. Quit your day job.

I am indebted to Jason Kersten's *The Art of Making Money* for information on the techniques of counterfeiting.

Thanks to Gerard at Murphy's Service Centre for answering my nagging questions about auto mechanics.

Glory be to God for dappled things . . . is from "Pied Beauty" by Gerard Manley Hopkins.

Men of England, wherefore plough . . . is from "Song to the Men of England" by Percy Bysshe Shelley.

Thanks to my first readers: Chris Bonnell, Rachel and Fletcher, Sarah and Pete, Paul Gardiner, David Hickey, Robin MacNeil, Elinor Gill Ratcliffe, Carm and Gerald, Brendan Sanderson, Mary and Mike, Jantje Van Houwelingen, John and Susan Venn.

Most of all, thanks to Fluff, my loving, in-house editor of a hundred versions of the story.

Part of the proceeds of this book will be donated to Team Broken Earth (brokenearth.ca).

PHOTO BY FLETCHER MADDEN

Leo Furey is a writer from St. John's, Newfoundland. His first novel, *The Long Run*, was a 2004 *Globe and Mail* Best Book and was chosen by Barnes and Noble for their 2007 Discover Great New Writers Seasonal Picks.

The Long Run received excellent reviews in various newspapers and literary journals across Canada and was on several bestseller lists. In the US, the novel received starred reviews from *Publishers Weekly* and *Booklist*.

Furey's short stories, reviews, and journalism have been published in several literary magazines, including the *Newfoundland Quarterly*, *Tickleace*, the *Antigonish Review*, the *Nashwaak Review*, the *Fiddlehead*, and the *Walrus*.

He is founder of Broken Earth Productions, a theatre company that raises money for Broken Earth (brokenearth.ca), a non-profit group of Canadian health care individuals providing medical assistance to earthquake victims.